MIDNIGHT CRAVING

SHARI NICHOLS

CITY OWL
PRESS

MIDNIGHT CRAVING
Raven's Hollow Coven, Book 3

CITY OWL PRESS
www.cityowlpress.com

Cover Design by MiblArt. All stock photos licensed appropriately.

Edited by Heather McCorkle.

For information on subsidiary rights, please contact the publisher at info@cityowlpress.com.

Print Edition ISBN: 978-1-64898-240-8

Digital Edition ISBN: 978-1-64898-241-5

Printed in the United States of America

PRAISE FOR SHARI NICHOLS

"Romance and intrigue collide in Shari Nichols' latest installment of the Raven's Hollow trilogy. Midnight Temptation is a can't-put-down read where the chemistry between Gillian and Garrett pulses with palpable desire, and the twists and turns keep you holding on for dear life. Buckle your seatbelts and enjoy!" - *M. Kate Quinn, Award-Winning Romance Author*

"Her plot was solid, her characters were complex and her writing hooks the reader right from the start and never let's go! Think of a multiple loop, fast, curving, upside down roller coaster and you have an idea of what you are in for with this book." - *Stephenee, Nerd Girl Official*

"Great read and start to a new series. I'm excited to see more of as it comes out!" - *Book Junky Girls*

"I was hooked from page one! A titillating, fast-paced read, this edge-of-your-seat paranormal romance kept me guessing." - *Sky Purrington, Bestselling Author of Time Travel Romance*

"An emotional, action packed, YUMMINESS ride!" - *Carrie Book Fairy*

"I can't wait for what is next in the Ravens Hollow series. I give this book 5 Fangs!" - *Maria Suarez, Paranormal Romance and Authors that Rock.*

"Action packed steamy paranormal romance with a host of intriguing characters." - *Crystal's Many Reviewers*

"The chemistry between the characters is awesome! You won't want this story to end. Looking forward to the next book by Shari Nichols." - *Chris Clemetson, Romance Author*

"I loved the take-charge heroine and the vampires! - *SFWBC*

For Mary Kate, I could've never finished this book without you. I will miss you forever!

CHAPTER 1

"*I*f you leave now, you'll miss the celebration."

Natalya Dubrosky glanced over at her roommate and smiled. Arabella found a reason to make every night a celebration. "I wish I could, but I have to work." Tonight's op required her to go undercover at a local pawn shop. She stood at the kitchen island of the three-story Victorian she shared with the five other women from their coven.

"What about afterward?" Arabella asked, tilting her dark head to the side. She pulled off boho-chic in a simple cream peasant blouse and ripped jeans. Longs strands of her hair fell out of a messy ponytail. Natalya admired her effortless style.

"I'll probably want to chill out, but I appreciate the invite." Natalya grabbed her trench coat off the hook and slipped it on, making sure to cover her gun holster.

"Let me know if you change your mind. Tonight's full moon ritual will go late." Arabella reached for a wicker basket off the counter and began filling it with sticks of incense, pillar candles and crystals.

Every other night seemed to be some kind of celebration around here. Between the esbats, sabbats and solstice festivals, the witches always found a reason to party throughout the year. "Let's hangout tomorrow and grab a drink."

"I'd love that. Be careful," Arabella called out.

"Always. Have fun tonight." Natalya walked out the back kitchen door and into the rain. Crossing the sidewalk, she headed up Park Street. The endless honking of horns and rattle of the subway beneath her were music to her ears. Raven's Hollow teemed with life and a pulsating energy. Gentrification had turned this city into a haven for supernaturals. The mixture of accents and ethnicities, from humans to vampires, demons, wolves and fae, intrigued her on every level. They all coexisted on one patch of urban sprawl. And the best part, it was only a stone's throw from Hoboken and a PATH train ride to the Big Apple. She'd been drawn to the cool history of the town, and the hotbed of myths and legends surrounding it. It dated back to the early 1600s.

Everywhere she looked gave spectacular views of the New York City skyline. She'd moved here almost a year ago, and loved the kitschy vibe and the friendliness of her neighbors. At this point, she couldn't imagine calling any other place home.

She tried not to walk around wide-eyed, but sometimes it was hard not to, maybe because it was a far cry from the Upper East Side where she'd lived for the past five years. There, everything depended on breeding, and the pressure to mate with a vampire from a proper bloodline. She'd be planning her wedding and the next charity ball if her sired family had anything to say about it. But they didn't. Not anymore.

She'd been there, done that and had failed miserably at the whole thing. Here in the Hollow, no one seemed to care about any of the superficial BS. They were all so ... normal. As she cut over to Washington Street, the scents of pizza and chocolate cake flared in her nostrils and made her sigh. She still craved the things she'd loved as a human.

A soft breeze blew her ponytail back as she darted across the block. Reaching into her purse for her comm piece, she placed it in her ear. Exhilaration and nerves pumped through her veins in equal measure. She walked through the door of Old World Capital and took a deep breath.

Time to catch some bad guys.

"Do me a favor, Dubrosky, try not to get us both killed." The deep male voice on the end of her earpiece pricked along Natalya's skin like barbed wire. Special Agent Cayden Teague of the Magickal Bureau of Investigations never missed an opportunity to give her a hard time. She'd worked with the demon on a number of cases over the last several months, which forced them together with uncomfortable frequency. To say they had never hit it off was probably an understatement. Lucky for her, his cover required him to appear as part of the staff.

"That's the plan." The inside of the store appeared gray and dark, except for a streak of moonlight shining in from a wall of windows at the front. No customers in sight. The place reeked of damp carpet, and metal. She turned her head and glanced at the glass cases of jewelry and rare coins. She hadn't come within a hundred feet of Teague, but that didn't stop the anticipation whipping through her veins in hot revolutions.

"No pressure, Dubrosky, but hell, if I'm going to die, I refuse to do it on your watch."

Gritting her teeth, Natalya turned her head to the side and her gaze locked with the object of her unhealthy obsession. The demon loomed large like some mythical creature from a dark fairy tale. He stood almost seven feet tall with short, spikey blond hair, and intense blue eyes. Short gray horns curled out of the sides of his head and rested against the wall behind the counter. He wore a red blazer with a Mötley Crüe T-shirt and a tie covered with cartoon monkeys loosely knotted around his enormous neck.

"Thanks. I appreciate the vote of confidence," Natalya shot back with a healthy dose of sarcasm.

Teague appeared to be around thirty at most, but the hardened look in his eyes made her think he must be older, like someone who'd lived a hundred lifetimes. He exuded strength and virility, the kind that practically oozed from his pores. But his personality left a lot to be desired.

She'd been called in by the agency to act as a liaison to assist on a stakeout related to a prison break at Hellios. The warden reported a fire that had resulted in a fugitive escaping, and now the vampire in question was still at large.

Coincidentally, three days later, Natalya got a tip from the owner of the pawn shop, Dan Jackson, about an anonymous person needing to fence some rare gems. Naturally, she passed the information onto the MBI, but so far none of the agents had shared why they thought the two were connected. Once their perp showed the ice, they'd take him in for questioning.

Teague stood at the far end of the counter. When his gaze locked with hers, all the air left her lungs. She should've been prepared when those baby blues did a slow sweep of her from the end of her ponytail to the tips of her low-heeled boots. It wouldn't be the first time she'd caught him checking her out, and her libido did a high five every time.

She saw their reflections in one of the mirrors and refrained from making a face. Under the spotlights, her olive skin took on an almost-greenish tinge, unlike Teague, who glowed like a bronzed god.

"Why so grumpy, Dubrosky? I hear the men's choir's in town. Let me guess, you made a pit stop on your way here and got a bad batch of B negative?" Teague asked with a smile.

Exhaling, she ignored him, refusing to go for the bait and focused on the op. Teague knew exactly what buttons to press. They'd been working together on a variety of cases for months. His teasing fluctuated from making cheesy vampire jokes, to goading her about her privileged upbringing. His open disdain for vampires didn't help the situation.

She'd been working her way up from beat cop to detective paying her dues, and had recently put in a request to transfer to the SVU—Sexual Victims Unit—her true calling. If she got the promotion, then she'd only be forced to see him on rare occasions. For now, he could think whatever he wanted. She didn't owe him an explanation, or the truth.

Her partner, Garrett Mulroney, was one of Teague's best friends and happened to be engaged to one of hers, a witch by the name of Gillian Howe. Now, they were forced to share the same oxygen even on their off-time. And so, Cayden Teague remained an unavoidable thorn in her side.

Typically, Garrett would've been right there with them on this kind of op, but he was on vacation with Gillian in some exotic locale. They were probably basking on a beach enjoying fruity drinks with umbrellas while she got stuck with her nemesis, scoping out a psychopath who got off on burning his victims alive while they slept.

"No sign of him yet," Dan said, interrupting her thoughts, drawing her attention to one the jewelry cases.

Natalya walked over and gave him a reassuring smile, hoping he'd relax. "You've got this, Dan. Try to act natural. I promise we won't let anything happen to you." Beads of sweat broke out on the human's forehead. He wiped them away with a handkerchief.

"I'm holding you to it, Detective," Dan muttered, some of the fear clearing from his eyes.

Natalya glanced at her watch and swallowed hard. Twenty minutes until closing. "We're cutting it close. Our guy's supposed to be here by now." After a few more tense minutes passed, she wanted to call it a night when the bell dinged. Senses heightened, Natalya leaned over the counter, pretending to peer closely at a ring.

"Look alive, people," Teague's human partner, Alex Denopoulos, said in her ear from a tech van less than a block away. His cameras allowed him to see and hear everything going on inside the store.

A tall, scruffy-looking male with a beard walked through the door and shook the rain from his long, dark hair. The water drowned out his scent. But from the wild beat of his heart and the rapid flow of his blood, she guessed him to be some sort of shifter. He ambled over to the case where Dan stood and pulled a velvet bag from inside his jacket, then set it on the glass. "I called earlier. The name's Wolf." His gaze darted nervously around the store before turning to face Dan once more. "I've got some ice I'd like to sell," he muttered in a deep voice.

Dan plastered a smile on his face and pulled out a velvet tray. "Yes, uh, of course, Mr. Wolf. I'm here to help. Let's see what you've got for us." Placing a jeweler's loupe to his eye, he opened the string at the top of the bag. A combination of rings, brooches, earrings and what appeared to be a jeweled collar spilled out. He whistled. "Absolutely incredible. I'll need a minute." He examined each piece closely before pulling the loupe from his eye. Then he reached over and thumbed through the pages of a leather-bound book on the counter, making notes on a pad.

"I'm in a hurry, man, just tell me how much I can get." Wolf sniffed the air as he glanced around the shop. When his gaze moved from Teague to Natalya, he visibly tensed.

"Shit, he looks suspicious. You two need to distract him," Denopoulos prompted in her ear.

Before she could think of something, Teague leaned over the counter and gave her a flirty smile. "While I appreciate you making a move, I'm afraid I have to pass on that drink. I make it a strict rule to never date the customers."

"I ... uh, understand," she mumbled, playing along. If she could still flush, her face would be crimson right now. Through the corner of her eye, she noticed Wolf turn back to face Dan, no longer paying them any attention as he slammed his fist on the counter.

"I don't have all day," Wolf snarled, his gaze darting to the front door.

Natalya kept her expression neutral as she checked Wolf out from the side. His clothing looked rumpled and torn in certain places like he'd been in a brawl. She made a mental note to check the database for any jewelry store or home robberies.

"We see guys like this trying to unload this kind of bling on the dark web," Denopoulos whispered in her ear. "But never in a local pawn shop. This guy must be desperate. I'm trying to get a face recognition on him. Hold tight."

"How much?" Wolf muttered, tapping his foot.

Dan's hands shook as he pulled out a calculator and pressed a few buttons. After a few minutes, he looked up. "The value of what you have here is determined by a combination of factors. What I can tell you is these pieces are extremely rare. Mind you, dating and period attribution aren't an exact science. I'd say they date back hundreds of years, if not more. All these pieces together are worth upward of over $400,000."

Bingo.

Teague moved to the end of the counter. A vibrant power emanated off him as he straightened to his full height. He moved with an animal grace that demanded attention. Wolf shrank back a step. "I'd like you to come with me, Mr. Wolf. I have some questions for you, particularly on how you came across these jewels and why you're trying to pawn them."

Wolf's gaze darted to Dan. "You little shit." His hand went inside his jacket.

Natalya leaped into action and pressed her Glock into Wolf's side. "Get your hands behind your back. I suggest you do as the big guy says," she warned, motioning to Teague. "You don't want to piss him off."

"You'll regret this," Wolf snarled.

"Is that a threat?" Teague made it to the other side of the counter and slammed a set of cuffs on Wolf's wrists. "I'll take my chances. Don't bother trying to break free. They're made of lead."

"You think these can hold me?" Wolf laughed but it came out more like a growl.

"Yeah, how about we put a tracking device on your ass just for shits and giggles?" Teague removed what looked like a guitar pic from his pocket and pressed it into the skin of Wolf's hand. "Let's go, tough guy." He nudged Wolf to the back of the store.

"Good work, you two. I'll meet you at the curb," Denopoulos piped into her ear.

Natalya helped Dan place the jewels back in the pouch. "Thanks for your help." Reaching for a Sharpie from the counter, she marked the bag as evidence.

"What if he comes back?" Dan asked in a shaky voice.

"I'm calling for a unit to sit outside to make sure you're safe." Natalya pressed a button on her phone and was automatically connected to the Raven's Hollow Police Department dispatch. She gave her badge number and the address of the store. "Can you send a patrol car over here ASAP." She ended the call and glanced over at Dan. "You should be good to go. I promise to check in on you. Call if you need me."

"Thanks, Detective."

"Anytime." Natalya crossed to the storeroom and cut through the back door to the alley. Moonlight reflected off the surface of a giant puddle. For a split second she swore an image appeared in the water. *What the hell...*

Her mind must be playing tricks from being in stress mode. Scanning the alley, she saw nothing out of the ordinary. And yet she couldn't seem to shake the sense of unease. After she took a giant leap over the puddle, she landed on the corner of Washington and Eighteenth Street next to a warehouse.

Her ears pricked from the steady drip of rain pouring out of the gutters and the whistle of wind through the buildings. Natalya lifted the collar on her trench coat, purely out of habit. She didn't feel the chill, but she supposed if she could, it would go straight to her bones.

Streetlights sliced through the darkness. A heavy fog hung in the air, adding to the eerie quality of the night. Throw in a killer who torched his victims while they slept, making a bust, and seeing Cayden Teague in a tie into the mix. Surely, Mars was in retrograde. She turned her head and found Teague standing at a curb with their perp muttering curses under his breath.

"I told you to shut it, man." Teague nudged Wolf forward. "We'll give you plenty of time to talk to a lawyer back at headquarters."

Out of the darkness, the clouds parted, revealing a full, blue moon. Wolf looked up at the sky and howled.

"Crap! He's a werewolf." Natalya shouted, but her words got swallowed by the wind. If she hadn't been so distracted and infuriated by Teague, she would have picked up on the signs.

Wolf flung the cuffs from his wrists like a plastic toy, while his nails sharpened into claws. His body elongated and became covered in long, shaggy hair. A beast emerged with snapping fangs and blood-red eyes. In a blur of speed, he took off down the alley on all fours and crawled up the side of the building. Natalya stared in horror as the wolf leaped from one rooftop to the next.

The surveillance van screeched to a halt in front of them. The side door slid open with a bang. "Get in," Denopoulos called from the driver's seat.

Natalya jumped in after Teague and the door slid shut. "Go!"

Denopoulos tapped a button on the dashboard. It lit up and turned into a map of the city. A black dot appeared, moving rapidly across the screen. "He's headed north. Hang on." He careened around a sharp turn, and she went horizontal, falling into Teague's lap.

When her ass brushed against the solid muscles of his thighs, he sucked in a harsh breath. "Sorry." Warmth crept up her neck.

One strong arm wrapped around her waist and held her in place. "I don't think now's the time to hit on me, Dubrosky, though I do appreciate the effort," he murmured close to her ear. His warm breath left a tingle along her skin. She caught his scent, a combination of clean laundry and woodsy aftershave. She had to admit he smelled incredible ... but still.

"Seriously?" He seemed to get some kind of perverse satisfaction in teasing her. Before she could wriggle away, he lifted her onto her seat. "Has anyone ever accused you of being a wiseass?"

"Every day of my life, sweetheart." The heat from the demon's big body caught her off guard and sent her pulse skyrocketing.

"Don't call me 'sweetheart.' What century are we in?" She'd worked her ass off to get promoted from beat cop to detective. She could do this job, and do it well. Now if only she could prove it to herself.

After she fastened her seat belt, she pulled the jewelry pouch out of her pocket and secured it in a secret compartment on the side door. "I'm leaving evidence," Natalya announced to Julia, the interface for the van's voice-activated computer system. Glancing at the map on the dash, she made sure to keep her eye on the moving dot.

"Evidence received," Julia responded. "The suspect is headed to the woods in the direction of Palisades Park."

"I'm on it," Denopoulos said, turning the wheel to maneuver the van in the direction of the park.

Teague's phone rang. "Jesus H. Christ, what now?" He pressed a button and the face of his boss, Commander Smith, a demon with reddish skin and dark horns filled the screen.

"I'm at Hellios. This place is a total shit storm. Here's what we know, prisoner number 137, Kyle Hawthorne, staged a fight with his cellmate so he could go to the infirmary, and then he torched the place."

"How many dead?" Teague asked in a grim tone.

A crease appeared between Smith's brows. "Five inmates were burned beyond recognition. The warden believes Hawthorne started the fire as a distraction, allowing him to escape."

"How?" Natalya asked, trying to process this new development. She'd never been to Hellios, but from all accounts, the high-security supernatural prison sat on the precipice of a mountain. The only way out was in a body bag. "Can someone please fill me in?"

"While the guards were trying to put out the fire, Hawthorne managed to escape in a medical-supply van with the help of an accomplice, a wolf by the name of Gregory Pike," Smith said over the noise in the background. "I'm still trying to make sense of this mess."

Teague frowned. Tension rolled off his broad shoulders in waves. "Pike's our accomplice. Now we have a connection between the jewels and the prison break."

"The plot thickens." Natalya turned to the demon in the dark. "Pike's not the pyro, but the accomplice. What do you know about Hawthorne?"

"He got off torturing his victims and then stealing their bling."

Natalya sucked in a harsh breath. "How awful." The cops around the station celebrated Teague like some kind of a god for putting a boatload of dangerous criminals in Hellios for a string of heinous crimes. She wondered if the former jewel thief might have been one of them. "If we can catch a break, maybe our wolf will lead us to Hawthorne."

"I sure as hell hope so." Smith said, drawing her attention back to the screen. "We're doing an all-out manhunt on the fugitives. I'm sending you intel on Pike now. Check back and let me know what you find."

The moment the call ended, a small hologram appeared, flashing images of their perp from the front and the side. "Male shifter, wolf, age twenty-five. Dangerous criminal alert. Name, Gregory Pike.

Natalya read over the details of the profile beneath his face, until now, Pike didn't have a criminal record. "Why would a vampire put his trust in a wolf? Those two creatures don't exactly get along."

"Greed can make you do funny things," Denopoulos called out from the front seat.

"You're probably right. And now they shared a common interest—survival." Natalya glanced over at Teague. "You think Hawthorne paid Pike in jewels for helping him escape?"

Teague ignored her question and leaned forward in his seat. She detected the fast pump of his adrenaline and the blood rushing though his veins. After a moment of tense silence, he pressed a button and the hologram disappeared like a wisp of smoke.

"Wow, I don't think I've ever seen you at a loss for words." Something was up. Could this case have touched a nerve?

"We're here," Denopoulos said in a tight voice.

A sense of dread settled over her as Natalya inhaled the scents of pine trees and fresh earth. She glanced out the window at the entrance to the park as Denopoulos maneuvered the van over the gravel and into the empty lot. After he cut the engine, he swiveled his seat around and pulled out what appeared to be a handgun from an ankle strap.

The small piece didn't seem like it could deliver a high-powered laser beam, but she'd seen it stop a supernatural in their tracks, and turn some into a pile of ash.

Denopoulos slipped on a Kevlar. "We need to bring Pike in for questioning, so let's try not to kill him. What do you say, are you ready to get the Big Bad Wolf?"

Teague shook his head. "No offense, buddy, but even packing heat, you're still no match for a werewolf. This is one instance where the bite is much worse than the bark. He can't turn me, but that doesn't hold true for you. I'm afraid I have to go at this one alone."

"What?" Natalya snapped and gripped the door handle so hard she nearly crushed it in her hand. Before she could climb out, hard metal closed around her wrist, binding her to the arm rest. Almost instantly she could feel all her strength leave her body. She rattled the cuffs, but they didn't budge. "What are you doing?" She looked up at Teague

"It's for your own good. Lucky for you I keep a spare set on me. My warning applies to you too, Dubrosky. Trust me, you'll thank me later. I've seen a werewolf rip a vampire to shreds, and the smell is like a dumpster fire," Teague said with a twist of his lips.

"I appreciate the sentiment, but there's no need to use your hero douchebaggery on me." Natalya tugged at the cuffs again. "I know how to handle myself. I'll decide what's for my own good."

"Try and calm down, Dubrosky. Teague does have a point. Let him handle this one," Denopoulos urged and turned to the computer now pinging on his dashboard. "I'll circle around the block and catch our perp from the other side."

The door slammed shut. Teague came around to her side of the van. "For once in your immortal life, trust me on this. Whoever said chivalry was dead." The demon winked at her and then took off at a sprint.

A buzzing began in her head. She sensed something bad about to happen. "You can't just leave me here. Teague?" Dread settled in the pit of her stomach. She needed to warn him.

But it was too late. He was already gone.

CHAPTER 2

*R*acing through the pine trees and bramble, Cayden followed the scent of wolf that now filled his nostrils. The rain had made it hard to detect the creature at first, but with every leaf and patch of dirt, the scent became more potent.

While he focused on tracking the werewolf, he let the beast inside him emerge. The gods took fallen angels like him and endowed them with supernatural strength and speed. His heightened senses allowed him to act as a guardian of nature. And unlike werewolves and vampires, he'd never been fully human. His demon essence lived inside him like a jacked up alter ego.

His horns resembled those of an animal. They helped him blend into his environment and protected him against his enemies. A scaly coating broke out along his skin. Cayden opened his mouth wide while his teeth turned into sharp, pointed fangs. His vision sharpened, making the colors on the leaves more distinct. Every raindrop that hit the ground echoed inside his head. The wind whistled through the trees and left a ringing in his ears.

He didn't want Dubrosky to see him like this. She already thought of him as some kind of brute. If she witnessed the full extent of his transformation, she'd never let him live it down. And he couldn't risk her getting mauled. He might give her shit, but he'd be damned if he let Pike lay a paw on her.

Most of the time she exasperated the crap out of him, but it didn't keep him from wanting to lick every inch of her skin. He pushed the one-sided attraction to the back of his mind and focused on the werewolf.

Sniffing the air, he continued forward, his heart pounding with every step. When he came to a clearing, his gaze cut through the darkness, searching for movement. Without warning, the werewolf darted out from a bush and lunged at his throat. Cayden blocked him and wrestled him onto his back. They rolled around on the ground, clawing and scratching, fangs snapping. Cayden roared, his head thumping with rage.

Dammit. If the wolf got through him, he might get to Dubrosky.

His body heated, burning from the inside, and suddenly burst into flames. Part of his skin felt like it burned off his body. The flames subsided and the scent of scorched earth and singed fur filled the air. *Holy shit on a shingle. What just happened?*

Two large streaks of burned hair ran down Pike's chest. Cayden lunged again and this time managed to get him in a headlock. The wolf whimpered and then sank his fangs into the side of Cayden's hand, tearing through his flesh.

Pulling his hand away, Cayden cursed in pain. His inner beast retreated. The wolf used it to his advantage and lashed out, biting him on the forearm, taking a chunk with him. When Cayden pressed his hand to the wound, blood spurted through his fingers. Legs wobbling, he grew light-headed. He swayed and sank to his knees, collapsing onto the cool grass.

Pain exploded through every nerve ending. Unable to move, he could only watch as the wolf sank his fangs into his own paw, digging until he caught the tracking device in his teeth. He spit it out and took off in the other direction. *Fuck!* They'd have a hell of a time trying to catch Pike now. Something wet and sticky dripped from his arm, and throbbed like a son of a bitch. He looked down at his blood-soaked T-shirt and the puddle on the ground. *Oh shit.*

Once Cayden forced himself onto his elbows, he ripped off a piece of his sleeve with his teeth. He pressed it to the cut, but the blood soaked right through. He swallowed the queasy feeling in the pit of his stomach. "I ... I need back up," he choked out.

Seconds ticked by and then he caught a rustling in the trees. Jolting upright, he immediately regretted it as burning pain seared through his arm.

Dubrosky ran toward him in a blur of speed. Her eyes grew wide as she sniffed the air. Her shocked gaze landed on the blood still spurting from his forearm. She rushed to his side, knelt on the ground, and pulled off the makeshift bandage. She gasped. "You've been bit."

"Yeah, but I should heal in a few minutes." No sense getting her riled up. "Along with ruining a perfectly good T-shirt, our perp got away."

"You don't have a few minutes from the amount of blood loss. I figured something was wrong when the tracker stopped working. Oh, Teague … it's deep. You should've let me go with you."

Better me, than you.

"Has anyone ever told you that you've got a hero complex?" Dubrosky took off his tie and wound it around his arm like a tourniquet. "At least this ridiculous tie is being put to good use."

"I … happen to like this ridiculous tie." Cayden breathed through the pain. He hated that she saw him weak and vulnerable. "Hindsight can be a bitch." Her previous attitude toward him ranged between open disdain and flat-out hatred. For the most part he couldn't blame her. His default mode had been major prick since day one. He'd been giving her a hard time to avoid the truth—he looked forward to their interactions more than he cared to admit.

"I've got to get the blood to stop." For a split second, her eyes widened with an unmistakable hunger as she stared at the blood dripping from his arm.

"If you dare say, 'I told you so,' there's going to be hell to pay." His voice sounded hoarse to his own ears. He wanted to shut his eyes and go to sleep. Maybe the pain and the guilt he'd been carrying around all these years would finally go away and then he'd be at peace.

"Stay with me, Teague." From the strain in her voice it was bad … real bad. "Try not to close your eyes. I'll be right back."

In a blur, she sprinted through the woods in the other direction while he tried to breathe through the pain. Sweat soaked through his shirt. Seconds later, she came back holding a first aid kit. "The ambulance is on its way. Denopoulos called for backup. He's circling the perimeter, trying to intercept Pike."

Uncontrollable shivers wracked his body.

"You're so pale." Dubrosky crouched next to him and fumbled around through the kit. Finally, she replaced the tie with a real tourniquet. "You've lost a lot of blood. Shit, it's not stopping."

"Yeah? Tell me something I don't know," Cayden mumbled, his heart skipping beats. He couldn't seem to move from the spot. Excruciating pain exploded through his nerve endings. His muscles began to constrict. Delirium must have been setting in.

Dubrosky sat on her knees. "You need a transfusion. We could wait for the ambulance or I could carry you to the van, but you'll bleed out before we get you to the hospital. There's only one option, but you're not going to like it."

"The bite burns like Hades's balls at a bonfire," Cayden panted seeing black spots. "Do whatever it takes to make the pain go away."

"You'll have to drink from me."

Except that. "Hold on, what are you talking about?"

"I refuse to let you die on my watch," Dubrosky said, mimicking his earlier words. "This will keep me from saying, 'I told you so.' Trust me." Before he could stop her, she sank two sharp fangs into her finger. When the blood began to flow, she held it under his nose. He recoiled. He might be inches from death but nothing—nothing in this world, could get him to drink from a vampire. "Drink," she insisted, "Or you'll die. Dammit, Teague, for once in your life stop being a stubborn ass."

"H-hard habit to break … I'd rather die." The last time he trusted a vampire, it ended in tragedy. All these years later his heart still hadn't mended from it. He turned his head away, making peace with his fate.

"I promise this won't turn you into a vampire." Dubrosky turned his head to face her, and held it in place. He tried to pull away, but she held tight. Her strength as a vampire almost matched his own. She pushed her finger into his mouth. "It's for you own good. Now drink." The second her blood touched his lips, heat burned through his veins like hot lava. Her blood tasted sweet, with a tangy bite.

Heat shot through his limbs like fire. Cayden became aware of the scent of her hair—strawberries and rain. Another spicy scent lingered in the air —something that smelled an awful lot like pheromones.

"What have you done to me?" he whispered as his whole body surged to life. Her blood pulsed through his veins and the pain began to ebb like a bad memory. When he glanced at his arm and the cuts on his hands, they mended together and faded right before his eyes. He could regenerate over time, but nothing like this.

He gazed over at Dubrosky, and his breath caught. Her eyes had rolled back in her head. Her lips had turned pink and swollen like she'd been kissed. He'd heard the rumors of vampires experiencing a kind of intense sexual pleasure when drinking, but could the same be true when someone drank from them? A moan slipped from her lips and called to his beast. The sound made him crazy. He didn't think he'd ever get it out of his head. As he stared at her flushed cheeks and a stray curl slipping out from her ponytail, he got a sudden urge to wrap the shiny strands around his fist. He wanted to bring those lips closer. The need became overwhelming.

But then what?

He'd been harboring an intense attraction to her for months now. This wouldn't be the first time he took notice of her warm brown eyes and full lips, or the way his dick stood up and saluted every time she walked into a room. He never acted on his attraction because they worked together, and Denopoulos told him she pretty much hated his guts. How could he ever be with a vampire? But now, the more he drank, the more he felt inexplicably drawn to her like an invisible chord pulling him closer. Cayden continued to suck, hell, he couldn't get enough. All the emotions he kept locked away flooded over him, lust and longing, along with an undeniable sexual hunger.

Her eyes widened. Could she sense the change? His gaze moved lower, to the pulse throbbing at her throat. He wanted to trail his tongue over the spot. Did she know drinking her blood would render this kind of connection?

"Your color is back," she whispered in a throaty voice, looking relieved. "You're going to make it." She pulled her finger away and he wanted to groan. "Don't sit up right away. Let me clean your cut so it doesn't get infected."

The soft lilt of her voice reminded him of fairy song. She dabbed at the wound with an alcohol wipe. He'd never been this close to her, never noticed the cluster of freckles across the bridge of her nose or the fullness of her upper lip.

Dubrosky sighed with relief. "Our patient's going to be okay," she whispered into her mic. Every word she flung at him might be filled with vitriol, but she did have an amazing mouth with full, pouty lips.

She never wore a stitch of makeup and kept her wavy, dark hair in a ponytail. While she might be uptight and a royal pain in the ass, her natural sex appeal sent his imagination into overdrive. Her eyes held a certain mystery he found mesmerizing. His gaze trailed lower to the starched white shirt buttoned up to her neck. He'd never seen a female try so hard to conceal her natural assets. It made him wonder what she wore underneath. Did she favor white bras and panty sets that were as prim and proper as the rest of her, or did she have a penchant for black lace?

Her chest rose and fell and pushed up her small breasts against the thin material of her white shirt with every breath. Her strawberry scent flared in his nostrils. Could it be her body wash or shampoo? He'd spent plenty of nights alone in his bed with his hand down the front of his boxers, imagining her naked, soaping her dark mane while hot water sluiced over her sarcastic mouth and smooth skin. He typically favored buxom blondes, not petite, brunette vampires. But *she saved your life*, his inner voice reminded him.

"What's going on in that head of yours?" she asked, interrupting the train of his wayward thoughts. Her gaze narrowed. Could she guess what he'd been thinking? Apparently, vampires couldn't read minds, but they were able to pick up on body language. The lot of them could tune in to a dozen conversations at once. He'd observed the annoying habit on more than one occasion. He hoped she couldn't figure out what he'd been thinking about or he was in serious trouble. He forced his mind out of the gutter and back to the case.

"I don't think Pike and Hawthorne are devious enough to pull something like this off by themselves." Only one name came to mind, a name that had been burned into Cayden's brain like a brand, Stephen Frost. He'd be willing to bet the vampire was behind this in some way.

Dubrosky cleaned the rest of his blood and drew her dark brows together. "Agreed. You're lucky Denopoulos had a key to those cuffs or we might not be having this conversation. I get the misguided chauvinist in you can't help yourself and you probably thought you were doing the right thing, but next time give me the option. I earned my place on the team and I make my own decisions. Understood?"

"Understood," he muttered. Putting a female in harm's way, no matter how much of a badass she was, went against his natural instinct to protect. He'd been treating her like a rookie for months now. She might be petite, but he knew she could hold her own. She kept him on his toes with that quick wit, and forced him to up his game. She genuinely seemed to care, and didn't let the job make her jaded. Not giving her the choice to come along, not trusting her to take care of herself had been a dick move. But he couldn't help it.

"May I ask how many males you have allowed to drink your blood?"

"You'd be the first." Dubrosky refused to look him in the eye. "Why?"

"I was just curious. How did you know it would work?"

"All the myths and legends about vampire blood having regenerative properties are true." Dubrosky's bright eyes sparkled in the darkness. "I found out by accident when I donated my blood to the hospital. The lab tested it and now it's being used to help human children suffering from a multitude of illnesses like diabetes and leukemia."

I've just been saved by an angel.

He nodded. "I'm sure the parents of those kids are grateful." He struggled to find the words to thank her. "Well, uh, thanks for patching me up."

Her big brown eyes filled with compassion. "Sure, don't mention it."

"Actually, I wish you wouldn't. The others will never let me live it down. Getting bitten by a wolf was bad enough, now I'll have to add drinking from a vampire to my reverse bucket list."

"The horror." She rolled her eyes. "Don't worry, your secret's safe with me." If he had to guess, from the mystery behind her eyes, Dubrosky had a few secrets of her own.

After she wrapped his hand in gauze, she packed up the kit and glanced around the empty clearing, then got to her feet. "What now? How do we find Pike or Hawthorne for that matter?"

"Once they identify the bodies at Hellios, I'll request the list from the warden and find out who's behind this." Sirens rang in the distance. The cops would be here any minute now.

His strength returned as he slowly got to his feet. He felt better than he should, considering he'd been inches from death a few minutes ago. He'd never admit it out loud, especially not to Dubrosky, but vampire blood rocked.

His partner jogged over to him, concern now etched on his bearded face. "You okay, buddy?"

"I'll live." Cayden dusted himself off and ran a hand through his hair. "What did I miss while I was in la-la land?"

Denopoulos glanced over his shoulder at the clearing in the direction the wolf took off in. "No trace of Pike. I sent the location of the park to the agents in some of the nearby field offices. We'll find him, one way or another."

"Where would you go if you were trying to avoid an all-out manhunt?" Dubrosky asked, lifting the first aid kit.

"I have a few ideas." Pulling out his phone, he scrolled through his contacts. "I've got a friend, I helped out a few times who's now a Confidential Human Source. She works at a bar in Hoboken. It's a big wolf hangout, and frankly, I don't know about you two, but I for one could sure use a drink."

CHAPTER 3

*A*n hour later, Natalya walked into the Wicked Wolf Tavern with Teague at her side. From the boisterous laughter and shouts, the place appeared to be hopping tonight. They got a few curious stares from the wolf packs congregated around the bar.

The loud thump of rock music pounded in her ears and pulsed through her veins, along with a half dozen conversations. Getting used to having supernatural abilities had been jarring at first, but over time she learned how to use them. Eventually, they became an asset on the job.

The pungent scent of sizzling meat permeated the air, along with sweat and leather. Natalya stole a glance at Teague, checking him for any lingering signs of pain. So what if she also took advantage of the situation to admire his strong profile and the sharp edge to his jaw. *It doesn't mean anything*, or so she told herself.

Shaking it off, Natalya took an empty seat at the bar while Teague remained standing, scoping out the place like only a special agent could. A combination of human and vampire couples gathered near a dartboard, while some congregated at the pool table. Sporting events played from flat-screen TVs around the bar.

"Where's this CHS of yours?" Natalya's gaze darted around the bar. "Unless of course there isn't one and you dragged me here because you're competing in some kind of wing-eating and beer-swilling contest." His reputation as a hard-drinking player had become water cooler fodder around the station. The demon might be ancient, yet he still behaved like an oversized frat boy.

"Ha. Not quite. But this place is known for their wings." Teague's eyes hardened a fraction at the dig. He angled his horned head to the blonde mixing drinks behind the counter. "The bartender owes me a favor, all right?"

Neither of them had said a word about him drinking her blood, both trying to cover with their usual snarky banter. But a palpable tension hummed between them. One of the demon barbacks walked to the bar carrying a case of beer. He loaded them into the cooler, and glanced over at Teague. "Andee knows you're here. She'll be right with you."

Teague nodded. "Thanks, man."

"Where's Denopoulos?" Natalya asked over the music.

"He's still in the van on the phone with his fiancée, something about wedding stuff that couldn't wait. Don't get me wrong, I love Willow like a sister, but I've never seen a man so whipped. He's entering into a lifetime of voluntary servitude."

"Don't let anyone ever accuse you of being a romantic." From what she'd overheard from Denopoulos, he'd been a great warrior on another plane until his people lost the war. She wondered if he could've become so battle-scarred that he'd cut himself off from love and relationships.

"Fat chance, Dubrosky." Teague's smile didn't reach his eyes. Could there be more to the jovial, ballbuster than what met the eye?

He plopped onto a bar stool and still managed to tower over everyone else. The heat radiating from his body made her warm all over. He'd changed into a fresh T-shirt in the van. The cotton stretched over his broad shoulders. Natalya sensed his power and couldn't ignore his magnetic personality. As much as she hated to admit it, the demon oozed sex appeal. The sweet scent of his pheromones lingered in the air. A shiver of awareness moved through her. She ignored it and set her purse on the bar.

Teague leaned closer and sniffed the air. "There's something I need to ask you."

She'd have fun with this one. "Go ahead."

"Is there any chance we're blood-bonded?" From the concern in his voice, he might as well have asked if they were now going to be fused at the hip.

"Since you drank from me, the sensations are only temporary. For it to be more permanent, I'd have to drink from you." She'd never experienced the physical, mental and emotional connection that took place during a blood bond. She'd overheard other female vampires talk and there was no act more intimate than that, except maybe for sex. "You have nothing to worry about." Turning her head, she glanced at the couples kissing in the dark corners of the bar, and her pulse kicked up a notch.

"That's a relief." He brushed his blond hair off his forehead, revealing scratches and cuts all over his face. Even scraped and battered, he oozed a raw, in-your-face masculinity and a toe-curling magnetism. At least until he opened his mouth.

Did the demon have any idea that when his lips closed over her skin and drank her blood, her whole body tingled with awareness? She hoped not, because if he did, he'd never let her live it down.

"As much as I'd love to sit here trading barbs with you, I need to head back to the station to write my report." She'd do whatever it took to get a lead on the case, but she couldn't wait to get out of there so she could soak in a hot bath with a glass of wine.

Before Teague could counter with a sassy comeback, an attractive blonde with a sizeable amount of cleavage walked over from the other end of the bar. "Hey, Cayden. It's great to see you."

Teague smiled. "It's great to see you too, Andee."

It became clear right away that the two shared some kind of connection. The hot sting of jealousy surprised Natalya almost as much as the CHS herself. She closed her jacket over her non-existent cleavage.

"Can I get you a drink?" When Andee set a cocktail napkin on the bar, Natalya glimpsed the handwritten words across the top. *What do you need?*

Once Teague pulled out a pen from his pocket, he turned the napkin over and wrote on the back. *The 411 on a wolf named Pike.*

Andee lifted the napkin and shoved it in her apron pocket. "I'll be back with your drinks." She turned and walked away, disappearing behind the bar. A few minutes later, she came back and set the napkin on the bar with a shot of amber-colored liquid for Teague and a glass of water for Natalya.

Natalya leaned over and read the words on the napkin. *Find Rocco. He's the alpha of his pack. He cleans ships at the Union Dry Dock Yard.* Natalya pulled out her phone and made a note to follow up.

Teague gave her a nod. "Thanks for the drinks, Andee."

"Anytime," Andee said with a wink.

Teague waited until Andee walked away to help a group of vampires at the other end of the bar before turning back to Natalya and whispering close to her ear. "Now we just have to find this Rocco."

"I'll make some calls and list the names of our fugitives on the NCIC (National Crime Information Center) database," Natalya said, hoping something would turn up fast. Two criminals as dangerous as Hawthorne and Pike roaming the streets together would be a recipe for disaster.

Andee came back holding a greasy basket of fries and a bottle of ketchup. She set both on the bar in front of Teague. "It's on me."

"Thanks, love. I'm starving." Teague lifted the bottle of ketchup and squirted some onto his fries. He dipped a fry into the ketchup and a spot dripped onto his tie. "Damn, first the shirt and now the tie."

"A pity." Natalya handed him a few napkins. When their fingers touched, it sent a shock of awareness up her arm. She ignored it, glancing at the tie covered in cartoon monkeys, sporting splotches of blood and now a giant ketchup stain. "I think it may be an improvement."

"Are you making fun of me?" Teague used the napkin to try and blot the stain. "I may not have worn a suit, but at least my clothes fit. What's your excuse?" he asked with a teasing smile.

His heated gaze traveled from her face to her baggy jacket. She suppressed a shiver from his flagrant perusal. His smile deepened, accentuating the dimple in his chin. *Great.* Had she become some kind of challenge?

"I'm not looking to impress anyone, least of all you." Not entirely true, but he didn't need to know that. An oversized trench coat, a blazer and low-heeled boots had become her uniform of choice.

"If you say so." Teague dug into his fries like he hadn't just dropped an anvil on her head.

"Have you thought about getting a hobby besides me?" *Damn that came out all wrong.* But she couldn't help it. He'd hit a nerve. Her sired mother would have a total shit fit if she caught Natalya in this shapeless pantsuit. Eleanora Dubrosky, had been coined the grand dame of vampire society. She sat on the board of numerous charities in New York City and always made sure to look the part. She'd never met a designer ball gown or gaudy piece of jewelry she didn't like. Needless to say, the news of Natalya joining the police academy hadn't gone over well.

Now for the first time in her life, she wanted to do things on her own terms without her sired parent's money or influence. She might not win any fashion awards, but she'd managed to turn her life around, forcing herself out from the black hole she'd fallen into. She was proud of how far she'd come, even if Eleanora wasn't. She refused to let someone like Teague second-guess her. What the hell was his problem anyway? She gazed into his eyes. *Big mistake.* Those baby blues burned into hers, and sent delicious sparks along her skin.

He pushed the basket off to the side and folded his arms across his enormous chest. "What's the matter, Princess, not your usual hangout? I'm sorry the waitstaff here doesn't wear white gloves or tuxedos."

Natalya got to her feet and placed her hands on her hips. "You don't know anything about me, so let's keep it that way."

Teague drew his brows together. "I can't help but wonder if you're trying to prove a point to your family."

You're not cut out to be a cop. Eleanora's harsh words stuck in Natalya's head and rattled her confidence. The need to prove Teague wrong rose to the surface like a crashing wave. "No need to pile on the gratitude."

Regret crossed his features. "I'm sorry. I went too far. Don't go. Let me give you a ride. Dubrosky, wait ..."

"No thanks. I'm getting a pounding in my head, probably from testosterone overload. I'll take an Uber."

"Hey, you two." Denopoulos walked in and took a seat next to Teague on an empty barstool. "You look pretty damn good for someone who almost died, so what'd I miss?"

"Perfect timing." Natalya reached for her purse on the bar. "The CHS gave us a tip on Pike that I'm following up on with the local and state police departments. Oh, and in case you didn't already know, your partner's an asshole."

Cayden lifted his glass to his lips and took a sip, letting Old Johnnie burn away the knot in his gut. "Don't let the door hit you on your way out," he murmured to Dubrosky's retreating form.

Maybe he did try to rile her up. Anger could be a familiar escape, but these new uncharted waters were a different story. Her words hung in the air, along with her exotic scent. He'd never been attracted to a vampire before and he wondered if her blood and her pheromones were messing with his head. His inner voiced mocked him.

Blood-sharing pheromones my ass. I've been pleasuring myself to her for months now.

"What did you say to her now?" Denopoulos asked, interrupting his wayward thoughts. "When are you going to let the past go? It has no place in this investigation. Are we back to the battle of Ramanya? It happened eons ago. You have to get over it at some point."

Talking about the past made Cayden's nostrils flare with rage. He'd never get over it. "Easy for you to say." His people had fought against the most ruthless group of vampires to exist, and lost. The Coterie murdered his family and took over the only home he'd ever known. *Those bloodsucking monsters somehow managed to turn a Shangri-La into a scorched piece of rock and enslaved every person I ever loved.* Dubrosky couldn't fault him for being bitter, but his partner did have a point. He'd been harboring a misplaced grudge against her for months.

Why take his anger out on her? It all happened before her time, and yet Cayden couldn't seem to hold his tongue whenever she walked into a room.

"What are you going to do when she's seated at your table at the wedding?" His partner's impending nuptials were only a few weeks away. Alex had been through hell and back with his fiancée, Willow, and somehow they still managed to come out the other side.

"Don't worry. I'll be the picture of grace. I'll be charm itself." He'd have to work hard to keep this mouth shut and not let Dubrosky rile him up. She could be stubborn, and persnickety. But she was also smart and sexy in an understated way. He found himself wanting to unpack the secrets behind her big brown eyes despite his hatred of vampires.

"I sure as hell hope so." Denopoulos shook his head and didn't look convinced.

Dubrosky had become friends with Alex's fiancée, Willow, and the rest of the witches from the coven when she met Gillian, Garrett Mulroney's girlfriend. Mulroney and Gillian fell in love during an investigation of a blood-trafficking ring orchestrated by a group of thug vampires. "Don't worry, nothing will get in the way of your big day." Cayden took another sip of whiskey, anxious to change the subject. "What did you find out about Pike and his buddy Hawthorne? This sounds like an inside job."

"We're checking out a few leads. We should know more in the morning. I need to stop by HQ to drop off the ice. I'll run the markings on the jewelry through our database and see if anything comes up stolen. Who knows, it could lead us to one, or both, of our fugitives." His partner's phone beeped. Denopoulos glanced at the screen and a wide beaming smile broke out across his face. "Sorry, man, I need to cut this short. Willow's waiting for me wearing only a flicker of candlelight and a pair of high heels."

"TMI, man, although I get it. If you're not into the woman you're about to get hitched to then what's the point? Go get her."

"You need a ride?" Denopoulos asked, getting to his feet.

"Nah, you take the van. I'll take a taxi. I think I'll stay and have another one." Drowning his sorrows in booze was one of Cayden's favorite pastimes.

"Are you okay, big guy?" Denopoulos looked him over, concern flashing in his partner's dark eyes.

Cayden shrugged. He'd been mauled by a werewolf and drank Dubrosky's blood, something he still couldn't quite wrap his head around. Other than that—he was great. "What can I say? It has been a hell of a day."

"If you say so, Spike."

Cayden's head snapped around. "Who the hell are you calling Spike?"

Denopoulos smiled. "Haven't you ever watched, *Buffy*?"

"No, I can't say that I have. Wait a minute, how did you know—Oh, right, the mics were on."

Clapping a hand on his shoulder, Denopoulos gave him a hard look. "All jokes aside, you need to cut Dubrosky some slack. Unless she's a history buff, I doubt she knows what happened to your people after Arcadia got taken over. She's damn good at her job and her record speaks for itself. She just saved your life."

"You wouldn't understand." Dubrosky represented all he had lost.

"I understand better than you think. I can't tell you the times Willow saved my life, metaphorically speaking. As for Dubrosky, she may be hardheaded and proud. But she reminds me of someone else I know." His partner broke into a fit of laughter.

"What's so damn funny?"

"Nothing. I'm just laughing at the irony. Dubrosky reminds me of the female version of you."

Bristling with irritation, Cayden emptied his glass. "That's not funny."

"She could've let you die out there. It would've served you right for being such a prick." Denopoulos nodded. "You two are connected now. I'll see you tomorrow."

Connected to Dubrosky? Funny, Cayden hadn't felt connected to another person in years. But his partner was right. Demons believed that when someone saved your life, it bound you together for eternity. He'd never tell Dubrosky or she'd never let him live it down.

Getting involved with someone he worked with would be a recipe for disaster. He should know. He'd been there and done that. Sure, it had worked out for Alex and Willow. But Cayden wasn't willing to take that kind of chance. Not now and not ever again. He'd never put stock in other people's opinion of him before. So why did he let Dubrosky's comments chafe? Should he stop giving crap to this beautiful, passionate woman? And what if he did? At least teasing her was safe.

Cayden exhaled a pent-up breath, and before he could shake it off, a heaviness settled in his chest like wet cement. Loneliness gripped him hard and hit him in the pit of his soul. Ever since the tragedy all those years ago, the pain never seemed to go away. It was his curse … his eternal punishment. He prayed for the guilt and sorrow to be numbed.

Random sex and booze were the only things that freed him from the pain, but even the sex often left him feeling hollow. He hadn't felt a woman's touch in months. Now everyone around him seemed to be falling in love and getting hitched—first Denopoulos and now Dubrosky's partner, Mulroney. Cayden didn't think Mulroney would ever settle into domesticity. But the former vampire fell ass over elbow in love with Willow's bestie, Gillian, and drank a potion that turned him human again. He could see those two popping out kids, getting a dog and driving a minivan.

It reminded him of how alone he was, and had been since the incident. Cayden planned on keeping it that way. His family had been gone for years now. How could he get over the past when the only woman he ever loved died in his arms? When he closed his eyes, he could still see Abigail's face in his mind.

He'd taken an oath to protect the innocent. It was his duty and the only thing that got him over the guilt. When he blinked, the image of Abigail's dead body gripped him by the throat like a vise.

Her blood ... everywhere.

His chest tightened with regret, forcing his thoughts back to the present. He needed something strong to knock him out and take the edge off. He signaled to Andee. "I'll have another. Keep 'em coming."

Several minutes ticked by before Andee sauntered back. She set another Johnnie in front of him, along with a shot. "What are you doing for the rest of the night?"

In the old days, Cayden would've jumped at the chance to keep the darkness at bay. But engaging in mindless sex always left him feeling empty and alone in the end. But that didn't mean he couldn't have a drink with a friend, anything to keep him from going home to his empty apartment. "What time does your shift end?"

CHAPTER 4

*R*ather than going home, Natalya found herself back at the station dividing her time between making calls to the local and state police departments, and tracking down leads related to their fugitives —but nothing new came up. While she tried to stay laser-focused, a bone-melting warmth spread through her limbs. It must have been the result of Teague drinking her blood. She could still feel the heat from his body and his tongue on her skin. Damn him.

She cleared the fog from her brain, and finished her report. At the crack of dawn, she headed to the Union Dry Dock Yard to find Rocco, the alpha of Pike's wolf pack. It didn't take long to discover he'd been fired the week before. None of his coworkers knew of his whereabouts. From there, she headed to the manor, hoping the rest of the day wouldn't turn out to be such an epic fail.

After a shower, Natalya changed into a pair of leggings and a comfy sweatshirt. She grabbed a few of her moving boxes, hoping to get most of her stuff into her new place in the next few weeks. For the past month, she'd been living here at the manor with the other witches from the local coven. She'd left her parent's townhouse in the city six months ago when Gillian's cousin Brooke needed someone to sublet her place after her kidnapping. The lease came up on the apartment, but Brooke chose to remain here with the manor.

It made Natalya realize she wanted a place of her own. When she found a condo for sale in an older brick building close by, she jumped in with both feet. The place needed a major overhaul. The women convinced her to stay on here while her contractor finished the renovations.

Natalya came out of her bedroom, and crossed the hall, passing the stained glass windows and redwood paneling. She loved the whimsical vibe of the old house. Antique lanterns lit her path to the kitchen. The moment she walked in, the scents of rosemary, lavender, and thyme mingled in the air. Herbs hung from dark wooden beams all around the kitchen. Mortar and pestles, along with votive candles filled the long wooden countertops.

Arabella sat at the table with a tin of Earl Grey and a fancy tea set. The steady sound of her heartbeat echoed in Natalya's ears. She wore her long, dark hair pulled back into a high ponytail. "What are you up to?"

"I'm about to load up my car with moving boxes. I thought I'd drink my weight in caffeine before I head out." Natalya headed to the coffee maker before facing Arabella once more.

"How about some tea instead?" Arabella lifted one of the pink, flowered china cups in front of her filled with what appeared to be brown gunk. "I'd love to read your tea leaves."

"What exactly does it entail?" She'd seen Arabella practice tasseography before, but this would be the first time she'd ever indulged in a reading. She'd always been fascinated by magick ever since she'd been a child. The summers spent at her aunt's cottage in Connecticut near the water were some of her best memories. She could still recall sneaking behind the staircase and listen to her do crystal ball readings. She'd been hooked ever since.

"This is just another form of divination," Arabella pointed out. "I can give you some quick predictions. C'mon, Natalya. Be bold."

"Why not." Foregoing the coffee, Natalya joined Arabella at the table.

"Step into my office." Arabella grinned and motioned to a stool.

The buzz of voices and loud banging climbed up from the window as a crew set up for Willow and Alex's wedding in the garden

"Where is everyone?" Natalya asked, glancing around the empty kitchen. She could hear the fridge hum and the fan spin.

"They're already at the shop." Arabella sprinkled some leaves from the tin into one of the cups, and then poured hot water in, and set the cup in front of Natalya.

Natalya became friends with this amazing group of witches a few months back after she'd gone undercover to protect Gillian from a blood-trafficking ring. The one bright spot in the whole ordeal had been getting to know everyone. These women had become some of Natalya's best friends and allowed her to explore her fascination with witchcraft. Outside of being a vampire, Natalya didn't possess any real magick of her own. Secretly she'd always hoped the gods would bestow her aunt's gift on her, but so far, no such luck.

"What now?"

Arabella pointed to the cup with a smile. "Go ahead and drink until you get to the bottom. Don't worry. The water isn't too hot. Think of this as a cup of destiny."

Excitement fluttered in Natalya's belly. "Destiny? I'm not sure I believe in such a thing, but I love anything to do with magick."

When Natalya finished, Arabella lifted the cup from the saucer and placed it facedown, spilling the contents on a paper towel. She turned the teacup three times in a circle before turning it right side up. She gazed deeply at the bottom of the cup. "Would you like to focus on your love life or career?"

"What love life?" Natalya chuckled. "Unless of course you see a charming stranger willing to go to a ball with me." When she clicked open her email this morning, an invitation to the Sexual Abuse Assistance Network annual charity event waited in her inbox. She prided herself on getting donations and sponsorships throughout the year. She usually skipped the thousand-dollar-a-plate, black-tie dinner, though. Unfortunately, she couldn't forgo the hoopla this time. She'd been nominated for an award to honor her work with sexual abuse victims.

Her sired family had been on the board for years. She preferred to do her part from the sidelines. The thought of showing up in a ball gown in a room full of society matrons made her break out in cold sweat. Besides making a speech, Natalya would be expected to bring a plus-one. If she showed up alone, she'd shame her sired family and their friends.

"Try and focus, Natalya. It helps with the reading," Arabella whispered, her voice breaking into her thoughts.

"Oh right, sorry." Natalya gazed inside the cup of scattered leaves, not sure where to look first, but trying to embrace the magickal aspect of the reading.

"I see birds in Leo's constellation, one has to do with your past and the other is your future." Arabella stared at the leaves. "Don't worry about finding a date for your ball."

"Easy for you to say." Male admirers flocked to Arabella's fun, outgoing personality and stunning good looks.

"Why don't we ask our resident matchmaker's opinion?" Arabella looked up at Brooke as she walked into the kitchen. "I thought you were at the shop?"

"I forgot my laptop and I have an astrology reading in thirty minutes." Brooke wore a fitted gray dress and knee-high gray boots. Her blonde hair fell to her shoulders in loose waves. She always looked put-together. Natalya envied her effortless style. "Ask me what?"

"Natalya needs a date for a ball," Arabella explained. "Don't you think her chances are better at finding one if she creates a profile on a dating app?"

"You don't have one?" Brooke's gaze narrowed in Natalya's direction.

"I, uh, well, I just never got around to it." Natalya ran her finger of the rim of the teacup. These conversations always made her stomach twist up into knots.

"I've met some good guys and some real a-holes." Brooke's lip curled into a smile. "I'm a big believer in throwing enough crap against the wall until something eventually sticks."

Natalya chuckled. "The prospect sounds about as romantic as a root canal."

"Brooke's still holding out for Mr. Right Now, not Mr. Right." Arabella winked. "Just sayin'."

"Says the woman who only dates guys who are well-endowed." Brooke's eyes sparked with mischief. "Pot, have you met cauldron?" She reached for her computer still plugged into a wall charger and slipped it into her tote bag.

Natalya laughed. She loved seeing Brooke take some good-natured ribbing and give it right back. Several months ago, she'd been completely lost after getting kidnapped. Natalya shuddered to think where she'd be right now if not for Garrett and Gillian's rescue.

"I'm here if you change your mind. I'd love to help. Sorry. but I've got to go. I'll see you two later." Brooke waved and disappeared out of the kitchen.

"How about I finish your reading before the tea goes cold?" Arabella glanced over at Natalya, and then gazed into the cup, turning it to the side. "I actually see two males entering your life. Both will be vying for your attention."

A thrill sparked in her belly. "Two men? These days the only boyfriend I've grown attached to requires AA batteries."

Arabella chuckled as she studied the leaves. "Not for much longer. One of these two men will be a kind of thorn in your side, and the other will be a sensual lover who eventually wins your heart. It's all part of your journey of accepting your opposite. You will be forced to choose between the two. This is going to be life changing for you, Natalya."

Natalya's cheeks heated. "I can't wrap my mind around the idea of two men. I'd be happy with one for now."

"I can't wait to see what unfolds." Smiling, Arabella rose and cleaned up the mess on the table, then put the cups in the sink. She glanced at Natalya her over her shoulder. "What about one of Alex's friends? They're all gorgeous. I hear Cayden's single. He stares at you all the time. Haven't you noticed?"

"What?" Why did her breaths grow shallow? "We work together," Natalya said, shaking her head. "And I hear he's a major player." The image of Teague sucking on her finger flashed through her mind. A hot flush spread from cheeks to her neck.

"I think there's a lot more to Cayden than meets the eye. He's a good guy. He volunteers with the kids at Hope House, the outreach organization Alex and Willow started for runaways and victims of sexual abuse. I hear he's amazing with them."

Hearing about Teague's volunteer work gave her a little jolt. Granted, Natalya caught a glimpse of vulnerability after he'd been wounded. For one brief moment, she got to see a different side to the demon. This revelation surprised her. She exhaled and pushed all thoughts of Teague from her mind. "I've got to go. I'll get some wine on my way home."

"Sounds like a plan. Oh, I almost forgot, Gillian and Garrett are headed back a week from Saturday so we thought we'd do a surprise welcome-home dinner for her the following day. Just the girls."

Natalya smiled. "Count me in."

"And of course we still have to plan Willow's bachelorette party."

"I can't wait. In my circles, women don't go to bachelorette parties. I've never been to one, but I've heard some crazy stories about them. Are you thinking brunch at a classy restaurant or a night of debauchery with penis-shaped lollipops and male strippers?"

"Everyone will take a vote, but with this group, my money's on the latter."

"Let me know what I can do to help. Thanks again, Arabella, for spilling the tea." Natalya headed out the door with thoughts of the two men in her future dancing in her head.

CHAPTER 5

The Avalon apartment complex on Madison Street sat less than a block from Dulce de Leche Bakery and Field Park. Natalya looked forward to jogging along the water and exploring the neighborhood.

After letting herself into the apartment, she placed the bakery box on the table, along with a paint can she'd picked up from the hardware store. "Honey, I'm home."

Her contractor, Adrian, a dark-skinned human man with glasses and a bald head, walked out from the plastic tarp in the kitchen with a smile. He sniffed the air and glanced at the box. "Is that from the bakery on the corner?"

"The best cannolis in town." Natalya opened the box and the scent of sugar, chocolate, and cream wafted through the air and made her mouth water. Turning her head, she gazed at the new crown molding in the hallway and the living room. "It looks like you've made some serious progress since the last time I was here. The place looks amazing. How much longer will it take?"

"Hard to say at this point." Adrian shrugged. "It could be a few weeks, maybe more. I still need to sand the floors, lay the quartz, and add the wainscoting. Be patient, have a cannoli." He took one from the box, broke off a piece and plopped it into his mouth.

She'd never been good at being patient. But she tried to look at the upside. She'd get more time to hang out with the witches from the coven and learn more about magick. She reached for a cannoli, took a bite, and sighed with pleasure. She didn't need to eat to survive, but she had lived on sweets as a human, a habit she couldn't seem to break. "Ah, breakfast of champions."

"I've already eaten a doughnut and drank a latte." Adrian wiped his hands on a towel and picked up the can of paint and a brush from his toolbox. "I'd better get to work before my sugar high wears off."

Natalya laughed. "I've got some boxes in my car. I plan to move more in next week." She'd ordered furniture from a local store, but her sales clerk said it could take weeks before they put her on the schedule for delivery. Throw pillows would have to do for now.

Adrian got to work priming the walls. "You hit gold getting into this building."

Before she could respond, the doorbell rang. Natalya glanced over her shoulder at Adrian. Almost no one knew the address to her new place. She brushed the crumbs from her hands. "Were you expecting someone?"

"Nope. It could be a delivery."

"Right." Natalya walked to the hall and caught a whiff of rose perfume. She opened the door to find a petite older woman with short, dark hair holding a small dog on the other side. "Mrs. Pearse?" They'd met briefly the day of her closing. She introduced herself while Natalya stopped by to drop off boxes. She had left out the part about being a vampire. In her experience, not everyone embraced vampires, especially the elderly human population.

"I thought I heard voices. I'm sorry to bother you, but I need your help. I think Andrea Lyon, the young lady who lives in 4G with her mom, may be in trouble," Mrs. Pearse explained. "She hasn't stopped by to walk Cody today." The dog yelped at the mention of his name. "It's not like her to flake out. She would've called."

"Could she be sick?" Natalya smiled at Cody and patted his head. "Good boy."

The dog growled, showing his teeth. She should have known better. She seemed to have this effect on dogs, cats and other domestic animals. Still, she had to try.

"Cody, no." Mrs. Pearse scolded. "I'm sorry. This isn't like him."

"It's okay." Natalya still missed her beloved golden retriever. He refused to go near her once she got turned. Everything in her life changed the night she became a vampire. Pushing the memory aside, she refused to fall down the rabbit hole. She shook off the past, focusing her attention back to her neighbor. Normally she wouldn't get involved in something like this, especially since she was off duty, but Natalya could detect the older woman's accelerated heartbeat. "Tell me about your dog walker."

"She works crazy hours," Mrs. Pearse said, shaking her head. "Her mother and stepfather are away and asked me to look in on her. She always shows up for Cody. She loves him. It's gotten harder for me to walk him these days. I've knocked on her door, but she didn't answer. Would you mind checking on her? Please, Detective. I'm worried. She's doing well now, but she got into some trouble in the past."

"Trouble? As in trouble with the law?" Natalya asked, now curious.

Mrs. Pearse nodded. "Sweet girl, but has the worst taste in men, always has. Her parents divorced years ago. The dad's not in the picture. So you see, Andrea's easy prey when it comes to matters of the heart. She got involved with a drug dealer and starting selling the stuff and became addicted. I swear someone upstairs was looking out for her. She got arrested and ended up getting probation."

"She could've gone away for a long time for a drug offense."

"Thankfully one of the agents on the case got her into rehab. After that, she turned her life around."

"Believe me, she was one of the lucky ones." Hearing those kinds of success stories was one of many reasons that made Natalya want to join the police force. She wanted to make a difference. "It sounds like Andrea finally got her act together. What makes you think something's wrong?"

"I heard a loud banging coming from her apartment earlier. Then a few minutes later, I heard the door open and shut, but the footsteps didn't sound like hers. They were too heavy. I looked through the peephole and caught a glimpse of a tall man in a black coat."

Natalya cleared her throat. Her neighbor didn't miss a beat. "Maybe she had a friend staying over." The banging could've been loud sex, but she didn't want to say that out of respect.

"At first I thought it was one of her male suitors, but not this one." Mrs. Pearse scratched her dog on the ears.

"How do you know?"

"By his coat. It looked too fancy for one of the fellas Andrea dates. I see them when they come to pick her up. The majority of her young men wear leather or fleece. You even get the occasional polyester, but this coat was long, and made of wool or cashmere, not something off the rack. If I had to guess, I'd say it was custom."

"And you got all this by looking through a peephole? Wow, I'm impressed." Mrs. Pearse was either a serious busybody, or an amateur sleuth. "I think I might have to tell my boss about you."

"I know my fabrics, my dear. My late husband and I used to own a dry cleaner."

"Well, that certainly explains lot, but it still doesn't mean Andrea's in trouble, Mrs. Pearse. Did you ever think this could be a family friend stopping by? Did you happen to see his face?"

"No. I only managed to catch a glimpse of him from the back. When I opened the door, I caught a whiff of a cigar. I must come off as some crazy old lady, but I'm not. Something's wrong. I can feel it in my gut." Mrs. Pearse pressed a withered hand to her stomach. "Cody keeps barking and sniffing at Andrea's door. Won't you help me, please?"

The pleading note in the older woman's voice tugged at Natalya's heartstrings. How could she say no? "Lead the way."

By the time they made it to Andrea Lyon's door, Mrs. Pearse appeared visibly shaken. The older woman knocked. "Andrea, I'm here with Detective Dubrosky. Can you open the door?"

They waited, but no answer came.

"Let me try." Natalya banged on the door. "Miss Lyon? Andrea? Open up." Natalya used her senses to tune into the energy on the other side. Sniffing the air, two things hit her at once: the scent of a demon, and freshly spilled blood. Her hand flew back to the door and she banged even harder this time, hoping she didn't leave a dent.

Cayden jolted up and glanced around the strange room, shielding his eyes against the ribbons of afternoon sunlight streaming in from the window. He rubbed the back of his neck, not sure if the pounding was coming from the door or his skull. At this point, he couldn't tell. A buzzing filled his ears. Everything from the night before became one big blur.

His tongue had gone fuzzy and it felt like someone had pulled his eyes from his sockets and put them back in his head. He sniffed the air. *Nothing.* Pushing a finger into his ear, he tried to dislodge the muffled sensation. *No such luck.* All of his senses seemed dulled. If he didn't know better, he'd say he'd been drugged. At least he hadn't woken up to a nightmare. He couldn't remember the last time he'd slept through the night without one.

Drinking himself stupid and passing out wasn't the smartest move, but at least it kept the nightmares at bay. His gaze darted around the room again and fragments from the night before came back like a movie in rewind. He'd gone home with Andee and passed out on her couch. But then what? Why couldn't he shake the fog from his brain?

Kicking off the cover, he breathed a sigh of relief to find he was fully clothed, He got up from the couch and a wave of dizziness hit him hard. Rubbing a hand over his eyes, a combination of drowsiness and nausea hit him like a right hook to the chin. He reached for his phone on the table. Thankfully, it held an infinite charge—one of the many perks of working for the MBI was all the cool gadgets.

He glanced at the screen. He'd missed a bunch of calls from his partner. In the ten years he'd worked for the agency, he'd never slept through a call. The banging on the door continued. He cursed and slipped his phone into his back pocket.

"Keep your bike shorts on. I'm coming." Grumbling to himself, he trudged to the front door, his head pounding with every step. He swung it open and found Dubrosky and a little old lady with a small dog standing in the hall. "W-what are you doing here?" Did his speech sound slurred?

"I could ask you the same question." Dubrosky's eyes widened as they roamed over him.

She cleared her throat, and then turned to the older woman and smiled. "I'll clear this up and meet you back in your apartment, Mrs. Pearse."

Mrs. Pearse sized up Cayden with a purse of her thin lips. "I think it's pretty clear what's going on here."

This situation is awkward as hell. "With all due respect, ma'am, nothing's going on. Andee and I are friends. She let me crash on her couch last night, end of story." Cayden's attention became focused on the dog. "Hey, buddy," he cooed and gave him a scratch on the head. The little guy wagged his tail in response.

Dubrosky cleared her throat.

"I'll leave you to it." Mrs. Pearse craned her neck to glance up at his face. "You seem to have a way with animals and apparently with women. The young men never looked like that back in my day," she muttered and retreated down the hall.

"Tell me again why you're here." Cayden's gaze rested on Dubrosky. Images from the night before flashed through his mind and forced blood to rush to his groin. Her strawberry scent invaded his nostrils and made the front panel of his jeans tight. All night long he'd been craving the sweet taste of her blood. He could still recall the way her lips had parted and turned a dark shade of red while he drank. He prayed she didn't notice.

"I'm here to check on Andrea. Clearly, she's a friend of yours." Dubrosky didn't wait for him to invite her in. She brushed past him and crossed into the hallway. "Where is she?'

"Do you have to talk that loud?" Cayden rubbed his throbbing head as his gaze roamed over her oversized sweater and loose-fitting yoga pants. He'd never seen her dressed this casually. And once again he wondered what her body looked like under the baggy clothes. "Andrea? Who the hell is Andrea?" And then it hit him. "Oh, you mean, Andee?"

"Andee … Andrea. Are you in the habit of sleeping with your informants?" Dubrosky asked with a note of irritation in her voice.

"If I didn't know better, I'd say you're jealous." Cayden ran a hand through his hair, amused. "Nothing happened. Just thought you should know."

"What you do during your personal time is none of my business. Although I'm not sure hooking up with an informant is wise." Dubrosky glanced around the apartment. "Where is she?" She turned back to face him, her gaze zeroed in on a few trickles of blood on his jeans. "There's blood on you, but it doesn't smell like yours."

Sniffing the air, his sense of smell returned full-throttle. When Cayden looked at the trail that led from the den area into the bedroom, the hair on the back of his neck stood on end. "What the …?"

"Is there anyone else here? I thought I smelled a vampire." Natalya removed the Glock from her holster and crossed into the bedroom in a blur.

Cayden followed her and froze in the doorway. Andee lay sprawled out on the bed, motionless and covered in blood, with a tie around her neck—

his tie. Bile rose up from the back of his throat. "Gods, no! No! Not again!" The stench of death and the smell of her blood made his stomach roil. An explosion of emotions tore through his chest.

Dubrosky blurred across the room and checked her pulse. She sucked in an audible breath. "She's dead."

Cayden followed her gaze to the blood-splattered tie wrapped around her neck.

She sniffed the air. "I smell ketchup." When Dubrosky turned to face him, a mixture of shock and disbelief flared in her eyes. She staggered back. "How could you?"

Adrenaline surged through his veins. He fell to his knees at the foot of the bed, willing Andee to open her eyes. "It's not what you think, Dubrosky. I didn't do it ... I wouldn't. I swear." Who in the hell could've come in and killed her without waking him? His mind blanked. *But what if I did? What if I blacked out?* Staring at the body, bile rose up from the back of his throat.

"That's your tie and there's blood on your jeans. Did you have too much to drink and engaged in a little rough sex that got out of hand?" The accusation in her voice forced his horns to elongate from his head.

"It's not like that." Cayden held up his hand. "You've got to believe me. I must've been set up. Pike must've followed me here and killed Andee to frame me."

Dubrosky's eyes filled with doubt. "Even if that were true, what am I supposed to think? From where I'm standing, all the physical evidence points to you. I'm sorry, Teague, but I have to follow protocol." She pulled out her cell, and pressed a button. "I have to call this in." After she repeated the address and her badge number, she ended the call, refusing to look him in the eye.

"I know this looks bad, but I'd never hurt her or any female." A cold dread settled in the pit of his stomach. Rubbing his forehead, he prayed this nightmare would end and he'd wake up. Guilt and rage surged through his veins. It felt like history repeating itself in some twisted way.

"You should call Denopoulos and Smith. They can meet us at the station. The Council can take things from there," Dubrosky said with a nod.

His hand shook as he pulled out his phone. After two tries, he pressed a button and Denopoulos answered on the first ring. "Where the hell are you? I've been calling you all morning."

"Listen to me, man. I'm in trouble." Cayden's chest heaved and he could barely catch his breath. "My ass is in the shit can this time. Andee's dead and I've been framed for her murder."

CHAPTER 6

"*I* swear I didn't do it. I was set up." Cayden sat at a table in the MBI conference room across from his lawyer, Mike Sierpina. Over the years, he'd bumped into the demon outside the courthouse on a number of occasions. From his shock of white hair and short silver horns, he'd been around the block a time or two, which seemed to jive with his reputation as a kick-ass criminal defense attorney for the supernatural.

Sierpina glanced at his legal pad before looking up. "The only reason the Council agreed to let you out on bail is because of your track record with the agency, but I'm afraid they won't be as magnanimous moving forward. There's an arraignment scheduled in two days where we will enter your plea."

"How do we prove I'm innocent?" The desperation in Cayden's voice sounded foreign to his own ears. He didn't relish the idea of going back to county lockup, or worse, a cell in Hellios. He ran a hand over the scruff on his chin. What he wouldn't give for a shower, a shave and a fresh change of clothes. He reached for a bottle of water on the table and took a sip

"We see what evidence the Council has against you and if it equates to probable cause," Sierpina said in a no-nonsense tone. "If so, then they can move forward with their case. They will deliberate as a final grand jury and be the ones to decide your fate."

"Great." Cayden's heart pounded, and his throat burned. What about finding Andee's killer? If the MBI didn't find the bastard responsible, he'd end up in Hellios. It would be game over the moment he stepped through the doors. As an agent, he'd be targeted and killed before the guards could do anything to stop it. He needed an outlet for the hot stab of anger racing through his limbs or he'd completely lose his shit.

Sierpina glanced over at his white–knuckled grip around the water bottle, and frowned. "I think you should start at the beginning. Don't leave out any details. I don't need to know if you're innocent or guilty, that's for the Council to prove."

Taking a deep, steadying breath, Cayden filled his lawyer in on everything from the prison break at Hellios, to the stolen jewels, the chase with Pike, the meeting with Andee and her tip on Rocco, and then finally to waking up at her place with a massive hangover and finding her dead. His stomach threatened to revolt thinking about it now.

Sierpina's pen scratched against a notebook. "Okay, we need to establish why these two characters, Pike and Hawthorne, might want to frame you. Pike's motive would be revenge. You confiscated his big payoff and now he'll be on the run for the rest of his immortal life with nothing to show for it, but what about Hawthorne?"

Cayden rubbed his jaw, ready to crawl out of his own skin. "Framing me would get me out of the way."

"I'll need to corroborate your story." Sierpina seemed to mull over this new information.

Unable to sit still any longer, Cayden got up and began to pace. "Someone else must've been at Andee's apartment that night and killed her." A riot of emotions swept over him—rage, guilt, remorse. He should've protected her somehow. How could he have slept through such an attack?

"We'll wait for the coroner's report to see if there's a forensic piece of evidence to prove reasonable doubt."

Cayden wondered if Pike could've followed him to Andee's and killed her while he'd been passed out on the couch, or got his buddy Hawthorne do the deed. He swallowed the lump in his throat. If he'd been awake and alert, none of this would've happened. The only thing he could do now was find Andee's killer.

"Tell me about your relationship with the deceased. Were you two ever involved romantically?" Sierpina asked, his gaze narrowing in Cayden's direction.

"No, never." Cayden pushed a hand through his hair, his nerves shot. "I thought of her like a kid sister."

"We need to prepare for the Council members to ask why you didn't wake up while your friend was being murdered." Sierpina folded his arms across his chest. "Can you fill in the gaps?"

Cayden stopped pacing and hung his head with shame. "I've thought a lot about this while I was cooling my heels in a jail cell. Sure, I imbibed during the night in question, but not enough to keep me from hearing someone enter the apartment and kill Andee. I was passed out for hours. I never sleep that long. I remember feeling spacey and disoriented when I woke up. Dubrosky ran a toxicology screen right away. I'm still waiting for the results."

"Are you suggesting you were roofied?" Sierpina scribbled another note on his pad.

"It's the only thing that makes any sense. There were a few people behind the bar the night of the murder. I suppose any one of them could've slipped something into my drink without anyone noticing. I've got no proof. My metabolism burns away booze quick, but not this time. I've never experienced that kind of hangover before."

Sierpina picked up his phone and began typing. "I just texted the lab and told them we need the results ASAP."

Cayden nodded, hope filling his chest. "If you can prove I was out cold when Andee was murdered, would that be reason enough to get the case dismissed?"

"It sure as hell would work in your favor," Sierpina said with a nod. "It really depends on what kind of physical evidence the coroner finds."

Sitting around waiting and doing nothing while they sifted through the mess would be agony. Cayden needed answers. He continued to walk back and forth, ready to burn a hole through the wood floor when an idea popped into his head. "What if we get additional evidence that isn't physical?"

"You mean like the testimony of a witness or an expert?"

"Exactly. What if we got a qualified psychic to try and pick up some clues when it's no longer an official crime scene? What if that person could testify that there was no way in hell I could've killed Andee?" Cayden would get down on his knees and beg Willow if he had to.

"It's possible. Do you have someone in mind?"

"My partner's fiancée is a top-notch psychic. She's well-trained and licensed. The agency used her as a consultant on a murder case a little over a year ago that got a ton of publicity. Do you remember the 'Crossbow Killer'?"

Sierpina nodded. "I read about that case. You must be referring to Willow McCray. I agree, she's certainly qualified. Has she testified in front of the Council before? Is she in the system?"

"Yes, on all counts."

"Hmm, you might be onto something, Cayden. The rules of evidence in the Council forum accept the accuracy and reliability of qualified psychics."

"Do you want me to give her a call?" Cayden's heart hammered away in his chest.

"Forward me her number. Let me handle the rest."

Cayden prayed for a miracle—for everyone's sake.

CHAPTER 7

$\mathscr{N}$atalya glanced over at Denopoulos as he walked around Andee's bedroom, crossing to the front of the bed where the yellow and purple crime scene tape used to be. The Council's office had reached out to her and asked if she'd return to the former crime scene in an unofficial capacity. Ribbons of late afternoon sunlight streamed in from the window, and cast a glow over the room. She inhaled and the scent of blood, chemicals, and death flared in her nostrils.

"Teague appreciates you doing this and so do I."

"I'll do whatever I can to help catch the killer." Blowing out a strangled breath, she turned her head, and it landed on Andee's blood-stained mattress. Her heart squeezed. This part of the job she'd never get used to—the senseless act of violence against an innocent woman.

"We should get this over with," Denopoulos said with a deep sigh. "Once Willow does her thing, then we can get the hell out of here. She should be here any minute now. I left the front door unlocked."

"Sounds good to me." Natalya tried to desensitize herself from the bubbly young woman she'd met a few days before, with the gruesome image of her lifeless body sprawled out on the bed. She couldn't help but think about all the things she'd never get to experience, like planning her wedding, having a family, or growing old.

Natalya didn't envy the officers assigned to the task of contacting

Andee's family. She'd been forced to relay the news of her murder to Mrs. Pearse before one of the officers interviewed her. She feared the ordeal had sent the poor thing into shock.

The front door opened and closed. Footfalls forced Natalya's gaze to the doorway. Willow walked into the room with a black bag over her shoulder. The fiery redhead wore a loose-fitting peasant blouse and a pair of green khakis that accentuated her tall, slender frame. "Sorry, I'm late. I got caught up at the bridal shop. Today was my final fitting."

The thought of having to pivot from something so happy and exciting to something so awful made Natalya's stomach twist. "I wish we were all here under better circumstances."

"Yeah, me too," Willow said with a sad smile. She used the tie on her wrist to pull her long, red hair into a ponytail. A radiant smile spread across her pretty face as she made her way over to Denopoulos. Stretching to her tiptoes, she placed a kiss on his cheek. "I didn't get to say goodbye before you left."

"Thanks for coming, babe." From the goofy expressions on both their faces, the two couldn't be more in love.

Natalya turned away to give them a moment of privacy and stared at the clothes still hung in Andee's closet, clothes she'd never get to wear again. Her gut told her Teague couldn't have killed her, regardless of the physical evidence. If he'd been lying, he'd given an award-winning performance. Until they found something concrete to clear him, he was still their prime suspect. But what if he killed Andee by mistake? One way or another, the truth would come out eventually. She turned back to face Denopoulos and Willow once more.

"Don't worry about contaminating evidence, Willow," Denopoulos said, motioning around the room with a sweep of his hand. "You can do what you need to. The crime scene has already been processed."

"Okay then. I'm going to get started." Willow pulled out two white pillar candles from her bag. After she lit them with a flick of her wrist, she sprinkled salt throughout the room.

"Are you ready? I'm going to record you." Denopoulos reached for his phone and pressed a button.

"Let's do this." Willow closed her eyes and whispered a few words. A pulsing energy vibrated throughout the room. She opened her eyes and walked around touching Andee's things, first her headboard, the lamp beside her bed, and then the knob on her desk drawer. She turned to Natalya and motioned around the room. "I'm sorry. I know this must be unpleasant for you, but can you show me where you found the body?"

"It's okay." Natalya swallowed the lump in her throat and pointed to the center of the bed. "Based on the pattern and splattering of blood, whoever killed her must've done it in the other room and then dragged her in here."

"I sensed her fear and pain the moment I walked through the door. Dear Goddess, poor Andee." Willow stopped at the foot of the bed. When she placed her hands on the edge of the mattress, she closed her eyes and sucked in a harsh breath. "She tried to fight back, but she was no match for him. He's strong ... powerful. His heart is black and filled with bitterness." She bent over the side of the bed, her face pale.

"What is it?" Denopoulos asked, alarm lacing his voice. He moved to stand behind her at the bed.

"I can see him ejaculating on the body."

Pain sliced through Natalya's chest. She exhaled and she tried to maintain a neutral perspective even though she wanted to hurl.

"I can feel his anger." Willow pressed a hand to her stomach. "He's hell-bent on revenge."

"Revenge for what?" Denopoulos knitted his dark brows together.

"I'm not sure." Willow rested her hand on the edge of the bed. "He believes what he did was justified. He's smart, and I'd go as far to say meticulous. He thinks he's smarter than the police. He has zero remorse for what he's done. He considers this as some kind of retribution. It burns in his veins like acid."

Denopoulos nodded. "Anything else?"

Willow coughed and made a face. "I smell cigar smoke. I'm also sensing emotional turmoil like Andee had been fighting with a lover."

"Do you see what the killer looks like? Can you give us a description of his face, his build, clothing, any distinguishing marks, tattoos, anything like that?"

Several tense minutes passed and then Willow exhaled a long breath. "I can see him coming into the room. He's tall with brown hair and dark, soulless eyes. As for the rest, I only see grainy, distorted images. Hold on, I have an idea."

She walked to her bag and pulled out a copper bowl and a small water jug. She set both on the dresser. After she poured some water into the bowl, she reached for the nearest candle, lit it and dripped the wax onto the water. She whispered a series of words and an image of a male figure rose up from the surface of the water like smoke.

Natalya gasped. She'd heard stories from the other witches about Willow's incredible gifts, but she'd never seen anything like this before.

Willow visibly tensed. "He wants something he feels was taken from him."

The smoke dissipated, leaving Natalya with more questions than answers. Every fiber of her being told her Teague couldn't have committed murder. The demon spent his every waking moment saving lives, not snuffing them out.

Denopoulos pressed a button on his phone and the recording stopped. He shoved his cell in his pocket and then walked over to his fiancée, and placed a kiss on the top of her head. "You were amazing. This proves Teague's innocent."

Natalya smiled at the genuine display of affection and for some reason loneliness gripped her by the throat.

Willow turned to her and arched her brows. "You okay, Natalya?"

Her cheeks heated. "Who, me? Yeah, I'm fine."

"I'll leave you to finish up. I'll wait for you in the hall." Willow gathered her things and walked out of the room.

"I'm going to send the recording to Teague's lawyer and Smith," Denopoulos said, looking relieved. "Willow's physical description of the killer doesn't mesh with Teague's. Let's pray this will help exonerate him."

"What happens now?" Natalya asked, sighing with relief.

"Willow sends a report to Teague's lawyer and then the Council has one of their own psychics corroborate it for legitimacy purposes. After that, we hope like hell the case against him gets thrown out."

"What about motive? Do you still think Wolf and Hawthorne are involved?"

"Frankly, at this point, it sounds more like a jealous ex or a stalker. It seems to me like the bastard killed the vic in an act of revenge when he walked in and found Teague here."

"Yeah, you're probably right," Natalya muttered, pulling out her phone and making notes. Why couldn't she shake the feeling that the killer wanted revenge against Teague and not Andee?

Denopoulos angled his head to the door. "What do you say, Dubrosky, are you ready to get out of here?"

Natalya took one last look at Andee's bed where her body used to be, and her stomach churned. She wanted to get the hell out of this room and never come back. "You have no idea."

A few days later, Cayden sat next to his lawyer at a wooden table in the Raven's Hollow Courthouse. Torches lit the dark circular room. Soundproofing kept it hidden from the general public. The layout resembled a regular courtroom with leather benches and a jury box. A cold foreboding energy hung in the air and forced the hair on his neck to stand on end.

Tapping his foot, he waited to make his statement to the four elder creatures of The Council. A demon, a witch, a vampire and a fae presided from a raised stone table that hovered in midair. He recognized a few of their faces, having seen them many times over the years.

The only sounds in the room came from the sand slipping through the witch's hourglass and the pounding of his heart. Taking a deep breath, he suppressed the urge to loosen his tie. He could barely breathe in this monkey suit Alex let him borrow, but he couldn't have been more grateful. He didn't know what he'd do or where he'd be without his friends.

Sierpina turned to face him, and motioned to the stack of papers piled up next to his computer. "Remember to stick to exactly what we talked about and whatever you do, don't lose your temper."

"Right," he whispered back. Tension coiled down Cayden's back like a snake.

"You may take a step forward, Cayden Teague." An older female demon with red skin turned her attention on him. "You have an excellent record with the agency. Your attorney has sent us quite a detailed list of the volunteer work you've done with the organization, Hope House. You're a contributing member of this society."

"However, you've been brought forth for the murder of the human female, Andrea Lyon," the vampire cut in, his deep voice echoed through the chamber and made Cayden's gut clench. "How do you plead?"

"Not guilty." Cayden's pulse raced. He'd never been this nervous before in his life. He wiped his sweaty palms on his slacks. Too much was riding on the outcome if things went south.

His lawyer stepped forward to make the opening statement they discussed. "If I may, Your Honors, my client had a relationship with the victim. He recommended probation for her from a drug-related crime. From there, he helped Andrea Lyon get into college and get a job. The victim turned her life around because of my client's influence. He'd have no motive for killing her. We ask this Council to take into account the expert report, as well as consider the toxicology report that shows traces of a potion used as a potent sleep aid that would've rendered my client unconscious at the time of Miss Lyon's death."

The panel of elders broke out in conversation. When the rumble of voices quieted, his lawyer continued, "After the Council reviews the overwhelming evidence proving my client's innocence, I'll be asking for all charges to be dismissed." Sierpina walked to the table and reached for the stack of papers.

"We've reviewed all the evidence and the expert report, and after careful consideration, and due to a lack of probable cause and exculpatory evidence, we've concluded that pursuing the case against you would be a waste of the citizens' money. All charges have been dismissed. You're free to go, Cayden Teague," the panel said in unison.

CHAPTER 8

"I can't thank you enough, man." Cayden shook hands with his attorney and practically sprinted out of the courtroom.

Denopoulos and Smith stood outside the double doors looking anxious. He'd never been so relieved to see them. Cayden loosened his tie, glad to be the hell out of there. "Thanks for coming."

"No need to thanks us. I'm assuming you were found innocent since you weren't taken away in lead chains," Smith said, patting him on the shoulder.

"All charges were dismissed," Cayden exhaled, long and hard, letting the news sink in.

Denopoulos bumped his arm. "We were worried there for a while."

The three of them descended the steps of the courthouse. Cayden turned his face up to the sky, basking in the late afternoon sunshine, glad to be free. "Let's take a walk. I need to stretch my legs and get some fresh air."

They made their way down Washington Street, passing brick office buildings, Cayden's favorite coffee shop, and throngs of both humans and supernaturals coming and going. He relished the sound of cars whizzing by. After they cut across River Street, the three of them headed to the waterfront.

The briny scent of roasted beef filled Cayden's nostrils and made his stomach grumble. Stopping at a hot dog cart, he pulled out his wallet. "Dinner's on me."

After the three of them dosed up their hot dogs with mustard and relish, they walked to a deserted area of the park. Once Cayden made sure they were alone, they sat on a large bench, and dug into their food. He glanced across the river at the New York City skyline and took it all in with a newfound appreciation.

"The toxicology report said I was I roofied, with what?" he asked his partner taking another bite of his hot dog, groaning with hunger.

"It referenced a potion made from henbane leaves found in your blood. I did some research. It's in the mandrake family and can knock even a big guy like you on his ass for a good, long stretch," Denopoulos pointed out. "It's odorless and tasteless."

"How in the hell could someone have slipped something in my drink with three cops sitting at the bar?" Cayden asked with a shake of his head. Sure, he'd imbibed a few the night of Andee's murder, but he'd barely caught a buzz. It took a hell of a lot of hooch to get him smashed. And he'd also been laser focused on his surroundings. Or so he thought. Guilt twisted in his gut. If only he'd had his wits about him, Andee would be alive today.

"Smith and I plan to get over to the Wolf Tavern and question the staff to see if anyone saw anything," Denopoulos said, diving into his food. "This had to be an inside job, someone who had easy access behind the bar like a waiter, or a fellow bartender."

Cayden shrugged. "I'll follow up with the witches at the shop and see if they can shed more light on this potion. As for the rest, I'm still trying to figure it out. Any new leads?"

Smith wiped mustard off the corner of his lip. "We went through the vic's computer and her cell phone. She was talking to a few different guys on a dating site called Plenty of Mage, or POM for short. That's where we start." The commander held up his phone to show him the app.

"Wait a damn minute." Cayden's jaw clenched to the point of pain. "Why aren't we going after Pike and Hawthorne?" The image of Andee's lifeless body flashed through Cayden's head, followed by Abigail's. Dark memories from the past came rushing back. *I may not have killed her, but I have her blood on my hands.*

"Dude, you need to lower your voice." Denopoulos glanced over his shoulder before facing him again. "I can't imagine the agony you must be going through, but you need to listen to me. Both Pike and Hawthorne went off the grid. They were nowhere near Raven's Hollow when the vic was murdered. We searched Pike's last known address. The place was empty. The dude hasn't been there in a while."

"Are you kidding me? How in the hell could two fugitives escape without a trace? They couldn't have just disappeared. It makes no sense. What are we doing to find them?" He couldn't take anymore. When would this nightmare end?

"We have agents combing the area near the park and the prison 24/7. The state police are assisting in the search efforts." Smith scratched his horns. "But nothing so far, I'm afraid."

"Andee's murder may have nothing to do with Wolf and Hawthorne and everything to do with the vic," Denopoulos continued. "The warden sent a copy of the coroner's report. The former head of the Coterie, Stephen Frost, turned out to be one of the prisoners who died in the Hellios fire. His body was burned beyond recognition. They identified him through dental records."

"Fuck." Cayden's mind whirled in a million different directions. He tried to control his demon, but it kept emerging, vibrating with rage at the news.

Smith held up his hand "We can't rule out the possibility that this could've been an ex-boyfriend, a lover, or some psycho she rebuffed. You, my friend, were just collateral damage."

Could Smith be right? Cayden gritted his teeth as reality set in. Could this be a case of him being at the wrong place at the wrong time? "How about the jewels? Did anything come up in the database?"

"The lab's still doing tests on them. No antique jewelry stores in the area were robbed recently." Smith glanced at his phone "I'm going to do some checking with the auction houses."

"Other suspects? Take me through what we have so far." Cayden's emotions ranged from sadness and guilt, to anger and frustration.

"No forced entry into her apartment." Denopoulos wiped his hands with a napkin. "Here's where it gets ugly, there were traces of semen found on the body. As horrible as that sounds, it seems to coincide with Willow's vision at the crime scene."

Cayden's hands curled into fists. The demon inside of him wanted to roar. He fought the pain and rage building inside by breathing deeply. "Your woman has come through for me on this one. I'll be forever grateful. Did Willow get a sense as to whether or not Andee knew her killer?"

His partner shook his head. "Willow believes the killer wants revenge."

But for what? "Revenge could be one hell of a trigger." Cayden often wondered how perfectly sane people could commit heinous crimes in the heat of the moment.

They finished the last of their food and threw away their trash. Voices pricked his ears. Turning his head, his gaze landed on a small crowd of what looked like tourists holding up a selfie stick and snapping away. "Let's head to the van for some privacy."

They walked to the lot across from the courthouse and hopped into the van. The second the doors slid shut, Cayden sat in the back seat, while Smith and Denopoulos slid into the front.

"How about security footage at the apartment?" Cayden asked, pulling out his phone, and glancing at a bunch of missed calls and texts. "What if someone saw something, but kept silent out of fear? Were there cameras in the hall?"

"We sent Nick to check. He said there were none." Denopoulos exhaled. "But he said there may be a witness. A little old lady who lives next door."

"I've got her statement right here. Dubrosky took it right after finding the body," Smith said, pressing a button on his phone. "I'll summarize. Mrs. Pearse heard banging coming from the vic's apartment sometime in the early morning. Shortly thereafter, the door slammed shut. The old bird took the initiative to look through the peephole and caught a glimpse of the back of some dude in a black coat, smelling like cigars. It's not much to go on, but maybe Dubrosky can get more out of her in time. It seems the two are neighbors."

Rubbing his chin, Cayden mulled the statement over in his head. "Now it's all making sense." He'd never forget the horror-struck look on Dubrosky's face when she found Cayden's tie wrapped around Andee's neck. Would the past haunt him forever? Regret settled over his limbs like wet cement. He still couldn't shake the feeling that Pike and Hawthorne had something to do with Andee's murder. "What's the plan moving forward?"

Denopoulos pressed a few buttons on the console, and the dash lit up with a computer screen. The homepage to the dating site POM, flashed across it. "I've been doing a background check on POM, the site Andee was on. Over the last seven months there have been a string of cold cases involving rape and sexual assault in both the city and the Raven's Hollow area."

Pressing a hand to his stomach, Cayden tried to ease the twisting in his gut. "I read something about that in the paper, none of the women could make a positive ID because the perp wears some kind of mask with a zipper over his face. He was coined some creepy nickname."

"The Zipper," Smith shot back.

"You think the two are connected?"

"All roads lead to users of POM," Smith said with a nod. "Three of the five vics reported getting pulled into a black SUV by a tall, jacked up figure with unusual strength and speed. They all claimed he wore a mask with a zipper. Based on their descriptions, I think it's fair to say we're dealing with a supernatural."

"Are you suggesting we have a serial rapist turned killer?" Cayden blew out air through his teeth. "Some twisted fuck called 'The Zipper'?"

"The name fits." Denopoulos pressed another button, and this time the coroner's report filled the dashboard screen. "We have a tie wrapped around the vic's neck like it was used to strangle her, or for some kind of kink like sexual asphyxiation, but here's what struck me as unusual, there was no sign of choking and no bruises on her neck. It's almost as if the killer placed the tie around the body for no other reason than to frame you."

Cayden rubbed his jaw. "It would be one way to get me out of the way. What about prints and the trace evidence?"

"No prints. The coroner found three sets of hairs, short blond ones, which belong to you, long blonde ones, the vic's, and short dark hairs around the body. They also found traces of a cigar fragment and cashmere fibers, along with four sets of different-sized footprints and the tread of a designer brand shoe. Bruno something or other."

"Magli?"

"Yeah, that's the one, size eleven," Smith said. "We're checking the database to see if there are any matches."

"What was the official cause of death?" From the bite marks Cayden recalled seeing on Andee's neck, he could already guess the answer.

Smith kept his gaze on the screen. "Blunt force trauma to the carotid artery. The murder weapon's listed as sharp, fang-like teeth."

Memories from the past flooded Cayden and made it hard to breathe.

Denopoulos's phone buzzed. He glanced at the screen. "Hold on, it looks like we're in. Nancy Slater, the CEO of POM, is meeting us at her office tomorrow. Once we have access to the vic's account, then we can see who she was talking to."

"Good thinking," Smith said with a nod. "We'll need to request a subpoena from the Council to get the names, addresses, phone numbers and IP address of whatever computer was used to sign into the vic's account."

"The way I see it, the only way to find Andee's killer is to lure him out." Denopoulos turned to face Cayden. "We need to get a trained female to catch the bastard in the act."

"I love your initiative, except for one thing, who do we know who's qualified for this kind of op?" Exhaustion pressed down on Cayden like a heavy weight.

"Hmm, I bet you can think of someone." Denopoulos rubbed his chin. "My advice, you should probably do some heavy duty groveling with Dubrosky—and if I were you, I'd do it sooner than later."

CHAPTER 9

*A*fter a hot shower, Natalya slipped into her favorite fuzzy pj's and then glanced at the stacks of boxes against the wall of her temporary bedroom. She planned to move the rest into her new place over the next couple of weeks. For now, she'd moved into Gillian's old room. Lucky for Natalya, the space was now free since Gillian had moved into Garrett's apartment. She glanced out the window, loving her view of the gardens from the second floor.

She reached for her laptop and a package of chocolate donuts from her desk and crawled under the covers, propping both up on a throw pillow. She opened the wrapper, broke off a piece and plopped it in her mouth. She didn't get a sugar rush anymore, but her craving for sweets never went away. They were like an old friend she turned to whenever she got stressed and kept her human memories close at hand.

Clicking on her email, she pulled up the coroner's report, poring over the findings. As she stared at the images of Andee Lyon's mangled body, her stomach roiled. When she closed her eyes, she tried to recall her own details from that night. Looking back, she could've sworn she'd smelled a trace of vampire. But she couldn't remember much more. Her stomach knotted with frustration.

She flip-flopped between restless and edgy and heartsick. She still couldn't erase the image of Teague standing over the body from her mind. Sighing, she pressed her head against the pillow, trying to relax.

She longed for the quiet. As much as she enjoyed the camaraderie of the other women, she relished being alone. She needed something to calm her frayed nerves. Setting her laptop and the donuts on her nightstand, she swiped a potion vial off the nightstand and downed the swirling liquid in one gulp. The sweet taste of lavender and peppermint exploded in her mouth. Their potions guru, Saje, sold concoctions like this at the shop and made sure to keep them well-stocked here at the manor.

After a few minutes, a sense of calmness settled over her limbs. The only downside was that it dulled her senses and left a gauzy filter over her brain. Her synapses slowed, along with her pulse. Turning on her side, Natalya closed her eyes, willing herself to push all thoughts of the investigation to the back of her mind. A sound coming from the window made her jolt upright. Sniffing the air, she caught a whiff of a demon. Her fangs elongated. Before she could get to her feet, a hand covered her mouth.

Her instincts kicked in. Thrusting up with her knee, she aimed for the groin. She rolled off the bed onto the wood floor, taking her attacker with her.

They both landed with a thud.

"Watch it, Dubrosky. You don't want to damage the jewels. Keep it up and you'll wake the whole damn house." Teague's masculine scent invaded her nostrils, a combination of sandalwood and pure male. The familiar scent comforted her, and sent a shock of heat up her arm, melting through her pj top.

"Teague? What are you doing sneaking into my room? Are you trying to get yourself killed?" His warm body pressed against hers and unwanted arousal left a hot tingle along her skin.

"I need to talk to you and it couldn't wait." She looked up into his blue eyes and they filled with storm clouds.

"How did you get in here?" Her voice came out huskier than she intended. For some reason the question seemed to make his horns turn darker, accentuating the broken one right at the tip. The imperfection made him even more attractive, and gave him character. She'd heard once upon a time that he'd been a fearsome warrior on another plane. Her fingers curled at her side with the urge to run her fingers over the tip. Had he injured himself in battle?

"Through the window. I knew I'd find you awake. I expected to find you hanging upside down."

Very funny. "If you came here to insult me then maybe you should go out the way you came. What's wrong with you?" She couldn't think straight having him this close. He radiated a palpable sexual energy that was hard to ignore. Teague stayed pressed up against her body. She could hear the rush of his blood and the hiss of his breath.

"Do you want the short list or the long one? My apologies for the drop by, but there's a lead I'm following up on and it couldn't wait. I should've called first. You're right by the way. I'm an asshole, but the reports prove I'm not a killer." The sincerity in his voice took her by surprise. Did he make jokes as an outlet for his pain? A better question, why wasn't he moving? And why didn't she want him to?

"You never mentioned that you had a history with the vic." He could've let her rot in prison, but instead he pushed to get her into rehab? In Natalya's experience, there were only a select few in law enforcement who cared enough to go the extra distance.

"I didn't think it was important at the time. We go back a long way." A deep sigh fell from his lips. "I can't believe she's gone." The vulnerability in his eyes drove a stake through her last shreds of caution. Her pulse quickened by the confidant way he held her, like he had every right to keep her there for as long as he wanted. And more importantly, like he'd never hurt her, but go out of his way to protect her at all costs.

If he'd helped Andee turn her life around, then maybe she'd been wrong about him after all. Could there be some chinks in his hard-ass armor? Her head spun.

"This was too important to talk about over the phone."

When he didn't make a move to get up, she cleared her throat. "If you want to keep those 'jewels' you seem to be so fond of intact, I suggest you let me up." Natalya could read his expression in the dark. His lips twisted into a smile. In most cases when a man was this close, let alone on top of her, she'd feel trapped. Panic would set into her limbs, but not with him. Her body became flushed, hot all over. Her breath came out in short little puffs.

"I want to talk about the evidence." His big hands left a blaze of heat over her bare arms as they retreated from her body. Rising to his feet, he extended his hand to help her off the floor. His shirt hiked up, showing a hard slab of muscle and a patch of golden skin. Her breath caught at the sight. *Holy hell.*

"I'd like to think this cigar paper's your smoking gun, but let's face it, the vic worked at a bar. She could've picked it up from anywhere. I'm afraid it doesn't prove anything."

"The fragment wasn't found on her body, Dubrosky, but right next to it." He moved to the chair across from her bed, sat down and tapped his foot. Lines appeared under his eyes and he looked like the weight of the world rested on his broad shoulders. Her heart stuttered in her chest.

"What about the theory that Pike set you up?" Natalya asked. "Do you think the wrapper could belong to him?"

"Smith and Denopoulos confiscated Andee's computer and her cell phone." Teague ran a hand through his hair, making it stand on end. "They believe this could've been a jealous lover, or someone Andee met on the POM dating app, someone who has a fondness for cashmere, smokes cigars and wears designer shoes."

From the way he couldn't sit still, she could see the toll this was taking on him. "What can I do?"

His expression grew somber. "There's been a string of unsolved rape cases connected to the POM dating site."

All of a sudden her stomach threatened to revolt. His words hit too close to home. She slumped on her bed and began to shake. After she took several deep breaths, she glanced up at him, trying to keep her expression blank. "Let's say you're onto something, how do we find this guy?"

His gaze narrowed in concern. Had he noticed the change come over her? "Andee was talking to a few guys on the site. The next step would be to lure them out into the open."

Natalya's throat constricted. "Where are you going with this?"

As Teague gazed at her long and hard, Natalya could almost hear the wheels in his brain turning. He appeared larger than life sitting in her room, especially in a house full of women. "We'd have to get the okay from your captain, but the best way to catch a predator like this is with bait."

"Let me guess, you want me to be the bait?" Natalya blew out the breath she'd been holding and shook her head hard. "No, not happening."

Teague's gaze roamed over her threadbare pj shirt, making her pulse jump. "You can team up with the other agents to find the real killer. I promise we'll protect you." The conviction in his voice forced a shaky breath from her lips.

"It's not that." Indignation warred with pride.

"For the love of the gods, then tell me what it's about." Fury sparked in his eyes. "Don't you want to find the scumbag responsible before he hurts another woman?"

"Do you even have to ask such a question?" An old familiar pain stabbed at her chest. "Of course I do. It's just I can't … I don't think I'm the right person for the job."

His jaw ticked. "What's the matter, you're not into swiping right?"

She couldn't tell him she'd never gone on a dating site in her life and that her last date had been in college, if one could even call it a date. He'd only tease her about it. *Wouldn't he?* But this wasn't about her dating history. It was about finding a killer, who they now suspected was also a serial rapist. "What I do on my personal time isn't the point."

"Okay, then fill me in, what is the point?" His face hardened with frustration.

Even if she wanted to, which she didn't, Natalya couldn't tell him the truth. She'd rather be thrown into a pit of snakes then go on an online date, even if it was part of a ruse to lure out a killer. Her stomach twisted. "I'd like to help you, I would, but I can't. I'm sorry, but you'll need to find someone else."

"You can't or you won't?" Cayden tried to keep the anger from his voice and failed. The rejection cut deep. They didn't exactly get along, but why wouldn't she want to work with him on this?

He gazed at Dubrosky and her eyes widened and the pulse point at her neck throbbed. Her heart rate sped up. Why was she so nervous? The evidence proved him innocent. Surely, she didn't still think him guilty. "There's no one else as qualified, no one else we can trust." Though he said, "we," he meant "he."

"There must be another way." Dubrosky paced the small room. "I can help you find another qualified female officer."

Glancing around, his gaze moved to her bed. Her simple white comforter caught his eye. An unwanted image of her naked with her silky dark hair fanned out against the pillow filled his head. *Get it together.* He cleared his throat. "You're already familiar with the case, and let's face it, you're more than qualified. Is there anything I can do to change your mind?"

When she remained silent, he sighed with frustration. He stood and turned to walk away, but he couldn't let this go, couldn't resist a chance at goading her to find out what made her tick. Could he have a conversation with her without it being tense and filled with landmines? He glanced at the boxes stacked against the wall. *Time for a different tactic.* "I hear your new neighbor is our only witness."

"Yes. Mrs. Pearse lives in the apartment next door to Andee. I met her a few weeks ago when I went to drop off some boxes. She knocked on my door and asked for my help the morning of Andee's murder because she sensed something was wrong. It's all been a terrible coincidence."

"If you have a place, then why are you living here?" In the confines of the small room, Cayden could smell her perfume. The intoxicating strawberry scent had kept him awake and hard long into the night.

Dubrosky stopped pacing and exhaled a long breath. "There's construction being done on my apartment at the moment, so I'm staying here until it's ready."

"What's the matter, things getting a little cramped at the mansion?" He'd heard about her parent's primo town house overlooking Central Park from her partner, Mulroney. He held up his hands, realizing he'd gone too far. "I'm sorry, my bad." Sometimes he couldn't help himself, old habits.

Hurt flickered in her eyes and it made him feel like crap. "Are we done with Q and A time?"

Sure, he might rib her for being some rich, spoiled princess, but he couldn't fault her record with the department. The more time he spent with her, the more he wanted to know what got her aroused. This gnawing impulse to explore the taste of her mouth, and drown in the sweetness of her lips grew stronger by the day. And the more he fantasized, the more conflicted he became, because he still held a grudge against all vampires. Pointing at the rumpled sheets, his gaze met hers once more. "I thought vampires don't sleep."

Dubrosky glanced at the floor, refusing to look him in the eye. "I shouldn't tell you."

"Why?" He wanted to do things to her body, wicked things to bring her pleasure.

"You'll only tease me about it."

Her words punched him in the gut. He never intended to give her a complex. Maybe at first, when he thought all vampires deserved his disdain. But not now… *I've gone too far.* "Try me."

"I got into the habit when my family sent me to a private vampire academy in Connecticut right out of college." She flitted around the room like a fairy. "All of my roommates used to stay out and party all night, which wasn't my thing. When I got tired of reading, I forced myself to crash. It was either that, or roam through the halls alone."

Cayden rubbed his chin. "I bet it was quite the posh place." While she engaged in pillow fights, he'd been battling his enemies.

"How did you guess?" He could hear the sarcasm in her voice, along with the hurt.

"Hey, what's going on in that head of yours, Dubrosky?" He took a step closer, fighting the urge to push her hair behind her ear. Gazing at her striking face, he tried to gauge her thoughts. In the past, he'd never been attracted to petite women for fear he'd hurt them, but with Dubrosky, he found himself wondering what it would be like to lay her on her prim white blanket and peel off those pajamas. His mind raced, imagining his big hands cupping her breasts, exploring all her luscious curves, stroking over her lithe body. He'd never hungered for a female like this. If she ever knew the extent of his attraction, she'd lord it over his head, so he settled for jabs and quips.

"I'm not about to leave you high and dry. Let me grab my phone and make some calls." When she turned away, he reached for her hand. A hot sizzle of awareness zinged up his arm. He immediately let go.

"I didn't mean …"

Her brown eyes searched his. She studied him like a puzzle she wanted to solve.

"Look, Dubrosky. I get that I'm not your favorite person, but this is about finding the killer. Trust me, I'm not thrilled with the idea of dangling you in front of a serial rapist and a killer to boot."

"As much as I appreciate your concern, I've told you before I can handle myself. The truth is I've never done an undercover op like what you're describing before. My lack of experience could put everyone at risk." Dubrosky exhaled a breath and Cayden picked up on the race of her blood. He scented her fear. What wasn't she telling him? "And what happens when this story goes viral? It will mean chaos for everyone involved."

They'd managed to keep Andee's murder out of the news so far, but that wouldn't last long. Somehow or another, the media would get wind of all the gory details and all hell would break loose. His jaw clenched to the point of pain. "Our agency will do our best to keep things under wraps. We're meeting at the corporate office of POM in the morning. I'll send you the details just in case you change your mind."

Her shoulders slumped forward. "I promise to find someone qualified to be there. But it won't be me."

"I'm glad we cleared that up. I'll get out of your way. I came to ask for your help. I don't know why I thought I'd get it. Sorry to have disturbed your beauty sleep." Cayden wanted to roar with frustration. He brushed past her and wrenched open the window. Now he'd have to come up with another plan.

Too bad he didn't have one.

CHAPTER 10

The moment the window slammed shut, Natalya plopped onto her bed and sighed. Tears stung her eyes. He didn't understand. How could he? After the way he constantly ribbed her, why did she care?

The buzz of her phone broke through her thoughts. Aside from a colleague, only one person would call her at this hour of the night. She hit accept and put the call on speaker. "Tessa? Are you okay?"

"I'm sorry for calling so late. How are you?"

Natalya glanced at the gold talisman dangling from her wrist. Three years ago, she had bought identical seeing-eye bracelets, one for her and one for Tessa, as reminders of all they'd been through and survived. "I'm good, busy with work. What's going on with you?"

"I've been asked to donate dresses on behalf of SAAN as part of the clothing kits offered at local area hospitals and shelters." Her best friend had become a darling in the fashion world. "Tessa Henry Designs" outfitted some A-list celebs and society mavens. Warmth filled Natalya's chest, upon hearing that some of her designs were going to such a great cause.

"That's amazing, Tessa." Natalya's heart radiated with joy for her friend. They pushed each other in their careers, offering a perfect measure of support and honesty. Her computer went into sleep mode and a picture of her and Tessa moved across the screen with the ocean behind them.

Wind blew in their hair. The camera caught the wide smiles on both of their faces. The two had met while organizing an event for SAAN and became fast friends.

"I wanted to be the first to call to congratulate you on being an award recipient," Tessa said with pride on her voice. "Why did you keep it quiet?"

"I'm sorry." Natalya fiddled with the sting on her pj pants. "I didn't think it was a big deal."

"Of course it's a big deal. I'm so proud of you. I want to dress you for the occasion. When can you come into the studio for measurements? I have a few things in mind. I promise it won't take long."

"I'm pretty busy this week," Natalya hedged and bit down on her lip.

"You can't keep hiding behind those baggy clothes forever, Natalya. You have an amazing figure. Don't you think it's time to show it off?"

"Can we talk about this later?" As much as she appreciated Tessa's efforts, she still had hang-ups about her body. Going to therapy and support groups helped, but she'd never been able to move past the shame. After hearing Tessa's story of sexual assault by her uncle from the age of nine, it made Natalya's experience seem relatively tame in comparison. Somehow Tessa had managed to move past her pain and not fall victim to it. Natalya wondered when she'd be able to do the same.

"You're being honored for a reason. You help victims by going out there on the streets every day and making them safer." Tessa's words filled Natalya with guilt.

"I think you give me far too much credit." By taking the easy way out of this case, she'd be allowing a rapist to go free.

"Is this about Charles?" Tessa asked. "Do you know if he's going to be there?"

Natalya sighed. "His family has been on the board for as long as mine. I haven't seen him since our divorce." The idea of facing her ex alone in front of a room full of people made her break out in a cold sweat. "I don't have a date and I can't show up there without a plus-one." If she did, she'd never hear the end of it from her sired family. Everyone on the committee assumed her interest in SAAN was philanthropic. No one outside her family and Tessa knew the real reason for her involvement in the charity. They'd be mortified if Natalya let the truth slip out.

"Who says you have to have a date? Why not shake things up for a change? I'd pay to see the look on Eleanora's face." Tessa chuckled.

"I need to stop caring so much about following the rules and staying in between the lines."

"Speaking of which, what's going on with your love life?"

An image of Teague's hard body pressed against her flashed through her mind. "Nothing new these days. I've been working a lot. There isn't much time left for dating. I'm not exactly out there looking. But it would be nice to have a sex life. I suppose I'll have to live vicariously through you and the witches from the coven." Natalya smiled.

"What's eating at you? I can hear it in your voice."

"It's this case I'm working on." *It's this case and Cayden Teague.* The combination of the two was turning Natalya inside out. She pressed a key on her keyboard and the coroner's report popped up. Another gruesome 3-D photo of Andee's body flashed across the screen. Her stomach tightened.

"I've got to fly. Matt just walked in and we haven't seen each other all day."

Natalya picked up on the excitement in Tessa's voice "Go."

If Tessa could have the courage to move forward with her life, then Natalya should be able to do the same. Finding the monster that killed Andee Lyon was bigger than her fears. She'd never forgive herself if the bastard went free.

"Let me know if there's anything else I can do to help."

"There is one thing." Natalya glanced at her closet. "Any suggestions on what to wear on a fake first date?"

CHAPTER 11

atalya's heart pounded as she stepped through the corporate headquarters for the app, Plenty of Mage. The team had set up a meeting that morning with Nancy Slater, the POM CEO, to give them access to the identities of the men Andee was talking to on the app.

"Welcome to Plenty of Mage. How may I help you today?" The pretty vampire who greeted Natalya sat at a mahogany desk. A POM sign in big, bold white letters covered half the wall behind her desk.

"I'm here to see Nancy Slater." Natalya pulled out her badge and smiled. Piped in jazz music filled her ears. The soft sound forced her to exhale the breath she'd been holding.

The receptionist held up a finger as the phone rang, her red lacquered polish glinting under the lights. Natalya glanced at her stubby nails and shoved her hand in her pocket. She didn't have time for manicures.

While forced to wait, she decided to have a look around the office. Turning away from the desk, her gaze darted to the open area of employees sitting at desks with large computer monitors, pounding away on their keyboards. *Could one of these millennials have inadvertently used their algorithms to match Andee with a killer?* The thought made her throat constrict. Last night, after she got off the phone with Tessa, she'd made her decision and put a call in to her captain, requesting to come onboard the case. From there, the agents sent her a ton of files on the string of cold cases involving rape and sexual assault connected to the POM app. Naturally, she spent the rest of the night reviewing them.

"Thanks for waiting. Nancy's in the conference room." The receptionist's voice drew Natalya's attention to the desk. "I'll be happy to show you the way. May I take your coat?"

"Uh, no thanks. I'll just hold on to it." In case she needed to make a hasty escape. Natalya followed her down a brightly lit hall, her stomach churning with every step. *Deep breaths.* She could do this. Her low, sensible heels clicked against the hardwood. They passed a sign for the restroom and she stopped outside the door. "I'll just meet them inside."

"Of course. It's the third door on the right."

"Thank you." The receptionist walked away and Natalya darted into the bathroom. Her chest heaved and her pulse pounded. She glanced at her reflection in the mirror. She'd pulled her hair in a ponytail and wore no makeup. Upon closer inspection, her brows needed grooming.

Her white blouse and conservative navy suit didn't seem appropriate for the occasion. She didn't look like someone who was about to explore the world of online dating. But this was just a meeting, she reminded herself. Then why did her stomach clench, ready to heave at any moment?

The question she dreaded the most, "Do you have a profile?" Everyone in this generation did, and on multiple sites. But not her. She refused to reveal that to a room full of male colleagues. The humiliation alone would be crushing. Teague would never let her live it down. He'd register her inexperience in a heartbeat. *I'm out my element.* Give her a room full of hardened criminals to interrogate over her knowledge on casual conversation with the opposite sex any day of the week.

Natalya turned, and right before she reached for the door handle, she shoved her hand into her purse and pulled out a package of mini chocolate doughnuts. After she tore open the top, she broke off a piece and put it in her mouth. She chewed and swallowed with a sigh.

One of these days she'd have to break her sugar crutch. Brushing the crumbs from her fingers, she squared her shoulders. She could do this. When she stepped into the hall, she picked up on two things at once, a female voice she didn't recognize and the flowery scent of her perfume. The words "Supernatural Swipe" were emblazoned across the frosted glass door in bold red letters.

She walked into the conference room and her gaze landed on a stunning female vampire with blonde hair sitting at the head of the conference table. Her honey highlights caught under the light, accentuating her stylish cut. Dark lashes made her eyes pop. Her cheeks glowed and pink gloss covered her lips.

Am I supposed to look like her?

"Sorry I'm late." Natalya smiled in greeting, then walked to the end of the table and took a seat across from Teague.

The demon pinned her with his intense blue gaze. A combination of shock and relief crossed his face. "Dubrosky? I didn't think you'd show. What changed your mind?"

She cleared her throat and tried to find her voice. "I'm doing this for Andrea. Fill me in." She took off her trench and draped it on the back of her chair.

"Miss Slater was giving me a list of the men Andee was talking to." Teague pointed to a smart board on the wall filled with messages. He pulled out his phone and pressed a button. "I just sent you a copy."

"Great. Thanks." Natalya didn't know how she'd pull this off without putting the entire op at risk. But there was too much at stake to back out now.

Teague swiveled in his chair, his broad shoulders casting a shadow through the room. "We appreciate your cooperation, Miss Slater."

"Please, call me Nancy. I need your help just as much as you need mine. We want this predator caught as much as anyone. This has all been so awful." Her eyes filled with tears. After a deep sigh, she seemed to gather her composure. "We hate the idea of putting any of our clients in danger."

"Do you do background checks on your clients, Nancy?" The deep timbre of Teague's voice filled the small space.

"We're not required to," Nancy said, shaking her head. "Unfortunately, when something horrible like this happens, it doesn't get reported directly to us. There's always a risk in all dating apps. We put a disclaimer on our site and make our clients sign waivers that acknowledge the client is solely responsible for exercising safe and prudent dating arrangements."

The image of the vic flashed through Natalya's mind. "I've done some research, and didn't you have something similar happen two years ago with a tier one sex offender?"

Nancy's face fell. "When we found out, we deleted his profile from our site immediately. Somehow he managed to hack into our system and change his identity. Thankfully, one of our IT guys found the breach and contacted the police."

"You did the right thing," Teague said with a nod. "Have you been able to establish a pattern of who 'The 'Zipper,' this alleged rapist, might be?"

"I'm afraid not."

Last night, Natalya had given herself a quick tutorial on how the site worked so she didn't look like a total newbie.

"Detective Dubrosky has agreed to go undercover to lure these men out." Teague got up and joined Nancy at the whiteboard. "The next logical step would be to create a profile based on the commonalties between Andee and her matches then give her those same qualities." He turned and gave Natalya a sidelong glance. "We'll need to get you a burner phone."

Trying to ignore the knot of nerves in the pit of her stomach, Natalya focused her attention on Nancy. "Once we create my fake profile, can you offer any tips on how to move the conversation to an actual date?" She hoped Teague didn't pick up on the catch in her voice.

"My advice, use wit and humor. Send something with emotion or challenge. Build banter and create intrigue. Remember, you want to create mystery, but your photos will get you matches. What's the story they're telling? Men are very visual creatures." Nancy glanced over at Teague and batted her eyelashes to emphasize her point. Her body language conveyed her attraction to the demon. Natalya couldn't blame her. Sexual energy rolled off the demon in waves. To his credit, Teague seemed oblivious.

"Even masked madmen like the Zipper guy?" Natalya kept her gaze on Nancy, refusing to look Teague in the eye.

Nancy frowned. "That, I wouldn't know."

Swallowing hard, Natalya tried to calm her nerves. "Any other recommendations?"

"I caution all of my clients not to show too much skin in their profile picture, not that we need to worry about that." Nancy gave her a once-over, frowning at her shapeless jacket and white shirt buttoned up to her neck. "Perhaps you might want to reconsider some of your wardrobe choices to look less like a cop. You don't want to stick out."

"No, of course not." Natalya forced a smile over the hot flush of mortification. She didn't know how she'd pull this off. *It's not about me*, she reminded herself. It's about saving an innocent and bringing a killer to justice. "I'm sure my friends can help me look less obvious."

Teague extended his hand. "Thanks, Nancy, for your help."

"It's my pleasure, Agent Teague. Stay as long as you'd like." Nancy gave him a flirty smile and walked out into the hallway.

The moment the door shut, Teague crossed the room, and folded his enormous body into the seat next to hers. "Thanks for coming through." His gaze flicked to hers like a laser beam. "You have something right there." He pointed to the corner of her mouth.

Before she could wipe it away, he shocked her by reaching out and pressing his thumb to the corner of her lip. When he licked the end of his finger, butterflies fluttered in her belly. "Mmm, chocolate, my favorite." Electricity crackled in the air between them.

"What can I say, sweets are my kryptonite."

He laughed, but it came out more like a groan. She hated the fact that the throaty sound sent a wave of heat from her head to her toes. "What made you change your mind?"

"Smith and Denopoulos were relentless, but that's not the only reason."

"Oh?"

"I can't sit back while a killer roams free." If Natalya could save one woman from getting raped or sexually assaulted, then it would all be worth it in the end.

His eyes softened. "I'm grateful."

She ignored the way her heart fluttered at his words and pulled out her phone and clicked onto her email, reading over the list of names Teague had sent her from Andrea Lyon's computer. "What are you proposing for an op?" she asked, redirecting the conversation.

"Denopoulos is the lead investigator on the case. The only reason he's not here right now is because he's with Smith interviewing the staff at the Wolf Tavern, setting up surveillance cameras, and establishing their covers before the bar opens." Teague blew out a breath.

"Take me through the plan."

"The goal is to get DNA samples off these guys. There's always the chance that the killer is none of those dudes on that list. We can't rule out the possibility that it was a customer at the bar, an ex, or someone Andee worked with." Teague scratched his horns. "Any questions?"

"Yeah, if one of these guys is our perp then don't you think he'd be lying low?" Natalya asked, trying to process this new information. "Why would he agree to go out with me and risk getting caught?"

"We go with the theory that this is his compulsion, or maybe his revenge for Andee jilting him. We follow some of Nancy's suggestions and put that sharp tongue of yours to the test and he won't be able to resist you."

If only it were that easy. Natalya swallowed the lump now lodged in her throat. "What's the timetable?"

"We need to create your profile and go over exactly what you're going to say from an agent's point of view. Let's meet at HQ tonight."

"I'm going to need time to prep for this." Natalya didn't know how long it would take to make her look like Nancy Slater or one of the women on the app. She fought the panic rising from her belly. *I'm in over my head.*

"What about the manor?" Teague asked, moving closer, his foot brushing hers. "But we'll need total privacy and confidentiality for the sake of the investigation."

Natalya laughed. "Privacy and confidentiality at the manor don't exist. If one of us so much as leaves a take-out menu on the counter, everyone knows about it and adds their two cents about the food and the service." Not that she minded, especially being an only child. She enjoyed having an amazing group of friends to talk to. She never realized how lonely she'd been until she moved in. If they worked in her bedroom, the other women would wonder why Teague was hanging out with her alone after hours.

"Well in that case, why don't we meet at my place? I'm not far from the manor and I can assure you we'll have total privacy." His deep voice sent heat unfurling in her belly.

Natalya drank in his features, the stress lines now around his expressive eyes. "We should probably go over my fake persona and the questions I'm going to be asking these guys before I try and set up any dates."

"We can work on it together." Teague began typing on his phone. "I just sent you my address. Why don't you text me when you're ready." The gentleness in his voice surprised her.

When Natalya thought about what a complete transformation would entail, her stomach bottomed out. *Can anyone say extreme makeover?* "Let's shoot for tomorrow, this could take a while."

CHAPTER 12

By the time Natalya got home, her nerves were shot. Thankfully, the place was quiet giving her a chance to get her thoughts in check. She took several long, deep breaths to dispel the tension in the pit of her stomach.

How am I supposed to pull this off without these men seeing right through me? She pushed her doubts aside, refusing to let a killer slip through the cracks.

The grandfather clock chimed, reminding her of the time. She planned to meet Brooke here to go over the plan for operation makeover. Her stomach churned with nervous energy. She needed to do something to relax, so she decided to check out the library.

She walked through the hall, glancing at the portraits of ancient witches displayed on the walls. The place held a certain mystique, filled with secret passages and endless rooms for her to explore.

Crossing into the library, she looked around the room in awe. Floor-to-ceiling shelves lined with leather-bound tomes, and ancient grimoires dating back hundreds of years from all over the world occupied almost every wall.

The scents of leather and incense mingled in the air. She glanced at the magickal tools randomly placed around the room—crystals, tarot cards, wands, copper bowls and candles for spellcasting. She perused through the numerous spines on the shelves, intrigued.

Through the corner of her eye, a small sphere of light above her head caught her attention. Craning her neck to get a better look, she found a good-old-fashioned crystal ball. Her gaze stayed focused on the light, which glowed even brighter now. She turned her head to the side and found a ladder with wheels at the end of the row. After she slid it over, she climbed onto the top rung, then stood on her tiptoes and stretched out her hand. Sometimes it sucked being short.

The moment she brushed her fingers over the glass, it turned from clear to blue. Holding the ball with one hand and the handle of the ladder with the other, she climbed down. She stepped off the ladder and set the glowing sphere on the table. When she gazed into the ball, an image swirled inside the glass. Her heart thumped against her ribcage. The front door opened and slammed shut, making her jump.

"Anybody home?" Brooke called out.

"I'm in the library," she called back. The crystal ball turned from blue to clear.

"Are you trying to scry?" Brooke asked, walking into the room. "What did you see? And does it have anything to do with these clothes that just arrived for you?"

"The clothes are here?" *Thank you, Tessa.* Natalya pointed to the crystal ball and laughed. "I was just playing around. I saw something move in the glass, but I don't know the first thing about scrying."

Brooke held a garment bag in her hand with the name "Tessa Henry Designs" in big, bold letters. "Scrying is just a fancy word for divination. It allows you to see outcomes."

"This might sound crazy, but I think it called to me."

"Trust me, nothing sounds crazy around here." After Brooke hung the garment bag on a wall hook, she sat on the leather couch and leaned against the cushion. "I could only read astrological charts when I first moved in here, but now I'm having premonitions. Magick lives and breathes within these walls, Natalya."

The eerie relevance of Brooke's words struck Natalya straight through the heartstrings. "I never imagined I could do magick."

"The ability to scry or perform spells and enchantments can be learned by practice and studying the craft."

A spark of hope fluttered in her belly. "My maternal aunt was a witch.

Clients used to line up around the block to get a reading with her. Do you think I could've inherited her gift? Maybe this is a fluke? I've never met any vampire witches." Natalya joined Brooke on the couch.

"Powers can remain dormant and then activate," Brooke pointed out. "Who says vampires can't be witches? Meditation helps, and you need to try and open your inner eye."

"My inner eye?"

"Let me show you." Brooke pointed to the center of her forehead. "This is where your inner eye's located. Think of it as another eye inside your head. It's the energy of your heart, the center of your intuition, and it's connected to your clairvoyance—the ability to see images, as well as your clairsentience—the ability to pick up on feelings. I use visualization to help me picture the third eye as a structure that receives light. Close your eyes, Natalya, and just breathe."

When Natalya closed her eyes, a soft flutter of air wafted across her skin. She breathed in and out, in and out. "Okay, now what?"

"Visualize a door in the center of your chest and picture light coming in and traveling up your spine. Imagine the light goes up through your brow and then moves through your whole body."

Natalya continued to breathe, blocking out everything around her, except for the sound of Brooke's voice. After several minutes, she saw nothing, but then as she grew more relaxed, something incredible happened—a faint haze appeared in her mind's eye. The haze misted away, revealing a beam of warm, yellow light. The beam traveled up into the center of her forehead and a sense of inner peace settled over her limbs. Her face grew hot. "This light will help me scry with the crystal ball?"

"Yes. The more you do this, the more you'll start to see images from any reflective surface like water and mirrors," Brooke said, squeezing her hand. "Remember, you're not seeing with your eyes. I've learned anything's possible with magick. It just takes practice."

The light continued to move around behind Natalya's eyes until her head began to pound. "Whoa, headache." Her eyes flew open.

"My bad." Guilt flashed across Brooke's pretty face. "I should've warned you that doing too much too soon will give you what we call, a serious eye-grain."

"It's okay." Natalya rubbed her temples. "Thanks for the crash course."

The smile she gave Natalya filled her with gratitude. "Anytime. We have ancient grimoires to show you how to interpret what the colors and symbols in the crystal ball mean." Brooke pointed to the top shelf of the bookcase closest to them.

"Thanks. I'll definitely check them out."

"Oh, I almost forgot to give you this." Brooke handed her a yellow sticky note.

Natalya glanced at the words and smiled.

Here are a few outfits that should get you through. Let me know if you need anything else. XO Tessa.

Natalya pointed to the garment bag. "The clothes were hanging on the door?" She'd been so caught up; she didn't hear anyone knock

"A messenger left them for you." Brooke got up from the couch and went over to the bag. "May I?"

"Go right ahead."

"The clothes are from your designer friend?" Brooke unzipped the bag and sorted through the clothing.

"I can't wait for you to meet Tessa. She's a lifesaver." Natalya appreciation and love for her friend deepened. "I don't know what I'd do without her, or all of you."

"Trust me, it's mutual." Brooke's phone pinged. She pulled it out of her pocket, glanced at the screen and smiled. "You're in luck. My hairdresser can sneak you in this afternoon. I put a call in to her right after I got your text about a makeover."

"Clothes and hair down, makeup still to go." Natalya sighed with relief. "Thank you."

"I'm guessing this has something to do with your ball?" Brooke asked with a teasing note to her voice.

"No, it's for an undercover assignment. I need to look the part and a lot less like myself." Natalya motioned to her shapeless navy suit jacket. After she left the POM offices, she headed to the station and worked until a few hours ago. The lack of evidence led her from one dead end to another.

Brooke smiled in understanding. "These things take time."

"Unfortunately, I don't have the luxury of time." Natalya could interrogate a perp, no problem. But don't ask her to teeter on high heels, or make idle chitchat with the opposite sex.

"In that case, I'm calling in the cavalry." Brooke began furiously typing on her phone. "I'm sending a group text to the rest of the troops."

"I need all the help I can get." She'd been going for the no-nonsense look, which worked great as a detective, but not so much to entice men. "I'm going to owe you big-time for this, Brooke."

"You don't me anything, honey." Brooke smiled. "That's what friends do for each other. I'm guessing you're working with Cayden on this one."

Keeping her expression neutral, she shrugged. "I'm sorry. I'm not allowed to say. Why do you ask?" Natalya thought about all he'd been through and her heart softened.

"I couldn't help but overhear some of the things you said to Arabella about him. He might come off a little overbearing at times, but he's a great guy. He saved my life. I wouldn't be here right now if it weren't for him."

Everyone seemed to love the guy, then why did he dislike her? "I admit he's got a hero complex ... "

"Trust me, there's a lot more to the story." Brooke cocked her head to the side. "I asked Willow about it and she confirmed that Cayden lost someone he loved in a horrible way."

An unexpected lash of pain cut across Natalya's chest. "I can't imagine how difficult that must've been for him." Maybe she judged him too harshly.

"Anyway, back to you." Brooke eyed Natalya's jacket and drew her brows together.

"What?"

"Has anyone ever told you that you're a small wearing a medium?"

Glancing at her jacket, Natalya exhaled, grateful for Brooke's honesty. "And your point is?"

Brooke laughed. "We have a lot of work to do."

The next morning, Natalya's desk had become transformed from a work space to a makeup table. Brushes, palettes and lipsticks covered almost every available surface. She'd been primped and primed within an inch of her life.

Brooke managed to tame her bushy brows. Arabella got to work applying fake lashes, liner, a boatload of mascara, and the final touch— bronzer to highlight her cheeks and pink gloss to accentuate Natalya's lips. She ran a hand through her new hair. Five inches had been cut and blown out into sleek, long layers. In between primping, she read everything she could pull up on her phone about online dating, which only served to terrify her, and make her more determined than ever to catch this guy.

"Time to choose your outfit," Brooke announced, pointing at the pile of clothing and undergarments spread out on her bed. They stopped at a cute little boutique on Washington Street on their way to the hair salon for some jeans, tops, a few blazers in her size, and new bras and matching thongs, to add to the pieces that Tessa had sent over.

Natalya picked up a short navy dress made of soft jersey material. "I'll go try this on." She walked behind the silk changing screen, slipped on the dress and then stepped out in front of the full-length mirror.

A loud wolf whistle came from Arabella. "Whoa, you're stunning. I'd do you."

Natalya laughed. "Thanks."

"You will knock those guys on their asses," Brooke agreed. "The dress looks great with your skin color."

"Are you sure you didn't use magick on me?" Natalya asked in disbelief. She pivoted in a circle then froze as she stared at her reflection in the mirror, barely recognizing herself after the transformation. Her eyes appeared bigger, with a smoky look to them. Whatever Arabella used on her skin made it glow. Her gaze moved lower and her breath rushed out. Thanks to the push-up bra, she now sported cleavage. The fabric nipped at the waist and flared at the hips. Feminine power surged through her veins. *Is this why women dress this way, to feel empowered?*

"Of course not," Brooke said, scooping up the rest of the outfits and hanging them on a garment rack. "Glamours work to make you look like someone else, not enhance what you've already got, and girl, you've got it."

Natalya swallowed hard. "Let's hope it works." She needed to come across as a single female looking for a date, not a detective in search of a killer. This outfit certainly seemed to do the trick, because she didn't look like herself at all.

"You look amazing. Now all you need is a great pair of shoes to match your dress." Arabella got up from the chair and handed over a pair of uber-high heels.

"Hold on." Natalya set the shoes on the floor and threw up her hands.

"I agreed to the fake lashes and even the thong, but I draw the line when it comes to wearing those torture devices."

"Mid-heels aren't going to cut it, not in that dress. Why not practice here first?" Arabella suggested, motioning for her to walk across the room.

Holding on to the side of the dresser, she slipped the skyscrapers on. Her toes pinched. Natalya took a step and her ankles wobbled. She attempted to walk across the room and tripped over her feet. She blurred over to the bed, and grabbed onto the post right before she face-planted on the wood floor. "This is harder than it looks." She had a whole new appreciation for women in four-inch heels. She'd cut off such a vital feminine part of herself. Maybe it was time to stop hiding and get it back.

"Allow me." Brooke expertly walked across the room in a pair of strappy gold sandals. "Keep your back straight and put one foot in front of the other. Lead with your heels, not your toes."

It took a few more tries, and finally Natalya managed to walk across the room without tripping. She glanced at her friends in gratitude. "What would I do without you two? You guys are the best."

After another look in the mirror, she couldn't help but think, *Take that Cayden Teague.*

CHAPTER 13

ayden took several long, deep breaths, which did nothing to ease the worry churning in his gut. He'd been seated at his desk, staring at his computer screen for the past few hours, reading over his notes. The cigar band they found next to the body was a primo brand, uber expensive and rare. He'd have to make a list of stores in the area and do his research.

They were still waiting for the results from the lab on the jewels. Pike didn't seem like the type to have that kind of loot available, which then begged the question, where had the bastard gotten them from? They must've been a payoff.

Both the local and state police didn't have squat on Hawthorne or Pike. They could be halfway to Mexico by now. Cayden pressed a few buttons on his keyboard and pulled up the warden's report, along with the autopsy reports from the prison fire.

Scanning the words, he tried to let them sink in. Stephen Frost had perished in the blaze. The only way to identify the vampire's body had been through dental records, whereas all the other bodies had been positively identified. Cayden read the words over again and his horns prickled with heat, something didn't sit right.

His mind drifted to the POM meeting, recalling the hacking incident Dubrosky had brought up. He spent some time researching the case, and it got him thinking about Frost. A perp had found a way to hack into the POM server after his profile had been deleted and created a new one.

Frost had been working as a ghost hacker when Cayden arrested him. He couldn't shake the gut feeling that Andee's murder was connected to the prison break somehow.

The ping of an incoming email stirred him from his musings. Their profiler sent him a report. He switched screens and read it over. The killer possessed above average intelligence and was a creature of immense strength and power, who believed he was smarter than the police. Cayden pegged him for a trained liar who could pass a polygraph test without a hitch. They'd continue to use bait to lure out this predator. Even though he pressed Dubrosky to do this op, he hated the idea of putting her in harm's way. How far would she have to take things before they could make an arrest? He hoped this op would lead them to the killer and not blow up in their faces.

Feeling antsy, he decided to do something productive while he waited, so he went about his standard agent operating procedure. Scanning his apartment for bugs had become part of his daily routine. He reached into his pocket, and pulled out an MBI issued microchip then pressed a button. A red blinking light arced through the room. No beeps meant no bugs. But that didn't mean he was in the clear. Whoever framed him was still out there and could be watching his every move. After he set the chip on the end table, he took out his phone and contemplated shooting Dubrosky a text when the doorbell rang.

Anticipation coursed through his veins as he walked to the door. He swung it open with a quip ready on his tongue and froze at the sight of the gorgeous woman standing in the hall. Her hair brushed her shoulders in silky, black waves and her eyes—*holy shit her eyes*—looked bigger, and were now lined in black with long, sweeping lashes. His gaze moved over her face. Her cheeks glowed and her pink lips glistened, just begging to be kissed. His mouth went dry.

Fuck. "Dubrosky? Is that you?"

"Who else would it be?" She tapped her foot, now encased in a high heel. His gaze dipped to the thin straps wrapped around her ankles, accentuating her bare, toned legs. "Are you going to make me stand out in the hall and teeter on these torture devices, or are you going to invite me in?"

"Yeah, it's you all right." Cayden bowed and extended his hand. "Welcome to my humble abode."

She walked in front of him and stopped at his hall table. A trench coat covered most of her body, but his heart pounded in his chest, ready to find out what she hid underneath.

"I'm trying to look the part, so no jokes, okay?" Her voice sounded tense. She looked up at him and he could make out the tension around her mouth.

Shit, he made her nervous. He nodded. "I promise. Can I take your coat?" He held out his hands.

Fumbling with her belt, she refused to look him in the eye. "I'm serious, Teague. No jokes."

"Try and relax. This is only the warm-up before the race." Moving behind her, he took the coat from her slender shoulders. He inhaled the sweet scent of her shampoo and the exotic smell of her perfume. "I promise not to—" His words got caught in his throat when she turned around. She wore a midnight blue dress with a slit cut up to her mid-thigh, showing off miles of creamy, olive skin. The fabric hugged her body like a second skin. He hissed out a breath.

"The dress isn't mine," she explained, shifting from one foot to the other. "It's for the profile pictures. I brought a few other outfits." She motioned to a black bag now at her feet. "Do you think it's too much?" The vulnerability in her voice made him want to put her mind at ease with soft kisses and caresses, but he settled for a shrug instead.

"It's perfect for what we're trying to do. No one will ever suspect you're a cop." *Hell*. His erection pressed against the front panel of his jeans. He prayed she didn't notice. Seizing the opportunity to walk a few steps away, he hung her trench on his coat rack. "Please come in and make yourself comfortable."

"Thanks, I've never been in one of these open layouts before," she said glancing around the room.

"My computer's set up in here." He led her into the loft, not sure what she'd think of his place.

Dubrosky took a seat on his couch. Cayden followed her gaze as it moved from the exposed pipe, to the stone wall, trying to see things through her eyes. When she stared at his bed, smack dab in the middle of the room, he picked up on the surge of her pulse. "Your place is super rustic. It's totally you. I mean that in a good way."

"Let me guess, you were expecting some dive filled with empty beer cans and posters of naked women?" His gaze dropped to her mouth and the way her upper lip curled in a smile. He wanted to taste her lips, and trail wet kisses down her neck. Ever since he drank her blood, his fantasies had become more vivid. They'd changed shape and texture. Now he couldn't stop thinking about her in his bed. *This is not good.*

She laughed. "How did you guess? Great visual by the way."

He enjoyed their playful banter more than he cared to admit. "I'm guessing this place is a lot different than your parent's townhouse." He took a seat in a distressed leather chair. *Dammit.* Why did he revert to being an ass whenever she made him uncomfortable?

"Yeah, but that's not necessarily a bad thing." After a moment of awkward silence, Dubrosky turned her head and pointed to the large row of windows. "I bet you get amazing light in here."

"I've never needed an alarm clock." Cayden left out the part that most days he woke up at the crack of dawn and not from the sun, but from the nightmares. They still plagued him even after all these years. He shook his head and forced the darkness away. "Would all this light be a problem for you?" He'd never broached the subject with Mulroney, but he'd always been curious.

"Don't believe all those myths and vampire legends. I can't burn to a crisp in the sun, but it does slow my speed and strength. What about you?" Natalya crossed and uncrossed her legs and then fumbled with the strap on her shoe, giving him a bird's-eye view of those gorgeous legs. "Is it true you don't always have control over your demon?" she asked, gazing at him in silent challenge.

Yeah, like right now. Every time he inhaled, he caught a whiff of her perfume and it stirred the beast within. He arched his brows, no sense in lying. "It's true, especially when I'm angry or aroused. But never in a violent way toward those I trust or care about." No denying the sexual tension arcing between them.

Her sharp inhale of breath confirmed his suspicions. "What kind of demon are you? I've always been curious."

"I'm a mix of Hymera and rage demon. Most Hymeras are more human than demon. They age and eventually die. But in my case, the rage part of me is stronger." Cayden folded his arms across his chest. "Any more questions?"

"'Yeah, how old are you?"

"Three-hundred and twenty," Cayden admitted. "I've got a few questions of my own. But they can wait." He wanted to know when and how she got turned into a vampire, but this wasn't the time or the place to ask. "Well, now that we've gotten that out of the way, can I offer you something to drink? You should probably loosen up a little before we get started."

"I'd love a glass of white wine if you have any." Dubrosky leaned against the cushions, chewing on her bottom lip.

"I'm more of a beer drinker myself. Well, I used to be." The moment he said the words, they tasted bitter on his tongue. After Andee's murder, he vowed to stop drinking. He drank to numb the pain, but it never truly went away. "I do imbibe in a little vino on occasion." He walked to the fridge, and grabbed a bottle of chardonnay for her and a bottle of iced tea for himself. He could use something stronger right now to ease the anxiety churning in his gut, but he'd have to suck it up.

"Where do we start?" she asked, pushing her hair behind her ear, drawing his attention to the slim column of her neck.

Everything about her appearance turned him on. He imagined what her naked body would look like and swallowed hard. Trying to rein in his urges, he looked away. He shouldn't be lusting after a coworker, not with innocent lives on the line. Not to mention, they'd been at each other's throats for months, whenever she came on board to assist with their caseload, or when they bumped into each other outside of work. Now, here she sat, a breath away, on his couch. He never brought women to his place. But this wasn't just any woman, and technically this wasn't a date.

"I got you a burner, compliments of the MBI." He pointed to the phone on the coffee table.

"Thanks." Dubrosky picked up the phone, pressed a few buttons. "I just downloaded the app. I went over the list of men Andee was talking to that the Slater woman gave us. I then cross-referenced them with both the RHPD and the MBI databases."

"Did anything jump out at you?" Cayden grabbed a goblet out of a cabinet and then reached for a wine bottle opener from a kitchen drawer.

"There's a mix of creatures: vampires, demons, fae, wolves, you name it. She'd been in contact with a number of them within days of her death. They all live within a twenty-mile radius of Andee's place. None of them list cigar bars on their profiles. I read over some of the names of the guys on the list, "Swingingjoe" and "Eeasy2plez" caught my attention." Dubrosky chuckled. "It appears I'm going to have my work cut out for me."

"No doubt. We need to create a username for your profile."

"What do you have in mind?"

"Let's stay within the common theme between Andee and the men she messaged, but I think we can come up with something a bit more original for you." After Cayden removed the cork from the bottle, he poured the wine, and set it on the counter. He brought their drinks to the couch. When he handed her the wine, his fingers brushed hers and that same spark of electricity shot up his arm. *Why do I have this intense reaction to her every damn time we touch?* It unnerved the hell out of him.

"Thanks." Dubrosky swirled the contents in her glass. Her pink tongue darted out and licked her lips. She took a sip and swallowed.

His gaze took in the way her throat worked. Who knew the sight of Dubrosky tasting wine would be this erotic? He subtly adjusted himself for good measure.

A crease formed between her brows. "There's something I need to know. I mean it has nothing to do with the case, but we'll be working closely together on this one and I think it's important moving forward."

"Okay, spill."

"Why do you resent me? Because my sired family has money? Or because I'm a vampire?" The hurt in her voice sent a punch to his gut.

Blowing out a breath, he ran a hand through his hair. "Look, Dubrosky, the past may have contributed to me making false assumptions about you and your family and that was wrong." Cayden refused to get into all the sordid details, knowing it would get deep and ugly if he did, so he settled on a piece of the truth and not the whole enchilada.

Dubrosky smiled. "Hmm, I think there's an apology in there somewhere."

"I've been a real tool to you. I shouldn't take old grudges out on you. I'm sorry." Cayden couldn't tell her that he'd narrowly escaped death on Arcadia by going through a portal, but his entire family and the only woman he ever loved hadn't been so lucky. All of the treasures, along with their history, were now gone, vaporized, thanks to the Coterie.

Her warm smile diffused any lingering awkwardness. "Apology accepted. I think for the sake of the op, we should call a truce."

"Agreed." He reached for his laptop off the table, grateful she wanted to move on. Once he logged into the POM website, he got into Andee Lyon's account. "I want you to know how much I appreciate what you're about to do. We're all going to owe you for this." He held out his iced tea bottle and she touched her glass. "Big-time."

When her dark eyes met his, an unfamiliar yearning washed over him. He pushed it aside and focused on keeping things strictly professional. "You won't owe me. Besides, this is what friends do for each other."

Taking a sip from his bottle, he nearly choked. "Friends? Is that what we are?" He wanted to be so much more, but he couldn't go there … he wouldn't, even if this case wasn't hanging over his head like a noose, his heart remained cold.

"I'd like to be," she murmured. "I want to start over. We have mutual friends that we both care about. We're connected, whether we like it or not."

He gave her a nod. "I'd like to think so. We might engage in the occasional banter from time to time, but we can have each other's backs when it counts."

Their gazes met and an unspoken energy pulsed between them.

Her face lit up and made his chest swell. "So we're good?"

"We're good. Friends it is." Her new appearance would attract a ton of male attention. The face paint and clothing accentuated her natural beauty, but Natalya Dubrosky possessed a killer wit, smarts, and innocence.

"I've checked out Andee's profile and compared it to the men she messaged and the common theme was falling in love or lust fast. Let me read you Andee's tagline." She glanced at her phone. "'I live for getting swept up in a new relationship.'"

"What about the responses?" Cayden asked, leaning forward.

"They range from, 'I'm into the whirlwind when you meet someone and fall for them instantly' to 'I think romance is all about the chemistry.'" She pushed her hair behind her ear. "Mrs. Pearse confirmed that Andee had a romantic heart, but terrible taste in men."

Cayden rubbed a hand over the side of his face. "Mrs. Pearse is spot-on.

How do you think Andee got into trouble with the law? She fell for the wrong guy." Exhaling a mournful breath, he never saw things ending this way.

"Would you say POM is a 'find your soulmate' kind of app? Or more of a hook-up one?"

"Definitely the latter. As for your tagline, we should come up with something similar, but it might help to know your hobbies and interests. What do you like to do?" Mulroney once mentioned something about a charity Dubrosky was involved in. Not that he inquired or anything. It all sounded pretty highbrow. Despite all the times they'd worked together over the past several months, Cayden didn't know jack about her personal life.

Memories clouded her eyes as she took another sip of her wine. "I've always loved to travel and I still enjoy cooking for friends. I love the way food brings people together in a communal way. It's something I miss as a vampire. I used to love Chinese food. I remember this restaurant we used to go to as a family every Saturday night. I used to order the same thing, dumplings and wonton soup. I never could get over the craving." She shook her head. "Sorry for rambling."

"Don't apologize." Cayden liked finding out personal things about her past. He wondered what else she craved besides food. What about sex? Did she crave it night and day like most vampires, or demons for that matter? "Okay, how about "Passionseekingsiren" looking for an adventure of a lifetime'?"

Dubrosky arched her brows. "Not bad." She set her glass on the table and began scrolling away on her phone. "How about "Loveseekingvampgirl?"

"I think we've got a winner," he agreed. "We can use that as part of your cover, 'travel agent looking for love in exotic places.'" He air quoted the phrase. "It has a certain ring to it."

Her damnable mouth slanted into a smirk. "It's a tad cheesy, don't you think?"

"Maybe, but not for "Swingingjoe," he said, adding the name to her profile.

The throaty sound of her laugh made his heart thump in his chest. This was the first time they'd ever joked around without it ending in an argument. "Does "Loveseekingvampgirl" want a real relationship or a fling?"

"According to Andee's profile, she was looking to casually date, but open to a relationship. I say we keep it the same." Cayden wanted to know more about Dubrosky's personal life, but he didn't want to push. "We need a name for your profile. It can't be your real one. The killer could look you up and figure out you're a cop."

"Any ideas?"

"We should use Natalya so you remember to answer to it." Saying her name out loud burned on his tongue. "Your last name should be Russian to match."

From the way she stiffened right before his eyes, he'd said something wrong. "Use Petrov. It was my biological father's name. You might find it hard to believe, but I was born to a working-class family."

Holy shit. Cayden's mouth fell open from the revelation. All this time he'd been giving her shit for hailing from one of New York's most bougee vampire clans, never bothering to inquire about her life before she got turned, and she never bothered to correct him. "Now I feel like an ass."

"You should," she said with a teasing smile. "After I got sired to the Dubrosky clan, they raised me as their daughter and asked me to legally change my name to theirs."

"I'm sorry for making assumptions about you."

She stared at him and exhaled a breath. "It's okay. I'm guilty of the same thing. We're starting fresh, remember?"

Thinking about the jabs and stupid jokes stabbed him in the gut. "Right." Cayden finished typing then glanced up. "How did your human parents handle you getting turned?" He held up his hand. "I'm sorry if that's too personal."

"No, it's okay. I haven't talked about this with anyone for a long time. I think they were in shock at first, the daughter they knew and loved was gone forever. Over time they were comforted when the Dubroskys became my surrogate family. They knew they'd help me with the transition."

The confession hit him in the pit of his stomach. "I'm glad you had that support when you needed it." Motioning to his screen, he attempted to clear the heaviness in the air. "Your profile's done. Now we need a few photos of "Loveseekingvampgirl." We can generate whatever background we need to. Are you ready?" He picked up his phone.

"Ready is a relative term, don't you think?" Squirming in her seat, she reinforced his suspicion that she avoided being at the center of attention. He wanted to ask why, but not here, not now.

"For the love of the gods, you look like you're going to the electric chair." Cayden got to his feet and took a tentative step closer. "May I?"

"Go for it," she muttered and sucked in a breath.

When he gently eased her shoulders back, his fingers skimmed over her bare, creamy skin. He tried to ignore the rush of heat coursing through his veins and cleared his throat. From the moment she took off her coat, he wondered if her skin was softer than the fabric of her dress. The fabric didn't stand a chance. His fingers lingered on her shoulder.

She gazed up at him with a question in her dark eyes. "Teague?"

Drawing back with a start, he held up his phone. "Okay, here goes." He began snapping away. "Can you smile? I got the feeling "Loveseekingvampgirl" was fun."

She rolled her eyes and then smiled wide and his heart began to pound. She seemed to have no clue about her appeal. He imagined trailing his tongue over every inch of her creamy skin and licking the wine from her lips. He pushed his lust-fueled thoughts to the back of his mind. There was no room for them in an investigation, period. But his demon nature got in the way, growing more enamored with each passing minute.

After Cayden finished, he walked to his chair, took a seat, and uploaded her photos. "Success. Natalya Petrov has a profile. Since "Loveseekingvampgirl" likes to travel, I added a picture of a landscape as a backdrop. Now we can message the men on the list."

Wariness crossed her features. "The dating coach said the best way to get dates is to be challenging and funny. I think that's more in your wheelhouse. Why don't you give it a try?"

"I'll do my best. I'm guessing from the deer in the headlights look on your face earlier today, that you're not into the whole swiping right thing?" he asked, gazing at her face, trying to figure out her aversion to online dating. There was definitely more to the story then she was letting on.

She shrugged. "And here I thought I was doing a good job hiding it."

Cayden observed the lines bracketing her mouth. "You have to be convincing to pull this off or we won't get squat from these guys. How do I sound like a chick, better yet, what does a guy want to hear?" Rubbing his chin, he hearted all the guys on their list. "Let's keep your tagline close to Andee's. How's this? 'I live for excitement and falling in love.'"

"Perfect. Now what?"

"We wait. You need to keep checking that burner phone. I almost forgot. There's something I want to give you." Cayden pointed to a small nylon zipped case on his coffee table. This is for you."

"What's this?" Natalya picked up the case, unzipped it and pulled out what looked like a pen with a metal point at the end.

"An Aluminum Summit Stake, the latest in vampire-hunting gear. There's an aiming point on the tip that allows you to hit your target in the center of the heart, even from a hundred feet away." Cayden smiled. "All you need to do is aim and throw."

"How efficient." Her hand moved to the bullets. "And what's so special about these?"

"Those are hollow points, coated with poison, meant to kill your garden variety demon."

"Lovely." Zipping the case, she slid it into her purse. "Some women get flowers or chocolate. I get weapons."

Cayden laughed. "Your dates won't know what hit them."

Her expression turned tentative and serious.

"What?" he asked, his gaze roaming over her face.

"The thing is I'm fine when it comes to trading jabs with you, but in terms of engaging with the opposite sex, well, not so much. I don't want to blow my cover." She toyed with an invisible thread on her dress.

The admission took him by surprise. "Imagine those guys are me and you'll be fine. Why don't we practice in the meantime?"

Her smile froze on her face. "Practice? What did you have in mind?" she asked, and once again he detected her pulse speed up.

"I promise nothing too crazy. If this is going to work, we need to get a few things out of the way first." Cayden got up and moved next to her on the couch. His leg brushed her thigh and blood, hot and heavy, rushed straight to his groin. "Do you think two people can find the real thing from online dating?" he asked, curious to hear what she'd say.

"I think I'm the wrong person to ask," she said with a sigh. "I know it works for some, but it all seems contrived to me. Love and attraction should happen naturally when you least expect it, not based on some computer algorithm."

The demon in him couldn't agree more. After the tragedy, he'd never tried to find love again, and never wanted to. Beating back the past, he forced the shadows from his mind. Funny, he never imagined Dubrosky as a romantic. "It's always good to ask questions. You want to show you're interested in the other person."

"Asking them flat out if they're a rapist and a killer is a nogo?" she suggested.

"Don't think it'll go over well."

"Fine, please enlighten me with your tips and pearls of wisdom."

"I'm by no means an expert, but I've done this sort of thing before." And he could say, without a doubt, that none of the women he met came close to being as smart, funny or sexy, as the woman sitting beside him on his couch. But he *wouldn't* dare say it, even if it would help boost her confidence.

Her breath became ragged. "I'm all ears."

"Keep it neutral, maybe offer a compliment." His gaze narrowed on her dress. "You look beautiful tonight. Okay, your turn."

When her gaze did a slow sweep of his arms and chest, an unmistakable heat flared in her big brown eyes. "You're in great shape. What do you do to work out?"

"I think you're getting the hang of it." A question still nagged at him. "I'm curious about something, how does a young, attractive female go about meeting the opposite sex if not online?"

Her expression became guarded. Why did he get the feeling he just opened a hot Pandora's box? "I haven't had much luck in that department. In my circles, arranged marriages are still considered the norm."

He became mesmerized by the rise and fall of her chest, like she needed to get something out. "I find it hard to imagine a modern, take-charge female like you buying into all that arranged marriage crap."

The spark faded from her eyes. "As archaic as it sounds, it's done to keep the wealth within the families, but you're right. I don't believe in arranged marriage, not at all. I guess that makes me the world's biggest hypocrite because it didn't stop me from doing it anyway."

CHAPTER 14

The moment the words flew out of Natalya's mouth she wished she could take them back. She braced herself for the onslaught of insults and innuendo. But to her shock they didn't come. Clearing her throat, she forced a smile. "Crazy, right?"

"I had no idea," Teague whispered. "When?"

"It's a long story, one I'm sure you wouldn't be interested in." She sighed, never intending to reveal such a deep, dark secret to Cayden Teague of all people, but the genuine concern in his voice completely threw her off guard. He didn't understand the stringent rules and expectations within elite vampire circles. She'd always be grateful to her sired family, but sometimes the responsibility could be overwhelming.

He pinned her with his intense blue gaze. "Quite the contrary, everything you do interests me. We're going into the foxhole together. I'm sorry. I didn't mean to pry … well maybe a little."

"It comes with the job, right?" she murmured, pushing past her disappointment. She stood and began to pace. He wasn't interested in getting to know her better. This was all for the case, which was exactly where her focus needed to stay. Any foolish romantic notions about him were now put to rest. But he did have a point. For all intents and purposes, they were partners now, and partners needed to have each other's backs.

"Who were you married to?" he asked in a voice that reminded her of smoke and whiskey. She couldn't deny the yearning he stirred in her body.

"He was a business partner of Pavel's, my sired father." Even after all these years, saying the truth out loud still stung. Thinking about it now twisted her stomach into knots. She teetered on her ridiculous heels and made her way over to the wall of windows. Staring out at the breathtaking view of the New York City skyline, she took a few deep breaths to ease the knot of tension in the pit of her stomach. She turned back to face him and forced a smile. "The wedding lasted longer than the marriage." Three days of smiling and faking conjugal bliss only to have the whole thing implode. She exhaled and tried to push the memory to the back of her mind.

"Go on, please," he urged.

Natalya swallowed hard, struck by the sincerity in his eyes. "He wanted to merge his company with Dubrosky Financials. Naturally, marriage became the next logical step. It was expected of me, so I agreed. This all happened five years ago, right after I got turned. You have to understand, I was only twenty-two and not prepared mentally or physically to handle the responsibilities and expectations that came with being a vampire. I didn't see how I could refuse."

"Marrying someone you didn't know or love must've hell. I'm sorry." Teague got up from the couch and joined her at the window.

The concern in his voice threw her for a loop. "The aftermath left a mark of disgrace upon my family."

"Did you ever consider refusing?" The air between them warmed and pressed against her chest. When he edged closer, his bare feet touched the tips of her toes.

"No," she said simply. She didn't think she'd ever experience the kind of heart-stopping love that Garrett and Gillian shared, or Alex and Willow for that matter. She still grappled with feelings of self-worth. Her therapist would say it came down to acceptance, something she still struggled with. She could feel the weight of his gaze from her head to her toes, now cramping up in her new strappy sandals "These are old vampire customs."

"I'm familiar with ancient customs. We demons have a few of our own." Teague folded his arms across his chest and the muscles in his arms bulged out of the sides of his short-sleeved, black T-shirt. She tried not to stare.

Talking about it now, even after all this time, left a bitter taste in her mouth. "My sired family thought they were doing me a favor by pairing me with a vampire from a proper bloodline. They put a lot of pressure on me. I'm sure you'd never do something against your principles." Of course he wouldn't, because Cayden Teague was his own man.

A defiant look flashed in his eyes. "Hey, it's not about that. Everyone deserves a shot at love."

Who knew Teague believed in love? The thought left her a little breathless. Her gaze trailed over the worn jeans that hung low on his hips. They fit him like a dream. He always loomed larger than life, but here in his own space, he just seemed more open and easy to talk to. She looked away to cover her appreciation of his body.

His thumb gently brushed her chin, forcing her gaze up to meet his. "You didn't answer the question."

"It's not that simple, Teague." How could she refuse when she owed them for saving her life?

"Why didn't you tell them to go to hell or fight back? It doesn't sound like the Dubrosky I've come to know." The admiration in his voice unnerved her, the kind that could make a woman flushed and weak-kneed.

Why indeed. It surprised her how much he seemed to get her. "I'm not the same person I was then. I broke away from that whole life when I left my family's place and never looked back."

Turning her head, a small silver frame caught her eye. A faded black and white photo of a beautiful demon woman sat on a table with a spotlight shining above her head. The edges of the photo had become frayed and yellowed from age. Curiosity overruled her better judgement and before she could stop herself, she crossed the room to the table. She ran her finger along the edge of the frame.

Teague's footsteps padded against the wood. He came up behind her, and she could smell his masculine scent, feel his heat. Her heart thudded against her ribcage. "Who was she?" Her hand fell to her side. Hot pins of jealousy snaked up her arm.

"Someone I knew many lifetimes ago," he whispered close to her ear, making her shiver.

She felt his pain like a physical ache. He moved to her side and adjusted the frame to the exact spot under the light. Maybe Cayden Teague wasn't the asshole she made him out to be. Anyone who experienced a love like that couldn't be all bad. Lately she'd seen his kindness and the patience he showed his friends and coworkers.

If someone had told Natalya that Teague had kept a picture of an old flame displayed in his apartment like some kind of shrine, she would've called them a liar. But here it was, plain as day. Then she wondered if she'd ever experience that kind of love. Her insecurities came rushing back tenfold. "I'm sorry. I didn't mean to pry," she murmured, echoing his earlier words. Turning to face him, she needed him to see the sincerity in her eyes. "What happened to her?" she whispered, adding a measure of compassion in her voice.

"She died in my arms." His gaze remained steely, but she could sense the grief brimming beneath the surface. "She made the mistake of trusting me."

"I'm so sorry." Now Natalya understood the pain beneath Cayden's wise-cracking demeanor. A part of her wanted to know more about his past. And another part of her warned her against playing with fire.

He remained silent. His gaze burned into hers.

Sensing his pain, she wanted to pull him into a hug and comfort him, but she stood still, too afraid to move for fear he'd shut down. Before she could ask him to elaborate, the burner phone began to ping, breaking the moment. She walked to the table and glanced at the screen. "Both "Swingingjoe" and "Easy2plez" responded."

"Good. Ask them to meet you tomorrow night at the Wolf Tavern, and make sure to space the dates so they don't run into each other."

Relieved to finally be making progress, Natalya shot out a few texts, and to her shock, both men responded within minutes of each other. "Done."

"You did great, Natalya." Hearing Teague say her first name in his deep, raspy voice sounded rich and decadent like warm chocolate.

"Thanks to you." She tried to play it cool and ignore the hot pins beneath her skin.

Teague moved closer, his heat surrounded her, and an altogether different tension thickened, sparking between them.

This attraction would only complicate matters. "I should head out. "Loveseekingvampgirl" has a big week ahead." She grabbed her purse and her coat and stopped in the hall.

The disappointment in his gaze didn't get lost on her, but then a second later it disappeared and she swore she imagined the whole thing. She felt his gaze on her, probing beneath her clothes. Her body got warm all over. "Any questions?" he asked, walking her out.

Natalya smiled. "Yeah, what kind of douchebag calls himself "Swingingjoe?"

CHAPTER 15

"*I*t's nice to meet you, Natalya. What do you do for fun?" It turned out nothing rivaled "Swingingjoes" penchant for boxing at the gym, except for maybe the vampire's love of tattoos. A sleeve of ink covered one arm and a giant skull covered the other.

"I love to travel and always enjoy a good cigar when I do," Natalya said over the blare of Top Forty in the background. A flutter of nerves turned the inside of her mouth dry. Glancing at Joe over the rim of her wine glass, his long dark hair almost touched his broad shoulders. He wore a black V-neck T-shirt and jeans. Sweat and cheap cologne wafted from his pores. "How about you?" The scent of werewolves caught in her nose. Turning, she gazed at the pack congregated at the bar, a few others engaged in a game of pool. No one seemed to notice her and Joe at a table in the dimly lit corner of the tavern.

After that, Joe talked nonstop about the shows he liked to binge-watch, his job at the tattoo shop, and his failed relationships with women he met online, but nothing about Andee Lyon, cigars, or if he had a nasty habit of raping and killing innocent women.

Natalya tried to add her own anecdotes and laugh at his jokes, but found it hard considering the knot in the pit of her stomach. Background noise from the numerous games playing on the flat screens, and the multiple conversations going on all around her made it difficult to focus on what he was saying, but she concentrated on blocking everything else out.

When she looked up, she caught a glimpse of Denopoulos behind the bar. He poured a draft and set the glass in front of a customer. Smith stayed in the back, posing as one of the dishwashers. Teague, on the other hand, remained in the parking lot, inside the van, watching and listening to everything through the surveillance feed in case the killer recognized him. None of them could wear a mic for this op, in case Joe, or any other vampire in the vicinity managed to pick up on their conversation.

"I was surprised you picked this place. I hang out here a lot. I would've remembered meeting you," Joe said, turning his head and glancing at the bar. Was he looking for Andee? Turning back to face her, he took a swig from his beer. "I can't believe we've never run into each other. This place is close to my apartment and you can't beat the wings."

Natalya smiled. "So I've heard. This is going to sound crazy, but I overheard someone say that one of the bartenders was murdered recently." She waited and tried to gauge Joe's reaction. "Did you know Andee?"

Shock lit his features. Natalya picked up on the surge of blood rushing through his veins. "What? Are you shitting me? Yeah, I knew her. I haven't seen Andee in a while. She wouldn't return my calls." Joe swiped a hand over his mouth.

Minutes later, Denopoulos appeared with their check and set it in front of Joe. He took her glass and Joe's beer bottle off the table, gripping it from the bottom. "Have a good night."

"Hey, I'm not finished yet," Joe snarled, looking affronted. "I'm still talking to the lady."

"Oh sorry, dude. Someone's waiting for this table and the lady's been here a while. Hell, you're the third guy tonight," Denopoulos said with a shrug and walked back to the bar.

She'd spaced the dates far enough apart so that none of the men would run into each other, but now it was time to poke the vampire. Natalya cleared her throat, "Look, Joe, it's nothing personal."

"In all matters of the heart, it's always personal. Look at me, Natalya."

When she did, she couldn't seem to pull her gaze away. His pupils grew large, saucer-like and hypnotic. She tried to speak, but her words became frozen on her lips. She fought against the pull and power of his trance by trying to reach for the Glock in her purse, but her arms wouldn't move. Joe had to be an Ancient for his trance to take hold of her like this. A flash of revulsion and panic threatened. The wave of helpless vulnerability brought her to a dark place. Old terrors rose up, stealing her ability to fight back or to run even if she could move.

"You females are all the same, always looking for the next best thing." His voice sounded muffled, as though coming from inside a wind tunnel. After several agonizing minutes, Joe blinked and the drugged sensation melted away. He got to his feet, showing a hint of fangs. "Nice to have met you." He stomped away, disappearing in a blur.

A wave of adrenaline rushed over Natalya. She inhaled in and out, trying to catch her breath.

Teague must've alerted Denopoulos that she'd been tranced, because a few minutes later he appeared at her table. "Are you okay?"

Panting hard, it took her a moment to answer. "I'm fine. I didn't expect him to turn into a creep quite so fast." Her phone buzzed with a text. Lifting it out of her purse, she glanced at the screen.

Teague: We're done here. Meet me in the rear lot.

Natalya sighed with relief. After she slipped her phone in her purse, she hopped off the stool and cut through the crowd. Wobbling on her heels, she bumped into the guy in front of her. "Sorry."

He turned and gave her a warm smile, showing a hint of fangs. "No problem."

Natalya moved past him, found a side door and exited to the parking lot. Sagging against the brick wall of the building, she breathed in a lungful of fresh air, trying to calm her frayed nerves and gather her composure. She found Teague pacing over the gravel with his phone glued to his ear. Blurring across the lot, she avoided a pothole and what looked like a pile of barf.

"I've got to go." Teague ended his call, pulled the wire from his ear and pushed his phone in his pocket.

Reaching for her shoulders, his warm hands brushed her arms, sending goosebumps along her skin. "He couldn't have gone anywhere with you. Do you hear me? We wouldn't have let him." The demon searched her face. The concern in his eyes chased some of the darkness away.

Natalya closed her fingers over his biceps, and picked up on the wild thump of his heart. "I know. His trance took me by surprise. "Swingingjoe" has a nasty temper."

Teague cursed under his breath and dropped his hands. "He's lucky I didn't rip him apart. Denopoulos talked to some of the employees before the bar opened. Apparently, "Swingingjoe" showed up here a few times looking for Andee and wouldn't take no for an answer when she tried to blow him off."

"No big surprise." Natalya bit down on her lip. "He's showing signs of resentment toward women. Do you think he agreed to meet me here because he genuinely didn't know about Andee's murder and was trying to make her jealous? Or could he be our man and he's a complete sociopath?"

Teague shook his head. "No, the dude seemed shocked by Andee's death. We'll get his DNA, and find out soon enough."

"Why not bring "Swingingjoe" in for questioning?" Natalya glanced around the lot, making sure they were alone.

"Not yet. There's not enough evidence and if we tip our hand too early, we risk "Swingingjoe" going underground and slipping through the cracks. Let's assume whoever framed me thinks I'm out of the way and they're off the hook. We let that play out for now." Teague rubbed a hand over the side of his face and Natalya caught a glimpse of dark smears under his eyes.

"If we can catch a break, maybe there's something incriminating in the recordings." In the course of the evening, nothing any of those guys said jumped out at her, but then again, she'd been too preoccupied trying to appear like a woman out for a good time and less like a cop.

"We'll listen to them again and see if we missed something." His gaze softened. A slice of pale moonlight illuminated his face. "You did great by the way, Natalya," he said with a note of admiration in his voice. Hearing him say her name sent a hot sizzle of awareness through her. "You were a real pro out there, despite those guys practically drooling all over you."

Her chest panged with relief, glad that her lack of experience didn't show. "I don't know about the drooling part, but I have you to thank for the private lessons." Why did her voice sound throaty all of a sudden?

"I'm open for private lessons anytime."

The familiar crackle of electricity warmed the air between them. His gaze roamed over her again. Her body came to life everywhere his eyes touched. Desire licked at her like flames. When he took a step closer, she inhaled the scent of his cologne, a combination of sandalwood and pure male.

Natalya fought the urge to sigh and swayed a little, losing her balance in her round-toe stilettos.

"Easy there." Teague wrapped a hand around her waist to steady her and it sent her heart galloping. The heat from his touch seared through the silk of her dress, leaving a trail of warmth and raw need. In a short span of time, things had shifted between them. Now they were sharing secrets and forging a bond of trust and friendship.

"It's these shoes. The whole balancing thing takes some maneuvering, but once you get past the pinching-the-crap-out-your-toes part, you're golden." She couldn't seem to stop rambling, or think straight with Teague this close.

His gaze darkened. "It sounds like you need a good foot massage." His voice dropped and came out like a purr. An image of him sliding off her shoes and rubbing her feet with those big callused hands made her draw breath. A dull ache settled between her thighs.

"Are you volunteering for the job?" She'd never said anything so bold to a man in her life, but with Teague she could be herself.

His gaze turned molten, searing into her like blue flames. This demon wasn't someone to be played with or managed. Gazing at her lips, he bent his head, tilting it to the side. "Natalya," he murmured.

She sucked in a breath and tilted her head to the side.

Abruptly, Teague pulled away and took a step back.

Standing there breathless and shaking, she heard a voice call out her name, and her brain stuttered into gear.

Oh crap, I've been recognized.

CHAPTER 16

"Who else knows you're here?" Teague asked, swinging his horned head to the female voice moving toward them.

"No one." Natalya's stomach lurched as she turned around and found Jade Hastings, a witch from a nearby coven, standing behind her with two other women.

"Jade? Is that you?" The last time she'd seen her, half of her face and arms had been covered in bruises. Now she looked happy and well. Natalya stole a glance over at Teague. He'd moved a few feet away and pulled out his phone. Then her gaze darted around the lot, checking to make sure none of her dates lingered. Praying her cover hadn't been blown, she turned to face Jade. "What are you doing here?"

"I'm here celebrating with some friends." Jade walked over and caught Natalya in a hug.

Natalya pulled away and smiled. "It's great to see you. How are things going?" They met at the hospital after Jade's boyfriend had beaten her up and sexually assaulted her.

"I'm well, back in school, working, all thanks to you," Jade said with pride in her voice. "I would've never gotten out of my situation if you hadn't given me the name of a counselor and put me in touch with the people from SAAN. I appreciate everything you did for me. I never got a chance to thank you."

"You don't need to thank me." Natalya reached out and squeezed her hand. Success stories like Jade's made the work she did for SAAN worthwhile.

"The nurses at the hospital told me you stayed at my bedside all night and into the morning until my parents flew in from California. You went above and beyond the call of duty."

"And I'd do it again in a heartbeat." When Natalya had been attacked and left for dead, no one came until it was too late. After that, she'd been forced to leave her human life behind, and start a new life … an undead one. She wanted to be there for someone else.

"I should go and let you get back to your date." Jade turned her head and eyed Teague with an appreciative smile. "Wow, he's hot. Go you."

"Oh, he's not my date. We work together." Butterflies fluttered in her belly, making her feel like a damn teenager. Jade must've seen her sexy-as-sin, pseudo-partner almost kiss her in the moonlight.

"I just assumed when I first spotted you two from your body language. My bad. I should go. It was great seeing you, Detective." Jade gave Natalya another hug.

"You too. Take care, Jade."

Minutes ticked by before Teague walked back over to her. He stared at her long and hard as though seeing her for the first time. "Chalk one up to you, Detective. Whatever you did must've made a real difference in that young woman's life." His praise caught her off guard. "Sorry, I didn't mean to eavesdrop on your convo. What's SAAN by the way? I've never heard of it."

"It's a charity I'm involved with. Nothing you'd be interested in." She didn't want him to know about her involvement with a sexual abuse organization. If he dug deep enough, he'd find out why and she couldn't bear his pity. "What's the plan for tomorrow?" she asked, eager to change the subject.

"We set up your dates, same place, same bat channel," he said, sounding all business, their near-kiss forgotten. "Hey, I wanted to ask if you've heard from "Hardluvingman?" We need to stay on him."

"I'll try messaging him again. I scheduled two more dates for the following evening. "Hardluvingman" has been the only guy who hasn't responded to my message." Aside from the blind dates part, Natalya didn't want the night to end. The more time she spent around Teague, the more she saw a different side to him—a side she wanted to get to know better. Sure, he could be a stubborn pain in the ass, but he made her laugh, and she sensed a gentleness hidden beneath his gruff exterior.

"Keep on him. I need to listen to the recording from your dates and see if anything comes up that we may have missed."

"I could go over them with you."

The heat in his gaze seared into hers. "I'd like that. But once they finish cleaning up, Denopoulos and Smith are headed out here with the evidence. We're dropping it off at the lab. Let me walk you to your car."

"I took a cab to be on the safe side." Natalya tried to hide her disappointment with a smile. Loneliness gripped her hard. *This is a work relationship*, she reminded herself. They couldn't blur the line, no matter how tempting. "Go do what you have to. I'll call an Uber."

"I can wait until it comes." He crossed his arms over his chest. The muscles in his shoulders and back flexed with the movement. She cleared her throat, trying not to drool.

"No, it's okay. I'm being extra careful."

"I'm not leaving you here alone, too many jerks out tonight."

"I'll be fine." His concern for her melted her insides. They stared at each other for several minutes with neither one of them saying a word. "Well, I should go."

"Text me when you get in." His gaze traveled the length of her and then he drew his brows together. "Didn't you have some kind of jacket over you?"

"Crap, it's not mine. I left it on the back of my stool. I need to go get it. I'll go in through the front this time."

"Okay, I'll see you tomorrow." He smiled and the heat in his eyes grew intense, almost painful. "Good night, Natalya."

Why would she do this to herself when she knew he was still hung up on his lost love? While she couldn't deny their sexual chemistry, this couldn't possibly lead anywhere considering they were colleagues. "Good night, Cayden."

Cayden almost kissed me.

Natalya pulled out her phone, clicked on the POM app and sent

"Hardluvingman" a quick text, while a giddy sensation spread from her head to her toes. After she ordered her Uber, she tried to get her head out of the clouds and make her way through the crowd without tripping. She rushed to the table she'd been sitting at earlier, relieved to find her borrowed jacket still draped on the back of the stool. Picking it up, she pushed her arms through the sleeves.

"Excuse me, miss? No one paid your tab." Natalya turned to find a waitress behind her looking annoyed. She handed Natalya the bill off her tray.

"I'm sorry, I'll take care of it." Natalya opened her purse and rooted around for her wallet. Unable to find it, she realized she'd left it at the manor, along with her credit cards and ID in preparation for her cover. She'd used the last of her cash on a cab. Her stomach dropped. "I don't have my wallet. I promise I can come back."

"It's on me."

Natalya turned and found the guy she'd bumped into earlier at the next table. He handed over a fifty to the waitress. "Keep the change."

"Thanks." The waitress smiled and walked away in the other direction.

"I don't know what to say except, thank you." Her cheeks heated with mortification.

"It happens to the best of us." The vampire stood out from the rest of the crowd. Between his ramrod straight posture and his sharp, honed gaze, she'd be willing to bet he'd been in the military.

"How can I pay you back?"

"Don't worry about it. Call me old school, but I don't approve of a male sticking a lady with the bill. I happened to be watching the game at the bar and I couldn't help but notice your steady stream of admirers," he said with a note of amusement in his voice.

Her cheeks heated. She could only imagine what it must have looked like to an outsider. "You must've been paying attention."

"Forgive me if I sound impertinent, but you're impossible to miss." His accent made him sound almost regal. Then again, it shouldn't surprise her. Most vampires emigrated here from other parts of the world. Natalya glanced at his face. His nose appeared to have been broken with a small bump in the center. A small scar marred his cheek. He wasn't classically handsome like Cayden, but she'd go as far to say his dark hair and green eyes made him striking.

"Trust me, it's not what you think." But then again, she didn't feel compelled to explain her dating habits to strange men she met in bars. She didn't owe him an explanation and yet she found the need to justify what he undoubtedly witnessed. The cop in her wondered if he'd been watching from the sidelines. At this point, any male who set foot through the door could've known the victim and could be the killer.

"I wasn't trying to probe. I'm James." He extended his hand and Natalya shook it, catching a glimpse of a Rolex on his wrist.

"Natalya," she said simply.

"A pleasure. I admit I'm fascinated by today's dating rituals. I grew up in another century where women had to be courted properly."

"My sired mother would love you."

He laughed. "I'm sure she's just as charming as her daughter."

James seemed harmless enough, but she could never be too sure. She wondered if he knew Andee. "Do you come here often?"

"I think that may be my line." He winked. "This is my first time. I eat on occasion as a novelty, and I hear good things about the wings."

Ahem. Her mind drifted to Cayden once more. Nursing an infatuation to someone who was unavailable made no sense, and there were non-fraternization rules at work to consider. As she casually checked out James, she found herself comparing him to Cayden. The two couldn't be more physically different. James was long and lean like a runner. Cayden, on the other hand, looked more like a linebacker, a giant made of solid muscle.

Her phone buzzed. She glanced at her screen. "My Uber's outside. I'm sorry. I have to go."

"Let me guess, you're being whisked away by another male suitor?"

"Definitely not. It's almost midnight and I'm about to turn into a pumpkin."

Aside from the fake lashes which made her eyes itch, and learning to walk in heels, she was starting to get the hang of this new undercover persona; practicing with Cayden had helped. She never imagined a figure-hugging dress and a new haircut could make her feel confident. Her phone pinged again. "My carriage awaits in a black SUV."

"Well then, Cinderella, if you'd like to continue the conversation, why don't you give me a call? I'd love to take you to dinner sometime, or even a ball." James reached into the front pocket of his jacket and handed her a card.

A ball? "It was nice meeting you, James." If anything, she'd check him out in the database.

"I'm sure we'll meet again, Natalya." Reaching for her hand, he placed a kiss on the back, and then disappeared into the crowd.

Blurring out the door, she got into the backseat of the SUV. She stared at James's card once more, and just when she thought this night couldn't get any more bizarre, it suddenly did.

CHAPTER 17

*C*ayden tapped on the glass door to the lab. "Anybody home?" The high-pitched notes of Motley Crue blared from speakers around the room. He found their MBI lab tech, Erika, sitting at her desk with half her face hidden behind a microscope.

"I figured you'd be stopping by any time now," Erika murmured from her stool, not bothering to look up. The witch changed her hair color like most people changed their socks. Today it gleamed under the lights to a dark shade of blue. "I pulled an all-nighter just for you, demon."

"Thanks, Erika, for doing me a solid. What do you have for me? I'm hoping something concrete." Taking a seat on a stool, Cayden glanced at her monitor.

"I superimposed a fragment of the cigar band found at the scene and was able to make out the letter *K*. I did some research. My best guess, it's a King of Denmark, one of the expensive brands you'd find at the more high-end smoke shops." Erika pulled out the pencil from her hair and tapped it on her desk. "Put it all together with our cashmere fibers and designer shoe print and I'd say we have someone with money and means who appreciates the finer things in life."

Rubbing the side of his neck, Cayden tried to puzzle this case out. "So far none of Dubrosky's dates fit that kind of profile. It blows the theory that it was someone Andee worked with, or was dating. None of those guys hanging out at the Wolf Tavern are walking around in cashmere or smoking fancy cigars. Our witness insisted that all of Andee's boyfriends were more the leather jacket and polyester blend types." Once they found the details on the cigar, then they found their killer.

"I hear Dubrosky is taking one for the team." Erika looked up and a curious expression spread across her face. "Lucky her."

A frown pulled at his lips. "Some of those guys were real tools. One of them tranced her when he found out he was her third date of the night." Saying it out loud made his horns burn with anger.

"And here I thought some of the guys I met online were dicks. All the good ones are taken," she said in a playful tone, but her eyes turned serious.

"Listen, Erika. I'm sorry. I never meant to lead you on, and if I did …"

"Don't sweat it. You've always been straight up with me, demon, which is more than I can say for most of the jerks I date."

Cayden smiled, happy they could move past any awkwardness. "What's your take on this guy?"

"He's not crazy, but organized with a high level of intelligence. The police report showed no sign of a break-in. I say the vic knew him, but he wasn't her usual type." Erika swiveled around in her chair, got up, and threw her gloves in the trash.

Her assessment of the killer came damn close to Willow's. He exhaled, holding on by a razor's edge. He'd been up all night, tossing and turning, not able to force the dark images from his mind, first Abigail and then Andee. Then it hit him. Maybe he was howling at the moon when he should be kicking coffins. "What if the killer tranced Andee?"

"It's possible." Erika shrugged. "No way to know for sure."

"What's his motive? We're still going with the jealous lover theory?"

"The way I see it, he didn't take the news well when the vic tried to break things off. Maybe he followed her, did a little stalking, seeing the vic go home with you set him off."

"Okay, let's run with that." Cayden nodded. "Why not kill me too and get me out of the way?"

"Simple, his anger was directed at the victim, not at you," Erika pointed out.

"I've put away some real pieces of shit over the years, some who'd probably love to see my horned head on a platter. Some of these dudes came from serious means, some like Stephen Frost."

"The former head of the Coterie?"

"I've been thinking, what if Frost didn't die in that prison fire? What if he's still alive and found a way to hack into the Hellios server, and switched the records to make it look like he died instead of Hawthorne?" Cayden rubbed his chin. "Frost was a cybercriminal, one of those black hats, a crackerjack in identity theft. Hell, it's not out of the realm of possibility."

Erika eyed him skeptically. "And what if the Easter bunny's real? I get someone's gone to a hell of a lot of trouble to get you out of the way, but I don't believe it's Frost. He's toast, literally. Do you have any solid proof he's alive?"

"No, not yet anyway."

"I'm sorry. I'm not mocking you. Maybe the job has gotten to you," Erika said, her voice laced with compassion. "Who could blame you? Your friend gets killed and you get framed for her murder. You're burned out, my friend."

Cayden hissed out a breath. "Maybe you're right. Any prints turn up?"

"Afraid not. He wore gloves. We're still trying to match up the fingerprints and saliva on the glasses from the bar with the DNA found at the scene. I'm comparing them to the body fluids, textiles and fibers from clothing and furniture from the vic's apartment. So far none of these are a match. We haven't found our killer yet."

"We keep trekking along until we do. Any luck with the jewels?" Cayden asked, curious. "What did you find?"

"It's not my area of expertise, but I've been doing a little research and I've become obsessed with the whole thing." Erika pointed to a stack of books. "Those gems aren't like anything I've seen before. There are symbols and markings that are indecipherable. I'm trying to decode them."

Hearing the words made Cayden's horns tingle. The jewels of his people were looted by the Coterie hundreds of years ago on Arcadia. As far as he knew they were lost forever, but he couldn't help wonder if there could be any connection.

"I'm sending the reports to your posse," Erika said, interrupting his wayward thoughts. "And your lady vampire."

"She's not *my* vampire." The thought forced Cayden's pulse to jump.

"Thanks for all your help. I've got a few things to do before I head over to the bar." Now he'd have to sit there and watch Natalya put herself in danger again, and there wasn't a damn thing he could do to stop it. "Let's talk soon."

Cayden spent the better part of the day scouring police reports and witness testimony. He chased down leads that only led to more dead ends. A designer shoe print, a cigar fragment, and cashmere fibers weren't much to go on. They were flying blind until they could get a match on the DNA. Something didn't add up—a piece missing.

He'd put a call in to Saje, the coven's potion guru, and scheduled a time to stop by the shop, in hopes of getting the scoop on the henbane leaves. By the time he pulled up to the Malibu Diner on 14th Street, he was running on fumes. Reaching for his phone from the cup holder, he sent Natalya a text, asking her to meet him and Denopoulos here before round two of the "Dating Game" commenced.

Mixing business with pleasure could get dicey, which was why he rejected her offer to listen to the recordings together. But no matter how hard he tried, he couldn't get her out of his mind. The demon in him wanted to soothe her pain after hearing about her divorce. He longed to taste her lips, explore every inch of her body with his tongue. The craving for her never seemed to go away. At this point, he didn't know how much longer he'd be able to maintain his distance.

Pulling off his T-shirt, he reached into the back, replacing his *Judas Priest* with his old standby, *Metallica*. He'd been eating most of his meals out of the van, dressing in it seemed apropos. He hopped out and walked to the front. The bright-blue moon cast an eerie glow on the street, which usually meant the crazies would be out in full force tonight.

Cayden made his way inside the diner and found his partner sitting at their usual table. His gaze darted around. The place was empty, except for a couple of old dudes drinking coffee at the counter. Taking a seat at the booth in the corner, he grabbed a menu and glanced at his partner. "Hey, buddy. What's up?"

"I hope you don't mind. I ordered for both of us. I couldn't wait. I'm starving. I haven't eaten anything all day except for wedding cake. We went to the tasting." Denopoulos's face lit up with a beaming smile. "We settled on the red velvet."

Seeing his partner so in love made Cayden's heart swell. "You deserve this, man, especially after everything you've been through together."

"The tux fitting's next week," he said with take a sip of water. "I'm sure it's the last thing on your mind, but I still want you as my best man. Let me know your thoughts. I get this case is personal to you on every level."

"There's nothing in this world that will keep me from seeing my best friend tie the knot."

Cayden's phone buzzed with a text. Glancing at the screen, he smiled, and then looked up at his partner. "Nat … er, Dubrosky, should be here any minute."

"Man, I never thought I'd see the day, you and Dubrosky partnering up. Have you been behaving yourself?" Denopoulos arched his brows. "Let's hope you two don't kill each other."

"What could go wrong?" He'd never tell him the truth—that he'd been looking forward to seeing Natalya all day. She somehow managed to make this nightmare almost bearable. Cayden shook his head. That kind of thinking would get him into trouble. He'd keep things strictly professional, no matter how much he wanted to spend time with her away from this case.

"I hope I don't have to keep cake knives far out of reach from you two."

Before he could respond, the waitress appeared with their food. She set their plates and their drinks on the table. "Enjoy."

"Thanks so much." The sizzling aroma of the beef made Cayden's mouth water. He took a bite of his burger and groaned. He chewed and swallowed, then wiped his mouth with a napkin. "I can't remember the last time I ate something that wasn't handed to me through a drive-up window. As for Natalya, you don't need to worry about me. We're getting along just fine. She's a lot different than I thought."

"How so?"

"She's complicated, that's for damn sure. But she's whip-smart, funny as hell, and she's got this whole Good Samaritan thing going on." Taking a sip from his glass, he shook his head. "Don't get me wrong. She's feisty as hell, headstrong, and as stubborn as a banshee." *She's gotten under my skin.*

"Uh huh. I know the look. And now you've started calling her Natalya. Well, I'll be damned." Denopoulos chuckled and reached for a fry.

"What look?"

"You like her."

"Like is a strong word." Lust was more like it. *Fine.* Cayden did like her, more than he should. A hum vibrated in his throat. She made him a little crazy, but in a good way.

"Do you remember when you accused me of having the hots for Willow and I denied it?" Denopoulos asked in a tone ripe with sarcasm. "Well, we both know how that turned out."

Cayden shot him a "don't go there" look. "Switching subjects, what have you been up to today? Tell me something good."

"I had an interesting chat with the manager from the Wolf Tavern. He gave me a copy of their employee list. I cross-referenced it with our database, but nothing came up," Denopoulos said, digging into his burger. He chewed and swallowed. "There was a barback by the name of Jason Michaels who worked the night of Andee's murder and he's been MIA ever since."

"It sounds suspicious. We should check him out. What about the names on our dating list? Any come up with a criminal record?" he asked, gobbling up a fry.

"Yeah, one. "Midnight Maverick" aka Scott Nelson." Denopoulos ripped open a couple of sugar packets and poured them into his coffee. "He's a person of interest. He's been arrested for sexual assault twice, but the charges were dropped both times."

"Did you find out why?"

"The victim recanted in one instance, and a bad bust in another, which resulted in the evidence getting thrown out." Denopoulos glanced at the door. "Dubrosky has a date with him tonight."

Cayden's gut tightened at his words. He'd practically begged Natalya to be a part of this ruse to lure this twisted fuck out into the open. "We'll have to keep a close eye on her. Did any of the staff at the bar recall seeing Andee go home with anyone they didn't recognize?"

"No one claims to have seen anything unusual." Denopoulos sipped his coffee.

"Something's not adding up." Cayden took a couple bites of his burger, and wiped his mouth with a napkin. "I pulled the police reports on the Zipper case going as far back as the last six months. Each victim couldn't give a positive ID on their attacker, but described him as a tall male wearing a leather mask with a zipper. Some reported getting dragged into a black SUV, and some say they were attacked in an alleyway."

"We find our masked man, we find our killer. Maverick definitely fits the profile."

"No argument there, but what made him graduate from rapist to killer?" Cayden finished the last of his food and pushed the plate away, trying to make sense of this case.

"Who knows, he could've been on drugs and snapped."

"Maybe, but here's the other piece of the puzzle that doesn't seem to fit. Andee was the only one out of the seven vics who wasn't actually raped. This scumbag jacked off on her body instead." Anger and guilt twisted inside Cayden's gut like a knife.

"Where are you going with this, Teague?"

"I still can't help but think Andee's murder and the Zipper case have nothing to do with each other, but are going on simultaneously." Cayden rested his arm against the back of the booth. "Hell, it wouldn't be the first time."

The click-clack of high heels drew Cayden's attention to the door. Natalya sauntered across the expanse of checkered floor. The two old guys at the counter turned their heads to get a better look at her in a short, fire-engine red dress that hugged her curves in all the right places. She might as well have waved a cape at a bull. His cock strained against the front panel of his trousers.

She slid into the booth next to Denopoulos. "What's up, guys? Where's the third member of the band?" she asked, setting her purse on the table. A curious expression spread across her beautiful face.

"He's already at the bar setting up, trying to fake his way through mixing a margarita." Cayden pursed his lips at the image.

"Why do I sense I'm interrupting some kind of top-secret meeting of the bro minds? What's got you two so tongue-tied?"

"It's about one of your dates, and I'm afraid you're not going to like it one damn bit." Turning to his partner, Cayden cleared his throat. "I'll let you fill her in." The impact of something happening to Natalya, losing her like he lost Abigail, became a suffocating squeeze to his throat. *What if?*

Cayden stared at Natalya, memorizing the curve of her face and the fire in her eyes. He waited for the hurricane of anger and frustration to dissipate, and when it didn't, he glared at Denopoulos. *Damn it to hell, why does he always have to be right?*

CHAPTER 18

*N*atalya's gaze cut through the crowd circling the bar. She'd been waiting for her last date of the evening, Scott Nelson, aka "Midnight Maverick" to show for the past thirty minutes, but so far there was no sign of the accused stalker yet. Lifting her phone out of her purse, she shot off a text to Cayden.

Natalya: How much longer should I give him?

Cayden: Five more minutes and then meet me in the rear lot when you're done.

Turning her head, she caught a glimpse of Smith sliding glasses into an overhead rack. He picked up a bottle of vodka and a shaker, looking right at home. He poured the red concoction into a martini glass and set the drink in front of a vampire seated next to Denopoulos who appeared to be watching one of the games.

None of her dates tonight had appeared to remember Andee Lyon, let alone harbor some twisted fascination with her when her name came up in conversation. Her first date of the night started out with a bang thanks to "Hardluvingman" who ended up drinking way too much. He finished the evening by asking her to be part of his succubi harem. She didn't know whether to be flattered or insulted. The final blow came when he leaned in for a kiss and whispered, "Don't be alarmed if my tooth falls out."

Shaking it off, she decided to pull up her email while she waited, and cross-referenced the list of the men Andee had met online with the tavern's employee list, looking for potential matches. Nothing new came up. Reaching into her purse for her notepad, her fingers closed over James's card.

She'd put his name in the police database, but nothing had popped up, which didn't mean much. She'd learned from experience that killers and serial rapists could have pristine records before they turned to violence. She supposed it wouldn't hurt to question him. Then again, he could simply be what he appeared, an attractive, charming vampire interested in getting to know her better.

The voice in her head told her something different. Adding his number to her contacts, she attempted a clever text.

Natalya: Hi, James. This is Natalya aka Cinderella. It was nice meeting you.

She hit send and tapped her fingers on the bar while she waited.

Almost instantly, three little dots appeared, indicating a response was being typed.

James: I looked for you at the bar, but no glass slippers were left behind. You made quite an impression on me the other night.

His text made Natalya smile, and got her thinking. How much longer would she be content to ignore her desires and her own lackluster love life? While she thought about a clever response, "Midnight Maverick" approached the bar and sat on the stool next to Natalya's. She recognized the demon from his profile pic. Immediately, she caught a whiff of beer and sweat, but nothing resembling cigar smoke.

"You must be "Loveseekingvampgirl." The lady in red. I liked your photo, but damn, you're even hotter in person." His words sounded slurred and she wondered how much he'd consumed before he got here.

"Thank you." She wasn't used to a guy referring to her as hot—witty, maybe, but never hot. She plastered a fake smile on her face. "It's nice to meet you." She slid her phone into her purse. "This is one of my favorite hangouts. Have you been here before?"

His eyes clouded over, a telltale sign he might be hiding something. "First time."

"I'm friends with one of the bartenders." Natalya glanced behind the bar before facing Maverick once more. "Funny, I haven't seen Andee around tonight."

His expression gave nothing away.

"Tell me about yourself." Natalya went through the checklist of her fake persona in her head while she checked him out. Maverick kept his dark hair cut short, accentuating an attractive face and short, black horns. He wore a flannel shirt and jeans. He didn't look like the kind of guy to wear cashmere or designer shoes, but he could be hiding his real identity.

"Where do I begin?" Taking her question as interest, Maverick nudged closer as he talked about himself. When he rested his hand on hers, she forced herself not to snatch it away. A creepy vibe oozed from his pores.

Smith walked up and set two cocktail napkins on the bar. "Evening. What will it be?"

"I'll have a draft. And what about for the lady?" Maverick turned to Natalya and looked her up and down, leering at her legs.

"Vodka and club soda please." He didn't need to know it was all soda.

After a few minutes, Smith returned with their drinks and set them on the bar. The conversation began to flow. Natalya nodded and laughed at Maverick's jokes. She tried to ask him questions and casually segue into his connection to Andee Lyon without being obvious. "How did you hear about POM?"

The demon finished his beer, wiped his mouth on his sleeve and set the glass on the bar. "A friend turned me on to the app. What about you?"

Natalya sipped her drink. "What a coincidence, mine too. Andee, the one I was telling you about, she's told me about some of the guys she met on the app."

This time his jaw ticked at the mention of her name. "Yeah, and what did she say?"

"She warned me about the creeps out there. Let's hope you're not one of them." A nervous giggle bubbled up from her throat. Could she be making small talk with the rapist/killer coined, 'The Zipper'?

"Only one way to find out, beautiful." Maverick ran his finger along her arm. She tried not to cringe. "Your skin's as smooth as your voice. I could listen to you all night. Are you ready to get out of here?" he whispered close to her ear.

"It's early. What's the rush?" From the reddish tint to his skin, Natalya guessed Maverick to be part fire demon. She'd clashed with one right after joining the force. He resisted arrest by creating fire and throwing it at her head. Swallowing hard, she kept her expression neutral.

"I know when I see something I like."

"We're just getting to know each other." Natalya chewed on her straw, trying to hide her reaction.

"I'd like to get to know you much better. You won't be complaining when my hands are all over you."

The comment made her skin crawl. Everything about him ignited dark memories—memories she'd rather forget. Natalya recovered by reaching for her purse, running her fingers over the outline of hard metal. "I have a better idea, why not go to the pier and keep walking until you hit the water?"

Smith strode over to them and swiped their glasses off the bar. A warning look flashed in his red eyes as he glared at Maverick. "I think it's time for you to hit the road. I'd be happy to call you a taxi."

"No need. I'm out of here." Maverick slapped some cash on the bar and then turned to Natalya and muttered, "You don't know what you're missing." He stumbled away without another word.

"Good riddance. Talk about some real winners." She took several deep breaths to calm her frayed nerves.

Smith's gaze narrowed at her in concern. "You good?"

She nodded. "I'm good."

When a customer called out his name, Smith turned and headed to the other end of the bar to maintain his cover.

At least she was done for the night. She needed a few minutes to pull herself together before she faced Cayden alone. She decided to make a pit stop at the restroom. Lifting her purse off the bar, she got up from her stool on shaky legs and made her way through the crowd.

The scent of sweat, cologne, and pheromones swirled in the air. Couples stood off to the side, their bodies pressed together in tight embraces. Voices and laughter drifted over the loud thump of the bass.

By the time she got to the bathroom, she couldn't stop shaking. She got in line behind a young woman with a sleek bob, rocking a pair of ripped jeans and an off-the-shoulder black top. Natalya smiled at her as they made their way inside. After she splashed cool water on her face, she reached for a paper towel and patted it dry. Heels scraped against the tile and then the door opened and shut.

Reaching into her purse, her fingers closed over her lip gloss. She rubbed the wand across her lips, needing something to do with her hands. She glanced at her reflection in the mirror, the more she stared, the more she tried to reconcile the memory of the scared young woman to the fanged creature with newfound confidence staring back at her.

She'd been scouring over every grimoire on scrying she could find in the manor library. Each night before she went to bed, she'd been practicing what Brooke had taught her, but so far no images or predictions had come to pass.

Taking a deep breath, Natalya closed her eyes and tried connecting with her third eye. If anything, it would help clear her mind and calm her nerves. Several minutes ticked by. Then she visualized a warm beam of light connecting to the center of her forehead and spreading to her limbs. The longer she breathed in and out, the more distinct and brighter the light became.

After several minutes, she began to breathe easier. When she opened her eyes and stared into the mirror, the hazy image of a young woman appeared in the glass, the same woman who'd been standing here moments before. She gripped the edges of the sink for support. The clink of glasses and the roar of a crowd echoed in the background. It was like looking through some kind of portal into the bar.

The scene changed like a wisp of smoke. The next moment, a man emerged from the shadows and tried to shove the woman into a car. Natalya sensed her fear and her shock. Before Natalya could contemplate what it meant, a scream tore from the woman's lips.

"Help me!"

Natalya reached out her hand to the mirror and the image disappeared. Icy fingers pricked along the back of her neck. She needed to find the woman, and fast. She blurred out the door and pushed through the crowd, trying to avoid knocking anyone over. Rushing through a side door, she found herself in the alley.

Shadows danced across the pavement like ghosts. Her gaze darted to a group of women walking past. Cars and trucks cruised along Frank Sinatra Drive and slowed to a stop. The woman could be anywhere.

Couples walked past holding hands. Nothing appeared suspicious. A cool breeze blew her hair in every direction. Closing her eyes, she tuned in to the conversations around her, and tried to block out the noise from the traffic. After a few minutes, she picked up on a woman's strained voice.

"I told you I'm not going home with you. Let go."

"Hey, I'm only trying to get to know you better."

She recognized that voice. It belonged to Maverick. Turning the corner, she cut across the alley, and spotted the demon hovered over the woman she'd seen in the mirror. "You don't take no for an answer, do you?" Natalya shouted as she approached the scene. Streetlights illuminated the sidewalk and the frightened look in his victim's eyes.

Maverick turned and his face contorted with anger, making him look every bit the monster she suspected beneath the handsome face. "You again? What the hell do you want? Why don't you piss off?"

"Get away from her." Natalya blurred across the alley, giving the woman an opportunity to take off in the other direction.

Maverick took a predatory step closer and moved into her personal space. "Where's your bodyguard from the bar? Funny, I don't see him right now."

Her phone started to ring. Would Cayden or the others find her in time? She sensed from the blades of fire burning in Maverick's eyes, she needed back up. *Now!*

"Take it easy. We can talk about this." Taking a step back, she reached inside her purse until her fingers closed over her badge.

"You'll regret getting in my way."

"Are you threatening me? Did you take your rage out on Andee Lyon when she rejected you?"

"What do you know about Andee? Who the hell are you?" Maverick's horns elongated from his head.

"Police." Pulling out her badge, she held it up. "Put your hands behind your back. You're under arrest." She hoped she could get her cuffs on him without getting turned into ash.

"You're a cop? The date was a setup?" Fury laced Maverick's voice as realization flared in his red eyes. "Fuck this. I'm not going to jail." He held up his hands, and fire pulsed from his fingertips. A fireball skimmed over her head right before she blurred out of the way.

Searing heat exploded over her skin. Her chest heaved. "Don't do this. You have options." Her hands shook as she fumbled for her Glock. Before she could get it out of her purse, his body went up in flames.

Where the hell did he go? Her heart went to her throat when he reappeared in front of her and closed his hand over her mouth.

"Why don't we chat in private?" His deep voice filled with menace and cut through the darkness. His words forced her brain to kick into gear.

Her hands curled into fists. A right uppercut landed at his throat, followed by a knee to the groin, giving her a chance to blur a few feet away. Before she could reach for her gun, Maverick came up behind her, trapping her arms in a vise-like grip. The strength and speed of him knocked her off-kilter.

Wobbling in her stilettos, she dug the spike of her heel into the tip of his shoe. He snarled and grabbed her by the hair, pulling her across the alley, away from the streetlights and the protection of any onlookers. He shoved her up against the brick wall of an abandoned building. The pressure of his hand digging into her waist and the weight of his enormous body forced a wave of helplessness to wash over her like a crashing wave. Old terror flashed through her mind and she froze, unable to fight back.

She tried to scream, but his hand remained on her mouth. Her vision darkened around the edges. With every inhale, she fought against her rising panic. Closing her eyes, she tried to stop the rush of memories.

Footsteps pounded through the field. When she tried to run, two of them tackled her to the ground. No!

Blinking, she came back to the present. She refused to let Maverick do the same thing to another woman. A burst of anger surged through her, forcing her fangs to elongate. She sank them into his flesh, tasting his rotten blood. Howling in pain, Maverick let go of her, allowing her to breathe.

"Get your hands off me right now or we can add assaulting a police officer to your list of felonies." Again she tried to reach for her gun, but it wasn't in her purse. A hard, cold pressure against her ribcage made her freeze.

Maverick's grip tightened. "Is this what you're looking for?"

CHAPTER 19

"What could've happened to her? She's not answering. Where did she go?" Hopping out of the van, a wave of emotions gripped Cayden by the throat. What if Natalya got hurt, or worse? His mind refused to go there. He'd watched and listened to her all night with rapt admiration and respect. She'd conducted herself like a pro. His gaze darted around the parking lot. *No sign of her.*

Denopoulos walked up to him with a frown. "Maverick's gone. I searched everywhere."

"Hold on, I have her location." Pulling out his phone, Cayden found her ping in the next alley over. "I got her. Let's go."

He raced across the lot with Denopoulos hot on his heels. Sniffing the air, he smelled Natalya's perfume. "This way," he said over the frantic pounding of his heart. Unwanted images flooded his mind: Abigail's lifeless body on the ground, blood seeping from her neck and bubbling out from her lips, followed by the agony of trying to bring her back when all hope had been obliterated.

In order to survive, he'd been forced to leave her and go through the portal alone. The guilt still choked him like a noose around his neck. But this time the memory didn't swallow him in grief. It forced him to take action, because somewhere along the way, he'd started to have feelings for Natalya Dubrosky.

He ought to know better than to care. He'd be putting both of them in jeopardy. A woman's scream pierced the air. Ice cold fear vibrated through his veins and forced his legs to speed up.

"Natalya!" Cayden darted across the alley, running at full speed toward the sound of her voice. His demon instincts took over, the rage building inside his body.

When he caught sight of her with Maverick holding her gun to her side, the monster inside him emerged. Cayden growled and lunged for the demon, coming up behind him and lifting him off the ground by the back of the neck. Slamming the demon's face up against the side of the building, he grabbed the gun from his hands.

"Now who's a tough guy?" He turned him around and held him in place.

Recognition flickered in Maverick's eyes. Did the bastard know Cayden? "Have I arrested you before?"

"Cayden, don't," Natalya shouted. "You can't assault him."

"Why not?" Cayden growled. "He deserves it." He could think of a few things he'd like to do to him right now. But deep down, he knew she was right.

"My lawyer will hear about this," Maverick hissed.

"Save it. You're under arrest." When his heart rate slowed and the beast inside him retreated, Cayden turned him around and threw a set of cuffs on his wrists. "You'll be coming with us."

Denopoulos came up behind him, panting hard. He turned his attention to Maverick. "We have a few questions for you about the murder of Andrea Lyon."

"I didn't kill her," Maverick said with a note of panic in his voice.

Cayden ignored the bastard and turned to Natalya who stood a few feet away. The look of shock on her face gutted him. His gaze trailed over her from head to toe, checking for injuries. "Did he hurt you?"

"No. He took me by surprise. He tried to pull a woman into a late model black Ford Bronco." Natalya collected her gun, put on the safety, and then shoved it in her purse.

"Where is she now?" Teague asked as his gaze darted around the deserted alley.

"I don't know, but I'm reporting the incident to the RHPD." Panting hard, Natalya pulled out her phone, pressed a button, and held it to her ear. "Hopefully she's okay and headed to the police station to file a report."

The tech van screeched to a halt in front of them. Smith got out holding a syringe. "Evening, everyone."

"What's the needle for?" Maverick snarled. "What do you think you're doing?"

"Nothing to worry about. This will settle you and give you a good buzz." Smith walked up to Maverick and plunged the needle into his neck.

"You're drugging me? Who the hell are you people?" The demon's eyes rolled back in his head and then he swayed. The three of them caught him right before he hit the cement. They loaded him into the van and slammed the door.

After Denopoulos and Smith jumped into the van, his partner pressed a button on the driver's side and the window slid down. He turned to Cayden. "Are you coming?"

"No." Cayden's gaze shot to Natalya, who stood shaking in her high heels. "I'm taking Dubrosky home. I suspect Maverick will be out for a while."

"See you at headquarters," Denopoulos called out and took off, leaving him alone with Natalya.

Crossing the distance between them, Cayden reached for her shoulders. "Natalya, talk to me, please. Are you sure you're okay?"

"I'm just shaken up. Trust me, it'll pass. I would've had him, you know." A challenge sparked in her eyes, but the way she couldn't seem to stop shaking didn't fool him for a second. And then an errant thought gripped him by the throat and wouldn't let go. *What if some bastard had abused her?*

"Come here." Unable to resist the urge, Cayden pulled her into a tight hug and pressed her up against his body. Rubbing her back, she surprised him by resting her head against his chest. He picked up on the wild thrum of her pulse.

"He knew Andee," she whispered. "I could tell."

"Agreed. We'll find out more when the agents interrogate him."

"Don't tell anyone about this, especially Mulroney." She looked up at his face, cracking a smile, but it didn't reach her eyes.

"Of course not." His fingers skimmed over her bare arms. "I don't want to think about what he could've done if I hadn't gotten here in time. He could've manhandled you, or worse."

"I can't lose it every time some perp tries to manhandle me." Cayden could hear the fear in her voice and smell it on her skin.

He huffed out a breath. "I'm getting you out of here, and then I'm going to make the bastard pay."

CHAPTER 20

They pulled up to the manor and Natalya exhaled with relief. She couldn't wait to take a hot bath, and collapse into bed.

Cayden turned to her in the dark, his exquisite profile caught in the shadows from the streetlights. Everything about him oozed strength and virility. But she sensed a gentler side to him, one he rarely showed to anyone. "How are you doing?" The genuine concern in his voice chased some of the darkness away.

"I'm fine, just drained." Natalya didn't want him to know how badly her hands still shook, so she opened her purse and fumbled around for her keys. She'd allowed that old sense of helplessness to rear its ugly head. Her gaze met his in the dark. "Do you think Maverick's our killer?"

His hand closed into a fist over the steering wheel. "It's hard to say at this point. We should know more in a few days, after we get the DNA results."

"If not him, then who?" Natalya stared at his face, trying to gauge his expression.

"Here's what I do know, a wing nut like Maverick isn't smart enough to pull this off. Willow believes this guy to be highly intelligent and meticulous. He doesn't appear to be any of those things. He's a hothead for sure, and hotheads usually make mistakes."

"What are you saying?"

"I've put away some of our world's most heinous criminals, and one in particular keeps

coming to mind." Cayden sighed with frustration. "What if Stephen Frost didn't die in that fire?"

His words boomeranged inside her head. "How could that be possible?" she asked. "I read the autopsy results."

"I know. It makes no sense, and yet, I can't help but think there has to be some truth to it.

I'm going to review all the evidence again." His phone buzzed. He glanced at the screen and cursed.

"I should go. Thanks again for the ride." Natalya held up her keys.

His gaze flew to her wrist. "I can already see the bruises that bastard gave you." He reached out and touched the black-and-blue marks starting to form. The warmth from his fingers sent licks of fire across her skin. Their gazes met and she could see the heat burning in his eyes, but it didn't scare her, it warmed her in all the right places. Cayden let go of her and rested his hand on the wheel.

"They'll be gone soon," she murmured, grateful for the ability to heal almost immediately. "There are some perks to being a vampire." She glanced at her wrist and her heart sank. "My bracelet is gone. Maverick must've ripped it off when he grabbed me. I need to go back. It has sentimental value."

"Why don't you let me? You should go inside and chill out."

She blew out a breath. "Thank you. I appreciate you going back there." She didn't have the stomach to right now. "What about Maverick? Don't you have to interrogate him?"

"Trust me, he'll be out for a stretch and I'm not allowed to because I was a suspect," Cayden said in his deep, raspy voice. "Besides, I'm filled with nervous energy. I need to do something to get my mind off things."

"I can relate. I'm still wired." She planned to take one of Saje's potions to calm her nerves.

"C'mon, let's get you inside." Cayden opened his door and got out of the car. Before she could reach for the handle, he appeared at the passenger side and held out his hand. "Allow me."

The van sat at least two feet above the ground. "This isn't made for short people." Grabbing her purse, she reached for his hand.

"That's because only one of us is short, Princess." Now, when he whispered the nickname, it sounded more like an endearment.

One minute she dangled in midair, and the next, she was pressed flush against the hard wall of his chest. She heard his sharp intake of breath right before her feet touched the ground.

"You kicked butt tonight. You held your own."

"Did I?" Luckily, he hadn't seen her lose it when Maverick grabbed her and pulled her deeper into the alley.

"Do you want to talk about what happened?" He kept his hand at the small of her back as they walked across the expanse of sidewalk to the outside gate. They stopped and faced each other. "It would've shaken up even the most seasoned of cops."

"Thanks, maybe later. I'm still trying to process the whole thing."

"Understood." Cayden gazed at her as though trying to dive inside her head and unearth all her secrets. "I've got your back, Natalya. You can trust me."

The genuine concern in his voice almost convinced her to confide in him, but she couldn't run the risk of him looking at her with pity in his eyes. Emotions clogged her throat. She looked away. "I'm fine, really. Thanks again for the offer." The teasing she could deal with, but this seemed different, and more intense. It made her stomach flip.

Taking a step closer, he now stood a breath away. She shivered at his proximity. His finger went under her chin. "I'm here for you."

Her resolve melted at his words. The stress of the last few days caught up to her and came to a head. "I don't know what would've happened if you hadn't been there." To her horror, the floodgates opened up and she couldn't stifle her sob. "Look at me getting soft. I need to toughen up."

"You saved that woman tonight. You're the strongest female I know." Cayden rubbed the tension from her neck. His affection and care sent her heart galloping.

Natalya curled her fingers into the soft cotton of his shirt, comforted by the steady beat of his heart. She wanted to stay right there in his arms and never let go. The overwhelming need shook her to her core. When did Cayden become someone good, someone she felt close to? The craziest part, she wanted more than close, she wanted in deeper. The sensation made her dizzy. His concern for her well-being wiped out her previous opinion of him.

"It's never okay to go rushing in without backup," Cayden whispered into her hair. "But you care deeply and that's what makes you a great cop."

Surprise jolted through her like an electric current. "You think I'm a great cop? That might be the nicest thing anyone has ever said to me."

"You of all people know by now I don't say things I don't mean." His hands moved to her arms.

Silence stretched between them. Things had shifted completely. He was the last person she ever expected to be there for her in her time of need. The whole thing threw her for a loop. How could someone who'd been so arrogant in the beginning now be so sweet and tender? "Why did you give me such a hard time at first? You do realize you acted like a prick?"

Cayden's mouth twisted. "Yeah, I do. At first, I judged you unfairly because you're a vampire. I was wrong."

"What about after that?"

"I figured you joined the force on a lark as a way to prove something to your family and I gave you shit for it. But then the more time I spent around you, the more I realized that you're doing this for the right reasons." His voice softened. "You're brave and you follow your instincts."

Those sweet words made her giddy with excitement. "Cayden ... I ..."

His blue gaze burned into hers and lit off a spark inside her body. "You deserve the praise. It's what friends do for each other."

Her heart skipped a beat. Natalya wondered if friends looked at each other the way they did. What she felt for him went far beyond friendship. Cayden ignited sensations in her that were both exhilarating and frightening all at once.

"Speaking of friends, are you free to stop by the shop tomorrow to ask Saje about the henbane leaves?"

She nodded. "Why don't you text me before you head out and I'll meet you there."

"Sounds like a plan."

A springtime breeze blew her hair in every direction. Cayden reached up and pushed a loose strand behind her ear. The familiar tension between them thickened. A voice in her head told her to walk away, but she remained rooted to the spot, every part of her body aching with need. He somehow managed to make her forget that she'd been attacked.

When their eyes met, the pull grew stronger. Her gaze dipped to the sensual curve of his lips. She wondered what his mouth would taste like and how his tongue would feel trailing down her neck.

An outside light turned on, breaking the spell.

"It's late. I should go." Cayden took a step back and she ached for the delicious heat from his body. "I'll let you know if I find your bracelet."

"Thanks, I appreciate it." She walked through the gate, past the weeping willow to the front of the house, and then turned to face him, and smiled. The slow ache pulled at her even more as their gazes locked in the darkness.

"Sweet dreams, Natalya." Cayden turned and headed to the van. His words sent a wave of heat and longing to her chest. She didn't want him to go. She wanted to spend the rest of the night talking to him, getting to know him better.

What if they slept together? It would complicate everything. Maybe they were just two people caught up in the stress and loneliness that came with the job. As much as her mind knew the answer, her body had other ideas. Her breasts ached. They were heavy and tender. And her clit throbbed. She couldn't wait to get upstairs and have some one-on-one time with BOB, her battery operated boyfriend, a poor substitute for the real thing.

Sweet dreams indeed.

After Natalya emailed her report to the team, and her boss, she soaked in a hot bath with the aromatherapy soaps Delilah made and sold at the shop. She lit a vanilla scented candle, and changed into her pj's. Slipping under the covers, she sprayed lavender on her pillow to help her relax.

Her mind drifted to Cayden. Somehow, he'd managed to take a frightening incident and make it bearable by being funny, sweet and downright chivalrous, everything she needed in the moment. She ignored the heat unfurling inside of her, and leaned against the pillow.

Her phone buzzed. She picked it up off the nightstand and glanced at the screen, surprised to find a text from James.

James: Good evening, Natalya. Glad you reached out. How was your day?

She began to type.

Natalya: Hey, James. Had a bizarre night.

James: Is everything okay?

Natalya: Rough day at work.

James: What do you do?

She couldn't tell him the truth, not yet anyway.

Natalya: I'm a travel agent. What about you?

She hated to lie, but even if he didn't have a record, that didn't mean she could rule him out as a suspect.

James: I'm in finance.

Natalya: Sounds interesting.

Could she ever be with someone who sat behind a desk all day?

James: I'd like to see you again. There's an art exhibit @ MOMA next Friday night. Would you like to join me?

Her mind drifted to Cayden. She tried to imagine him wandering around an art gallery and suppressed a smile.

Natalya: Can I look at my schedule and get back to you?

James: Sure. I'm sending you a link so you can see the art work.

Natalya: Thx. Talk soon.

A moment later, her phone beeped with another text from James. Clicking on the link to the art exhibit, she contemplated how she'd respond to his offer as she scrolled through the images. How could she go out with one man when she couldn't stop thinking about another? She thought about Arabella's prediction about having to choose between two men. She tried to focus on anything but her attraction to Cayden, no matter how tempting. It would put a strain on the case, and everything she worked so hard to build over the last three years.

Setting her phone on the nightstand, she reached for the remote. Through the corner of her eye, she caught sight of a large shadow at her window. Her stomach dropped. She jolted out of bed, grabbed her gun from her purse, and removed the safety. Stalking closer to the window, she pulled the drape aside.

A large hand tapped against the glass. Her heart went to her throat when she found Cayden hanging on the old wrought iron trellis.

Sighing with relief, she put the safety on her gun, and set it on the dresser. She lifted the window. "I almost shot you. What are you doing here?"

"You want to shoot the guy who just found your bracelet?" Cayden held a fleck of gold in his hand.

"I can't believe you found my bracelet. Please, come in." She stepped out of the way to let him climb inside.

"The clasp's broken, but it shouldn't be hard to fix." After he shut the window, he placed the bracelet in her hand. "You said it was important to you."

His consideration and thoughtfulness blew her away and somehow made him even hotter. "Thank you. My best friend Tessa has the same one." She left out the part about it being a reminder that they were survivors, not victims. She slipped the bracelet in her jewelry box. "I can drop it off at the jeweler on my way to work. You didn't need to come all the way back here."

"It was on my way home. It was no big deal. You had a shit night." His blue gaze pierced hers as he motioned to the window. "I would've knocked on the front door, but I didn't want to wake the other ladies and have them razzing you about me stopping by at this hour."

He did have a point. "You know them well," she said with a smile. "You could've waited until the morning." He loomed over her in the dark, tall, broad, and gorgeous. The sheer size of him made her room seem smaller.

"You're right, but I wanted to check in on you and make sure you're okay." His words took her by surprise.

"I'll live." She smiled in gratitude. "Thanks, that was sweet of you."

"I can tell Maverick spooked you." He held up his hands. "We may be cops, but we're not infallible."

One thing became clear; the man who stood in front of her was different than the person she'd pegged him for. This man was kind, thoughtful, and someone she could get close to. The realization made her knees a little weak. "I appreciate what you're trying to do."

"Hey, you don't need to hide from me." Closing the scant distance between them, he caressed her cheek. His touch sent a shiver along her skin. "What were you doing before I barged in on you?" His gaze started at the top of her head and trailed over her pink pj top, then moved lower to her bare legs peeking out of her shorts. The air became electric between them.

"I was about to watch something to unwind." She angled her head to the TV.

"Would you care for some company?" She picked up on the heaviness in his tone. When she gazed at his face, stress lines appeared around his eyes. It seemed both of them could use some company and a distraction tonight.

A smile tugged at her lips. "That depends. Do you like old movies?"

His blue eyes sparkled in the darkness. "Are there any other kind? I'm a sucker for anything in black and white."

"I pegged you for more of an action genre, blow-everything-up kind of guy. My mistake."

"I think it's fair to say we've both made assumptions about each other that weren't true."

"Well then, take a seat." A sensation of warmth spread from her head to her toes and everywhere in between.

He moved to the chair next to her bed where all her books were piled up—books on forensics, psychology, and surviving sexual assault. "It looks like you were you doing some light reading?"

"I'm sorry about the mess. I've been living out of boxes." Blurring in front of him, she attempted to move the books out of the way, but he waved her off and took a seat at the end of her bed. It bowed from the size and weight of his big body. She motioned to the stacks of cartons in the corner. "It didn't make sense to unpack."

"When do you move into your new place?"

"As soon as my contractor finishes up. It's an older building and the apartment needed a refresh. Things are taking longer than I expected."

"It's ironic, you buying a place in the same building as Andee." The words snapped Natalya back to reality. The case beckoned. Something neither of them could forget anytime soon.

"We were about to take our minds off things. I think we could both use a break." She sat next to him on the bed and picked up the remote.

"Agreed." He stretched out his legs, and his thigh brushed hers. His body tensed with awareness as hers prickled with heat. "What are we watching?"

"Have you ever seen *Vertigo*?" Everything about this felt surreal, Cayden Teague hanging out in her bedroom, about to watch a movie.

Turning to face her, his eyes glittered in the darkness in an enticing way.

"I saw it when it first came out in the fifties. It's still one of my favorite movies."

"You've got great taste, because it's mine too. Who knew we would have something in common."

Cayden flashed a smile so bright she swore it could power the sun. "Imagine that, Natalya, and hell didn't freeze over."

CHAPTER 21

One hour and twenty-five minutes later, Cayden glanced over at Natalya and suppressed a groan. She sat at the end of the bed, her gorgeous legs front and center in those little pink shorts. At some point during the movie, they both had moved closer to each other and now he sat only inches away.

Cayden tried to keep his focus on the movie, but her strawberry scent kept invading his nostrils and the demon in him responded. His cock strained against his jeans. Grabbing one of the throw pillows off her bed, he casually placed it on his lap.

"I never understood why the husband wanted Madeline out of the way." Her question snapped him out of his sexual haze.

"He did it for the money, of course." The light from the TV cast a shadow over her breasts and the outline of her nipples, igniting a hot stab of lust. He imagined sliding his tongue over every inch of her skin, exploring her lush little body all night long. But it would be a bad idea. For one, he'd never be able to stop, and for another, they worked together.

The back and forth continued throughout the rest of the film and he found himself enjoying the hell out of their banter, considering the circumstances they found themselves in. He couldn't remember the last time he could breathe without thinking about Andee's murder. The guilt weighed on him 24/7. But sitting here chilling with Natalya brought on a sense of contentment.

When they got to the scene where Kim Novak's character falls to her death for the second time, they both gasped. "Wow, even though I knew what was coming, it's still chilling," Natalya said with a shake of her head.

"Losing someone you love once is bad enough. I can't imagine having to go through such an ordeal a second time." The pain over losing Abigail still hurt like a fist to the chest, even after all these years. He should've been the one to die, not her. Then Natalya showed up in his life like a force of nature, interrupting his monotonous world.

The force of nature picked up the remote and lowered the volume as the credits began to roll. "You sound like you speak from experience." Her gaze filled with compassion.

"It happened a long time ago, another lifetime when I lived on Arcadia."

"The demon plane taken over by the Coterie?" Natalya crossed her legs in front of her body, drawing his attention to her pink-painted toenails. His demon rose up and took notice. He'd never been drawn to feet, but hers were as pretty and delicate as the rest of her.

"One and the same." The vampires had decimated his people and killed the only woman he ever loved. All these years later, he still carried a misplaced grudge against all bloodsuckers, Natalya included. Now that he got to know her better, he realized he had no right to take his anger out on her, period. "I've given you some shit in the past and treated you unfairly."

"I get how you could be resentful, but underneath all those rough edges, I see a good man," she said in a soft voice. "Mrs. Pearse only hinted at what you did for Andee. The rest I put together myself. You kept her from going to jail and that's how she became an informant for the agency, isn't it?"

Cayden sighed. "Andee started doing drugs and then selling them after she got involved with one of the members of a demon-run crime syndicate we busted up a few years ago. The Shadow Cabal dabbled in everything from drugs to money laundering. Anyone left from the organization was either dead, or behind bars. She was just a kid. I helped her get into a program and she got clean."

"You made sure she got probation over a jail sentence?"

"I may have pulled a few strings. No one knows, and I like to keep it that way. Eventually, Andee went back to school, got a job at the tavern and turned her life around." Cayden leaned on his elbows. "And then in the blink of an eye, some maniac snuffs it out right under my nose." Guilt twisted in his gut.

"Stop beating yourself up, Cayden. You went above and beyond what most cops would've done given the situation." Her gaze narrowed on his chest. "I suspect there's a lot more beneath the heavy metal T-shirts and the sarcasm."

Surprise jolted through his body. The warm fuzziness in his chest expanded at the compliments. He wanted to be worthy of her praise. "Now that you know the truth, how will I ever maintain my badass image?"

Her warm smile thawed a part of his soul. He tried to keep his eyes on anything but the tantalizing way the top of her shirt opened on every exhalation. "I'm sure you'll think of something."

Seconds ticked by and then her expression grew serious. She reached out and caressed his arm. Her touch seared through him, a fire that spread to his chest.

"You've never had a chance to grieve. I'm sorry you lost someone you cared about in such a horrible way."

He tried to shrug it off. "Hey, everyone's got a story, right?" The words got sucked right back into his throat, along with all the air in the room.

"Yeah, I suppose we all do." Something dark and volatile flashed in her eyes. "Thank you for trusting me with your secrets." He got the feeling she had a few of her own. No doubt there was more to the story behind marrying her father's business partner. He'd wait for her to tell him when she was ready. He wouldn't push. He thought about getting the hell out of there. But the sound of her breath and the rise and fall of her chest kept him glued to the spot.

"I must be feeling comfortable with you because I've never told anyone about my involvement with Andee, except for Denopoulos." Natalya made him feel things he hadn't in centuries. She managed to still see the good in him, something he thought died in that damn war. He'd never been able to move past the pain. He stayed numb, unable to open his heart again.

His thumb caressed her fingertips. Heat radiated from her body and a deep yearning he'd been carrying around for months now burst open and flowed out like a waterfall.

"I feel comfortable with you too."

The air sizzled, snapping with sexual tension. He became filled with such longing, a longing that only intensified with the look in her eyes.

"Cayden," she whispered. The way she looked at him made his chest swell.

He wanted to nuzzle her throat. He moved closer and glanced at her lips when his ring tone shattered the air. Muttering a curse, he let go of her hand. "Sorry." He sat up, pulled out his phone, and then glanced at the screen.

Smith: Maverick's still out cold. Still waiting for DNA results. We've got agents searching his place as we speak.

Cayden: What about his wheels?

Smith: Already sent Nick to pick them up. Sit tight for now.

Cayden: Keep me posted.

Setting his phone on the night table, he looked over at Natalya, and ran a hand over his face. "Maverick's still out cold. The waiting is pure torture." He didn't know what he would've done these last few days if it hadn't been for her. If they crossed the line, he'd jeopardize their friendship, and it was the best thing that happened to him in years. He couldn't lose her now.

"Let's hope we get some answers to end this nightmare." The longer Cayden stayed, the longer he found himself not wanting to go. This bubble could burst at any moment. His head pounded with overload. "I've got an idea on how we can pass the time."

"Oh?" His horns burned as his head filled with possibilities, making her scream with pleasure being one, and taking her in every possible way being another. Flames of heat shot to his cock and made his balls ache.

Clicking on the remote, she turned to the screen. "It looks like *Rear Window* is on. What do you say to one more?"

Every moment he spent with her took away the ugliness of the job and replaced it with something light—something he wanted to explore. "I say count me in."

Sunlight streamed in from the window. Cayden opened his eyes and blinked. His arms were now wrapped around a soft, sleepy woman. Her hair fanned out on the pillow like black velvet. His heart sped up. For the first time in years, he'd slept the entire night without a single nightmare. A sense of peace filled the emptiness inside his chest.

He'd been rock-hard all night long. How could he not be with Natalya's tight, little ass nestled against his crotch? His cock ached. The demon in him wanted to brand her, make her his own.

Natalya stirred and then jolted upright. When she opened her eyes, fear burned in their depths. Bolting out of bed, she blurred to the opposite corner of the room. Her chest heaved and her dark eyes became wild.

"I'm sorry. I never meant to fall asleep." But he'd been so weary. He thought if he shut his eyes for a minute then maybe, he'd finally get some peace. And lying beside her, he had. "I didn't mean to frighten you. I got excited waking up next to you." Did she have any idea how beautiful she looked right now with her shiny hair and bright eyes?

"It's not you. I was having a nightmare about Maverick … about the past." Her chest rose and fell with the admission.

"Talk to me, please." He held up his hands. "Hey, it's just me," he whispered. "It's okay."

"I can't … not right now. I'm sorry." The tremble in her voice got his hackles up. "It's my day off and I have a million errands to run. I need to shower and change and help with the decorations for Gillian's welcome home party tonight."

Scratching his horns, he got to his feet. He wanted to pull her into his arms and wipe the fear from her eyes, but he kept his distance. She needed space. "Are you sure you're okay?" His voice sounded hoarse to his own ears.

Her hand shook a little as she ran it through her tangled hair. "I'll be fine, Cayden."

"What's going on?" he asked in a gentle voice. Something had spooked her. He wanted to find out what, but didn't want to push and scare her away. "I can't imagine you'd want to be in the room when the team interrogates Maverick. I'll stand by whatever you decide. The choice is yours."

"I'd rather not. I thought I'd stop by Mrs. Pearse's place and show her a picture of Maverick and some of our other suspects to see if they ring any bells," she said in tight voice. "Even if she only caught a glimpse of him from the back, she might remember something."

"Good idea. I should get over to headquarters." He ran a hand over the scruff on his chin. He didn't want to leave her, not like this. I'm here when you're ready to talk."

"Thanks. Let me know what happens with Maverick."

"Will do. I'll call you later." He walked to the window and heaved it open. He decided to go out the way he came. He didn't want the other women speculating about their relationship and giving her shit about it, especially when he had no idea how to define it himself. Climbing down the trellis, he exhaled when his feet touched the ground.

He'd never been so torn and confused in his life.

CHAPTER 22

"Vhat was the nature of your relationship with Andrea Lyon, Mr. Nelson, aka Maverick?" Smith asked from the head of the conference table. Denopoulos sat across from him with Nelson hunched in the corner.

Cayden peered into their interrogation room from the other side of a one-way glass. He wanted to wring his neck for laying his hands on Natalya, but he couldn't.

"I should remind you that your answers are being recorded." Smith pointed to his phone.

All around them, life-size moving holograms of their most-wanted criminals beeped and floated around the room.

"We went out a few times," Nelson muttered, not looking up. Scruff darkened his jaw and his hair stuck up in all directions. His bloodshot eyes remained unfocused and glazed over. His hands were cuffed behind his back to keep him from throwing a fireball. "What the fuck did you people do to me? It feels like the worst hangover of my life."

Smith took a sip of his coffee and set the mug on the table. "Don't take it personally. We do it to all our guests. We needed to keep you from figuring out our location. Our offices are strictly off-limits to the general population."

Denopoulos stood and moved to the corner of the room. Picking up a pitcher, he poured water into a mug, and set it on a small table in front of Nelson. "You claim your relationship with Andrea Lyon wasn't serious, and yet we found your hairs and your footprints at her apartment the night she was killed. We got your DNA and it's a match. I suggest you start talking."

Nelson licked his cracked lips and eyed the water. "Fine, I admit we'd been dating and I stopped by her place after she got off work, but I swear I didn't kill her. I'm innocent."

Smith stood up and walked around the desk, stopping in front of Nelson's chair. "Did anyone see you after you left her place that could vouch for you? A neighbor? A friend?"

"It was late," Nelson shook his head. "I didn't see anyone."

Smith pressed a button on his phone and Nelson's file appeared on their wall-sized monitor. "Interesting resume. It looks like you've got a little bit of everything—sexual assault, stalking, and harassment under your belt. You fit the profile of a serial rapist. Right now, murder doesn't seem like a big stretch for you. Why were the charges for sexual assault dropped in both incidences? Did you threaten the victims?"

"No, this is all a big misunderstanding," Nelson said, motioning to the screen, a defiant note in his voice.

Denopoulos pulled out a key from his pocket "I'm going to unlock your cuffs so you can have a drink of water. If so much as a spark comes out of those fingertips, you're going into a cell at Hellios for a good long stretch. Am I clear?" When Maverick nodded, his partner removed his cuffs. "What happened the night Andee was killed?"

Gulping the water, Nelson wiped his mouth with his sleeved. "Andee and I had been dating on and off for months, but this time when she broke up with me, I knew it was for good."

Cayden smiled, impressed. His partner's good cop routine never failed.

"Why did you two break up?" Smith asked, taking a seat on the table.

Nelson shrugged. "She accused me of being jealous and possessive. Maybe I was, but now I've lost her for good this time."

"You must've been angry over getting dumped. I'd say that gives you a motive. I suggest you try telling us the whole truth," Denopoulos said over the constant beep from the holograms. "Things will go easier for you if you do."

"Andee refused to take my calls or answer my texts. I couldn't sleep so I went to her apartment to talk."

"At what time?" Denopoulos asked, checking his notes.

"I'd say it was around three in the morning. When I found the other agent, the big blond demon passed out on her couch, I got the wrong idea." Anger flared in Nelson's eyes. "We had a fight and I left. It was the last time I saw Andee alive."

Shit. Cayden never figured out why Nelson seemed to recognize him out in the alley. Now he knew.

Hopping off the table, Smith walked around the room, his back now to the one-way glass. "We're reasonable people, Mr. Nelson, but you're asking us to believe that you're a grieving ex-boyfriend. If that were true, then why agree to go out with Detective Dubrosky so soon after Andee's death?"

Pain flickered across Nelson's face. "For the same reason every other dude is out there. I was lonely."

Cayden could relate. He'd been there himself on more than one occasion. He read over the evidence again and rubbed his chin.

"How was I supposed to know she was a cop?" Nelson visibly swallowed. "She sure as hell didn't look like one. I just wanted to have some fun with her until she tried to pull her weapon on me."

Anger coursed through Cayden's veins like battery acid. He couldn't bear to think about what Nelson could've done to Natalya if he hadn't shown up. He'd never seen her so frightened, and he'd learned, from working with her over these past few months, she didn't scare easily. His fingers clenched at his sides, fighting the urge to open the door to the conference room, grab Nelson by the throat and beat the shit out of him. His rage surged. Leaning forward, Cayden placed his hands on either side of the table as heat pulsed through his body. His demon started to emerge, a slow flame burning through his skin.

Get it under control.

He breathed in and out slowly until his demon retreated. He listened to the rest of the interrogation.

"You'll face the consequences for stealing an officer's weapon and menacing them with it. Here's the way I see it, you stopped by Andee Lyon's place, found Agent Teague on the couch and went into a rage," Smith said matter-of-factly. "You killed her by accident and fled."

"I'm not saying shit until I speak to a lawyer." Nelson slammed the mug on the table. The sound echoed throughout the room. "This is a case of bad luck."

The door squeaked open and in walked Nick holding a plastic evidence bag. He whispered something and then set the bag on the table.

Denopoulos nodded, slipped on a pair of gloves and opened the bag. A leather mask with a zipper and two holes for horns fell into his hands. "My guess is your luck's about to run out."

A few hours after leaving the manor, Natalya walked through the door of Enchantments and found Saje behind the counter. She planned to meet Cayden here so they could pick her brain on the herb found in his toxicology report. They hadn't spoken all day. She'd been ignoring his calls and texts, still not sure what to say. Guilt slid in her belly.

The dull ache inside her chest intensified, leaving her feeling raw and vulnerable. She'd replayed the pained look on his face a dozen times in her head and couldn't help but cringe. She'd acted like a total head case. He deserved an explanation. But she wasn't ready to give him one, not yet anyway. She still didn't trust him completely.

She needed to put a call in to her therapist. It had been a few months since she'd seen her, and if anything, this morning proved she was long overdue. Exhaling, she crossed the expanse of black tiles to the front, passing shelves of copper bowls, tarot decks, and spell candles on her way.

Smiling at Saje, she met her at the counter. "Hey stranger, do you have a minute?"

"For you, anytime." A loose strand of dark hair fell out of Saje's messy ponytail as she lit a bundle of incense. The sweet scent perfumed the air.

"I've been meaning to stop by. I wish I had more time to browse around."

"You should check out today's potion. I just mixed up a batch." Saje motioned to the tray of Dixie cups filled with pink swirling liquid on the counter. "It's for good fortune."

"I'll take all the help I can get." Lifting the cup, Natalya downed the potion in one gulp. She tossed the empty cup in the trash, praying it might help them find their killer.

Saje greeted a few customers as they browsed around the shop and then turned to Natalya, tilting her head to the side. "We've missed you around here."

"I've been busy with work." Natalya left out the part about her growing infatuation with Cayden. The fact that they were knee-deep in a murder case complicated matters even more. The sooner they found their killer, the sooner she could stop doing this online charade and breathe easier. If she could catch the maniac responsible for killing Andee and framing Cayden, then it would all be worth it in the end. Turning her head, she caught a glimpse of Delilah, who stood in the reading area helping a few customers. She caught her attention and waved.

The bell dinged and the door swung open. Heavy footsteps scraped against the wide planked floor. The woodsy scent of Cayden's aftershave and a hint of leather filled the air. A rush of excitement washed over her.

"Sorry I'm late. I just got out of the interrogation with Maverick." He wore a light blue flannel and a pair of jeans. The color brought out his eyes. Her gaze roamed over the muscles in his sculpted chest, admiring the way the material accentuated his broad shoulders.

"What happened?" She hoped he didn't notice her checking him out and cleared her throat to hide the raw appreciation for his body.

"I'll fill you in on the details when we're alone, but the gist is, we got evidence on the bastard. It looks like he's our man."

"You found evidence?" Her stomach twisted.

"Whatever we find here will help to build our case against him. Can we talk privately for a minute?" His soulful blue eyes drew her in like a magnet.

Natalya nodded. "Sure."

Cayden led her by the elbow into a quiet corner and whispered close to her ear. "You haven't returned any of my calls."

"I'm sorry for avoiding you."

"If I did something to make you uncomfortable …" The concern in his eyes disarmed her, and broke through the wall she used to keep her emotions at bay.

"No, you did nothing wrong. It's not you," she whispered. "I owe you an explanation."

"You don't owe me anything." Staring at his face, blond scruff darkened his jaw, and shadows appeared under his eyes. The pain of losing a friend was bad enough, but then to be accused of her murder had to be taking its toll.

Her heart ached for him. "What about you? How are you holding up?"

"I can't sleep. The last time I did was with you." She shivered at his words.

A whispered conversation involving her and Cayden pricked at her ears. Through the corner of her eye, she caught Saje and Delilah staring at them with curious expressions across their faces. *Great. Now we've attracted an audience.*

"None of it makes any sense," he continued. "Maverick claims he didn't kill Andee."

"Do you believe him?"

"I'm not sure what to think, but there's no way in hell he's that good of a liar. He had motive and no alibi. But not all of the evidence points to him." Cayden ran a hand through his hair, clearly torn. "Any luck with Mrs. Pearse?" he asked, switching subjects.

"I showed her a picture of Maverick, along with our other suspects," Natalya said, recalling he grief on her face. "She recognized Maverick from his horns and confirmed she'd seen him leaving Andee's apartment around three in the morning when she looked through her peephole."

Doubt flickered in Cayden's eyes. "The time corroborates with what Maverick said. But I thought she heard the banging early the following morning."

"Mrs. Pearse said the guy in the cashmere coat left around six, right after she heard the banging coming from Andee's apartment. She didn't recall seeing horns. The poor thing's still in shock." Recalling Mrs. Pearse's testimony forced a ball of dread into the pit of her stomach. "We may have found our rapist, but not our killer. What do you think? Should we take her peephole observations into consideration?"

Cayden shrugged. "Her word is as good as any. The timeline doesn't match."

"If we can figure out who drugged you, things might start to make more sense." Natalya held up a finger. "There's one more thing, I'm waiting to hear from a contact at the state police. They may have gotten a bead on our friend Rocco, remember him?"

"The head of Pike's wolf pack? How could I forget? Where?"

Before Natalya could respond, Saje walked over to them, and gave

Cayden a quick hug. "Hey, big guy. I pulled some receipts on all of our recent purchases of henbane leaves. Why don't we talk somewhere more private?"

"Thanks for doing this." Cayden's smile filled with gratitude.

"Anything for you guys." Saje led them to the back of the shop, through a gauzy purple curtain to the stock room. She motioned for them to sit at a small table where a laminated map of the city was spread out, and dotted with splotches of candle wax.

Natalya's gaze darted to the candles of different shapes and sizes that covered almost every available surface. Stacks of leather-bound grimoires lined the bookshelves. Glass jars filled with herbs took up the entire wall.

As Cayden folded his big body into the metal chair across from her, his knee brushed her thigh. She sucked in a deep breath, trying to ignore her constant awareness of him. But it was impossible.

"We only had one customer in the last two weeks who bought a sleep tonic made from henbane leaves." Saje pulled a receipt off a spindle. "It's not one of our more popular herbs. We use it mainly for sleep tonics."

"Do you have anything that could help us find him?" Cayden asked, glancing at the slip of paper. "A name, an address, a phone number, anything like that? I know I'm asking a lot, but this is a matter of life and death."

"It looks like he paid in cash. I could try using divination to find him." Saje got to her feet and walked across the storage room. She filled a cauldron of water at the sink and set it on the table, along with a white candle. After she whispered a series of words, she lit the candle. The wax dripped into the water and after a few minutes, an image appeared out of the smoke. "I see a house with a red door, tall buildings and rocks that look like trees."

"Rocks that look like trees?" Natalya repeated the phrase, racking her brain, trying to remember where she'd heard it before.

"It's what the Lenape used to call Weehawken," Cayden chimed in. "You're aces, Saje. I'll be right back. I'm calling for backup." He stood and disappeared behind a bookcase.

Natalya got to her feet and pulled out her phone searching through the RHPD database for perps with formers in the area. When she finished typing, she turned to Saje, and gave her a hug. "Thanks. You're the best."

"My pleasure. I hope you find this guy."

Cayden returned looking tense. His gaze cut o Natalya. "Nick and Tom, you probably know him as Big Red, are headed over to Weehawken now. Are you ready to head out?"

"Let's go." Grabbing her purse, she met him at the drape.

"Ladies first," Cayden motioned for Natalya to walk in front of him, and she could feel his warm gaze on her back.

Chatter and laughter echoed from the other side of the wall. After the three of them made their way to the front, they found Arabella, Delilah and Brooke hanging out, leaning against the counter.

"We're headed over to Grand Vin for happy hour," Arabella said, turning to face them. "Do you guys want to join us?"

"I wish I could, but I'm still on duty." Natalya smiled. "Next time."

After saying their goodbyes, they walked out of the store and stepped onto the sidewalk. Natalya looked up at the sky. Dark gray clouds hung overhead. The smell of rain hung heavy in the air. Her gaze moved to Cayden. From the tension in his shoulders, it looked like he wanted to crawl out of his own skin. Too many unanswered questions remained. Maverick didn't match Mrs. Pearse's description, and if he wasn't their killer, then who was? Then the worst question of all pounded through her head. *Who will be next?*

"What now?" she asked, tapping her foot.

"We find something to do while we wait." When he took a step closer, his cologne caught in her nostrils and her frayed nerves sparked at the ends.

"Cayden …" Her phone buzzed with a text, breaking the tension. She glanced at her screen and her heart raced. "It looks like my tip panned out. Apparently, Rocco's in the woods for some kind of pack ritual. It's the eve of the wolves' spring equinox. They were spotted at a stone circle in Putnam Valley. I could ask the cops up there to go check out the scene, but the wolves are out of their jurisdiction."

"But not ours. If we can find Pike, then we find out who paid him off, and then we'd know once and for all if the prison break is somehow connected to Andee's murder."

"You're not supposed to be doing an op alone. How do you think Rocco's pack will react when we show up?" Natalya asked with a humorless laugh. "I doubt they'll welcome a demon and a vampire into their midst."

"I can't help but think that if we don't check this out, Andee died in vain by giving us Rocco's name." Cayden exhaled in a rush. "It has to lead to something."

"Okay, I get what you're saying, but why not call one of the other agents? There must be someone who could back us up."

His gaze stayed locked on hers as though weighing the pros and cons of her every word. "All the agents are tied up. If we don't go now, we could lose Rocco for good. You don't have to go with me if you're not comfortable." Cayden motioned to the bright orange muscle car parked on the curb. "If I throttle open the four barrels, I can be there in no time."

"Your muscle car isn't going to make it through the mountains in the rain. I can smell a storm coming." She pointed to the sky.

Sniffing the air, he nodded. "Good point."

"What about following procedures and protocols? There are rules about this sort of thing." What would this mean for her promotion if she did go? She'd been working toward this for months.

Cayden gave her a playful nudge. "Sometimes you need to bend a few rules to get things done."

"We can't just bust in on their turf without a plan." Natalya calculated all the potential risks in her head. "Trust me, it won't go over well."

A disarming smile tilted up the corner of his lips. "What if I told you I have a plan?"

"I'd say I'm driving." Reaching for her keys, Natalya clicked her fob. "My cruiser has four-wheel drive. Let's go before I change my mind."

CHAPTER 23

$\mathcal{C}$ ayden gazed over at Natalya and exhaled the breath he'd been holding. In the dark confines of the car, he couldn't read her expression, but he could smell her inner turmoil. And in that moment his admiration for her grew tenfold. She came with him to chase down this lead, despite her misgivings.

"I believe you were going to fill me in on this plan of yours. And how do we get the pack to hand over Pike?" she asked, keeping her gaze focused on the road.

"We threaten to expose the whole pack to the misdeeds of one of their own. It violates a treaty they signed." Cayden left out the part that it was signed over a hundred and twenty-years ago, probably by their ancestors. He'd spent the majority of the car ride on his phone, scrolling through the MBI database, researching everything he could find on tribal laws related to wolf packs. Fortunately, he'd found some signed treaties.

"Let's hope the threat works."

Pounding rain forced Cayden's gaze to the window. Damn, maybe this wasn't such a good idea after all. A loud crack of thunder boomed, drowning out the screech of the wiper blades. He cranked on the button to push his seat back, but it didn't budge. He looked over at Natalya, his gaze drawn to her small hands gripping the wheel. "You okay?"

"Yeah, visibility is horrible, even for me," Natalya said, maneuvering the cruiser through the storm.

"You concentrate on the road. I'm still doing research." A strike of lightning illuminated the night sky.

"I'm trying. But it's difficult when you keep moving around." She bumped his arm. "You're distracting me."

Welcome to my world. In the confines of the car, the smell of her perfume flared in his nostrils. The wild scent made him want to run his tongue along the slim column of her neck. His blood felt hot, snapping with electricity. "I'm not used to being in the passenger seat." For one, he could barely fit, and for another, he didn't relish giving up control. The demon in him liked to take over.

"Take me through the ramifications for violating this treaty?"

"The pack could be kicked off the land for harboring a suspect, which in turn keeps them from participating in their ceremonial rituals." Cayden pointed at his screen. "Granted, it's a long shot, but it's the best we've got to go on for now."

"Okay, it's worth a try." Her shoulders relaxed. "And here I thought we were going to wing it with a hope and a prayer."

"Have a little faith, Natalya." He didn't dare tell her his brain was still formulating the finer details of this so-called plan. He'd die before he'd let her anything happen to her. On the other hand, he wouldn't be caught dead saying those words out loud to such a take-charge, headstrong female. She'd accuse him of being a misogynist and some kind of dinosaur.

Her burner pinged. "Can you see who it is? The phone's in the back seat inside my purse."

"You want me to touch your purse? I thought the purse was sacrosanct." If someone had told him he'd be rummaging around through Natalya's purse a few weeks ago, he would've called them a liar. Now nothing seemed to be off the table, even handbags. Cayden turned and reached into the backseat for her bag. When his fingers wrapped around the burner phone, he held it up and glanced at the screen. "It's a text from "Carefreeadventurer." He wants to know if you're still on for your date. It might be a moot point if we can get "Midnight Maverick" to confess." Something about this case still didn't add up.

Natalya shook her head. "Maverick checks all the boxes in terms of physical evidence, motive, and opportunity, except he's not the type to wear cashmere, designer shoes or smoke fancy cigars."

"True, unless he didn't want to get his hands dirty and hired someone to kill Andee and let me take the fall." Cayden scratched his head. "Unfortunately, it blows the theory that he killed her in a fit of rage. We still have quite a few suspects to interrogate while Maverick sits on ice."

Her phone beeped with another text. This one was from James.

"Who's James?" Cayden rubbed his chin. "The name doesn't sound familiar."

"No one important." Turning away, her body language became guarded. A sting of jealousy burned though his chest like a hot poker.

Cayden wanted to know more about this James since he'd texted Natalya on the burner phone, but decided not to pursue the subject for now.

"I'll fill you in later. We've got more important matters at hand." She leaned over, took the phone out of his hands, and set it in her cup holder.

The GPS on her dashboard beeped. "It's right up ahead." She turned off Route 28 to a gravel road. When she came to the end, she parked in an open field and cut the engine. Lifting her pant leg, she checked the safety on her Glock. "Okay, ready. I loaded the bullets you gave me."

"Good girl," he murmured, pulling his flannel over his shoulder holster. "Let's do this." He got out of the cruiser, pulled out his phone, and pressed a button. The hologram of the stone circle rose up from his screen as a floating blue light.

"How far away are we?" After Natalya got out of the car, she walked up and stood beside him. He followed her gaze to the rows of stones surrounded by towering pines. The scent of rain, grass, mud and wolf caught in his nostrils.

"We're looking for the Sisyphus Stone Circle. According to the map, it's in a clearing about a half mile due north from this point." Cayden pointed to the path up ahead. "We'll have to trek it from here."

"Lead the way." Natalya leaped over the puddles with the speed and grace of a gazelle. A gust of wind whipped through the trees, sending leaves and branches flying in every direction.

They hiked up the muddy trail, passing shrubs and gnarled tree roots. After a while, their clothing and shoes became soaked and muddy.

"The weather sucks. But we can use it to our advantage." Gripping his phone, he hoped the wind wouldn't knock it out of his hands.

"If I'd known we were going on this kind of mission, I would've dressed for the occasion. I thought I was going on a date," she shouted over the rain. "I prefer this kind of op any day."

The demon in him wanted to know why. But this wasn't the time or the place to ask. "Your new clothes suit you, by the way." Her badge gleamed in the darkness, forcing his gaze to the chain around her neck. It settled between her breasts, drawing his attention to her soaked sweater now plastered to her chest. The shape of her small, round breasts became visible through her bra. He caught a glimpse of her nipples poking through the thin fabric, and stifled a groan. He wanted to look away. He knew he should. But he couldn't. Blood, hot and heavy, rushed to his groin.

"Thank you. What? No jokes?"

"No jokes. It's the truth." He couldn't tell her the *whole* truth. The poking and teasing seemed much safer than the alternative. "Thanks for coming through for me on this one, Natalya."

He'd started to depend on her more than he should, but he was still messed up in the head, and broken on the inside. Pulling off his flannel, he draped it over her shoulders, so the wolf pack wouldn't get an eyeful of every one of her luscious curves now on display. He knew it would make her uncomfortable.

"What's this for?" she asked, surprise lacing her voice. "I don't feel the chill, although I appreciate the gesture."

"Your shirt, it's, uh, see-through." Images of licking her breasts and sucking on her nipples flashed through his mind with vivid clarity.

"Oh." She closed the flannel over her chest. "Thanks."

After a few moments with neither of them saying a word, he pointed to the circle in the distance. "We can get close. They shouldn't be able to detect our scents over the rain."

Natalya motioned ahead of them. "I read these stones are magickal. Witches used to gather here for ceremonies hundreds of years ago before the wolf packs took them over. If I close my eyes, I swear I can hear voices reverberating from them." Cayden caught a wistful note in her voice.

The path narrowed as they headed deeper into the woods. Her warm breath whispered against his neck as they walked. A hum of chanting and animal sounds echoed through the trees. Cayden picked up on the wild thump of her heart. They stopped a safe distance away from the massive stone cavern. He turned to her and put his finger to his lips.

His gaze zeroed in on the seven men in the circle covered in animal skins, dancing around a fire. Flaming torches surrounded the perimeter and somehow managed to stay lit despite the downpour. Wisps of fog curled around their shadowy forms, adding to the eerie scene. Some kind of scented oil emitted from the fire and swirled in the air.

"Don't move," a male voice shouted from behind him. Something sharp poked into Cayden's side. "Get your hands up where I can see them, demon. What are you doing bringing a vampire out here? Do you have a death wish?"

"We mean no harm. We come in peace." Slowly, Cayden turned and faced the shifter with his hands held high. Ceremonial makeup covered his weathered face. He wore a choker made of leather, and animal skins and furs on his back.

"Great, now we've pissed off the alpha," Natalya muttered as she lifted her hands in the air and faced forward.

"Let's all take a deep breath." Cayden kept his voice calm. "We're looking for a wolf in your pack. We're told Rocco knows where he is."

"I'm Rocco, but none of us answer to cops or bloodsuckers," he growled and took a menacing step closer and prodded Cayden with his spear.

"That plan you were telling me about in the car, I think it's time to put it into action," Natalya whispered with a note of panic in her voice. "Don't do anything foolish. We're outnumbered."

"Who do we have here?" Rocco turned his head, his attention focusing on Natalya.

Seeing his chance, Cayden lunged, grabbed the spear from the alpha's hands, broke it in half, and threw it in the fire. The ground rumbled beneath Cayden's feet. The trees swayed. Why did he get the feeling he'd just released hellfire? The demon in him stirred, the rage building inside, the need to protect taking over. His skin burned from the inside. His body grew hot all over. "Back off. She's with me."

CHAPTER 24

*N*atalya stole a glance over at Cayden and gasped. His skin took on a reddish hue and looked almost reptilian. His horns began to elongate from his head into sharp points, even his voice sounded deeper. She'd never witnessed his full-on rage state before. She hoped it could buy them some time and give them a chance to escape.

"What do you want?" Rocco snarled. "You two are trespassing on private property."

"You've reneged on the terms of your treaty," Cayden shouted over the wind. "A wolf in your pack broke the law. I'm sure you wouldn't want more cops showing up and sniffing around this place. You're aiding and abetting a fugitive."

The rest of the pack surrounded them, growling and showing teeth, closing in.

"Leave now or the female dies," Rocco snarled.

Natalya's heart thumped wildly in her chest. Her fangs elongated. Her gaze darted around, but there was nowhere to go, nowhere to run. There were simply too many of them. "Take another step closer and you'll all be under arrest."

When she went to pull out her gun from her ankle holster, two shadowy figures grabbed her from behind. Before she could blur away, they wrestled her to the ground. The move took her by surprise, rattling her for a second. "Get off me." She tried to break free, but they held her down, the effortless grip of captors who knew how to immobilize their victims. One of them sniffed her hair and she tensed, her stomach twisting into knots. Their grip tightened. The smell of their sweat and adrenaline caught in her nose and her throat.

Her cop training kicked in. Suddenly all her options exploded through her head. But none would get them out of this alive. Sucking air into her lungs, she tried to breathe through her fear. Her vision blurred around the edges as dark memories rose to the surface.

Her father called out her name, but she was too weak to respond. He picked her up off the ground and carried her through the field while her blood spurted out from the wound in her stomach. Tears streaked down his cheeks and made her face damp. She took a final breath, knowing, it would be her last.

She awoke to razor sharp fangs sinking into her neck. The pain had been unbearable, like fire burning through her nerve endings.

A rush of anger surged through her, and made her teeth clench so hard that she pricked her lip with her fangs. Rearing up, she head-butted the first one, knocking him sideways into one of the large rocks. His head smashed against the jagged edge with a sickening thud. Her other captor loosened his death grip on her neck, and she used it to her advantage by pushing him off her with both hands.

He landed on his back in a heap of twisted limbs. Rolling, she climbed onto his chest and sank her fangs into the pulsing vein on his neck. She tried not to gag as the foul tang of his blood flowed into her mouth. She spit it out, along with a chunk of his flesh. Howling in pain, he hightailed it out of the clearing in the other direction. Her bite couldn't turn him into a vampire, but the sting from her fangs would cause some serious damage.

A bloodcurdling scream pierced the air. Her gaze flew to Cayden as he lifted the wolf closest to him by the throat. He threw him across the field like a football. Before he could go after the next one, a spear flew through the air, piercing his shoulder.

"Cayden!" A stab of fear lashed at her chest. "No!" When she blurred over to help him, a wall of blistering heat enveloped her like an oven. The scent of burning flesh and hair filled the air. The pack took off, running toward the woods. Her gaze darted through the trees, making sure they were gone.

Cutting across the empty circle, Cayden closed the distance between them, pulled a small stick out of her hair, and threw it on the ground. The heat from his body radiated into hers. His gaze roamed over her as though checking for injuries. "Are you okay?"

"I'm fine, just shaken up," she said, panting hard. Her head throbbed, still fuzzy around the edges from the shock of having two males hold her down. But she survived.

When his face, coloring and horns slowly returned to normal, he gripped her arms, and she became struck by the wild pump of his heart. "Now that's what I call kicking some serious wolf ass. We make a great team."

As the last of her adrenaline wore off, shock swept over her and made her sway. Cayden caught her, wrapping a strong arm around her waist. Leaning into his touch, she tried to force those old images from her mind, but the past clawed at her like a snarling beast. Before she could protest, he lifted her off her feet. He carried her out of the clearing to a copse of trees. Once he set her on her feet, she leaned against the bark, breathing in and out through her nose to diffuse the onset of a panic attack.

"I can tell you're not okay. I should've never brought you here," he said through gritted teeth. "I don't know what I was thinking."

"We were chasing a lead. I made the choice," she panted. Her chest heaved from her fast breathing. She couldn't stop shaking. "I just need a minute." Closing her eyes, she pictured a warm bright light in the center of her forehead, radiating throughout her body. She imagined the light banishing all the frenzied thoughts in her head. Several minutes ticked by and the light expanded. Once a sense of calm washed over her, she opened her eyes.

The concerned expression on Cayden's face made her throat thick with tears. "I'm here for you. Please, talk to me." His comforting words wafted over her shocked body like a warm caress. He ran his thumb along her chin.

Sharing the details of her past with Cayden seemed like an impossible task. A part of her wanted to, and another part of her feared what his reaction might be. One thing she did know, she trusted him. Tensing her jaw against the burn of tears, she willed them away for now. "Not here, Cayden. Let's do what we came here for." Right now, she needed a distraction to move past what just took place.

Cayden looked like he wanted to argue, but then he shook his head. "Fair enough."

"Did Rocco tell you where Pike's been hiding out?" Her voice came out shaky, betraying the tornado going on inside her.

Cayden pointed in the other direction. "It's a shack straight up the hill. But there's no way in hell we're going there. I'm taking you to the car and getting you home. We've had enough adventure for one day."

"We've come this far. We can't go back now."

"I'm so sorry I put you in harm's way. Seeing those men on top of you freaked me the fuck out. When I think about what could've happened …" Cayden trailed his fingers along her arms and goosebumps broke out along her skin.

The admiration in his eyes made her melt. A thrilling, unfamiliar sensation shot through her body like a drug. "Cayden…"

His hands moved to her shoulders. Regret burned in his eyes. "I've been selfish. I've gone too far."

She became aware of her back getting pressed further against the tree, the cool wet bark scraping against the bare skin beneath her sweater. Their breaths mingled together as he curved over her, his gaze full of warmth and need.

"You didn't force me to come here. I agreed."

"Maybe, but I won't take any more chances with your life." His words ignited something inside her, a mixture of anger and arousal. She became so overwhelmed with emotion, it almost hurt. She wanted to move past the memories. Cayden could help her forget.

"I make my own choices," she whispered and became filled with such longing, a longing that only intensified because she knew it might be reciprocated.

"Why do you have to turn everything into a fight?" He came closer, his heat and scent made her ache. A flame ignited from the sheer stress of the situation. His stance became rigid and filled with tension. He reached for her shoulders, his lips came closer, now a breath away. "Answer me."

Gasping at the sudden contact, a bead of panic laced with her desire. She couldn't think with him this close. "You bring it out in me. It's what we do. We fight …"

He groaned and bent his head, sealing his mouth over hers. The wild taste of him exploded in her mouth. Shock rippled through her at the softness of his lips. He exerted just the right amount of pressure to make her melt. Delicious tingles exploded all over her body.

His tongue tangled with hers in slow wicked laps. She moaned, exhilarated. The delicious scratch of his stubble brushed against her skin. In all the times she'd imagined kissing him, nothing could've prepared her for the hot sweep of his tongue. Her body caught fire, flames licking at her breasts. Desire rippled through her as she wound her arms around his neck.

His hand moved along her rib cage to the underside of her breast. Heat pooled between her legs. A distant voice in her head told her to stop, but she couldn't. The kiss was just too good. Pulling her closer, her breasts pressed against the hard wall of his chest. She found herself losing control. Her skin became heated, her fangs tingled.

Cayden growled, deepening the kiss. He kept her firmly anchored to him by keeping his hands on her hips. With every lush glide of his tongue, forgotten parts of her blazed to life.

More. The word reverberated through her head like a drum. She became painfully aware of the softness of his lips and the wild beat of his heart. Her panties grew damp from the skill of his kiss and months of anticipation.

His erection pressed against her thigh, and at first she drew back on instinct. But the longer the kiss went on, the more she became aware of every magnificent inch of him. A low rumble of arousal vibrated from his chest and the sound turned her on.

Natalya got so caught in the heat of the moment, she almost forgot where they were and what they were about to do. She pulled away, panting hard, dazed and aroused. "We have to keep going."

"I'm sorry." Cayden hissed out a breath. Confusion clouded his eyes. His enormous chest heaved.

"Don't apologize. I wanted you to kiss me." Her face flushed hot. The combination of his proximity and his warm breath made her world spin. She tried to get her breathing under control and pointed up the hill. "We're already here." Her mind whirled in a million directions, trying to make sense of the last few minutes.

"I can see there's no arguing with you. Why don't you get on my back? Let me do the work." He turned and bent down.

She didn't have the strength to argue at this point. Hopping on his back, she wrapped her arms around his neck. "Lead the way."

Cayden could be both attentive and caring, and despite her freak-out, it made her wonder what he'd be like in bed. She imagined his lovemaking would be wild and passionate, just like his kisses.

Hiking north through the woods, he moved at a fast pace. At some point, the rain had stopped, leaving a cold chill in the air. When they reached the top of the hill, he stopped and she jumped off.

They came to a dilapidated shack surrounded by weeds and stumps of wood. A wolf statue sat out front. "Let's see if Rocco was telling the truth about our fugitive Gregory Pike. This matches the description of his place," he said, pointing to the door.

The putrid scent of a dead animal and freshly spilled blood flared in her nostrils. "I don't like this. Something smells rotten." She drew her Glock and held it in front of her, hoping she wouldn't have to use it. Her fangs elongated as they climbed the rickety steps. "I'll cover you."

Pulling out his gun from the holster under his shirt, Cayden turned the knob on the old wooden door and it creaked open. "MBI," he called out.

No answer came.

Natalya followed him inside, pointing the barrel of her gun into the darkness. Her breaths grew shallow. The only sounds came from the squeak of the floorboards and the squeal of rats behind the walls.

Piles of logs sat in one corner, garbage and rotten food in the other. Cobwebs hung overhead and tangled in her hair. She batted them away, hating anything creepy crawly. She spun around, staring into the shadows. "I don't detect a heartbeat or a pulse anywhere, except for the rats. We should find out where the dead-animal stench is coming from."

"Agreed. Let's have a look around."

The constant drip of water splattered on the floor. Through the corner of her eye, she caught sight of dried muddy shoe prints. She followed the trail to a closet and opened the door. She blurred out of the way right before something big and heavy fell onto the floor with a loud thump. *A body*. Her heart banged away in her chest. "I think I just found Pike."

Cayden rushed to her side and crouched. He put a finger to the werewolf's bloodied neck where two fang marks stood out. "He's dead. No big surprise. Someone went to a hell of a lot of trouble to cover their tracks. The body's still fresh. He hasn't been dead for long."

Her gaze darted to the footprints next to the body. "Look at these. I can make out the tread of a boot."

Pulling out his phone, Cayden snapped a few pictures of the body, and then some of the footprints. "How much do you want to bet they match the ones at Andee's apartment?"

"I'm going to give a heads up to the state police when we finish up here."

"There are gloves in the front pocket of my flannel."

She reached inside the front pocket and pulled out two pair of gloves. She handed one to him and slipped on the other pair. "What are we looking for?"

"Pike has to have a cell phone or a computer somewhere around here." Cayden put on his gloves and motioned to an upturned table and chairs. "It looks like someone's already been here and ransacked the place." He angled his horned head around the room then sifted through stacks of papers on the floor.

"My guess is whoever killed Pike took anything that could be traced back to them." She blurred to the other side of the room. Something silver caught her eye. A small key dangled from a hook. She pulled it down and examined it. "This looks like a safe deposit key."

Cayden turned and stared. "Holy shit. Let me see. How much do you want to bet there's a payoff inside that box waiting for Pike?"

"A payoff from Kyle Hawthorne for helping him escape from Hellios?"

"Don't you find it odd that no one's been able to find Hawthorne, none of our agents, no one from Hellios, and none of the local or state police?" He tore off a piece of paper towel from a roll on the counter and walked to her side. "Here, wrap it in this. We can put a trace on the key."

"Well, now that you mention it, but the warden's report detailed Hawthorne's escape with Pike in a medic van." After she wrapped up the key, she slipped it in Cayden's jacket pocket to be marked as evidence.

"What if Stephen Frost is the one who escaped with Pike, and Hawthorne is the one who's dead?"

Her stomach dropped to the floor. "But how? They found Frost's body, burnt to a crisp."

"Frost was an identity thief adept at hacking into some of the world's most secure systems when I arrested him."

Her mouth fell open. "You do realize this sounds insane. And you still think the jewels are somehow connected to Andee's murder?"

"Once we get the 411 from Erika on the serial numbers and markings, then we play connect the dots."

An icy chill settled over Natalya and made her throat tight. "If it turns out the murders are connected and Maverick's behind bars, it can only mean one thing, the killer's still out there."

CHAPTER 25

The next morning, Natalya stretched, still shaken up from the day before. She kicked off the covers and hauled herself out of bed. The last twenty-four hours became one big blur. She tried to block out the ugliness of the attack and finding a dead body. She chose to focus on Cayden's awe-inspiring kiss instead. Her body liquefied thinking about it now. His concern and consideration warmed her heart.

Walking to her dresser, she pulled her bracelet out of her jewelry box. For a moment, she indulged on a floating cloud of possibilities. Shaking off the gooey sensation in her stomach, she decided to see what the crystal ball had to say.

She left her room and descended the stairs. She headed for the library to practice gazing. The crystal ball sat in the same exact spot on the bookshelf. The moment she touched the glass, it lit up.

After she set the ball on the coffee table, she lit a bundle of incense. Breathing deep, she focused her mind on opening her third eye and bringing in the light. A soft flutter of air touched her skin but this time it expanded and whipped around the room. Her heart pounded. What if she saw something she didn't want to see?

What if I can't stop it from happening?

She'd stopped a perp from attacking an innocent. She couldn't help but think she'd been given this power for a reason. When the beam of light floated to her third eye, she gazed into the glass. At first nothing happened. The glass remained hazy. She concentrated, imagining her heart opening. Several minutes ticked by, then the clouds parted and the glass turned from clear to purple.

A woman with bluish hair, black glasses, dressed in white appeared in the glass. She held her phone to her ear, deep in conversation. Natalya recognized her voice, but from where? She could feel the other woman's excitement. But then as the glass clouded and turned to black, she sensed something sinister lurking in the background.

Natalya blinked and the image disappeared. Her heart stuttered in her chest. What did it mean? She'd ask Willow about it later. Maybe she could shed some light on the whole thing. From the knot in her stomach, she sensed this could be some kind of omen.

The line at the coffee shop circled out the door and Natalya wondered if they were giving free coffee away. All morning long, she kept glancing over her shoulder as she'd walked, not able to shake the feeling that she'd been followed.

As the line moved along, she caught part of the conversation in front of her, even though she tried not to listen. An elderly couple decided to stop for lattes before their walk around the pier. They held hands and gazed into each other's eyes, lost in their own private little world. Could she ever experience that kind of love and devotion?

Her phone pinged with a text, pulling her out of her head. Reaching inside her purse, she glanced at the screen.

Tessa: I wanted to give you a heads up. Eleanora wants to host the charity luncheon @ the townhouse. She asked me to tell you.

Of course she did. Natalya sighed and began to type.

Natalya: Eleanora luvs to be in charge of every last detail. It gives her a twisted sense of purpose. :)

Tessa: LOL. Don't worry. I'll be there.

Natalya:. I can't wait to catch up. Sorry GTG. xoxo

She hadn't seen much of her best friend since Tessa started dating her new man. Before she could slide her phone in her purse, it rang. Eleanora's name flashed across the screen. She must've summoned the grand dame.

She pressed accept, and put the phone to her ear. "How's it going, Eleanora?"

"I'm surprised I caught you since you never seem to answer your phone or return any of my calls."

Guilt slid in her belly. Natalya tried to ignore the dig and decided to change the subject. "How's Pavel?"

"Oh, you know him—when he's not at the office, he's on the golf course or in a meeting."

Natalya caught the loneliness in Eleanora's voice. "Are you okay?" Her sired father still worked nonstop. They rarely spent time together as a couple. Eleanora seemed content to go along for the ride, loving the lifestyle and her place in vampire society. It wasn't what Natalya wanted for herself, not even close. Cayden's words popped into her head. *How could they have encouraged their daughter to marry someone she didn't love?* He'd never understand. These things were considered normal and acceptable in their world.

But that didn't make it right.

"Being on the planning committee this year means I'm up to my eyeballs in preparations for the gala. You never responded to my email, Natalya."

"I'm sorry. I've been busy." She took a step closer to the front of the line. The scents of fresh coffee, cinnamon and pastries wafted through the shop, making her crave something sweet.

Eleanora rattled on about this year's society mavens who'd be attending. Natalya braced herself for the questions that were sure to follow. "Who will be your plus-one?" And of course, "Does he come from a proper bloodline?" And the biggie, "What will you wear?"

As much as Natalya cared about raising money for the victims, she couldn't think about ball gowns and baubles when trying to solve a case involving rape and murder.

"Natalya? Have you heard one word I said?"

"Sorry. It's noisy here. What can I do to help?"

"We need to go over the final seating arrangements, the flowers and the entertainment."

She'd also been asked to help plan Willow's bachelorette party. "I have plans in the morning, but I promise I'll be there afterward." She'd already secured some great silent auction items from a number of local businesses for the gala, but she needed more.

"You know how important this is. Don't make me look bad in front of the other women." Over the years, Eleanora's subtle digs about her appearance and her lack of suitors had taken their toll. Natalya was a grown-ass woman. She needed to stop letting it affect her confidence.

"I promise I'll be there." Someone called out her name. Natalya turned and found James standing at the end of the line. "James? What a surprise." A flush spread from her cheeks to her neck. She never got back to him about the art exhibit.

"Who's James?" Eleanora asked, sounding curious.

"Uh, sorry, Eleanora. I have to go. I'll talk to you later." She ended the call and smiled as James walked up to her with a smile. He rocked business casual in a gray sweater and dark slacks.

"We have to stop meeting like this. What are you doing in my neighborhood? I've never seen you around here before. Believe me, I would've remembered." Aside from Cayden and the few males she'd met online while pretending to be someone else, she wasn't used to men flirting with her.

"I was next door at the jewelry store." She pointed to the red brick building across the street.

"I hope you weren't picking out engagement rings with one of your many admirers from the other evening." James arched his brows.

Natalya laughed. "Definitely not."

"Well, then I'm relieved. I was beginning to think you were blowing me off because you might be taken."

Cayden's magnetic presence filled her head. She sensed that he understood her and could satisfy her deepest desires. But at what cost? If she opened her heart, would he break it? How could he not, when he was still hung up on his lost love?

They let the people behind them go ahead.

"I've been meaning to text you. I'm sorry. I've been busy with work." *And lip-locking with a guy I thought I hated.* She got up to the counter, and ordered a tall green tea with steamed almond milk, but before she could pull out her cash, James placed a twenty on the counter.

"My treat."

"Thank you. I'd still like to pay you back for the other night." Before she could reach into her purse, he held up his hand.

"Please, don't, you'll insult me."

"It's kind of you." Natalya waited as he ordered his coffee, a cappuccino with extra foam. She couldn't imagine Cayden ordering anything but strong black coffee. Everything about the demon embodied masculinity and virility. Funny, they'd spent all this time together and she still didn't know how he took his coffee and vice versa. So why was she thinking about Cayden when she was here with another guy? Her body seemed to know the answer. She still felt flushed and aroused after their kiss. The craving for him never went away.

They made small talk about the weather and how Hudson Street had changed over the years due to gentrification. James asked her questions about her job while they waited for their drinks. She hated to lie because he seemed like a nice guy.

After their names were called, James motioned to a table in the corner. "Shall we?"

"Sure, why not. I can hang out for a few minutes." She grabbed her cup, some napkins, stirrers, and a few packets of raw sugar.

"Am I keeping you from something?" he asked, taking a seat across from her in a plush leather chair.

"I have a lot going on today." After she added sugar to her tea, she blew on the top of her cup and took a sip. "I live with a group of witches, and we're making a welcome home dinner for a friend. I've been assigned to the food and wine committee for fiesta night."

James nodded his approval and took a sip of his coffee. "How do you like living with all those women?"

"It's never boring."

"I bet. I've been thinking about you and then we run into each other like this." His voice took on a husky tone. "It must be kismet."

"Kismet? Wow, I haven't heard that word in a long time." Natalya ran her finger along the edge of her cup, not sure how to respond. The cop in her told her maybe this wasn't such a coincidence after all. She hated being a cynic and looking over her shoulder every minute of the day. Would she regard every man she met who seemed interested in her as a potential killer?

"I'm still trying to adjust my vernacular for the times, but as someone who's lived for centuries, some habits are hard to break." His green eyes glowed against the sunlight peeking in from the windows.

"I find it charming." She finished the last of her tea. "Thanks again. I'm afraid I have to go." As much as she found herself enjoying their conversation, there was something about him she couldn't quite put her finger on, and it put her on alert. Why couldn't she believe a normal guy liked her without being suspicious of his intentions?

"I understand. Fiesta night awaits." James flashed a smile, showing a hint of fangs. "What are you doing next Friday night?"

"Next Friday night?" Cayden's face flashed through her mind. Her head spun with confusion.

"I thought we'd hit a museum and then grab a cocktail afterward."

Natalya looked into his eyes, seeing only kindness and friendship. She didn't detect anything calculating or malevolent. Maybe James liked her, or maybe he was lonely. She chose to believe decent men still existed. Maybe he could turn out to be a friend or someone she could date. What if she did accept? She could fake her way through the pretend dates with potential serial rapists and killers, but what would she do on a real date with a guy like James? Her lack of experience would show, and she'd be mortified.

When she hesitated, he knitted his brows together. "I'm not asking for a marriage proposal." He studied her face like a puzzle piece.

She shook her head, embarrassed. "I'll check my schedule and get back to you. I promise."

"I'm looking forward to it," he murmured and placed a kiss on her cheek.

Natalya watched him disappear through the crowd and out the door and wondered when life had become so complicated.

CHAPTER 26

$\mathcal{N}$atalya helped her friends set up tonight's feast on a long wooden table outside on the deck. Gleaming chafing dishes filled with bean burritos and veggie tacos covered almost every available surface, along with cast iron pots of rice and beans. Giant cauldrons filled with frozen margaritas added to their Mexican theme.

Everyone sat outside at picnic tables under a canopy of stars, lanterns, and fairy lights. The scents of lavender, basil, rosemary, sage, and lemon balm perfumed the air, courtesy of their herb garden. The trees had been trimmed and the flower beds planted in time for Willow and Alex's big day.

While everyone ate and chatted, Natalya approached Willow and pulled her off to the side. "Hey, can I talk to you for a minute?" Natalya sensed if anyone would know what to do in this situation, it would be her.

"Of course." They walked to a corner of the garden. Clay pots painted with symbols and runes sat under a pergola covered in vines. A breeze blew Willow's red hair in every direction. "Your new look is stunning, by the way. I meant to tell you earlier."

"Thanks, I had a little help from some friends." Natalya glanced over at Arabella and Brooke, and her chest filled with love for them. "They make me feel a part of something aside from my job and my charity work. I cherish the friendships that have grown and blossomed from living here."

"This crew can be a lot to handle sometimes, but they all pull together when it counts." Willow reached out and touched Natalya's arm. "I can sense your tension. What's going on?"

"I'm sorry to bring this up now, but it can't wait." Pushing a hand through her hair, Natalya sighed. She filled Willow in about the image of the woman in the mirror at the bar and included what she saw in the crystal ball this morning.

Willow sucked in a breath. "It sounds like you're developing your gift as a clairvoyant based on the events happening in your life right now."

"I can't help but think this might happen again and for a good reason. If I did inherit my aunt's gift, then I feel like I should hone my skills." If she hadn't stepped in, Maverick could've lured that woman into his car. Natalya refused to imagine what could've happened. "I can't help but feel I'm destined to save this woman I saw in the glass earlier, whoever she is."

"You should carry a type of crystal ball with you at all times like a hand mirror or a compact."

An idea popped into Natalya's head. "I have a compact from my aunt."

Willow nodded. "Your compact might have an added psychic punch since it has your aunt's energy still inside of it. Why don't you leave the compact on the kitchen table and I'll replace the glass with a scrying mirror. It will only take a few days."

"I can't ask you to do this so close to your wedding." Natalya reached out and squeezed Willow's hand, warmed by the gesture. "You must have a million things to do. I don't want to add to the list."

"Trust me, it would be my pleasure." Willow smiled. "It will give me something to focus on besides the wedding. As for your vision, I hate to say this, but from what you've described, I'm sensing this is more of a premonition related to Andee's murder."

Natalya mulled the information around in her head. "I was afraid you'd say something like that."

"You need to tell Alex," Willow said, taking on a serious tone. "He can generate a computerized picture based on your description. My guess is your powers will continue to grow with practice."

"Thank you." Natalya pulled out her phone and shot Denopoulos a text. He responded immediately and they set a time to meet.

Willow gave her a hug. "I know this is a lot to take in, but I promise it gets easier."

They returned to the group without anyone noticing and sat at the table. Natalya took a seat next to Saje and tried to push the sensation of unease to the back of her mind. She turned her attention to Gillian, glancing at the rock on her finger. "Tell us how Garrett proposed. We want to hear every detail."

Gillian finished the last of her burrito and then pushed her plate away. "We stayed at this hotel on the northern tip of the island. It sat at the top of a mountain that went clear to the heavens. The views were breathtaking."

The chatter, laughter, and clink of forks became nonexistent.

"We ordered room service on our last night. Garrett suggested a midnight dinner on the balcony," Gillian whispered with a dreamy look in her eyes.

"Don't you just love room service at midnight on an exotic island?" Delilah asked with a giggle.

"Continue," Natalya urged, taking a sip from her margarita glass and grinning from ear to ear.

"The cart arrived, covered in rose petals. I figured Garrett had pulled out all the stops for our last night, but when he lifted the lid over my plate, there was a ring box underneath. Before I could process what was happening, he got down on one knee and told me I was the most important person in his life and that his soul was connected to mine. Then he asked me to be his wife." Gillian's eyes filled with tears.

Hearing about Garrett's romantic proposal made Natalya's heart tug. Could she dare to dream for the same kind of passion for herself? A gentle breeze blew through the air, adding to the dreamlike quality of the night.

Deep sighs could be heard all around the table.

"What a beautiful proposal," Brooke murmured from the other side of the table. "I wish I could meet someone so wonderful. This place has turned into couples central. There must be something in the water." She motioned to Saje. "Or in this case, the potions."

Everyone in their happy little group seemed to be finding love, first Willow with Alex, and then Ellen with Commander Smith. Saje had moved in with her special agent boyfriend Nick, and now Gillian and Garrett. Natalya wondered who'd be next. She couldn't be happier for them.

"To Garrett and Gillian," Saje said with genuine affection in her voice and lifted her glass.

"To Garrett and Gillian," the ladies repeated. When they lifted their glasses, visible sparks flew up in the air. Natalya stared in awe, mesmerized by the display.

Ellen used her napkin to dab at her eyes and then turned to Willow with a curious expression on her face. "As long as we're on the subject of romantic islands, has Alex given you any hints as to where he's taking you for your honeymoon?"

"He's keeping it a surprise. He did say something about a private beach where clothing is optional." Willow's cheeks flushed.

Ellen fanned a hand in front of her face. "Whoa, I just got a visual of that gorgeous fiancé of yours walking around in the buff." She pulled out her phone. "I need to see what the commander's doing later tonight."

All the ladies laughed.

Natalya could only dream about having such a sensual connection with someone, and she realized she wanted that someone to be Cayden. A delicious thrill spread from the center of her chest to the rest of her body.

"Speaking of gorgeous men, what's going on between you and Cayden?" Arabella's curious gaze slid to hers. "I saw him crawling out of your window the other day like freaking Tarzan. I waited for him to beat on his chest. He doesn't have to sneak around if you want him to stay over. He can use the front door."

Natalya's face heated. "Uh, about that, it's not what you think."

"As long as he didn't ask you to let down your hair." Gillian chuckled. "I'm sorry. I couldn't resist."

"Nothing happened. We were just hanging out watching movies and he fell asleep. Cayden didn't want any of you giving me crap about it, which of course is a lost cause." Natalya cracked a smile. She left out the part about acting like a total head case.

"If you say so, but your aura's turning colors." Brooke ran a finger along the side of her giant margarita glass. "How could you just hang out with a smoking hot, seven-foot-tall demon, and not want to jump his bones?"

Heat crept up Natalya's neck. "I'm pleading the fifth."

"Don't deny it, honey. It's not only your aura that changes color, but your voice gets higher when you talk about him. It's a sign of sexual attraction." Willow sipped her margarita.

"Okay fine, I admit I'm attracted to him, but he's unavailable and we work together. It's complicated." She'd never met a man she could talk to or confide in like she did with Cayden. He made her feel things—warm, wonderful things that woke up her body and melted her heart.

Willow inclined her head to the side and her long red hair fell over her shoulder. "There's something I should tell you. I don't want to betray his confidence, but we're among friends and I wouldn't want to see you get hurt, Natalya. I've known Cayden for a while now and he doesn't do relationships. He's never gotten over the brutal murder of his first love. He told Alex it really screwed with his head. I mean, how could it not?"

Natalya's stomach grew queasy. "I had no idea he's been through so much." Willow had to be referring to the beautiful demon woman in the photo at Cayden's apartment. "Does he know who murdered her?"

"I don't know all the details, except that she was killed by a vampire." Willow gave Natalya a sympathetic smile.

"How horrible." Natalya swallowed hard and tried to digest the eerie relevance of her words. The room fell silent. "I appreciate you telling me." She kept her tone casual, hoping the women didn't pick up on her disappointment. "Actually, I met someone. He asked me out a couple of times, but I'm still debating if I should go out with him." The moment she brought up the subject, she regretted it.

Arabella glanced over at her as she wrapped a throw around her shoulders. "Did you mention you need a date for your ball?" she asked, breaking through the heaviness in the air.

"In the total of the five minutes that we actually spoke in person, I forgot to ask," she joked. Too bad she wasn't the least bit attracted to James. Natalya's mind drifted to her searing kiss with Cayden and her face flushed. The demon had probably ruined her for all other men.

Brooke beamed. "He sounds perfect. Why do I detect a 'but' in there?"

Natalya shrugged. "I'm not good at dating and all the things that go along with it, like sex." There, she said it. Mortification set in. She expected everyone to stare at her with shock in their eyes, but to her surprise, their expressions filled with compassion.

"You don't need to be embarrassed in front of us." Saje reached out and touched Natalya's shoulder. "We're all here for you."

"Thanks. It means everything." Natalya's smiled, filled with gratitude and love for this group of women. "I'm sure you're all wondering why, but are too good-natured to ask." An explanation bubbled up from her lips, but she held back. She wanted to confide in them, tell them about her past, especially since they'd been nothing but good to her. But she couldn't come up with a good enough reason to drop a bombshell on their heads, especially since this night was supposed to be all about Gillian. "I guess that part isn't important, but my willingness to change is."

"Why don't you practice with someone you feel comfortable with first before you go out with your new guy?" Brooke suggested with a mischievous gleam in her eyes. "You should ask Cayden for some lessons. I'm sure he'd be up to the task. The demon has lived for centuries. If anyone is experienced sexually, it's him. At least you know he's not about to make any false promises. What do you have to lose?"

"Besides my dignity?" When Natalya tried to envision having such a conversation, a mixture of embarrassment and excitement fluttered in her belly. "I don't know if I could." How would she even broach the subject? Before she could contemplate it any further, her phone buzzed. She glanced at the screen and swallowed hard.

Cayden: We need to talk.

Natalya's heart banged away in her chest. No time like the present.

CHAPTER 27

*M*oonlight glistened off the dunes. Cayden glanced over at the
woman standing beside him, and her dark hair blended into the
inky sky. When he reached out to touch her, she slipped through his fingertips like
sand. He couldn't lose her. Not now.

A growl pierced the air. Maverick appeared out of nowhere in a cloud of smoke
and launched a fireball at his head. Cayden darted in front of his beloved to save
her from the blast. But before he could reach her, a snarling beast lunged,
disappearing with her into the night.

I need to save her!

Cayden tried to run, but his feet sunk in quick stand. No!

Bolting upright in a cold sweat, Cayden's heart pounded. His throat
burned. "It was only a nightmare," he muttered out loud.

Kicking off the covers, he crawled out of bed and tried to get his
bearings. He'd been waiting to hear from Natalya and must've dozed off. It
had been days since he'd taken a drink. He didn't want to, but he didn't
know of any other way to numb the pain and the loneliness, or make the
images in his head go away.

He cursed, refusing to give in to his weakness. The jittery, sweaty,
crawling-out-of-his-skin tremors would pass. They always did, eventually.
He made his way to the shower and turned on the spray.

He tried to block out the memories as the hot water ran over his sore muscles. First, he'd failed Abigail, and now Andee. Why did he have this sick feeling in his gut Natalya would be next? She'd been the woman in his dream, not Abigail.

After he turned off the water, he stepped out of the shower and reached for a towel. Tying the end around his waist, he headed out of the bathroom straight to the liquor cabinet. His hand shook as he wrapped it around a his old pal Johnnie

The craving consumed him, body and soul. One sip would make it all go away. *Fuck it.* As he lifted the bottle to his lips, the doorbell rang.

Who would be stopping by at this hour? He secretly hoped it was Natalya. He walked to the hall and caught a whiff of her strawberry scent.

Looking through the peephole, he found her standing in his hall moving from one foot to the other like she might bolt at any minute. He opened the door. "Natalya? I've been texting and calling you all night."

Her eyes widened as they roamed over his bare chest, making the water droplets on his skin heat. "I thought I'd surprise you. I'm sorry. I … I don't know what I was thinking coming over here at this hour," she said with a note of panic in her voice. The sound kicked him in the gut. "This was a bad idea. I should go." She moved in a blur to the elevator.

"Natalya? Wait." He shoved the umbrella stand against the door to keep it from shutting. He jogged over to her holding his towel. "You didn't come all the way over here to leave."

"I should've called first." She pressed the button. "C'mon, c'mon," she mumbled, her gaze darting from his to the elevator. An explosion of scents lingered in the air—tequila, Mexican food and rain. He couldn't bear to see someone as confidant and ballsy as her this skittish. But then that same nagging question popped into his head, making his gut clench. Had she been abused in some way?

This time when she reached out to press the button again, he closed his hand over hers, rubbing his thumb over her knuckles. "Please don't go," he whispered. He still couldn't believe he'd been dreaming about her only minutes before. She'd kept him from falling off the wagon.

The elevator dinged. The doors opened and he held his breath, hoping she didn't step inside. "Come back to my apartment and let's talk." After their kiss, he could still taste her on his lips.

Natalya turned to him and blew out a breath. Her big brown eyes locked with his. "Okay."

He wanted to take her in his arms, peel off her clothes and make love to her until they both couldn't think straight anymore, ease her worry with long, deep kisses. But it would be a mistake to let things go any further. He led her across the hall by her elbow, making sure she couldn't see his back. Once she did, then she'd really be scared shitless, and right now he didn't need to pile it on.

Maybe he should let her go and talk to her in the morning when he wasn't at an all-time low. She deserved more. But he continued down the hall. His gaze moved to her shapely backside and the alluring sway of her hips. Bare, toned legs peeked out from a black trench coat. The swishing sound made his dick harden under his towel.

He'd never seen a female so unaware of her looks or her feminine appeal, but why? The question nagged at him like a raw open wound. When they reached his door, he pressed his back to the wall, motioning for her to step inside.

"I'm sorry for stopping by so late. I wanted to talk in person." Natalya ground out the words and crossed the threshold. Her high heels tapped against the wood floor, mimicking the rapid beat of his heart.

"Why don't you sit?" Cayden slid the umbrella stand away from the door, and motioned to the couch.

"Thanks." She walked past his computer on her way and glanced at his screen. She took a seat at the far end of the couch, and the overhead light cast a glow on her heart-shaped face. Her dark hair curled around her shoulders in loose waves. Gods, she was beautiful

"Can I get you something to drink?" Reaching for a jacket off the coat rack, he threw it on, secured his towel. He wanted to put on some clothing, but he stayed in the room, too afraid she might take off. "If I remember correctly, you enjoy white wine. How about some chardonnay?" He'd been meaning to dump all the booze in his place—better for her to drink it than him.

"I'd love some. Thanks." Natalya unbuttoned her coat, took it off and laid it over the arm of the couch. She wore a short brown dress that showed the outline of her small breasts, the kind to fit perfectly in his hands and mouth.

He walked to the fridge and grabbed a bottle. After he pulled out the stopper, he reached for a wine glass from a cabinet and filled it to the rim. Her kind may be immune to alcohol, but imbibing might soften her nerves.

"Any ideas on who killed Pike?"

"I'm still waiting for Denopoulos and Smith to send me a copy of the coroner's report. We want to see if the shoe prints at Pike's place match the one at Andee's apartment."

"What's your take?"

"I think we may have found our rapist, but not our killer."

Natalya sighed. "So two separate cases we believed to be connected, but aren't?" Her voice wavered. "Part of me is relieved and the other part fears we're back to square one on solving the murders."

"Have some faith. I'm going to Hellios to get to the bottom of this mess and check it out for myself."

"Do you still think Frost is alive?" Natalya asked, looking more relaxed.

"Until I have something more solid to go on, my theories on Frost still being alive would have to go on the back burner for now." Cayden walked over to the table and set the wine glass in front of her, then ran a hand over his face.

"Thanks." She took a sip of her wine and his gaze focused on her mouth, mesmerized by the way her tongue darted out to wet her lips.

Right now he didn't want to think about the case. Cayden wanted to taste her, lose himself in her moist heat, and push all this ugliness and death behind them, if only for a little while. Taking a seat next to her on the couch, he looked her in the eye. "We could talk shop all night, but my guess is you didn't come over here at this hour of the night to chew on the case. Is this about our kiss?"

"Well, that's part of it. But it's also about my reaction to you the other morning when I freaked out." Her gaze roamed over his bare chest where his jacket opened and her eyes flared wide. She proceeded to cross and uncross her legs, and it forced her dress to hike up her thighs, drawing his attention to her shapely legs. He tried to stop the mindless surge of blood to his dick. But how could he with her luscious skin on display?

"Why don't you start at the beginning?"

"I don't know how to put it into words. I'm not sure how you'll react." Her expression became even more guarded.

"Hey, it's just me." He moved closer to her and reached out to rub his thumb over a silky curl, then pushed it behind her ear. "Whatever it is, I'm not going to judge you. Talk to me."

Her eyes sparked with tears and clung to her lashes. "I want to, but it's not that simple. I guess I didn't think about how hard this would be."

"Take your time. We've got all night," he murmured. "Whatever it is, Natalya, you can say it."

"Okay. I've noticed you checking out my new look. I want to be sure you still see the real me under all the lip gloss and bronzer." She visibly swallowed.

"I always have." He'd taken plenty of notice of her in those baggy pants and ill-fitting blazers. "It was your sass and wit that got my attention, even when you drove me crazy, I wanted you. Showing off your sexy little body was just an added bonus." He angled his head and brought his lips closer so they breathed the same air. He reached out and placed her hand on his chest to the wild thump of his heart to prove his point. The heat from her fingers made him burn.

Her eyes grew wide. The pulse jumped at her neck. "Cayden," she murmured on a whispery catch of breath.

"I do see the real you," he whispered, running his thumb along her cheek. "Your natural sex appeal is incredibly hot. The hair and clothes seemed to make you more confident. Is that what's on your mind?"

She shrugged her slender shoulders and moved her hand to her lap. "A few of the ladies saw you leaving my bedroom the other night and started asking questions."

"I see." He cleared his throat, not surprised it might come to this. "What kind of questions?"

Tension crackled in the air. "If you and I ever …you know." The pulse throbbed wildly at her throat.

"Had mind-blowing sex all night long?"

Her eyes widened, and her breath came out in a rush. "That was the general inference and it got me thinking."

Cayden should probably redirect the convo, but he needed answers like he needed air to breathe. "Thinking about what?"

"Have you ever thought about us hooking up?" The words seemed to rush from her lips like she couldn't wait to get them out.

He crossed his arms over his chest, amused. If she only knew how many times he'd laid awake alone in his bed stroking himself, imagining her hands and her lips on his body. He wanted her naked, spread out before him so he could touch her, taste her, worship her for hours on end, and give her unimaginable pleasure. He didn't think she was ready to hear all the dirty details yet, so he'd settle on a version of the truth. "We're colleagues, and I think we both know what would've happened if you had any idea I've been lusting after you. I figured you had rules about that kind of thing."

"I did. I mean, I do," she amended.

If she knew how much he wanted her it might freak her out. He'd fantasized about taking her up against the wall of the shower too many times to count, but if what he suspected about her was true, then he'd take things slow. He'd start with tender kisses and hugs, let her set the pace. He leaned in and whispered close to her ear, earning him a delicious shiver. "I look forward to our bantering." The air grew thick with sexual tension.

"There's more." Her body language became guarded. "I'm not experienced with sex," she blurted out.

He leaned against the cushions, trying to process the weight of her words. "Are you a virgin?" But she'd been married. None of it made a lick of sense, unless her husband abused her in some way. The thought made his gut clench and his horns burn.

"I had one awful experience in college. I wasn't able to …you know."

"Have an orgasm?" He never imagined in his wildest dreams talking about orgasms with Natalya Dubrosky. *Never say never*, he supposed.

Humiliation flashed in her eyes. "No," she said simply. The admission hung in the air.

"I'm sorry you had such a bad experience. Clearly the stupid boy didn't know what he was doing."

Her lip curled into a sad smile. "Let me guess, you do."

"If you're asking if I know how to give a woman an orgasm, the answer is yes. I'd love to make you come, Natalya. It's something I've been fantasizing about for months now."

Her pulse throbbed at her throat. Her chest rose and fell from his words. She brought out every one of his primal urges. "I've heard you had quite the run."

"I'm not going to lie. I had a lot of empty hookups, and in the end they left me feeling worthless and empty. I let everyone continue to think what they wanted. I stopped having meaningless sex ages ago."

"I didn't know."

"What about after the guy from college?" When Cayden thought about how she'd been treated, he gritted his teeth to the point of pain.

The question seemed to cut her to the quick. "He called me a 'frigid bitch.' Word got passed around campus, and well, you know how that goes."

His hands clenched into fists at his sides. He breathed in and out, trying to control his rage. "Those poisonous words rattled your confidence. The bastard tried to crush your spirit. None of what he said is true. You're passionate and sensual. He deserved to have his ass handed to him. I only wished I could've been the one to do the honors. There had to be other dudes who asked you out." If circumstances were different, he would've been one of them.

Regret pulled at her features. She stood and began to pace. "I've lived a sheltered life, Cayden. My sired family kept a close eye on me, and I let them. Men were never allowed into our home. I wasn't permitted to date, not that I got a lot of offers. I did what I was supposed to." A note of anger filled her voice. "But not anymore."

"Didn't you have sex with your husband?" he asked, confused. "When you said he filed for an annulment, I just assumed it was a formality for financial reasons. Did it mean you never consummated the marriage?" If she'd been his, he would've taken her in every position possible. His towel tented around his growing erection just thinking about all ways he wanted to bring her to orgasm.

She stopped pacing and stared at him with regret in her eyes. Could she sense what he'd been thinking? *Shit*, he hoped not. He didn't want to scare her away. He needed to tread lightly or she might bolt.

"When he tried to have sex with me after the wedding, I cried. I couldn't go through with it. I wasn't attracted to him."

"Who could blame you for not wanting to sleep with someone you weren't into?" Something in his chest shifted.

"The Dubroskys for one." The admission tumbled out on a sigh.

He blew out a breath through his teeth. "I'm humbled you trust me with your secrets, Natalya. I promise to keep them locked away with my own." He stared into her eyes and her pupils dilated. There was more to the story than she let on. "Tell me what can I do? Whatever it is."

This time when she sat next to him on the couch, she moved closer. Her knee brushed against his thigh and a spark of heat shot up his leg, jolting through him like an electric current. Did she feel it too?

"I have my reasons for telling you all this." Her gaze moved to the tenting under his towel, shooting more blood to his groin. Their breaths became shallow, the familiar tension arcing between them.

For a moment they stared at each other. He wanted her with a ferocity he could no longer ignore. Could she want the same thing? Of course he knew the answer, but he needed to hear her say the words. He skimmed his fingers over her arm, awed by the softness of her skin. "What are you asking, Natalya," he whispered on a breath.

The pulse pounded at her throat. He wanted to flick his tongue over the spot, make up for the pain she'd experienced and fill it with pleasure. "I want to have a normal sex life like every other woman." Her voice sounded hoarse like it would crack at any minute, but to her credit, she kept on going. "You can help me."

His heart thudded against his ribs. "You don't know what you're getting yourself into."

"I get you don't do relationships." Her assessment about his love life stung.

"Have you been asking around about me?" He couldn't blame her for doing her research, especially in matters such as this.

"Not exactly, but you have a reputation for being a love 'em and leave 'em kind of guy."

"I won't deny it. I've slept with my share of women over the years." Some he'd genuinely cared about. "I always made sure to be honest from the beginning so no one got hurt. Tell me what you want from me." All these years later, his heart remained closed. But she tempted him to open it again.

"Somewhere along the way, I've unintentionally cut myself off from having a normal sex life after that awful experience in college, but I don't want to live that way anymore. I want passion in my life." Moving closer, she filled the scant few inches between them. From the sudden movement of her hand to her hair, he knew she wasn't telling him the whole truth. As much as he'd started to care about her, there had been only one love of his life and she died because of him. Since then, his heart stayed cold, for fear the same thing could happen to someone else. Call it superstition or fate from the gods.

"I've been so cold." She reached out and pressed his hand to her face. "I don't want to be cold anymore." Her words flayed him like a knife to the chest and spoke to the man he used to be, the man with a romantic heart.

He shook his head hard. If she came any closer and continued to pour out her soul, he wouldn't be able to stop himself from taking her in his arms and making love to her all night long. But in this case, he needed to tread carefully, especially after everything she'd been through.

Full disclosure time. "There are some things you should know about me before we go any further." Seeing what she might be working with might make the decision for both of them.

"I don't know if I'm the guy to help you with this kind of thing." What if he messed up? Then again, mind-blowing sex might be just what the doctor ordered. At least they'd get it out of their systems. He could fill the ache inside him, if only for a little while. *Yeah right.*

"I'm not expecting anything in return, and I know neither are you," she said with conviction as though she'd already weighed the pros and cons.

After everything she told him, her cavalier attitude sent a kick straight to his gut. He ran a hand through his wet hair. "True, but not the point. I'm ancient and jaded, flawed to the point of no return. For all intents and purposes, you're an innocent." How could she ask him to place a piece of glass in his hands and not break it?

Her gaze narrowed in confusion. "What are you saying?"

"You should probably see what you're getting yourself into before we continue this conversation any further." Her innocence blocked out all the ugliness and brought him to a time before bitterness took root inside him like a patch of thorns twisting out his virtues. He surged to his feet, his pride be damned. They were both scarred. The only difference, his marks could be seen on the outside.

"Cayden?"

"See for yourself." Now it was his turn to show his hand. He took off his jacket and tossed it on the couch. Turning, he stood frozen, hoping he didn't send her sprinting out the door.

"Oh, Cayden." Her gasp of horror shook him.

He realized two things. The marks and bumps on his back were even uglier than he thought, and dammit to hell, he wanted her more than he had any right to.

CHAPTER 28

"Who did this to you?" Natalya reached out and ran her fingers over the deep welts and scars across Cayden's reddened flesh. His sharp intake of breath told her no one had touched him like this in a while, if ever.

"It happened when I was a slave on Arcadia. The royal guards took pleasure in torturing us, especially me," he said in a humorless voice.

Natalya never imagined Cayden enduring such horrific physical abuse. Tears stung her eyes as she stared at the numerous raised red scars. She could see him bucking authority and letting the consequences be damned. "I'm so sorry," she whispered and continued to roam her hands over his marks, sickened by what he'd endured.

"After seeing the road map on my back, are you sure you still want to go through with these lessons of yours?" he asked, glancing at her over his shoulder. The rawness in his voice tugged at her heartstrings.

"Your scars don't change anything." In fact, they only made Natalya want him all the more. She shook her head at the irony. "Who knew we were kindred spirits." Cayden's scars marred his body, hers marred her soul.

"Talk to me. What are you thinking?" Shadows danced across the sculpted angles of his body.

"I don't see these as scars, but as symbols of courage." As she traced each raised bump and blemish with her fingertips, her heart broke and threatened to shatter. She moved the tips of her fingers beneath his shoulder blade to a dark red welt and his breath came out in short rasps. "This one is a mark of strength." Her fingers moved lower to the middle of his back, where the red marks and bumps became even more distinct.

"Don't stop." The raw need in his voice surged into her blood.

"This one's honor." She moved to one under his shoulder blade. "Valor," she whispered.

"Your touch unravels me." When he turned around to face her, his eyes filled with hunger.

His words emboldened her as her fingers roamed over his bare chest. The sight of his sculpted muscles and washboard abs made her want to drool. His body reminded her of an artist's rendering of Raphael, beautiful and broken.

His brows drew together in question. "No one's ever seen me the way you do."

"That makes two of us, Cayden." Her gaze moved lower to the deep V of his hips where his towel dipped. She'd never seen anything so sexy in her life.

Her body responded in an unfamiliar way. Delicious tingles broke out along her skin. A deep ache throbbed between her thighs. The tattoo above his hip caught her eye. Her gaze moved lower to the small scrolling letters with a number above them. "What's this? *Condemnant quod non intellegunt.*"

"The number is how the guards kept track of us. The phrase is Latin, but the origin is Demonish. It means 'they condemn that which they don't understand.'"

"You forgive them for what they did to you?" Her gaze moved to his face. She practiced learning to forgive, but she didn't think she'd ever forget.

He stared at her lips. The scent of soap and his arousal mingled in the air and her body shivered with awareness. "I try not to let my past define my present. It's something I'm still working on, but it speaks to me every day."

"Well, Socrates, in terms of lessons, is that all I get?" Disappointment gripped her by the throat. "I was hoping for a kiss." She'd been dreaming about one all day.

His breath came out in a hiss. His horns flared red. He groaned a feral sound that got her heart racing. He wrapped a hand around her waist and then pushed the other one through her hair to angle his head close to her lips. "Careful what you wish for."

A blaze of emotion flared in her chest as he covered his mouth with hers, stealing her breath. When he sucked on her bottom lip, she opened for him on a moan. He stroked into her mouth with deep, velvety sweeps of his tongue. He tasted like mint and something deliciously male. She melted into his arms, warm and wanton.

Sensations wracked her body. Stubble scratched against her skin as he deepened the kiss. Her fingers curled around his neck, needing him closer. Her heart hammered in her chest. Her senses went into overload. The scent of his skin wound its way into her head like a drug. His heat and his strength surrounded her and made her burn. He pressed her flush against his body and she felt the pounding of his heart and the pulse of his erection.

Her hands twined around his neck. The kiss turned raw and passionate and made her toes curl. They kissed until she had to pull back to draw breath. "Cayden."

His eyes turned a fiery shade of blue. "What are you doing to me?" he whispered.

She'd been asking herself the same question.

His computer pinged, followed by his phone. "Shit, it's probably Smith. His timing sucks, but it must be important for him to reach out at this hour." He untangled his fingers from her hair. "Don't move," he said and darted to his desk.

She pushed her hair off her face, flushed and aroused, with Cayden's words reverberating in her head. *Don't let your past define your present.* Too bad she didn't have the guts to tell him the whole story. She couldn't. Her chest panged with anxiety. The guy from college didn't ruin her. The incident that happened the night she got turned did.

The group of them came out of nowhere, and tackled her to the ground. Their dirty hands roamed all over her, ripping at her top, pushing it up along with her bra, groping at her breasts.

She tried to get away ... to fight but there were too many of them holding her down. She managed to kick one in the shin, and he spit in her face. One whispered something about teaching her a lesson.

A hand covered her mouth, muffling her scream. A glint of a blade caught in the sunlight. No one saw her...no one helped.

The leader of the group plunged the tip of the knife into the side of her belly. Gut-wrenching pain exploded through every cell and nerve ending. She thought she'd pass out from the agony. Blood dripped down her legs, mixing with the grass stains on her new jeans.

To this day she didn't know all of their names, but their faces still haunted her nightmares, forcing her to relive the horrors of that fateful night over and over again. As for those boys, they probably forgot what they did, or the pain they inflicted. They never knew it had changed her life forever.

"Natalya?" Cayden's deep voice pulled her back to the present. "What's going on?" The concern in his voice chased some of the darkness away.

Turning to face him, she forced a neutral expression. "It's nothing."

Concern etched between his brows as he stared at her face, and she swore he could see inside her soul. "I'm dropping it for now because I don't want to push you."

His consideration for her made her throat tight. How had she been so wrong about him? She motioned to his phone, hating to leave their private little bubble. "Any news?"

"We got a tip from Erika on the cigar brand. We located a few places in the city. Denopoulos and I will check the place out in the morning. It's a long shot, but hell, it's the best we've got right now. As for you, I think you should take a few days off. "

Sighing deep, she nodded. "I'm not going to argue."

"Shh, I don't want to talk shop." He moved closer and placed his hand to the back of her neck.

"Okay, what do you want to talk about?" she asked over the thrum of blood through her veins

"Who says we have to talk at all?" She caught the searing heat in his eyes right before he angled his head and covered her mouth with his. His tongue stroked hers, teasing at first, and then turned wicked. The kiss went from soft and sweet to searing hot in a matter of seconds, and she felt like she would melt into his body.

He pulled away, his broad chest rising and falling, panting hard. Nipping at her neck, he trailed open-mouthed kisses along her collarbone, sending sparks of heat under her skin. "You're so beautiful." He lifted his head and placed a sweet kiss on her cheek.

When she gazed into his eyes, she saw nothing but raw sincerity and deep emotion shining back at her. "You make me feel beautiful." Every touch and brush of his lips made her pulse skyrocket.

"Talya." The way he murmured the nickname spurred her desire even more. Her nipples grew hard, heat pooled between her thighs. He gently pulled down the edge of her sweater and licked her shoulder, exposing the top swell of her breasts.

Her body caught fire. She wanted him to touch her so she could continue to ride this sensual high.

"I think that's enough for now. Consider this lesson number one, the art of the slow burn. Anticipation can be a good thing." He reached under her knees, and pulled her onto his lap. He ran his hand through her hair, massaging her scalp until her body became boneless.

"And just when things were getting interesting," she murmured, resting her head on his shoulder.

"What do you say to picking up where we left off tomorrow night?" he asked in a husky voice.

"I say yes, slow burn it is." The tremendous yearning she felt for him excited her on every level. "I can't wait for lesson number two."

CHAPTER 29

The next morning, Natalya took a quick shower, and then slipped one of the cream pantsuits from Tessa for the SAAN brunch. The team had suggested she take a few days off after the attack, and she was grateful for the reprieve. She needed some time to get her head together and talk to her therapist. Fortunately, Dr. Cruz had agreed to squeeze her in at the last minute. The case lingered in the back of her mind as she applied her makeup and ran a blow-dryer over the ends of her hair.

Glancing at her watch, she grabbed her purse and rushed downstairs. She made a beeline for the kitchen, needing a jolt of caffeine before she headed out. She found her compact sitting next to the coffee maker with a sticky note attached to the top. Pulling it off, she read the words.

Natalya, the more you practice the art of spheromancy, the more your powers will grow. XO Willow.

She glanced at her watch. The coffee would have to wait. If she didn't leave right now, she'd be late for her appointment with Dr. Cruz.

Natalya parked on River Street and walked a block to Dr. Cruz's home office. Nerves fluttered in her belly as she made her way through the front door and into a hall that served as her waiting room.

Dr. Cruz greeted her right away. She smiled and shook her hand. "It's good to see you, Natalya."

They talked for a few minutes about Natalya's job and then the doctor motioned to a couch and an arrangement of comfy-looking chairs. "Please, sit anywhere you'd like."

"I appreciate you squeezing me in on short notice."

Soft beiges and greens added to the tranquil vibe. Relaxing music played from a small speaker on the desk. Slowly, the muscles in her neck and shoulders began to relax.

"My pleasure. I do it as a courtesy for my existing patients. It sounded important. May I get you some water or coffee?" Dr. Cruz pulled out an old-fashioned pad and pen and scribbled some notes.

"I'm fine. Thank you." Natalya bit her lip and took a seat on a wingback chair while Dr. Cruz sat across from her on a cream sofa.

Dr. Cruz glanced at her and pushed her glasses up the bridge of her nose. "You're looking well, Natalya. Your new haircut suits you."

"Thank you. I'm feeling more confident too. It's one of the reasons I came to see you today."

"What brings you in?" Dr. Cruz asked with a friendly smile.

"I'm considering sexual experimentation with a colleague. I don't think it can lead anywhere because it's my understanding that he doesn't do relationships," she said over the dull pain in her chest. She waited a heartbeat for the doctor to respond.

Dr. Cruz took off her glasses, her green eyes alert. "This is a big step for you. Go on."

"As it stands, my sex life is nonexistent. But I want to change that. I'm done with being afraid. I want passion and love in my life." The words fell from her lips, forcing her to swallow hard.

"Making the choice to have a normal sex life and refusing to let the events of your past dictate your happiness is the first step in getting your power back." Dr. Cruz pointed out.

Tears welled in Natalya's eyes. "I want more." She'd do anything to make the ache inside her go away. Now that she'd had a taste of what it felt like to be touched and held by Cayden, she wanted to let go of the excruciating memories and move on.

Dr. Cruz reached across her desk and handed her a tissue box. "This is the first time you've opened up in this manner. I see a big change in you."

Blowing her nose, she balled up the tissue in her hand. "I realize I'm stronger than the pain those guys inflicted on me." But she guessed Cayden may be behind the real reason. His words still echoed in her head. *Doesn't everyone deserve a shot at love?*

"But why not find a man who's open to having an emotional connection, a real relationship?"

Tension gathered in Natalya's shoulders. "I'd like to experiment with someone I trust before I dive into the dating pool. This will be a turning point for me either way. I'm done lamenting about my loss of innocence." She didn't plan on going out with James, although he did give a boost to her confidence. He got her thinking about dating and putting herself out there more. Closing her eyes on a breath, an image of Cayden appeared behind her lids.

"May I ask why you feel the need to experiment first?"

"That's a fair question." Sighing, Natalya opened her eyes. "I guess I'm afraid I might be a disappointment in bed. I've always felt I must be lacking in some way. This is the first time I've admitted that to anyone out loud." She twisted her hands together. "It's the same reason I never bothered to do my hair, and put on makeup, or wear sexy clothing. It's kept me from asking for what I want and need."

Dr. Cruz nodded and her gaze filled with compassion. "After everything you've been through it makes perfect sense. Have you thought about how this could set you back if you develop an emotional attachment to this man? There's a good chance you will."

Could she have a sex-only relationship with Cayden and then just walk away? The question burned in her mind. "I have thought about it and it's a risk I'm willing to take."

"It sounds like you've already made your decision. I think it's a great step forward." Dr. Cruz reclined on the couch and took a sip from a coffee mug.

"I get this could get messy. But I'm done playing it safe. Where has it gotten me?" Natalya sucked in a harsh breath, waiting for her reply.

"I can't tell you what you should or shouldn't do, but your determination to move forward is a big breakthrough. I do think it's worth exploring as long as both parties know what to expect going in, and no one gets hurt."

"Thank you, I appreciate your help." A tingling sensation spread through her limbs, and got her thinking about this new unknown place she couldn't wait to explore.

CHAPTER 30

Cayden walked up West 29th Street with Denopoulos at his side. The subway rattled beneath their feet. The scent of roasted peanuts mixed with exhaust, and a hint of freshly baked bagels lingered on the breeze. Cars and taxis whizzed by at breakneck speed. The blare of sirens pierced the air. He ate up the sights and sounds, enjoying the vibrancy of the city.

Through the process of elimination, they narrowed their list of cigar shops that sold the King of Denmark brand to three in the area. One said they hadn't carried that brand in their shop for months and the other one was closed. "It looks like Martindale's it is. What's the plan?"

"We see if anyone from Martindale's recognizes one of our suspects." Denopoulos sipped his coffee. "I hope like hell this tip from Erika pans out."

Cayden shook his head. "You and me both. The designer shoe prints and the cashmere fibers don't seem to match with our suspect. It looks like we need to do some more digging to connect the dots."

They'd spent the better part of the morning talking to one of Andee's ex-boyfriends, a guy by the name of Bryce who lived in the West Village. His alibi checked out for the night of her murder.

When they asked him flat out whether or not he'd killed her, the answer had been a resounding no. In fact, he didn't appear to have any sort of attachment to her anymore. The poor guy's reaction to her murder was one of genuine sadness.

Guilt gnawed at him. If Cayden didn't catch Andee's killer, how could he ever rest? "I had Nick pull the photos of the men Natalya met online." He held up his phone. "I just sent you the video surveillance from the bar on the night of Andee's murder. What about the jewels? Any word at the auction houses?"

Denopoulos's eyebrows shot up. "Smith checked with some of the local places, but nothing so far."

Now as they made their way to their last lead of the morning, Cayden's whole body tensed.

"Hey, you okay, buddy?"

"Who, me?" Cayden waited until the people behind them passed. His mind flashed to the moment right before Natalya showed up at his place. He came close to falling off the wagon and spiraling into hell. "I've got a problem with booze. I need help." The words hung in the air, thick and heavy like fog.

Denopoulos stared at him long and hard as realization sparked in his eyes. "I'm here for you, buddy. I could put you in touch with my brother Gus. I used to go to meetings with him. I'm sure he'd be happy to talk to you."

"Thanks, it means a lot." If Alex's little bro could get sober, then so could he. Cayden wanted to lighten the mood as they maneuvered their way through the crowd. "After this, you can enjoy the rest of the day with Willow."

What would it be like to have someone waiting for him at home? To his shock, Natalya's face came flashed through his mind and not Abigail's. He'd been up half the night thinking about her. After she left, he jerked off twice and still woke up rock-hard and shaking. He meant what he'd said about taking things slow, even if it required a cold shower or two.

Denopoulos waved a hand in front of his face. "Where did you just go?"

"Sorry. I didn't get a lot of sleep last night. Catch me up about wedding stuff. Anything I should know as the best man?" He prayed they'd find their killer and wrap up this case before the big day.

Running a hand over his beard, Denopoulos mumbled something

about seating charts and Cayden tuned out. "I plan on having an early dinner and soaking in a bath with my girl."

"She's got you totally wrapped around her little, witchy finger." Cayden chuckled. "I couldn't be happier for you, man." He suspected Natalya could have the same effect on him if he let her in. But would things get that far?

"We'll need to take a look at the footage from the bar. There's got to be something there." Cayden pulled up an app on his phone that would allow him to download the feed in seconds. He'd do everything in his power to find this maniac before he hurt someone else he cared about.

By the time they left Martindale's smoke shop and walked across the street, the sky had turned gray, much like Cayden's mood. Clouds loomed overhead, blanketed by a thick layer of fog rolling in from the Hudson. "I want to compare Martindale's security feed with the one from the bar, to see if anyone matches up."

"I just sent everything to Erika," Denopoulos said, shoving his phone in his back pocket. "Let's see what she comes up with. She's running a scan on the safe deposit key to see what bank it can be traced to. We should know more in a few days. Let's hope we can continue to keep Andee's murder out of the press." They stopped next to Cayden's Challenger parked on the curb.

"Yeah, you and me both." Whoever drugged Cayden had been waiting and watching in the wings. He needed to get answers. He wouldn't rest until he did. "The more I try to put the pieces of the case together, the more something still doesn't add up. Any luck locating the barback from the Wolf Tavern?"

"We found his last known address, but he hasn't been there for a while," Denopoulos said with a sigh.

"What about Maverick?"

"All the evidence has been sent to the Council. My guess is he'll be spending the rest of his days in Hellios."

Cayden sighed with relief. "Best news I've heard in a while."

"I think we should wrap up and call it a day, buddy." He could hear the exhaustion in his partner's voice and the frustration.

"Yeah, I suppose you're right." Cayden ran a hand through his hair. "We got something, but I was hoping for more. I wonder if Natalya recognizes anyone from the footage at the bar. She might've seen someone from her vantage point that you and I might've missed." He decided to shoot her a quick text and pulled out his phone.

Cayden: Any chance you can check out some video footage? Are you around today?

Natalya: Sure. I'm on the Upper East Side @ my family's place. Where are you?

Cayden: West 29th· There's something I need you to look at. Can I pick you up early?

Blood throbbed in his veins waiting for those three little dots to appear. He wanted to see her and finally take her in his arms.

Natalya: Yes. I'm sending the address.

Cayden: See you soon.

"You're texting Dubrosky now?" Denopoulos asked, pointing to his phone.

"It's about the case. What's the big deal?" His words belied the pounding of his heart. Anticipation coursed through his veins when he thought about meeting her later for lesson number two. After last night, the ball remained in her court. No one needed to know if they did decide to hook up. Mind-blowing sex might be the only thing to take away their pain and turn it into pleasure. He'd make sure they kept things on the down-low.

"It's okay to admit that you want to see her, dude." His partner smiled and gave him a pat on the back. "I've been there, my friend. But stick to your story if it makes you feel better."

Exhaling a pent-up breath, Cayden opened his door. *So much for keeping things on the down-low.*

CHAPTER 31

*O*oices drifted over the distinct notes of Chopin's *Nocturnes.* Natalya reclined on a velvet bench in her parent's living room with Tessa on one side of her, and a stack of charity brochures on the other. The scent of expensive perfume and roses, Eleanora's favorite, lingered in the air. The champagne flowed like blood at a guillotine.

The females from the committee mingled with the other volunteers, most of them decked out from head to toe in designer wear. Women in this group prided themselves on their grace and style.

Every now and then, one of the women would stare at Natalya with a curious expression on her face, fangs flashing, and then she'd simply look away. Some of these women had lived for centuries and still clung to arcane ideas like hierarchies and mating within their species, one of the many reasons these kinds of gatherings always made her nervous. Having an annulment marked her as damaged goods, and becoming a cop had put her on the fringes of this group even more.

She didn't have any interest in becoming the perfect wife and society maven then, and certainly not now. After a while, she stopped trying to blend in. Her decision to leave this life behind and never look back had been her best one yet, so why did their rejection still chafe?

Tessa must've picked up on her unease because she reached out and touched her arm. "Natalya? Are you okay?" She looked like the picture of class in a simple black sheath dress, one of her signature designs.

"Who me? I'm peachy, just peachy." Natalya needed to do something with her hands to keep them from shaking. She picked up a brochure and flipped through the contents, not able to process what she read, her thoughts diverted to the night ahead with Cayden.

Tessa eyed the brochure gripped in her hands. "If you say peachy one more time there's going to be paper everywhere and I don't think Eleanora will appreciate confetti on her Aubusson rugs." She removed the brochure from Natalya's clenched fingers. "Easy there. You look amazing by the way."

"All thanks to you." She wore a black lace bra and thong underneath her pantsuit. Every time she moved, the silky fabric brushed against her nipples. She'd been up half the night thinking about Cayden and still woke up flushed and aroused.

"What's going on?"

"I'll tell you everything when we're alone." Natalya smiled at a white-gloved waiter holding a silver tray of champagne flutes.

Thinking about having sex with Cayden filled her with a sense of excitement and ice-cold fear.

The waiter stopped in front of them. "Mimosa?"

"Yes, please. Thank you." Natalya reached for two flutes off the tray and handed one to Tessa. They clinked glasses.

"Drink up. I see Eleanora making her way over and she looks like a woman on a mission," Tessa whispered over the rim of her glass.

"Trust me, Eleanora's right in her element." Bouquets of roses in crystal vases adorned every table. The nineteenth-century Viennese chandelier above them glowed, illuminating the shine on the parquet floors. A fire sparked in one of the eight fireplaces.

The Dubroskys' had bought the three-story townhouse in 1940 and had it renovated to rival the New York City mansions from the Gilded Age. What would Cayden think of this vulgar display of wealth?

"Do you think she'll try and play matchmaker?" Tessa angled her head in Eleanora's direction, taking a sip from her glass.

"This is Eleanora we're talking about, need I say more?" She couldn't resist trying to meddle in Natalya's personal life. She meant well, but it left her feeling inadequate. "How are the dresses coming?" she asked, anxious to change the subject.

"It's an enormous task, but I'm thrilled to be doing it. I've focused on making the designs simple. I don't want to show too much skin." Tessa smiled. "There's something different about you and it's not just the hair and makeup. What's up?"

"I've been meaning to tell you." Butterflies fluttered around her belly. Natalya glanced around the room to make sure the ladies were engrossed enough in their own conversations that they wouldn't be listening to hers. "I've been spending a lot of time with Cayden and I'm thinking about sleeping with him. It would be a friends-with-bennies kind of arrangement." Under normal circumstances, she wouldn't even consider it if it weren't for her pending transfer to the SVU. If things went south, they could get awkward.

"Have you told him?" Tessa's gaze narrowed with concern.

Natalya's stomach tightened into knots. "No, not yet. I didn't see any reason to."

"Don't you think you should, especially if you're thinking about getting involved?"

Anxiety panged in Natalya's chest. "I will at some point, but it's not a conversation I'm looking forward to having."

"If you're even thinking about having sex with him, then you need to." Tessa's eyes clouded over. "I told Matt everything before we got intimate."

When Natalya thought about the sensual way Cayden kissed her, goosebumps broke out along her skin. "He gets me in a way no other guy ever has." How would she ever walk away unscathed? Her heart seemed to know the answer. She felt a connection to him like no else in her life. "I wouldn't know where to start."

Tessa gave her an encouraging smile. "Have you written your speech yet? It may help you find the words."

"No, I've been struggling to put my thoughts on paper." She'd never felt good enough, or accepted in this tight-knit little group. Natalya wanted to express how much she related to the pain and shame of the victims, but she'd promised to honor her family's wishes and keep her story a secret.

"I'm here if you need me."

"Thanks, you're the best." Natalya smiled and gulped the rest of her champagne. It didn't give her a buzz, but the bubbles managed to ease some of the tension she'd been carrying around.

"I hear Charles's new wife is here. She's now on the committee." Tessa turned to glance at a stunning blonde talking with a group of females in the corner. "I hope it won't be too weird for you."

"Charles and I are ancient history." After their annulment, she'd read about his elopement immediately afterward. She couldn't blame him for wanting to save face. Natalya, on the other hand, hadn't come out quite as unscathed.

Of course everyone assumed the deficiency had to be in her and not him. Something no one talked about in polite conversation. They all knew of her single status, something virtually unheard of in these circles. A female from a prominent, purebred vampire family was expected to find a mate or be ostracized from society. These rules bordered on the archaic and yet everyone still abided by them.

"I say to hell with rules and silly expectations," Tessa said, setting her glass on the table, and stealing two more flutes off a tray from a nearby waiter. They left her alone because of her success and the prestige that came with being a fashion designer.

"If anyone has any other expectations, they can shove them right up their Pilates-toned asses." Natalya downed the second glass of champagne.

Tessa laughed. "What's gotten into you?"

"My job and living with a group of powerful witches might have had something to do with it." Natalya set the flute on a tray and considered. "The friendship and camaraderie from the other women has been priceless."

"I'm glad you got some armor. You might need it today."

The conversation shifted to the event, and the topics ranged from corporate sponsors to silent auction items. The donations went toward rape kits, the distribution of information to victims, conferences, emotional support hotlines after reporting, and forensic exams.

"Natalya?" Eleanora emerged from the throng of women looking regal in a fitted gray suit with a broach of the family crest attached to her lapel. She kept her black hair pulled off her face in a tight chignon. She took one look at Natalya and froze, her mouth falling open, her fangs slipping out. "You look …"

"Different?"

A few heads turned in their direction.

"I was going to say lovely." Eleanora air-kissed her on both cheeks and did the same to Tessa. "I'd love to hear all about what brought on this magnificent transformation. All these years of me trying, what finally took?" she asked, arching her dark penciled brows.

"I did it for a case, and then it kind of stuck." Finally, after all these years, she'd started to feel comfortable in her own skin. Natalya could chalk it up to her budding relationship with Cayden, and from living at the manor with an empowered group of women. But deep down, she guessed it had more to do with a wellspring from within.

From the way Eleanora's lips thinned, she'd never approve of Natalya's job. She recovered by pressing her hands together and smiling "Frankly, this couldn't have come at a better time. I found a proper gentleman to escort you to the gala."

By gentleman, she meant someone from a wealthy, old vampire family. "Not here, Eleanora. We can talk about this later."

"It's only a few weeks away," Eleanora whispered, sounding annoyed.

Natalya's anger flared. When would she ever learn? "Excuse me," she mumbled to Tessa and the group of women around her, before rushing to her feet. "I need a moment of fresh air."

She walked into the study, past the leather couches and matching chairs, and exhaled the breath she'd been holding. Gold tone draperies adorned the windows and French doors. Crossing the room, she pushed them aside and turned the knob.

A hint of freesia perfumed the air. After Natalya stepped onto the balcony, she leaned her hand against the railing, soaking up the view of the garden, a place she used to escape to, her own little sanctuary. A springtime breeze blew across her face. She gazed out at the towering willows and the lush junipers and inhaled their fragrant scents.

She let herself bask in the quiet reprieve, needing a moment to herself when the loud rumble of an engine roared across the block. She spotted Cayden's muscle car, pulled out her phone, and dialed his number.

He answered on the first ring. "Talya," he whispered in his smoky voice. "I missed you." A hot spark shot to her belly.

The green and red hues of the garden became more vivid somehow. "Me too." Nothing about this felt casual anymore.

"Are you almost ready to go?"

Natalya could make a hasty escape and meet him out front. But Eleanora needed to know once and for all she couldn't run her life anymore. "I have a better idea. Why don't you come up?"

Silence filled the line.

"Cayden?" She didn't want to embarrass him in any way for the sake of making a point. But he was a big boy. He could handle himself with Eleanora. Maybe it was time to shake things up at the Dubrosky household.

"Are you sure that's such a great idea?"

"Frankly, I think it's the best one I've had all day. Come through the gate. I'll meet you in the hall." Natalya hung up and put her phone back in her pocket. The knot in her stomach loosened, replaced with giddy butterflies.

The patio door opened and closed. High heels scraped against the stone floor. She instantly recognized Tessa's flowery scent. Her friend walked up and stood next to her at the railing.

"I thought I'd come check up on you." Tessa eyed her with a curious expression, "What's with the goofy smile on your face? What are you up to, Natalya?"

The prospect of being alone with Cayden made her belly flutter with anticipation. "I'm doing what I want for a change. Eleanora, on the other hand, is about to get the surprise of her life."

Cayden pulled up to the corner of Lexington and East 64th Street behind a line of town cars that stretched halfway around the block. In one of these posh neighborhoods, he expected nothing less. From the lack of parking spots, it appeared something was going on here, and Natalya had failed to mention it.

He got out of the car, not bothering to lock his door. He doubted anyone in this neighborhood would steal a muscle car. As he made his way up the tree-lined block, he stopped outside a luxurious three-story town house with a black wrought iron gate.

Once he approached a set of fancy double doors, he pressed the buzzer. He glanced down at his worn jeans and the concert T-shirt he wore under his flannel, and made a face. He wasn't exactly dressed for a soiree. His hand trailed over the scruff along his chin. If he'd known he'd be invited inside, he would've at least managed to shave.

An older human male opened the door wearing a dark jacket and a frown. "You must be Mr. Teague."

"I'm here to see Talya, uh, Miss Dubrosky."

"She's expecting you." He glanced at Cayden's clothing and a curious expression appeared across his haggard face.

Cayden stepped inside the town house and wiped his boots on a mat. The butler led him across a black and white tiled floor into an enormous hallway. Glancing at his surroundings, he noted a fancy chaise lounge and a grouping of nude statues on a table. Luxury oozed from every corner of the room. He walked deeper into the hallway, stopped, and stared.

Murals that could rival the Guggenheim lined the walls. Cayden sucked in a breath at the collective opulence. The scent of expensive perfume and vampire floated in the air.

"I'll let Miss Dubrosky know you're here," the butler muttered and disappeared through the hall.

The hum of voices drifted through the room and Cayden wondered if Natalya had ever invited a demon into her home. Staring at the paintings reminded him of the watercolors from Arcadia. He'd scoured every corner of the planet searching for lost demon treasures, only to come up empty.

"Are you a fan of Keith Haring?" The soft lilt of Natalya's voice pulled him from his reverie.

Turning his head, Cayden caught her silhouette in the frame of the doorway. Seeing her standing against the backdrop of light and color left him a little breathless. "I've seen his work before at a local gallery. Mind you, I'd been undercover busting a drug smuggling ring at the time."

"It would be nice to check him out when you're not working. We could go sometime." She crossed into the hall. "I mean, if you want to."

A spotlight glowed above her head, accentuating the silky strands of her dark hair and the flecks of gold in her eyes. His gaze moved lower, devouring every inch of her with a single glance. He took in the outline of her breasts, the curve of her hips, and those shapely legs of hers encased in a pair of dress slacks. He couldn't look away. From his vantage point, not an inch of skin showed. She reminded him of a forbidden fruit he wanted to savor.

"I appreciate pop art as much as the next guy. I'm certainly no connoisseur. But I know beauty when I see it. You look gorgeous." Her exotic strawberry scent flared in his nostrils. A jolt of unexpected lust pooled to his groin. He couldn't stop his body's instant reaction to her if he tried.

Her eyes warmed as she took a step closer. "I never took you for a sweet talker. We've come a long way from all the bickering back and forth."

"I think we can chalk it up to six long months of foreplay." Last night he'd been so caught up in this insatiable need to please her and fulfill every one of her desires, that he hadn't taken the time to think about the repercussions of what they were about to do.

"You said you had something to show me."

"I have hours of video footage from the cigar shop and the bar. I thought we could go someplace quiet and go through it together. See if you recognize anyone."

"Of course."

Motioning to her outfit, Cayden hoped he wasn't busting up a private party. "What's the occasion?"

"It's a charity meeting. This is what females in my circles do when we're not shopping and going to lunch," she said with more than a healthy dose of sarcasm.

"Hey, I might like to give you a hard time, but I'd never try to minimize what you do for those in need."

"Thank you." Natalya swallowed and turned her head. From the change in her body language and her breathing, she was hiding something. A part of him wanted to find out what and the other part of him didn't want to push.

"Do we have a visitor?" A tall, well-dressed female who appeared to be in her late fifties walked into the hall. She took one look at Cayden and froze. "Natalya?"

"Eleanora, I'd like to you to meet Cayden Teague." Natalya turned in her direction. "We work together."

Why did her scrutinizing gaze make him feel like a warrior gearing up for battle? Cayden took a step closer and extended his hand. "It's nice to meet you, Mrs. Dubrosky. I've heard a lot about you from Natalya."

Eleanora had to be an expert at social niceties because she recovered with a tight smile as she shook his hand. "Funny, I've heard nothing about you, Mr. Teague, but then again Natalya doesn't tell me much."

When he glanced over at Natalya, her spine visibly stiffened. "On second thought, I think we should go. Please say my goodbyes to the others." She reached for a small purse off the table and pulled the strap across her body.

"What's the rush?" Eleanora took a step closer. "Do you work as a police officer, Mr. Teague?"

"No, but I'm in a branch of law enforcement," Cayden confirmed, crossing his arms over his chest.

"You can imagine our shock when Natalya announced she was joining the police academy. With all due respect, it's not something we do in our circles." Eleanora drew her perfectly shaped brows together. "You must have observed Natalya in the field. I'd love to hear an objective point of view."

When he glanced over at Natalya, her face fell. "You don't have to answer that, Cayden."

Talk about being put on the spot. "No, but I will." Cayden inclined his head to Eleanora. "Natalya makes a difference every day. She leads with her heart. She genuinely cares about the people she's helping. She's brave and stubborn." He smiled. "A little unwavering at times, but frankly those are the best skills you can have on the job. I've been in law enforcement for over fifty years in one capacity or another, and I've never seen someone who stands out like she does. She's special. The RHPD's lucky to have her."

This time when he looked over at Natalya, an expression of pure joy crossed her face. "Wow, I don't know what to say except thank you."

Eleanora cleared her throat. "Well then, there's my answer. Why don't you come in and have a glass of champagne? I'm sure our other guests would love to meet one of Natalya's friends."

He'd never been one to back down from a challenge. The offer made him long for a glass of Johnnie with his name on it. He shook off the temptation in favor of keeping his wits about him. "I'd love some coffee if you have any."

"Are you sure?" Natalya whispered, her eyes grew wide with apprehension.

"I'm sure."

Eleanora led them through the hall, her heels click-clacking across the tile floor. They entered a large sitting area where a group of well-dressed female vampires were gathered. The room fell silent as he walked in. Some of the women sniffed the air and frowned, probably not used to hobnobbing with a demon.

They gazed at him with various expressions of shock across their faces. No one said a word, but he could feel the tension in the air. You could cut it with one of their stilettos. He did his best to ignore their stares, turning his head to more artwork lining the walls. He walked under the curved arches, taking in the grandeur of the place, and noting the differences in their homes. While Natalya spent her time here, living in the lap of luxury, he'd been turned into a slave, forced to live in a tent with a sand floor and a slab of stone for a bed. Swallowing hard, he shook off the pettiness and resentment coursing through his veins like a toxin, and focused on staying in the moment.

"Come with me." Natalya pulled him through another hall, even larger than the last one. The moment they left the room, it began to buzz with chatter. They walked into an alcove. She pressed her finger to a button on the wall and it opened to a secret passage with an antique-looking desk, chair, and a computer.

"Is this your office?"

"No, Pavel's. Don't worry. No one can hear us. He made this vestibule soundproof for his meetings. He wanted to make sure no one could pick up on any of his business dealings when Eleanora entertained. I'm sorry she put you on the spot. She can't help herself." Regret pulled at her features. "We don't have to stay. We can leave right now."

"First off, why don't you tell me why I'm here? I could've waited outside. Why did you want me to come up?" Cayden didn't know what he'd been thinking stepping into the Dubrosky digs. He was in over his head, out of his league, and clearly out of his damn mind. He should get out before things got messy, but he hesitated, torn by what he wanted and what he should do.

Hurt flickered in her eyes and stabbed him in the gut. "Please, let me explain. I didn't invite you up here to embarrass you. It's the last thing I'd ever want to do." The sincerity in her voice softened the crux of his anger. "Maybe I did want to prove a point, but not at your expense." She got up on her tiptoes and placed her slender hand to his chest.

A spark turned into a slow simmer as her warm hand caressed him through his shirt. Irritated and wanting to stay that way for the moment, he took a step back.

"What did you think would happen? Do you see me sipping Bellinis with your family and some of the Upper East Side's vampire-elite? I can't help but think this is some kind of test. Or a way to get back at them."

"They have nothing to do with this."

"I'm sorry." He sighed deep, immediately regretting his words. "I didn't mean to be callous. But I had to see your reaction to know I'm not some kind of social experiment."

"Of course not. I want you to know the truth about me, Cayden, the real me." She motioned to her surroundings with a sweep of her hand. "This might be where I came from, but this isn't who I am. It never was. All this privilege never felt like mine to begin with, maybe because I wasn't born into it."

"What would your family think if we got together?" Cayden sat on the edge of the desk to make them eye level.

"I don't care what anyone thinks. You asked me before if I was trying to prove something to my family and the answer is no. I'm trying to prove something to you." Her voice cracked on the last part and it made his gut twist. "I'm sorry. I didn't mean to make you uncomfortable."

This woman who stood before him, part warrior, part goddess, took all his preconceived notions and threw them out the window.

"Cayden?" The uncertainty in her eyes gutted him.

His anger melted away. She didn't need his wrath. She needed his acceptance. "You're forgiven. You want to exchange truths, fine by me, let's exchange truths. Why do you let Eleanora intimidate you?"

"Whoa, don't beat around the bush."

"I'm sorry. I'm not trying to be flippant." Reaching out, he ran a hand through her hair.

"I'm working on changing our dysfunctional dynamic." Pain flicked in her eyes. "I can't believe I'm going to say this, but I still feel like I've never quite measured up." The rawness of her confession made him swallow hard and warmed an icy part of his soul.

"You do measure up, Talya, in every way possible, in every way that counts. Your kindness and sincerity draw people in and put them at ease. I've seen it firsthand. It's what makes you so special. But it's also your heart." Pulling her to his chest, he hugged her close, wrapping his arms around her waist, inhaling her sweet scent. The feel of her in his arms felt so right.

When Natalya pulled away, a breathtaking smile spread across her face. "I can be myself around you."

"That makes two of us. You blossom like a flower when you smile." Cayden moved his thumb across her bottom lip.

Those big, beautiful eyes swam with tears. "You see me like no one else ever has."

"Don't cry. I owe you an apology for giving you a hard time in the beginning, and for being an arrogant jerk. But there were reasons behind the teasing."

"Such as?"

"I'll tell you one of these days." He tilted her chin up with his thumb. "Since we've partnered up, you've forced me to up my game and work harder and be better."

"Likewise. I've never worked with anyone with your bravery or sense of honor. I misjudged you."

These confessions gave him hope. "Are you ready for another truth?"

When she nodded, he whispered close to her ear, "Last night, after you left my apartment, do you want to know what I did with your scent still in my nostrils and the taste of you still on my lips? I'll give you a hint. I pleasured myself all night long."

"Cayden." Her chest rose and fell from the admission.

The passion she showed him made him wonder now more than ever the real reason behind her lack of sexual experience. "Now I've gone and scandalized you. If you were hoping for sonnets and love poems, then you have the wrong guy."

"I just need you," she whispered, pressing into his body.

Thinking about all the things he wanted to do to her stirred the demon inside of him. He pulled away to look at the slim column of her neck. The urge to mark her flesh became overwhelming. He had zero claims on her and intended to keep it that way so things didn't get complicated. He closed his eyes against the onslaught of lust and moved his thumb to her bottom lip. "All I can think about is making you come."

Her strangled moan got his heart hammering in his chest. A mixture of desire and uncertainty flashed in her eyes. "Show me, Cayden, please."

He didn't need to be asked twice. Moving his hand to the back of her neck, he tilted his head to the side and covered her mouth with his. He licked at her bottom lip, teasing at first, turning his ardor into the soft whisper of a kiss. Holding her face in his hands, he took his time, learning her mouth. His fingers brushed across her cheek as their breath mingled together.

Groaning, he flicked his tongue into her mouth to get a thorough taste. The kiss grew hotter and more intense sending a rush of heat to his groin. When her fingers plunged into his hair, he switched their positions so his head leaned against the wall, letting her take the lead.

Soft breathy sounds fell from her lips and called to his demon. Her breasts brushed up against his chest in the most tantalizing way. His cock swelled against his jeans. He wanted to rub up against her lush little body, but he didn't want to scare her away, recalling her reaction the last time.

She met his ardor stroke for stroke, kissing him back with lush sweeps of her tongue. Her fangs brushed against his lips and he growled at the sensation. His hand moved under her jacket, to caress a patch of silky, bare skin. He wanted to learn every sensual curve of her body. *Take it slow*, he reminded himself.

Gripping her hip, his fingers massaged her through her slacks. The sweet scent of her arousal flared in his nostrils. His erection throbbed against his jeans. He wanted to lift her up and feel her legs wrapped around him. He'd press his cock against her wet heat and make her scream with pleasure, but he held back, refusing to dry hump her at her parent's house.

It took every ounce of willpower to pull back. He cursed under his breath and pressed his forehead to hers, panting hard. "We need to stop. We can't do this here."

Her eyes popped open, still drowsy with lust. "I know." She glanced at the door that led to the hall. "Eleanora will have a search party looking for us," she joked, breaking the tension.

"Uh, I'll need at least a minute." Cayden motioned to the bulge in his jeans. He didn't want to leave their bubble. This connection was developing fast and deep between them.

"Oh right." Her gaze trailed over him, and this time her eyes filled with wonder instead of fear. They were making progress.

He took in the red marks on her chin from the scratch of his beard and the smudged lip gloss at the corner of her mouth and guilt slid in his belly. Brushing his finger to the corner of her lip, he wiped the last remnants away. "It's probably best not to look like you've just been ravaged before facing everyone again."

"Who says we have to? Let's sneak out before anyone sees us."

"And solidify whatever negative impression Eleanora might have of me? I don't think so." He wasn't about to let some society matron chase him out with his tail between his legs.

"You don't need to prove anything."

"I've got a backbone. I'll go in there and show my face." He refused to negotiate when it came to proving his worth as a male. And despite their past history, maybe a small part of him wanted to prove to himself that he was worthy of Natalya. He let his job define him, but sometimes loneliness would sneak in through the cracks of his heart. She'd managed to fill them in with her warmth and her beauty.

"Fine, I'll say my goodbyes, and then we're out of here." She ran a hand through her hair.

"Deal. I want to be alone with you." He'd take things at her pace, even though his cock ached and his balls throbbed.

"Yeah? Me too." After she straightened her jacket, she reached into her purse and pulled out an old-fashioned compact mirror. She opened the top and the glass inside glowed bright like a crystal. She brushed some powder over her chin.

"Nice mirror. It reminds me of a looking glass."

"It's my most prized possession. It belonged to my aunt. She was a clairvoyant. People came from all over to get a reading with her. Willow replaced the glass so I can use it as a scrying mirror."

"A scrying mirror? I'm not following." Cayden tucked his shirt in his jeans.

"I've been having visions. I keep seeing one in particular, of a woman who I believe is in danger." A line of tension formed between her dark brows, and he got the feeling she'd been carrying this around for a while now.

"Strange things tend to happen to anyone who spends time with the witches from the coven, but a vampire practicing witchcraft?" Cayden shook his head. "Now that's a new one."

"I'll explain everything, but not here." Natalya shoved the mirror in her purse. "I'm supposed to meet up with Denopoulos so he can generate a picture through his face recognition technology."

"You never mentioned it. What do you think it means? Hold on, do you think this vision of yours has something to do with Andee's killer?"

She shrugged her slender shoulders. "I don't know, but I can't help but think …" A noise outside the door made her spin around. "We should go." Her gaze cut to his. "Are you ready?"

"I'm right behind you." He followed her through the hall, doing his best to smooth down his hair. They walked into a living room where a cluster of well-heeled women in fancy dresses lounged on silk sofas and chairs. When a few of them turned and glanced in his direction, their eyes filled with ice. Cayden could practically feel the temperature in the room drop.

An attractive female with short, dark hair walked over and glanced up at him with a warm smile. "You must be Cayden. It's nice to finally meet you. I'm Tessa, the official best friend." She shook his hand.

Tessa turned to Natalya and whispered, "You've been holding out on me."

Natalya shot her a look. "Tessa."

So she's been talking about me to her friend. Interesting.

"You're a metal fan?" Tessa pointed to his T-shirt.

"Tried and true, and apparently you're the ice-breaker," Cayden said with a chuckle. Aside from Eleanora, she was the only one in this group with the cajones to speak to him.

They talked for a few minutes about some of their favorite bands and commiserated on how much music had changed over the years. The conversation flowed and Cayden understood how Natalya would be drawn to someone with Tessa's cool, laid-back vibe.

"Eleanora sent me to find you two. I should let you go." Tessa angled her head to the hall. "The grand dame's waiting for you two in the kitchen."

Tessa walked over and pulled Natalya into a hug. "I'm headed out. Good luck. And by the way, I like him."

Cayden waited until Tessa walked away and then bent his head and whispered close to her ear, "You've been talking about me to your friends?" He wouldn't dare tell her how much he liked the idea.

"I think you misunderstand."

Reaching out, he brushed his fingers across her hand, needing to remind her of their connection. "I want you to know I do see the real you. And from where I'm standing, I see a strong, intelligent woman."

"Cayden." Joy blossomed across her face.

"I like making you smile. Your whole face lights up when you do." He motioned for her to walk in front of him, giving him the perfect view of her shapely ass. By the time they made their way into the kitchen, his cock twitched. He couldn't wait to get her to open up to him more, find out what had spooked her the other morning.

Cayden whistled as they crossed the threshold into the kitchen. "This is easily the size of my first apartment." White marble surfaces and commercial grade appliances gleamed under the shine of numerous chandeliers. The scent of coffee and roses wafted through the air.

Eleanora stood at the island with a pinched expression on her face. "I wondered what happened to you two. May I speak to you for a moment alone, Natalya?" The older woman's eyes shot daggers across the room. "It will only take a moment."

"Don't worry, Natalya, I'll be fine." Cayden walked over to the coffee urn. "I'll just help myself."

"I'll be right back," Natalya whispered, and blurred away with Eleanora at her side.

Reaching for a mug off the counter, a colorful brochure next to the sugar bowl caught his eye. He read the words emblazoned across the top. *SAAN Charity Gala.* He'd heard that name before, but where? He read on. When he scanned the words, "sexual abuse assistance network," he froze. It felt like he'd been punched in the gut.

A dark and disturbing insight took hold of him by the throat. All the pieces suddenly fit together, Natalya's desire to work for the SVU, dressing to hide her body. This wasn't simply a case of her living a sheltered life, or some guy smearing her name. No. The reason she had almost no experience with men was because she'd been abused.

His vision swam. Rage twisted his insides. Digging his fingers into his palm, he concentrated on keeping his demon from emerging. He breathed deeply through his nose, refusing to turn into a beast in front of this group of women.

Why didn't she tell him before she'd allowed him to put his hands on her? If he demanded answers she might shut down. His need to comfort her overtook his torment. He walked through halls, darting into empty rooms. In his desperate search to find her, he realized he needed to wait until she was ready to tell him the truth, and find a way to gain her trust in the meantime. He'd be there to listen and comfort her when she did.

Cayden stopped outside a closed door when he picked up the hum of voices.

"How could you invite a roughneck in a T-shirt here? A demon of all things?" Eleanora demanded. "You disappeared with him and embarrassed me in my own home."

"I'm sorry, Eleanora, but I needed a moment to breathe."

"You belong with a gentleman. He seems pleasant enough, but he's not what we want for you. He's not a part of our world."

"This isn't about what you want. You tried to run my life and we both know how that turned out." The humiliation in Natalya's voice twisted Cayden's gut. "You see me as a failure because I chose not to follow your path, but it's my life, my choices to make."

"We only want what's best for you," Eleanora whispered. "You should've been thrilled a fine gentleman like Charles wanted to marry you, but you burned that bridge. As for your demon, you're only using him as a pawn to get back at us."

"You're wrong. You're the only one who plays chess with people's lives. Congratulations, Eleanora, I'm all checkmated out. Cayden's kind and caring. He's more of a gentleman than Charles will ever be."

Natalya's words ignited an unexpected surge of emotions in the center of Cayden's chest. Somewhere along the way she'd started to believe in him. Now he finally understood why she'd brought him here, not to prove a point. She needed an ally besides Tessa.

"If you walk out that door with him and disrespect us in front of everyone, then perhaps we shouldn't see each other for a while," Eleanora warned.

His adrenaline spiked. He'd heard enough. Cayden hated threats. Opening the door, he stormed into the room.

Two sets of eyes darted to his.

"Cayden?" Natalya froze.

After he made his way over to Natalya's side, put his arm around Natalya's shoulders and squeezed. "I think it's time to go. I'm ready whenever you are."

Eleanora looked shell-shocked, but she remained silent, apparently at a loss for words.

"I couldn't agree more." Natalya looked up at him with a grateful smile, and then turned to Eleanora. "I'll see you at the gala."

She led him out of the room and into the hall. "How much did you hear?" The hitch in her voice tore at his heart.

"Enough." *It was more about what I read in that brochure.* "And here I thought this kind of gathering would be dull. Boy was I wrong." He cracked a smile, trying to lighten the mood. Needing to touch her, he placed a hand at the small of her back as they walked to the front of the house. He looked straight ahead to avoid the gaggle of prying eyes.

"No one's ever stuck up for me like that before." Her fingers laced with his and sent warm tingles along his arm.

"Get used to it. Let's go somewhere we can be alone." Cayden reached for her hand, and tangled their fingers together.

Her face broke out in a smile. "That's the best idea I've heard all day."

CHAPTER 32

They walked out the front door and descended the steps to the sidewalk. Natalya exhaled in a rush, trying to push the episode with Eleanora to the back of her mind.

"Do you want to talk about what happened in there?" Cayden asked, keeping stride beside her. "Are you okay?" He lifted their joined hands and placed a kiss on her fingertips. She wanted to lose herself in the affectionate gesture and forget all about what just took place, but Eleanora's ugly words still tugged at her insides.

"Maybe later." She sucked in a breath and blew it out. Her mind reeled in twenty different directions. "I'm sorry you overheard us. I should've never brought you here."

"We shouldn't let it ruin our night." His lip curled into a smile but she could see the tension in his broad shoulders. He opened the car door for her, and reached for her hand. "Think about it this way, at least now we know where everyone stands."

"Good point." But where did *they* stand? The question burned on her lips. But why ask when she didn't know herself? "Subtlety never was Eleanora's strong suit." She got in and then adjusted the seatbelt across her lap, anxious to get the hell out of there.

Cayden shut her door and came around to the driver's side. While he maneuvered his enormous body into his seat, his horns skimmed the roof of the car. His profile caught in the shadow, accentuating his strong jaw and the sensual curve of his lips. "Let's put it behind us." Reaching for her hand, he placed another kiss on the inside of her palm. Her skin warmed from the brush of his tongue. "Where do you want to go?"

"Just drive, please. In spite of all the drama, something wonderful came out of this. In time, my family might start to see my job as more than some kind of latent rebellion thanks to you." They'd turned a page. His sincere words made her feel worthy of the badge.

Natalya had heard the stories about his boozing and brawling. She'd overheard Garrett rave over his dedication to the job, his brilliance when it came to cracking a case and his unwavering loyalty to his friends. She'd never realized he valued humility and honesty, everything she'd ever wanted in a partner. *Whoa, where the hell did that come from?* She'd seen a different side to him, a soft, gooey middle beneath the hard shell.

Revving the engine, he peeled down the street at breakneck speed, leaving a plume of smoke and the smell of burned rubber in his wake.

Her head fell against the headrest. "Whoa, I've never been in a car this fast."

"She can go up to a hundred-thirty in a quarter mile." Cayden slid his fingers across the dashboard. "She's growing on you, isn't she?" Turning on the radio, he cranked up the volume of heavy metal music over the honk of horns and the blare of traffic.

"I can see how much you love this car. I'm sorry for referring to it as a phallic symbol."

"I do believe you said, and I quote, 'It's probably an attempt to compensate for something small.'"

Her gaze trailed over his crotch to the sizeable bulge in his jeans. Nothing about the demon appeared small. "It was juvenile of me."

"Not to mention untrue." When Cayden glanced over at her, heat and humor blazed in his eyes. "Sorry, bad joke. Apology accepted, but as I recall, I gave as good as I got."

"You were a worthy adversary." Traffic came to halt and the vibration of the car got her to relax. Natalya admired the way he drummed his long, tapered fingers on the steering wheel.

"Will you do something for me?"

"What did you have in mind?"

"Crank down the window and stick your head out. It's a total rush." He reached out and caressed her knee. "Trust me."

She did as he suggested and breathed in a lungful of warm spring air. A sense of exhilaration pulsed through her as wind whipped around her face and blew her hair in every direction. After a few minutes, she stuck her head back in and smiled. "You're right. The fresh air cleared my head. I couldn't wait to get out of there."

"I can understand why. Aside from Tessa, that group's a lot to handle. No wonder you came looking for me."

"What do you mean I came looking for you?"

Cayden held up his hand. "I'm just making an observation."

"Any others?"

"Yeah, as a matter of fact. The way you defended me to Eleanora surprised the hell out of me, and for someone who's lived as long as I have, I don't surprise easily. Did you mean what you said?"

The scent of his cologne and the husky sound of his voice drew her in like a magnet, pulling her closer. "Yes, every word." He somehow managed to make her feel supported and understood. "You surprise me too." But could she keep things casual without getting her heart involved? She glanced out the window to the fields beyond the tree line and her whole body tensed. "Where are you going?"

"I'm taking a short cut to the tunnel." Cayden cut across West 71st Street and traffic came to a grinding halt outside the entrance to Central Park. "We might be here for a while."

Dark memories flashed. She never imagined that the guy next door could be such a monster. Looking back, he'd always been troubled and got some kind of sick pleasure from tormenting her.

Have you ever played the rape game? Her stomach twisted with revulsion thinking about it now.

"Natalya? What's wrong? You've gone pale." The note of alarm in Cayden's voice forced her gaze to his.

"Nothing. It's just weird being here." No matter how hard she tried to force the memories to the back of her mind, sometimes they reared their ugly heads like venomous snakes.

Finally, traffic eased up. When they shot through the tunnel, she began to relax. They passed the sign for Raven's Hollow and she got an idea.

"Can you cut across Willow Avenue to Madison Street? There's something I want to show you."

Pushing her key into the lock, Natalya turned the knob to open her door. The scents of fresh paint and polyurethane mingled together and hung heavy in the air. She glanced at Cayden over her shoulder. "I'm sorry if coming back to Andees's building is painful for you. I haven't shown anyone my place yet, and I wanted you to be the first."

"I'm honored." Cayden followed her inside, his heavy footsteps trailing behind her into the hallway.

Natalya walked across the newly polished floor, surprised to find no squeaks in the floorboards. She set her keys on the counter, and turned to face him.

"I haven't been here since the murder." He ran a hand through his hair and sighed.

"I'm sorry, Cayden." Thinking about how he must be feeling made her heart ache. She lit a candle and the fresh scent of evergreens filled the air, calming her frayed nerves. "If Maverick's not our killer, then who is?"

"We can link Maverick to the rapes, not to the murder," he said with a shake of his head. "I have a few theories I'm batting around, but I don't want to share them until I have something concrete."

In this light, the dark smudges under his eyes became more pronounced. She couldn't bear to see the toll this case had taken on him. As much a she wanted to press him on his theories, she decided to hold off for now.

Cayden glanced around the empty space, and it became clear he wanted to change the subject. "Nice place."

Natalya followed his gaze to the open kitchen that led to a small living room and the boxes lined up against the wall. Several paint cans sat on the counter. "It's old and still needs a lot of work, but it's mine." Craning her neck, she looked up at his face, trying to gauge his reaction.

"I learned about renovations when Alex and I went undercover as part of the construction crew at the manor." Cayden turned in a circle, nodding his approval. "I can see this place has great bones."

"Yeah, I think so too." His praise lightened her mood, wiping away the scene from earlier. She angled her head to his phone now clutched in his hands. "You have some feed to show me?"

He nodded. "Let's get this over with."

At first, the black and white, grainy images didn't ring any bells. After about an hour of hitting pause several times, the mannerisms of one guy walking away from Andee's door sparked her memory. Natalya pointed at the screen. "Something about him seems familiar."

"Do you recall seeing him at the bar?" Cayden replayed the feed several times until her head began to spin.

She rubbed her temples, feeling the start of a headache. "I can't put my finger on it, but I've seen him before."

"Let's take a break. My eyes are starting to bug out." Taking off his holster, he set it on the counter along with his phone.

"I'm sorry it still smells like paint in here." Turning, she walked to the window and wrenched it open. Fresh air wafted into the room. When Cayden came up behind her, she could detect the fast beat of his heart and the blood rushing hot through his veins. Drinking blood wasn't something she craved anymore, not since the early days of her transition, but she imagined his would taste rich and bold.

"The only thing I smell is you," he whispered close to her ear. Blood rose to the surface of her skin. The air became thick with electricity. He moved closer still, his warm breath fanning her neck, and her body responded, tingling all over.

"There's something I want to talk to you about." She wanted to mend the broken pieces of her life once and for all.

"I'm listening." He moved his hands to her shoulders and turned her around. The concern in his eyes hurt more than the words still stuck in her throat.

Tears burned and threatened to fall. She swallowed hard, misery lodged deep in her throat. Her body wanted to move forward, but her mind still lingered on the past. Letting go opened the door to the possibility of more frustration and disappointment. The damn flood gates opened up and a sob escaped from her throat. "Maybe I'm more messed up than I thought."

"Talya. Don't cry. I can't bear to see it." He stroked her hair with such tenderness it made the lock around her heart burst open.

"I haven't been totally honest with you." The need to come clean and tell him the truth outweighed the risk of revealing the most traumatic event of her life and having him look at her with pity in his eyes instead of awe.

"Go on." He caressed her cheek, and she leaned into his touch. She'd never been this attracted to someone, and yet she held back.

"The reason I can't have an orgasm in front of another person is the same reason I'm inexperienced in bed. When you asked me why I seemed to hide under my clothing it's because I never felt comfortable showing that side of myself."

"You're beautiful. You always were." He ran his knuckles along her chin.

"You're the first person who has made me feel beautiful." She smiled through her tears. "I never felt like I could please my sired family. At a certain point I gave up trying. I don't want to sound like I'm blaming them. I'm not. I've worked through a lot of these issues in therapy."

"Thank you for trusting me with your secrets. I know it must be hard to talk about." Cayden kissed both of her cheeks and she melted. "You can trust me, Talya. I'd never judge you."

"Okay, but there's something weighing on me—something I need to address before we go any further. We're a complete mismatch, sexually speaking." She swatted away her tears. "You're used to women with experience, and I have none."

"I don't care about your lack of experience, and if a man would leave you over it, then he's not worth your time." When his gaze met hers, she inhaled sharply at the raw need in their depths. "You're naturally sensual."

The emotion in his beautiful words forced another wave of fresh tears. "What I'm trying to say, the reason I'm like this is ... I was sexually assaulted."

Hot fury burned in his eyes. For a split second his body went rigid, and then he pulled her into his arms. "Shh, come here." He stroked her hair while tears splashed to her cheeks. "It's okay. I've got you, baby." The words wound through her heart like a thread. "I'm sorry. I'm so sorry."

"It happened a long time ago, but it really screwed with my head." Her body shook with the revelation. Resting her head against the hard wall of his chest, she sobbed into his T-shirt.

"Talya, my Talya," he soothed with such torment in his voice, an icy pain stabbed at her chest from the weight of it. After a few minutes, the tears finally began to subside. "I figured it out. I read the charity brochure."

"What?" Her stomach knotted. "Why didn't you say something?" She tried to pull away, but he held tight.

"I needed you to say it first," he whispered against her hair and brushed a kiss on her temple. "I needed you to trust me. Please, don't be mad."

She took a deep, calming breath. "I'm not mad. I appreciate you giving me space. In all the other areas of my life I'm good, but when it comes to sex, the memories are still twisted up inside of me. I guess this case brought everything to a head. In some ways it's been a real kick in the ass, and in some, it's been like a living breathing nightmare coming back to haunt me. But you've been the one bright spot in it all."

"You've been my bright spot too, baby. What can I do?" he rasped against her ear.

"You can help me forget. Won't you?" She couldn't stand to be broken anymore. Deep in her soul, she sensed Cayden could make her whole again. Her feelings for him overwhelmed the painful memories and gave her hope.

"Yes …" The word came out as a frantic groan. Pulling back, he gazed into her eyes and wiped her smeared mascara with his thumbs, now black with her tears. "If only I'd known." His eyes filled with regret. "All those times I teased you and gave you shit."

"I wouldn't have had it any other way. I couldn't bear the thought of you treating me with kid gloves."

He pushed her hair off her forehead. "I won't hurt you." She knew he'd never hurt a woman, at least not physically. He might be a giant on the outside, but inside he was a big teddy bear. "You tell me to stop and I will. You take the lead."

"I want to be with you, Cayden. I'd invite you into my bedroom, but I don't have a bed yet. My furniture's getting delivered next week. I hadn't thought that far ahead. I've wasted so much time. I don't want to waste anymore."

"There must be something we can use around here to get comfortable," he said, glancing around the empty apartment.

"Hold on." Natalya went to one of the boxes marked 'towels and blankets.' She dug around until she found a throw and pillows. She pulled them out. "How's this?"

His hot gaze burned into hers. "Perfect." He helped her move everything to the center of the room. Together, they spread out the blanket and laid the pillows on top.

"We haven't talked about being with other people." She smiled over the wild thump of her pulse. She'd never ached for a man like this before. "I wanted to ask if you're seeing anyone."

"No, and I have no plans to."

Her stomach somersaulted. "What now?" She took a tentative step closer and her breasts brushed against his chest.

Tilting his head, he sniffed her neck. "I want to touch every inch of you." He trailed warm fingers along her ribcage, to her waist. "Are you able to come by yourself?" The question sent a wave of heat through her body.

"Yes, I think about you when I do." Her skin tingled with the admission. At this point it made no sense to hold back. "I've never had a healthy romantic relationship." This didn't feel like a practice run. It felt like the real thing.

"I've been masturbating to you for months. All the damn time." Cayden lifted his head and looked her in the eyes. His had turned dark, almost molten. His hands moved to her ass and gave a little squeeze. "You're killing me right now." He slipped off his boots and flannel jacket, revealing his broad shoulders encased in a worn black T-shirt. He sat on the blanket and patted the space next to him. "We take things slow and go from there."

Her heart pounded in anticipation. A million thoughts jumbled together. Did she remember to shave her legs, and did her bra match her panties? After she kicked off her heels and shoved them in the corner, her jacket came next. She slipped it off, leaving her in a sheer white V-neck. She laid the jacket on the counter next to her keys.

"I want to touch you, but I won't." He kept his hands at his sides. The pleading note in his voice made her skin flush with a mist of perspiration. No man had ever looked at her with such heat in his eyes. "Why don't you change into something more comfortable? Do you have any clothes here?"

"I plan on moving in some things next week. I ..." Her words got caught in her throat when he slipped his shirt over his head. Swallowing hard, she stared at his chest. Even though she'd seen him before, she didn't think she'd ever get used to all those sculpted muscles. She swore her skin caught fire.

"Why don't you put this on?" He handed her his shirt and smiled. "On you it will fit more like a dress."

"Thanks." A pang of nerves and excitement took hold. She ducked into the bathroom and changed, not bothering to turn on the light. His scent flared in her nostrils, putting her at ease. After she hung her pants and blouse over the towel bar, she turned and glanced at her reflection in the mirror. She sucked in a breath at her black, tear-streaked cheeks. She washed her face and dried it with her only towel. Taking a deep breath, she came out of the bathroom and resumed her place next to him on the blanket.

"Better?" Cayden eyed his shirt, now hanging to her knees.

"Much." She wanted him with a single intensity that frightened and exhilarated her all at once. What if she disappointed him?

Desire burned in his gaze as it trailed over her, settling on her breasts. Heat burned through the thin layer of cotton and snaked over her nipples like a fuse. "I'll take it easy. I promise. I can do this slow, even it kills me."

"Kiss me, Cayden." She didn't want to think. She only wanted to feel.

His lips brushed hers once, twice. When he licked along her lower lip, she moaned and tilted her head to the side to deepen the kiss. He stroked his tongue into her mouth, teasing at first. He tasted like cinnamon and sugar, sweet and decadent, just like his kisses.

She dug her fingers into his shoulders, silently begging for more. She realized, as her body stirred and flamed to life, this was what she'd been missing out on.

A low masculine groan rumbled out of him and made her belly clench with need. Every stroke of his tongue infused her senses with his wild taste. Moving her hands to twine around his neck, she pressed her breasts against the hard wall of his chest.

Every touch and kiss made her shiver with pleasure. She'd never experienced this kind of burning desire before and she didn't want it to end. His scruff brushed against her jaw, and tickled her cheeks.

His hands moved alongside her ribs to the underside of her breasts. His warm touch became sensual torture as he explored patches of her bare skin. He took his time while she felt like she might combust at any second.

He pulled away and trailed open-mouthed kisses down her neck. Brushing her hair away from her face, heat and reverence sparked in his gaze. "You're beautiful and so brave. Tell me to stop and I will."

His words made her melt. "Don't stop."

"Talya." The endearment sounded sweet on his lips. He guided her down on the blanket and moved onto his side. The press of his erection against her thigh set off a fire alarm inside her body.

"Touch me," she murmured.

This time when he claimed her lips, she could feel the urgency behind the kiss. He cupped her breast through the thin layer of cotton while his finger brushed her nipple in lazy, teasing strokes. He broke the kiss and rubbed his thumb across her lips. "I want to make you feel good."

She had no doubt he could from the skill in his kisses. "Cayden."

"Is this okay? Am I going too fast?"

"It's more than okay." Heat pooled at her thighs.

Her attention dropped to the thick ridge of his erection, heavy and insistent between them. She licked her lips.

"I need you." He ran his fingers through her hair.

"I want to ... but ..." She glanced at the outline of his cock and swallowed hard. She wanted to learn every ridge of his body, but not knowing what to do, her hands stilled at her sides.

"But what? I promise *he* won't bite." Mischief sparked in his eyes. Cayden glanced at himself with a quirk of his lips. "Although he does tend to have a mind of his own."

She burst into a fit of nervous giggles. "Only you could make me laugh at a time like this." His humor broke through the awkward tension and put her at ease.

"I'll do whatever it takes to see you smile."

"Well, for starters, I'd like to see what *he* likes." She rubbed her hand over the denim, and a hiss of pleasure fell from his lips. She'd waited most of her adult life to do this. How had she gone all these years without experiencing something so erotic? She wanted to take in each breath and whisper of pleasure, relish every delicious moment.

"Yeah, just like that, Talya," he urged. Instead of shining a light on her inexperience, his words emboldened her to keep going.

She pulled his zipper down, and dug her fingers under the waistband of his boxers. When her hand closed around his shaft, she gasped. "Whoa, there's a lot of you." He was silky smooth and pulsating in her hand.

He pulled his jeans off and kicked them to the side, revealing a sexy V of muscle and long, brawny legs. "Where were we?"

"I believe *we* were getting acquainted." She ran her fingers over the crown and continued her exploration of his penis. Hunger spread from her fingers to her toes and everywhere in between.

"Touch the tip. Use your thumb, whisper-soft. What you're doing feels so good." His praise touched her like a caress. From the way he threw his head back and growled, she'd gotten the hang of this.

"How does this feel?" She realized how much she must trust him to ask such a question.

"You're driving me out of my skin," he groaned. "You need to stop. I don't want to lose control. I won't last long if you keep it up."

A heady rush of excitement surged through her. She might be green, but knowing that she'd gotten him to the brink gave her a boost of confidence.

Before she could ask him how long it had been since he'd had sex, he reached for her hand and placed a kiss on the inside of her palm. "Now it's your turn. I need to see you, Talya." His hand snaked under the hem of the T-shirt. "Can we take this off?"

"Yes." She tilted her head back as his warm fingers trailed over her skin, barely recognizing the sound of her voice.

He lifted the cotton over her head, leaving her in nothing but her thong. A rough sound rumbled from his throat. "Beautiful," he murmured, his gaze filled with hunger.

Running her hands over his sculpted chest, she pushed through the instinct to cover herself. She wanted this, and wanted her first pleasurable sexual experience to be with Cayden.

"I need to taste those pouty nipples," he panted. "Tell me it's okay, Talya."

"Please," she moaned. Her breasts ached and her nipples begged to be licked and sucked by him.

He bent his head and his tongue darted out and licked her areola, slow and sweet. When his mouth covered her nipple, her pulse went haywire. Sensations rocked her body. Moisture pooled at her core, dampening the silk of her panties.

"You okay? Should we slow down?" His hand stilled, concern etched between his light brows.

"No. I need you to keep going." When she looked up into his gorgeous face, she saw concern and tenderness shining in his eyes. The promise of pleasure overruled any remaining anxiety.

"Mmm, baby. Good news for a change." He sucked and licked her other nipple, giving it the same attention. His hand moved to her inner thigh. He drew lazy circles with his fingers, making her skin tingle. When his hand moved between her legs, she nearly leaped off the blanket. "Talya?"

"Don't stop," she rasped over the pounding of her heart. Unintelligible sounds fell from her lips.

His thumb rubbed her clit through the thin layer of silk. Her fangs grazed against her lips. She whimpered and gripped the edge of the blanket. Arousal took over, singeing through every nerve ending and erogenous zone. His fingers moved under the silk and her hips shot up.

"You're so warm and wet. I can smell you. I can't wait to taste you, lick you all over, especially here." He put his hand over her mound. "But not yet." The throaty sound of his words ignited another spark of heat. Searching her face, he waited for her to give him a sign before he continued.

"Keep going." The ache between her thighs throbbed, begging for release.

"I want to see you come apart." Cayden slid her thong down her legs with one hand and increased the pressure on her clit with the other, rubbing the moisture across her sensitized flesh. Curling a dexterous finger inside her, waves of heat licked across her body like flames.

"I'm close," she panted.

Could this be happening? But when she looked up and found him concentrating hard, trying to get her off, a shudder racked her body. She stiffened beneath his fingers. All those delicious tingles disappeared and her arousal faded. Her gut clenched with frustration. Her eyes stung with tears.

"What's wrong?" Cayden removed his fingers from her body. The last traces of warmth disappeared, leaving her cold again.

"I'm sorry. It's not you."

"Whatever you're thinking you can tell me." Cayden placed a soft, wet kiss on her shoulder. The gesture brought warmth to her skin. For a split second, her body stirred again, but the mood was gone, shattered like broken glass.

"I guess it has something to do with being vulnerable in front of another person." The excuse sounded lame, but there was truth in the confession. For some reason, the memory of those guys watching her took hold and now she couldn't seem to shake it off.

Her rational mind knew it made zero sense and yet the memories played in her head and dragged her down like a dead weight in the depths of the ocean. The wild eyes of her attackers, the heinous laughter, and the shame, flashed through her mind. *That's in the past*, she reminded herself. She tried hard to keep those vicious memories buried deep. But every now and then they reared their ugly head, robbing her of pleasure.

The ringleader of the group got his revenge when she refused to go out with him. She'd never forget the smug look on his face while he attacked her. She didn't go to the police and still regretted it to this day. She wondered if he'd done the same thing to some other innocent woman. She'd kept quiet. But the guilt still plagued her.

"How can we get you comfortable and make you come?" The honest question pushed her back to the present.

"I want to, believe me I do." She exhaled long and deep. "You have no idea how much."

"The fair maiden who's locked in the darkest tower guarded by the cruelest beast, never believes herself to be in danger, only suffering from sorrows untold and a heart untouched," he whispered and moved his hand to massage her scalp. "I promise there are no monsters under the bed, just you and me."

The words brought another wave of tears to her eyes. "It's beautiful. Who knew you quoted poetry?"

"It's Hudson, and it reminds me of you." His fingers moved from her scalp to her neck. The warmth from his touch forced her out of her head. "I want you, any way I can get you. How about we try a different tactic?"

"I'm willing to try anything at this point."

"I'm a big believer in having a plan B." Cayden sat up and his erection strained against the front of his boxers, reminding her of his desire. She'd gotten him to this point and the thought filled her with hope.

"Talk to me about plan B." Forcing a smile, Natalya hoped the embarrassment and disappointment didn't show on her face.

"You need to let go and not be self-conscious of me in the room," he said with conviction. How could practically read her thoughts?

Her arm draped over her eyes as she stretched out on the blanket. "How?" The present and the past converged, leading up to this moment.

"After everything you've been through, I'm not surprised that you're having a hard time trusting a dude, or being vulnerable. On some level you think you don't deserve this. But you do, Talya," he whispered and came closer, moving her arm.

The intensity in his gaze warmed the cold place inside her chest. "You sound like my therapist." His compassion and understanding unlocked a closed part of her heart.

"When you're on the job for as long as I've been, you see your share of horrors, rape and sexual abuse victims." His mouth turned into a grim line. "I'm no expert by any stretch, but I have a few ideas if you're game."

If she could still blush, her cheeks would be crimson. "Cayden … I …"

He cut her off by holding up a hand. "Please, let me finish." His voice became gentle, but coaxing. "This is important. What if instead of me trying to make you come, you get yourself off, but I do it too, at the same time? We both get vulnerable with each other."

When she gazed into his eyes, there was no trace of judgment, only pure arousal and sincerity. His honest words blocked out the demons in her head, the ones still overruling her life and her happiness.

Before she could contemplate the idea any further, he stood and moved his hands to the waistband of his boxers. He pulled them down and his beautiful cock sprang free.

Her mouth fell open. Her insides liquefied.

Holy hell.

Touching him didn't prepare her for the sight of him up close. His penis was long and impossibly thick. She tried not to stare, but when he gripped the base in his hand, her mouth watered. She licked her lips, taking in the pink, satiny skin and heavy-veined crown.

"Talya? What are you thinking?"

"I'm thinking you're too beautiful to be real." Her body stirred to life once more, her clit tingling. "You may be onto something."

His desire to make sure she'd be taken care of melted her defenses. Their gazes locked, and unlike the faces of her attackers, there was no malevolence or smugness in his eyes, only sweetness and searing heat. *He's a good man with a kind heart.* By taking his time and making such an effort, he showed her that it was okay to be vulnerable and flawed.

He wrapped one big hand around his erection and moved it back and forth, sending heat to her core. She became mesmerized by the moisture beaded at the tip.

"Do you want to know what I'm thinking about right now, Talya?" His seductive voice brushed over her skin.

"Yes." She drew in a deep breath, still a little uneasy.

"I'm thinking of you naked." His hand moved a little faster now. "I'm imagining you coming apart. All you need to do is say something. I get aroused by the sound of your voice."

The sight of him gripping his cock, and all those powerful muscles stirred her hunger. Her heart thundered in her ears. "Your body is a thing to behold."

"This is my fantasy come to life." His voice sounded hoarse, thick with lust. She couldn't help but be encouraged. "Okay, turnabout is fair play. Now it's your turn."

CHAPTER 33

*J*n all his years of playing the field and engaging in his fair share of hookups and flings, Cayden had never jerked off in front of a woman before. The act itself felt intimate, and doing it with Natalya made it even more exciting. He moved his hand to the center of his shaft, avoiding the tip. He wanted to arouse her without freaking her out.

"I'm glad I agreed to the waxing," she joked, a note of hesitation in her voice. He'd seen her use humor whenever something made her uncomfortable. He should know. He did the same thing.

"I want to watch what you do when you think of me. Part your legs so I can see all that beauty," he urged, rock-hard and hanging by a fucking thread.

She hesitated at first and then brushed a finger over her folds, drawing his gaze to the thin strip of dark hair between her legs.

"Beautiful." Licking his lips, he wanted to devour her slowly. The demon in him stirred to life, ready to take over.

Her legs fell open on a breath. Her fingers roamed over her flesh and all the air escaped Cayden's lungs. "Have you ever done this before?" she asked in a tentative voice.

"You're the first and there's nothing to be embarrassed about. I've got you."

The wariness faded from her eyes, replaced with desire. Her fingers moved faster as she got more into it. After everything they'd been through together, he couldn't believe she was lying before him like this.

"That's it, Talya. Touch yourself." The scent of her arousal made his cock swell. He wanted to lick all that luscious pink flesh, but he resisted the urge. He refused to risk whatever progress they'd made. He needed her to feel comfortable.

"I've never been this wet before," she whispered. Her head fell back, accentuating the slim column of her neck. A fine sheen of perspiration glistened on her skin. When she squeezed her breast, he wanted to roar.

It was all he could do not to explode right there and then. He'd been fantasizing about her for months now. "I can't stop thinking about you." His gaze trailed over her breasts. They were small but perfect with rosy tipped nipples and dark areolas. He continued his perusal of her naked body, admiring her narrow hips and toned legs.

"I think about you too, even when we're fighting," she panted.

"This is the culmination of months of fantasizing, baby." He gave his cock another stroke and groaned. His body was strung tight. No matter how turned on he got, he needed to take things slow and use some finesse to prolong her pleasure. If he came too fast, he might scare her away. He'd hold out for as long as he could to make sure she got off. "How are you doing over there, Talya?"

"I feel like I'm going to come." She picked up her pace while her gaze stayed glued to his penis.

"Watching you lose yourself in front of me is sexy as hell. What are you imagining me doing to you right now? Tell me." His voice sounded hoarse, thick with lust.

"I'm thinking of how good your mouth would feel on me right now." Color spread from her cheeks to her neck and turned her nipples a deep shade of pink. Her finger brushed back and forth over her clit. Her eyes closed on a moan. The pace increased as soft flutters of her breath filled the air.

"Every sexy word out of your mouth's driving me wild." He pumped faster. "Do you know what you're doing to me?" *Fuck.* He was ready to explode. "I'm getting close. How about you?" The words came out on a strangled groan.

"I'm not quite there, Cayden." The sound of his name on her lips forced him to slow down to match her pace.

A part of him was thrilled that she seemed to be getting into it, and the selfish part of him regretted the whole thing—watching without touching was pure torture. But he'd do just about anything to help her let go of her fears. He wanted her to trust him enough to give her the ultimate gift —pleasure.

"Tell me what you're thinking?"

"I can't wait to taste you." Muttering a curse, he tried to hold on. "I'm not going to last, baby." He stroked again as waves of heat overtook his body.

"Cayden …" She squeezed her eyes shut as one hand roamed up her body and toyed with her nipple while two fingers tended to her clit. He'd never experienced this kind of satisfaction before. He might not be touching her, but his presence was turning her on. Her chest heaved, her breaths became ragged. "I'm coming." A hiss fell from her lips. He could scent her release, which spurred his own.

"Open your eyes, Talya. Watch me come apart. Watch what you do to me." A feral groan erupted from his lips. His body caught fire. He stroked faster and harder. His head fell back. His pleasure coated his hand and the edge of the blanket as wave after wave racked his body, stealing his breath. His legs felt like wet noodles from the power of his release.

After a moment, he shot her a lazy grin. "I'll be right back." He went into the bathroom and cleaned up. When he came out, he reached for his boxers off the floor and slipped them on. When he finally caught his breath, he gazed over at Natalya's mussed hair and swollen lips. His chest tightened. *Gods, she looks inviting.* "Please, say something."

"You helped me. You made me feel comfortable." Pure joy flashed in her big brown eyes. She slipped his T-shirt on and shot to her feet. She moved to his side, wrapped her arms around his waist and hugged him hard. "I orgasmed in front of another person. I can't believe it. All thanks to you."

Cayden swallowed the lump now clogging his throat at the raw honest show of emotion. He placed a kiss on her head. "I'm glad I could help."

"This was a huge breakthrough for me," she whispered against his chest. Eventually she pulled away and craned her neck up with a smile playing across her lips. "You gave me my power back."

His heart hammered in his chest. He didn't want to think too much into whatever they just did. One thing he knew, it meant something. "I didn't do anything. All that power has been there all along." He placed his hand above her heart "You're a strong, incredible woman."

"I'd like to bask in the afterglow." She went over to the blanket and laid her head on the pillow. Lifting her arms over her head, she stretched like a cat. "I feel more relaxed than I have in a long time."

"I'm feeling pretty good myself." He didn't want this little bubble to burst, so he joined her on the blanket and ran his fingers through her hair.

"There's something I want to come clean about." Natalya sat up and looked him in the eye. "I met a guy at the bar the other night. He asked me out and we've been texting. I want to be up-front with you."

His gut twisted with irrational jealousy. "Do you want to go out with him?"

"No, I thought I did for a nanosecond. I guess I was flattered by the attention." She glanced at his scattered clothing across the floor before her gaze met his once more. "I wasn't too sure about us. I'm still not."

A wave of possessiveness took a hold of him by the throat. "We haven't put a label on what we're doing, and it could get awkward if anyone gets wind of our involvement," he said in a voice thick with regret. He'd blurred the lines between his personal and professional life. But lying here with Natalya made it feel like that other world didn't exist. For the first time in years, he didn't care. *But I have nothing to offer?* Shaking off the sexual fog occupying his brain, he couldn't ask her to go there with him, not when he came with centuries worth of baggage. She deserved better. It would be selfish to jump in with both feet.

"I've given some thought to this. As long as we're discreet, I think we can keep seeing each other." Excitement spread across her face.

"I can't let you risk your promotion for me." Could Cayden give himself to Natalya and take the risk of opening his heart again? Old wounds rose to the surface, guilt and a sense of loss.

He'd been numbing himself to this kind of joy for years. He didn't know how to open himself up to it again. And what about her family? Being with him would only drive a deeper wedge between them. Granted, Mrs. D. was a pill and a half, but she was the only family Natalya had left. He couldn't let her take such risks for him when they were just messing around. His stomach clenched as he got to his feet, and picked up the rest of his scattered clothing off the floor. After he got dressed, his gaze found hers once more. "I'm sorry. I have to go."

"You're leaving?" The vulnerability in her eyes called to him and yet he remained where he stood like a coward. "I thought we could cuddle."

Everything in him wanted to rejoin her on the blanket and hold her in his arms all night long. But things would only get messier if he did. "I've got a lot to do before Alex's bachelor party." He might not have slept with her, but his heart told him he'd gotten in deep.

"Cayden? What just happened? Why do you feel a million miles away? Is this about me texting another guy? I only told you to clear the air."

"I'm glad you did." Cayden wanted to run his fingers over her soft skin and make her purr with contentment, kiss away any lingering doubts she may be experiencing, but he wouldn't, because cuddling led to intimacy. And right now he couldn't afford to get high on post-coital hormones. "How about I call you tomorrow?"

Confusion clouded her beautiful eyes. She gazed up at him like she'd done something wrong. "Yeah, sure."

He didn't want to leave like this, not when she looked hurt and vulnerable, but it wouldn't be fair to lead her on or go forming attachments. His inner voice mocked him. *Too late.*

CHAPTER 34

The next day, Natalya sat in a leather chairs across from Denopoulos in the manor library. "This woman I keep seeing in my mirror is in danger. Don't ask me to explain how I know, I just do." Reclining against the cushion, she tried to think over the pounding of her heart.

"What can you tell me about her? What does she look like? Give as much description as you can. Take your time." Denopoulos looked up from his laptop.

The smell of leather, books and incense surrounded them, unraveling the tight knot in the pit of her stomach. The voice activated device she'd been hooked up to would capture the images floating around in her head.

"She has medium-length bluish hair, dark glasses, a narrow-shaped face, and green eyes. I'd say she's in her early thirties. I sense she's in danger." She exhaled a pent-up breath. "I know it's not a lot to go on."

A sudden flash of recognition passed over Denopoulos's face. He pressed pause on his device. "Oh shit. I think I know her. We both do."

"What? Who is she?" Natalya asked with a deep sigh.

Denopoulos pointed to his screen. "You're describing our MBI lab tech, Erika, to a T."

"Erika? We've talked on the phone, but we've never met in person.

Now I know why her voice sounded familiar." Natalya wanted to warn her, but about who, or what, she didn't know. "What do you think this means? We have to tell her that someone's after her."

"Do you think this is related to Andee's murder?" Denopoulos asked, scratching his beard.

"I wish I knew. I've got this tight knot in the pit of my stomach, but no solid proof that she's in danger. Erika might think I'm nuts. Crystal ball gazing isn't an exact science."

He shrugged. "After living with Willow and spending time here at the manor, nothing sounds crazy to me at this point. I'm not sure if you knew, but Erika's a witch. I'm sure she'll take your vision seriously. We can send some agents to her place and the lab to keep an eye on her. I'll be giving her a call myself."

"The witches can pool their magick and make her a protection charm." Natalya got up from the chair and walked around the room, her thoughts jumbled in a million different directions.

"Good idea," Denopoulos said in an encouraging voice. "Don't worry. We've got all hands on deck. Something's going to pan out."

"I saw the results from the lab. The shoe print at Pike's place matches the one at Andee's apartment. So it looks like whoever killed Pike, killed Andee. What about the safe deposit key?" Natalya's mind drifted to Cayden. The memory of the way they'd left things yesterday flashed through her head. Her eyes misted. She didn't want Denopoulos to see, so she turned and pretended to be interested in one of the books on the shelf.

"We traced it to a bank southeast of Hellios in Albany. Smith's headed up there now to check it out."

"So we've got one dead wolf and still no leads on Hawthorne?" Turning to face him, she wracked her brain, trying to fit the missing pieces of this puzzle together.

"Pretty much."

"It doesn't make sense. Do you think there's a chance Hawthorne is the one who died in the prison fire and not Frost?" Could Cayden be onto something?

"Anything's possible at this point." Denopoulos gathered up his equipment and headed for the door. "I'll be in touch."

An icy chill settled over her, and pressed against her chest. Natalya didn't see this nightmare ending anytime soon. In fact, she sensed things were about to get a whole lot worse.

The manor kitchen buzzed with voices and boisterous laughter. Natalya pulled out trays of fruit, truffles and penis-shaped cake pops from the fridge and set them on the counter.

All the women from the coven showed up for the occasion, along with some of their clients from the shop. The topic of conversation revolved around wedding festivities of course, everything from the bridesmaid's dresses, Willow's gown, and what it took to write their own vows, to how outrageous Cayden's best man speech would be. When Natalya thought about Cayden, a dull ache spread from the center of her chest to every part of her body, she didn't want to go there, not tonight.

"Let me help you." Arabella walked up and peeled the foil from the trays. She gave Natalya an approving smile. "Not bad. The guys are throwing Alex's bachelor p arty tonight. It should be interesting."

"I'm sure, but I think we're ahead of the game. So far no one's gotten plastered or puked on any of the furniture, but then again the night's still young." Natalya smiled and put on a brave face for the ladies, but inside she still hurt. What had she been expecting, Cayden to declare himself as her boyfriend? *Ha.* Pushing all foolish romantic notions about him to the back of her mind, she'd make Willow's big night epic, no matter what.

She'd been in charge of the food, while Arabella and Brooke had been in charge of decorations. Purple beads, pink balloons and pink margarita glasses filled with some of Saje's signature party concoctions sat on the table next to pink gift bags. The plan was to hit the bars in Hoboken and paint the town after the shower games.

"What's in the bags?" Willow asked as she walked into the kitchen wearing a pink bride sash over a fitted gray top and jeans. A crown sat on top of her mane of long red hair. She snagged a pink glass off the table and lifted it to her lips.

"Every girl brought a pair of underwear, and you have to guess who brought what," Arabella explained. "If you guess right, she drinks. If you guess wrong, then you do."

"I might need to cheat. Whatever Saje put in these cocktails will probably knock me on my ass," Willow said with a chuckle, reaching for a penis-shaped cake pop off the tray. "These look so real, kudos to the bakery."

Shouts drifted into the kitchen from the living room. Delilah walked in looking chic in a black camisole, jeans, and high heels. "The girls are getting rowdy in there. We have to move this party along. I'm about to get my tarot decks set up."

"When are the strippers coming?" Arabella turned to Delilah, and then glanced over her shoulder to the kitchen door.

As Willow turned to Delilah, her maid of honor, a line formed between her brows. "You promised no strippers."

"Don't worry, honey. There are no strippers coming to this party." Delilah put her hand on Willow's shoulder. "When you're marrying a guy as gorgeous as Alex, why in the world would you need strippers?"

"Good point." Natalya reached for a glass off the table and took a sip. An image of Cayden buck naked, jerking off and moaning her name danced through her head with vivid clarity. Her cheeks instantly heated.

"Whoa, Natalya? Are you okay?" Willow's gaze narrowed in her direction. "I just got a strong whiff of pheromones off of you." She fanned her hand in front of her face. "What gives?"

"Oh …I, um …" She'd been caught. She decided to do what any self-respecting woman in her position did in the face of such scrutiny and deflected the question. "Who's ready for the underwear game?"

An hour later, Ellen walked into the living room carrying a Chinese take-out bag. She set it on the table in front of Natalya with a curious expression across her face. "I intercepted the delivery guy. He said this was for you."

"For me? But I didn't order any food." Natalya's words got caught in her throat when she smelled dumplings. Cayden was the only person she shared those happy childhood memories with, the only person who knew about her human family's affinity for Chinese food. Warmth slid in her belly and made her cheeks burn. She didn't know what to make of the gesture. Could this be his way of apologizing for how he'd left her apartment? Or did he send this over out of guilt? The thought forced her muscles to seize up.

"When men screw up, they typically send flowers," Ellen said with a throaty laugh. "But Chinese takeout? Now that's a new one."

Natalya took a sip from her whiskey sour, enjoying the tanginess as it slid down her throat. Glancing at her friends saddled up to the bar, most of them looked pretty buzzed. They chatted about men while eighties music played in the background. Every time her thoughts drifted to Cayden, she pushed them aside, still confused about what to do.

"What's going on?" Brooke came over and gave her a hug. Pieces of her blonde hair fell from her clip in messy waves around her face. "Thanks for making everything purr-fect for tonight," she slurred.

"Whoa, the matchmaker's officially shit-faced. I've never seen you with as much as a hair out of place. I think the bigger question is what's going on with you?"

"I'm surfing for hot guys." Taking a sip from her cocktail, Brooke scoped out the bar. A woman got up from the next stool and she sat in her place. "I still don't have a plus-one for the wedding."

"How come?" Natalya asked, turning to face her, running her finger along her glass. "You must meet eligible men all the time."

"Yeah, but you know the old adage, a cobbler never has any shoes but scuffed up Manolos."

Natalya laughed. "I don't think that's the saying, but okay."

The bartender walked up and set a row of shot glasses in front of her and the rest of their party seated at the bar. He lifted a bottle of high-end tequila and poured. "The gentleman would like to buy you lovely ladies a round."

"The gentleman? What gentleman would that be?" Natalya asked, turning her head, looking around. She spotted James on the other side of the bar. He lifted his glass in salute and smiled.

Pointing at the shot glass, she turned to Brooke with a smile. "Go easy. I'll be right back." She hopped off the barstool and wobbled a little in her heels.

Natalya wound her way through the crowd and stopped when she came face-to-face with James. "What are you doing here?"

"I could ask you the same thing." James bent and kissed both her cheeks. He wore a blue button-down and jeans. "I'm just chilling with some friends." He motioned to a few vampires sitting at a table in the corner.

"Thanks for the shots."

A tinge of guilt settled in her belly. She'd never responded to his text, which only reinforced her lack of interest. She didn't get butterflies in her stomach or the rush of heat in her erogenous zones when she looked at him like she did with Cayden. *Too bad, because he seems like a nice guy.* The realization forced her to admit the truth. *I'm totally into Cayden.*

James stared at the purple beads around her neck and then turned his head in the direction of the loud, boisterous laughter coming from her friends seated at the bar. His gaze met hers once more. "Let me guess, one of the guys from the other night proposed and you're getting married?"

Natalya laughed. "Definitely not. It's my friend's bachelorette party. I'm sorry for not getting back to you. I've been busy with work." The excuse sounded lame. A few weeks ago, she would've jumped at the chance to go out with a guy as charming and attractive as James, but ever since she and Cayden had taken their bickering into the bedroom, she'd been totally preoccupied only with him.

"It's been great bumping into you again, but I know that you're not interested."

"Listen, James, it's not you ..."

James reached out and squeezed her hand. "It's okay."

"I'm sorry. I didn't mean to lead you on. I'm seeing someone. It just sort of happened." No matter what went on between her and Cayden, it didn't change her goal, to catch the sonofabitch who killed Andee Lyon and framed Cayden in the process. If all went according to plan, she'd get her promotion, and help more women like her, but that was a big *if*.

"I appreciate your honesty," James said, interrupting her thoughts.

Shouts rang out from the bar.

Natalya turned to find some of the ladies dancing on the tables. She turned to face James once more. "I should get back to my friends." And then an idea popped into her head. "Speaking of friends, I have someone I think you'd hit it off with. Can I give her your card?"

"I don't usually do fix-ups, but if she's anything like you, then sure, why not." James gave her a quick hug and disappeared into the crowd.

As Natalya walked back to the bar, she could hear her friends belting out "Tainted Love." She could relate. Taking a seat on the stool next to Gillian, she cracked up. "If we manage to get out of here without anyone getting arrested, it'll be a miracle."

"Fortunately, a few of us are in bed with the cops." Gillian arched her brows and angled her head to the crowd. "Who's the hottie you were chatting up?"

"Oh, James? He's just a friend." Natalya decided to switch the subject to wedding talk. "Where are Willow and Alex having the rehearsal dinner?"

"They're doing a bonfire at the manor in lieu of the traditional rehearsal dinner." Gillian sipped her drink.

"It sounds fun. I've never been to a bonfire." Excitement fluttered in Natalya's belly. "We haven't had much time to talk lately. What's it like being engaged?"

"It's the best. I'm happy Nat, more than I've ever been." Gillian rested her elbow on the bar and her face lit up with a smile.

Natalya blinked away tears. "If any two people deserve to be happy it's you and Garrett." At one point, she swore they'd broken up for good, but somehow they managed to find their way back to each other. Seeing her friends so happy and in love shined a light on what she'd been missing. She couldn't be satisfied with simply existing. She wanted more.

"What's going on?" Gillian reached out and touched her hand. "I'm sensing something's up. Is it about Cayden?"

"What makes you say that?" Natalya sucked in a breath.

"It helps being a psychic, and he's been seen sneaking out of your room." Gillian finished the last of her cocktail and set the glass on the bar. "Fess up."

"We've been messing around, but I'm not sure what it means … if anything. It's not like he's ever opened up to me." Natalya picked up her straw, and chewed on the end. "I spotted a photo of his lost love in his apartment. She was wispy and ethereal." How could she ever compete? "I wonder if he's ever talked about her with anyone. I'm sorry. Am I rambling?"

"No, not at all. Garrett said he only confided in Alex about her, and even he doesn't know much. I'm guessing Cayden keeps his feelings locked up, which isn't unusual for males from a different era and all."

"Yeah, I'm sure you're right."

"Have you talked to him?" Gillian's phone pinged. "Hold that thought." She glanced at her screen. "Garrett's texting me."

Cayden struck Natalya as a guy who would make no bones about what he wanted, and yet he was giving her mixed signals. Could she be crushing on someone who didn't feel the same way? Could knowing her secret have something to do with it? His response had been nothing short of incredible. He'd surpassed any and all expectations. She could only imagine what sex would be like with him. Would things even get that far?

"The guys are calling it a night." Gillian looked up from her phone. "The timing's perfect for you to go ask Cayden yourself. I find face-to-face works best."

"Now? Even if I had the guts to go over there, I can't leave the party." When Natalya glanced over at the ladies, they were lounged in their chairs, looking spent. Willow's head rested on Saje's lap. "On second thought, it's probably time to call it a night."

Gillian turned her head. "It looks like this party's officially over. The limo can drop you at Cayden's on the way to the manor. What do you say, Nat?"

Go there and look like a clingy one-time hookup? "I say I love your enthusiasm, but I can't just show up at Cayden's apartment unannounced. It's something a girlfriend would do." Natalya didn't know if what took place on the floor of her apartment would even happen again. Lifting her phone out of her purse, a tingle shot up her spine when she glanced at the screen. Three missed calls from Cayden and a few texts.

"Why not? You look gorgeous. You should torture him a little first. Show Cayden what he's missing. The demon won't be able to resist you," Gillian teased.

The thought made Natalya warm all over. "I want to, but I grew up with all these rules about how a woman should behave and be courted."

"There are no set rules when it comes to love and relationships, Garrett's words, not mine." Gillian patted Natalya's arm. "It's okay for things to get messy. Trust me on this."

Natalya contemplated waiting to call Cayden later when she got home, but she supposed Gillian did have a point. She wanted to see him in the flesh and get this confusion cleared up once and for all.

"What did you decide?" Gillian prompted.

When it came to her career, she'd always gone after what she wanted, no hesitation. Why shouldn't she give the same attention and consideration to her personal life? "Maybe you're right. Why wait?" She exhaled, not sure if she'd won a personal victory or set herself up for more disappointment.

CHAPTER 35

There's nothing quite like watching boxing on pay-per-view with a group of your buddies. Cayden got up from the couch while the guys grumbled over who should've won the fight. They huddled in the hall, saying their goodbyes.

All of the dudes in the wedding came to hang out for Alex's big night. The groomsmen consisted of Alex's two brothers, Gus and Nico, his cousin Dave, Smith, Garrett, and Nick. As for Cayden, he'd managed to snag the honor of best man. Alex didn't want anything too splashy, no girls jumping out of a cake, no drunken debauchery.

His partner wanted a simple night of fun, which seemed at odds with Andee's unsolved murder. But some things took precedence, giving his best friend a proper send-off being one of them.

"Are you sure you don't want to hang out for a bit? I could heat up some more ribs, open a few more beers." While the other guys imbibed, Cayden spent the night chugging diet soda.

"Nah. Thanks anyway, man. The Ubers are here," Smith called out. Everyone shook hands and headed out the door. "You two coming?" His boss glanced over at Garrett and then at Alex, who slumped on the couch with his chin resting on his chest.

"My cruiser's outside. I'll make sure our bachelor gets home safe," Garrett said, plopping in a chair across from him and pulling out his phone. "I'll drop him off then I'm headed to the station. Dubrosky's meeting me there."

Cayden swallowed hard at the mention of her name. He'd acted like a total dick leaving so quickly after what they did. Waiting a beat, he looked over at Alex and shook his head. "We need to sober up our groom."

"I think some strong coffee's in order before we send him home to his future bride," Garrett agreed looking up from his screen.

"High octane coming up." After Cayden went into the kitchen and filled the water tank on his coffee maker, he pulled out a bag of coffee from the pantry. He reached for a mug off the rack and pressed a button. A loud noise echoed throughout the room.

Alex jolted. "I'm getting up. Is it time for work?"

Garrett laughed. "No, not yet, buddy. Take a load off." He turned his attention to Cayden. "I'd say you pulled off one hell of a party. Alex passed three sheets to the wind an hour ago." He sniffed the air as the scent of coffee filled the apartment. "I'll take one of those."

"Yeah, he's going to feel it in the morning." Cayden reached for a couple mugs off the counter. "Maybe Saje has one of those hangover potions she can give him."

"I'll ask Gillian. She's with her right now. The bachelorette party's over. The ladies are leaving the bar."

"Did they have strippers?" Cayden tried to sound casual, but when he imagined some dude sticking his junk in Natalya's face, he squeezed his hand into a fist, shattering the mug into pieces. Shards of ceramic scattered all over the counter. Muttering a curse, he grabbed some paper towels, wiping up the mess and a few trickles of his blood.

"Everything okay?" Garrett called out.

"Yeah, fine." Cayden threw the broken mug and the paper towels in the trash. Reaching for another mug, he filled both to the rim, and then walked over to the side table and set the mugs down. "Drink up, buddy. You don't want your woman to see you like this."

"Do you need any help cleaning up," Garrett asked, waving his hand around the room. "You've made quite a few trips to the incinerator. We were taking bets as to what you were really doing out in the hall."

"You guys made a lot of empty beer bottles," Cayden mumbled. "What did you come up with?"

"I said you were calling your bookie after you lost your shirt on the fight." Garrett's lip twitched with amusement.

"Nice, except I don't have a bookie."

Garrett sipped his coffee and stared at him over the rim of his mug with a smug smile. "Admit it, you were sneaking out to call Natalya. What's going on with you two?"

No use lying to his friends, especially when they saw right through him. "Okay fine. I may have started something with Natalya, but it's not going anywhere and please, for the love of the gods, don't tell anyone."

Cayden hoped sending over her favorite food might let her know he'd been thinking about her, and maybe make up for the way he'd bolted out of her place. He walked around the apartment, picking up the empty bottles wondering why she still hadn't returned any of his calls.

Hell, I didn't even kiss her good-bye. What an asshole.

He helped her with her problem and now she could move on with her life, end of story. He'd only end up hurting her in the end. Did she have any idea that he struggled with addiction, nightmares, and lived in a constant state of guilt? How could he indulge in the sweet pleasure of caring for a woman like Natalya when Abigail died because of him? What if he took a chance with Natalya and something happened to her? He wouldn't survive another tragedy. He'd have to be satisfied with the fantasizing, something he couldn't seem to stop doing.

"We all saw it coming with all the bickering and teasing." Garrett laughed. "You might as well have pulled on her braids."

"You couldn't have been less obvious if you'd stuck a rose between your teeth," Alex chimed in, sitting up and sipping his coffee, starting to look more alert.

Great, just great. "Did she uh, ever say anything about me?" The moment Cayden posed the question he swore his sack shriveled up. "Forget I asked."

Garrett nodded. "Oh she said a few things, but none I can repeat in mixed company. Let's face it, you have a rep for being a Lothario."

"A Lothario?" The label probably gave Natalya even more reason to assume he'd hit it and quit it. He'd stopped engaging in empty hookups a long time ago. He sure as hell didn't miss the self-loathing he felt afterward.

"You might have some competition, and it serves you right." Garrett finished his coffee, set the mug on the table and stood. "Gillian said Natalya was talking to some vampire named James. He bought them a round of pricey tequila, probably just showing off."

"James?" Why did his name keep coming up? The vampire probably liked to throw his old money around, platinum to Cayden's nickel. Walking up to Garrett, he looked him square in the eye. "Anything else?"

Garrett craned his neck. "As a matter of fact, there are a few things. If anything, I hope this little chat gave you the kick in the ass you need. Make a move or walk away. But if you hurt her, I might have to kill you."

"Hold on, Garrett." Cayden held up his hand. "While I appreciate you looking out for Natalya, she's an adult who makes her own decisions."

"True, but I want to make sure she doesn't get hurt," Garrett shot back. "She saved Gillian's life at the risk of her own, and by some miracle managed to convince her that I'm not a soulless bastard. Let's face it, this isn't the first time you engaged in a dalliance with a colleague. Natalya hasn't been out there. She could get her heart broken."

"You're referring to Erika?" Cayden lifted an empty bottle and slammed it on the end table. "We're ancient history. We both knew what we were getting into up front, so no one got hurt. I don't need a warning from you." The worst part—Garrett was right. Cayden needed an outlet for his misplaced anger. He took a step closer to his friend, coiled and ready to spring.

Alex shot up from the couch and moved in between them. "Okay you two, why don't you both cool off. The fight ended a half hour ago. Tensions are running high. It's time to call it a night."

Garrett took a step back, regret flashing in his eyes. . "I'm sorry, Cayden. I didn't mean what I said. It was a cheap shot."

"It's okay." Cayden huffed out a breath. "I'm glad Natalya has someone in her corner who cares about her." *But I do too.* They man-hugged it out. "Apology accepted."

"I'm glad we're all back on the same side. Now, it's my cue to go." Alex shook Cayden's hand. "Thanks for everything. You're the best. Love you, man. Look, for what it's worth, I can tell you like her, a lot, but if you're not going to offer her anything, then leave her alone. My relationship with Willow started out as a fling, but she turned out to be the love of my life."

Cayden wished he could be like Alex and Garrett where everything around them seemed shiny and ripe with possibilities, but too many pieces of his soul had been stripped away. "It's probably for the best. It's complicated." Natalya deserved more than he could give.

"Okay then." Alex patted him on the shoulder. "See you tomorrow."

The second Cayden shut the door behind them, he felt a little numb. Going into the kitchen, he replayed the last five minutes in his head as he threw out the rest of the plates and empty bottles.

He walked to the window, and wrenched it open, allowing the sounds of the city to float in. When he turned around, his gaze settled on the blood from the broken coffee cup. The sight triggered a host of gut-wrenching images he didn't want to think about—Abigail's mangled body lying in a ditch. Blood dripped from the bite marks in her neck ... so much blood everywhere. A wild sorrow had gripped him and never let go. He'd been living in a constant state of grief, regret, and remorse ever since.

Lifting a sponge from the sink, he scrubbed the spot until his fingers went numb. He tossed the sponge into the trash and pulled the bag from the can. He headed out the door to the incinerator in the hall.

Once upon a time he envisioned a life with Abigail, a forever after. He still remembered the joy of first love. He'd never wanted to think about another woman in the same way, even after all these years, until he met Natalya. How could she know the impact of her sweet affection? Could he leave himself open to something happening again, considering what they both did for a living? She might be a vampire, but she could still be hurt, or worse. The thought was too horrible to bear.

The more time he spent with her, the more she opened up a part of him he thought died in the war. He had vowed to never let his guard down again, or let anyone in. Somehow Natalya had managed to sneak under his defenses. Now he didn't know how to cut off his feelings and stick to the script. Thanks to her, the hollowness inside him didn't seem as great.

Once Alex and Willow got married, there'd be no more hanging out watching b-ball or hockey until the wee hours of the night. Things wouldn't be the same. Soon Garrett and Gillian would get hitched. As for Nick, he'd probably pop the question to Saje any day now. Even Smith and Ellen seemed to be going strong, creating a life together. And where was he? In the same place he'd been for the last three hundred years—alone. Loneliness crept in like an unwanted visitor. There he stood, enveloped in his own misery.

What would it take to make him forget the pain and the ugliness of the job when the cold of the city settled into the bones? Everyone he'd ever loved had perished. But with Abigail, that blow had shattered something inside of him—something he didn't think would ever heal. Somehow Natalya had managed to open up those old wounds and make him rethink his whole existence. Could he open himself up again?

The click-clack of heels jolted him out of his head. The sweet scent of strawberries filled the air. He turned and his heart pounded in his chest when Natalya appeared at the end of the hall. She wore a short, hot-pink dress that showcased her toned, legs. Her hips swayed as she came closer. How could he resist her?

His demon rose up and took notice. He'd have to end this before they crossed any more lines, or she jeopardized her future. His cock mocked him, hardening instantly against the front panel of his jeans.

"Natalya? What are you doing here?" His palms began to sweat. He wiped them on his jeans.

When she stopped a few inches away, the scent of booze and vampire flared in his nostrils. His gut twisted. Her expression changed from excitement to apprehension in the blink of an eye. "You don't look happy to see me."

"You surprised me." His resolve lost steam the moment he gazed into those warm brown eyes. He should do the right thing and send her home, suffer another night alone with a raging hard-on.

"I was at the party and thinking about you, but from the look on your face I've made a huge mistake by coming here." Cayden could hear the hurt in her voice, and it shredded him. She turned on her high heels, ready to walk away.

"Natalya, wait, please." His guard dropped like a dead weight. Reaching for her waist, he turned her around. A strange combination of panic and relief set in. *She'd missed me?* His chest swelled with the revelation. "I'm glad you're here. I don't want you to go." He motioned to his door. "Please, come inside."

"I'm sorry for just stopping by without calling. I guess I got carried away on wedding talk, a few too many cocktails, and all those penis-shaped cake pops."

"Penis-shaped cake pops?" Cayden laughed. "Do I want to know?"

"Absolutely not."

"Why don't you come inside?" He could practically smell the estrogen emanating from her pores. Her hair fell out of a messy ponytail. His fingers curled at his sides, wanting to push those silky strands behind her ear. But if he touched her, it would be all over. *You've got me twisted up in knots.*

"Okay."

He forced himself not to sweep her up in his arms and carry her to his bed. It became almost impossible to cut off the riot of emotions she dredged up inside him. He led her into his apartment and shut the door.

Natalya stood in the hall, her expression guarded, and he didn't like it at all. He followed her gaze as it darted around the living room, taking in the chips still on the cushions and the spilled beer across the coffee table. "It looks like you guys had fun. How was the bachelor party?"

"You'd have to ask Alex, but I think everyone enjoyed themselves. I'm sure you didn't come all the way over here to talk about the party." Gloss covered her lips. In all pink, she looked like a confection he wanted to eat.

"Does there have to be a reason?" Her eyes searched his for answers. "I'm not familiar with mating rituals and dating habits. I'm not even sure what we're doing. I'm new at all this."

The honesty in her words snuck under his defenses. "I think we should start by getting a few things out of the way."

Nodding, she looked a little wary. "Okay, you first."

"I smell a vampire on you." Cayden ran a hand through his hair. "I've got no right to ask, no right whatsoever." But he couldn't help himself. His gut burned with irrational jealousy. "Who is he?"

"He's the guy I told you about. We met while I was undercover at the tavern. He asked me out a few times." Her shoulders relaxed. "At first I was flattered. I'm not one to date much, as you've probably figured out, but I have this charity event coming up and he seemed like the type that would be into it. I would've asked you, but I figured it might not be your thing."

Cayden laughed. "Can you see me rubbing elbows in a room full of blue-blooded vampires?" He wanted to be there for her, but he wouldn't fit in, and he didn't want to embarrass her in front of her people. *Shit, this kind of thinking will land me in dangerous territory.*

"I don't blame you," she said, sounding disappointed.

"Aside from your shindig, are you into this guy?" His heart went to his throat. How would it change anything? A conflict waged inside him.

Nothing made sense anymore. All the meaningless hookups started to blend together.

"You're jealous?" Her gaze burned him alive.

"What if I am?"

"He's perfect on paper, but he's not you." Her voice calmed him like ice on a slow burn. "To be honest, your reputation as a player scares the hell out of me."

Ever since she showed up with her challenging looks and sassy comebacks, he'd been less content, wanting more of whatever she could give. He could no longer bury his impulses any more than he could stop breathing. "I was trying to fill a void and never could. Any more questions?"

Her lips parted and her breaths came out in short little puffs. "Only one. What happened to Abigail?"

Natalya moved to the kitchen island, trying to ignore the potent scent of Cayden's blood. The intoxicating smell made her want to lick the spot on his hand, graze it with her fangs and taste his essence. Hunger spread from her lips to her fangs. She'd never experienced such a visceral craving.

"You don't beat around the bush, do you?" Cayden motioned for her to take a seat on a barstool. He looked mouthwatering in a threadbare T-shirt, ripped jeans and bare feet.

"I hoped we could talk, and you might feel comfortable opening up."

"Can I get you anything? I've got ribs, wings?" Cayden began opening and closing cabinets, putting dishes away.

"I'm fine. Will you answer the question, Cayden?"

"I'm afraid the subject's off-limits." Pulling a couple of glasses off a rack, he filled both with water, and set them on the island.

Her stomach tensed at the rejection. "I've opened up to you, poured out my heart and told you my darkest secret. There are only a few people in this world who know the truth and you're one of them. Why won't you trust me the way I trust you?"

"Dammit, Natalya. This isn't about trust." Cayden gritted his teeth.

"I don't want to make you do anything you don't want to, but can you look at this from my point of view?" Natalya tried to keep the emotion of out of her voice, and failed. "We're spending time together. Things have turned physical, and I still don't know anything about your past, nothing personal about you at all. This might be routine for you, but I'm not into casual hookups. I know I'm changing the rules and I'm sorry. I thought I could do this without an emotional connection, but I was wrong."

"Don't ask me this, anything but this, Talya. You won't look at me the same way." The pain in his voice tore at her heart. He gulped the water, drawing her gaze to the sensual curve of his lips. She wanted to kiss him, touch him and feel their connection, now more than ever.

"This needs to be a two-way street." She could leave this subject alone, but she knew if they were ever going to get closer, they'd have to talk about the demon woman still in the room. Something told her to smash the wall he'd put up now, otherwise this would always come between them.

He leaned forward, his lips a breath away. His masculine scent invaded her nostrils and made her ache. "I'm here with you now, Talya." Reaching for her hand, Cayden placed her palm on his chest where his heart pounded. "Isn't that enough?"

"Why won't you talk about her?" She should probably leave this alone, but something inside of her wouldn't let him push her away. "It might make you feel …"

Cayden cut her off by releasing her hand, and storming out of the kitchen. He paced across the room like a beautiful caged animal. When he turned, a muscle ticked in his cheek. "This is where you and I are different. I don't want to feel. I've spent the last hundred years trying to forget."

Her death still tortured him, even after all these years. How could she get him to move past his pain? All this time she thought they were different, but she realized they both struggled with the ghosts of their pasts. He needed her, even if he'd never admit it aloud. Hopping off the stool, she moved next to him, making sure to tread lightly. "Have you ever talked to a therapist, or a grief counselor? There's no shame in getting help. I still talk to someone."

He walked over to the glass liquor cart, picked up a bottle, and held it up. "Do you want to know who my therapist has been for all these years? Big Johnnie, that's who."

"Do you have a drinking problem?" Natalya held her breath, waiting for his reply.

A vulnerability she'd never seen before flared in his eyes. "I don't know. But I went to my first AA meeting a few days ago and got a sponsor. A friend helped me get things rolling from there."

"Oh, Cayden." She closed the scant distance between them. Rising to her tiptoes, she reached up to caress his stubbly cheek. "I'm proud of you for getting help. I know of some local support groups. I could go with you if you wanted me to."

Cayden sucked in a breath. "Thank you. I appreciate what you're trying to do, believe me. I've been searching for the lost pieces of myself, and being with you is helping me get them back."

Hearing him admit those words scared her and exhilarated her at the same time. Did it mean he could be himself with her? Did he need her? She wanted him more than ever. After all her attempts to fight her feelings for him, she'd finally let him in, more than anyone else in her life.

"Abigail and I grew up together, and then eventually fell in love. We were supposed to get married, be together forever."

Her heart plummeted, hearing about the depth of his feelings for another woman. *You asked,* she reminded herself.

"It should've been me that died and not her."

"Don't say such things." She rubbed his arm. "How did she die?" She wanted to be the one he confided in, the one to ease his pain.

When he closed his eyes, a swirl of emotions emanated off of him, regret, guilt, and anger. Finally, he opened his eyes and sighed deep. "I think we should sit down for this." He led her over to the couch.

"Please, go on."

"After Arcadia was taken over by the Coterie, I went from a being a general in the army to a slave overnight. A vampire by the name of Lilith rose to power and became queen. She got off by inflicting pain on her subjects. Hundreds of my former soldiers perished at her command."

"How horrible. Did anyone try to stop her? What about the king?" Hearing about the needless suffering of his people made her heart break.

"King Stephen? The former head of the Coterie was more of a monster than his wife. Who do you think gave me most of my scars? When he wasn't busy fighting wars and overtaking kingdoms, he was wreaking havoc on our land. But he and Lilith weren't the only culprits. The entire ruling class used demons as blood slaves and took whatever they could get from us. Rape typically followed. We lost half of our population from the abuse."

Tears welled in Natalya's eyes. "What about you?" She prayed this strong, fearsome warrior had been spared.

"I managed to avoid getting raped or turned into a feedbag, mainly because of my standing as a former officer, but most of my brethren weren't as lucky."

"Now I finally understand the crux of your resentment against vampires." She'd worked with him all these months and never had any idea the extent of the atrocities he'd faced. He'd been reliving the horrors of his past all this time alone. She wanted to wrap herself in his arms and soothe him, but she pushed on. "What about Abigail?"

He bowed his head. "Somehow Lilith caught wind of my relationship with her and propositioned me out of spite. She demanded my allegiance be only to her."

"What did you do?" Natalya hung on his every word, hoping to keep her heart out of it so he'd continue.

"When I refused her advances, she took her wrath out on Abigail." His voice came out sounding raw. "We were supposed to run away together. She was killed before we ever got the chance."

Tears burned behind her eyes. "You can't blame yourself, Cayden."

His gaze seared hers like a brand. "But I do, every day of my life. I should've been the one to die and not her. Now do you understand why I don't get close to anyone? When I close my eyes, I swear I can still hear the sound of Abigail's last breath. I've never told a soul the whole story until now."

"I'm so sorry. I can't imagine what you must've gone through." Swallowing hard, she pulled him into a hug. "I've got you, warrior."

"Talya," he breathed and placed a kiss on top of her head. They stayed that way for several minutes. "I've carried this around for most of my adult life." Finally, he pulled back, his gaze softened and filled with need.

"You don't have to carry it around anymore." A million more questions raced through her head. "How did you escape?"

"I came through a portal. I slept in the woods and hunted for food like some *Survivor* reject. I couldn't get myself out of the mental stupor I'd fallen into. The loss had rendered me incapacitated for months on end. I don't know how to let go of the past or the bitterness." His voice sounded raw.

"Abigail will always be in your heart, Cayden, but it's okay to let her go." She placed a kiss on his cheek. "You have nothing to feel guilty about. Her death wasn't your fault. She wouldn't want you to go on grieving for her all this time. Keep her memory alive by focusing on how she lived, not how she died."

"I wish I could. I want to." His shoulders slumped forward. "The anger and guilt almost ate me alive. It consumed every part of me. I buried the pain, hoping it would go away, but it never did."

"I can relate to wanting to curl up in private and push the memories back to the dark hole where they came from better than anyone. But it won't help you heal. What about now?"

"I'm better since you've come into my life." He reached out and caressed her cheek with his knuckles.

Her heart sped up and somersaulted in her chest. "What happened to your family?"

His gaze turned steely, blazing with anger. "The Coterie tortured and killed my parents. My brothers fought to the bitter end, dying in battle as heroes." He sighed. "After all the losses and tragedy, I eventually became hardened."

"I'm so sorry. Thank you for trusting me enough to tell me the truth."

"I do trust you, with my life." His gaze filled with warmth. *Can this be real, or is it a dream?*

"I didn't mean to drudge this all up for you." Her arms tightened around him as she breathed in his scent. The warmth from his body and all those hard muscles made her feel safe. The pounding of her heart should've scared the hell out of her, but it gave her strength.

After a few blissful minutes, relief crossed his handsome face. "I never thought I'd say this, but talking about it helps."

"I'm glad."

"I'm still me. Don't expect unicorns to sprout out of my ass." His lips curled into a smile.

"Of course not." She laughed.

"But I want to move on, Talya. For you." The sheer emotion in his words made her throat tight with tears.

"I want to move on for you too." Hope blossomed. Now if she could only convince him that nothing bad would happen to her, despite being in dangerous situations on the daily.

"Don't move." Cayden walked to the table and picked up the framed picture of Abigail He stared at the photo for several minutes and then finally, some of the fog cleared from his eyes. "You're right. It's time to move on." Crossing the room, he stuck the picture in a drawer on his night table. She caught a glimpse of a velvet jewelry box.

"This is for you." He pulled out the box and placed it in her hand.

"What this?" Her heart sped up and panged away in her chest.

"I planned on giving this to you later as a surprise."

She opened the box to find a silver bracelet with a crystal in the center. Her breath caught. "It's beautiful."

"Here, let me." He took the bracelet out of the box and clasped it around her wrist. One thing became clear to her, they were both twisted up in each other. "I wanted to get you something to say I'm sorry."

"I'll treasure it. You didn't need to buy me anything. It was so thoughtful of you."

After he sat on his bed, he rested his horns against the wall. "Yes, I did. Bolting out of your place the other night was a shitty thing to do."

"It hurt when you pulled away from me." A few things became clear. She'd need to give him time, patience, and assurances to help him get over his fear of loss. He'd go to great lengths to protect the people he loved. All of these things doubled her attraction to him and increased her chances of getting hurt. But she realized he was worth it. She moved closer to him on the bed.

"I'm sorry." He ran a hand through his hair. "I'm so damn sorry." The light from the moon shone through his arched window and highlighted the torment on his face.

"Let me help you. Let me, this time," she whispered, too afraid to say or do anything that might push him away again.

She stared at the bed where Cayden slept and touched himself while thinking about her. The smell of him emanated off the navy comforter, and the soft gray sheets. She found it both comforting and arousing at the same time. When their chests touched, their breaths mingled together, their hearts beat in the same steady rhythm.

His gaze smoldered. "Talya ..."

The magnitude of his interest in her may have been something he'd buried for a long time—something she'd missed, but not anymore. He seemed to be wrestling with his lust like a stand-off with a tiger. Leaning over, she placed a gentle kiss on his lips.

Cayden groaned and deepened the kiss, tilting his head to the side. His tongue swept into her mouth and twined with hers in slow, wicked licks. The wild taste of him exploded in her mouth, and heat rushed over her skin. She wanted whatever he could give. She couldn't get enough.

She could feel his anger and his grief. He communicated both with his mouth and his hands, now roaming over her body, caressing her through her clothing. She wanted to take all of his pain away, absorb the hurt, and the grief into her own body.

She no longer worried about the impulses he stirred inside her, or the fear of getting overpowered. She trusted that he'd take care of her in the most sensual way. Moaning, she sucked on his lower lip and found herself flat on her back.

Pressing her into the mattress, his thick erection pulsed between them. No more taking things slow. His hand threaded through her hair and positioned her head at just the right angle to deepen the kiss, devouring her lips in the most sensual way. She wanted to be the one to unleash his passion more than anything.

The hot lash of his tongue left her breathless and shaking. He rubbed his erection against her core, soaking her panties. But then in another distant part of her brain, she worried if she could handle a creature as large as him.

The most exquisite male sounds of pleasure came from deep in his throat as the kiss raged on. Her confidence surged. Arching up, she lost her mind from the hungry sweeps of his tongue. The taste of him could easily become addicting. His hands trailed over her body, cupping her breast, tracing over her nipple with his thumb. Delicious shivers rippled through her body.

He broke away on a gasp. His gaze met hers, and hunger bled from his eyes and liquefied her insides. "I want you, Natalya," he murmured against her lips. "You tell me how and in whatever way that makes you comfortable."

"I want you too," she murmured over the rapid beat of her heart.

"I'm all yours." Pulling his T-shirt over his head, Cayden threw it to the side. The sight of his broad shoulders and rock-hard chest never got old. He was a primal male with the kind of body and virility she'd always dreamed about.

"I don't think I could ever get tired of looking at you." Natalya tilted her head and pressed her lips to his skin, starving for a proper taste. She'd never gotten the chance to explore a man's body before. Her tongue swirled over his pecs, tasting soap, salt, and man. Her lips moved to his nipple and grazed the tip.

He groaned. "I want those gorgeous legs wrapped around me. Leave the shoes on."

Turned on by his take–charge attitude, she felt safe and taken care of. She wanted to drive him out of his skin.

"Come here," he growled and lifted her onto his lap. Taking her lips for another searing kiss, he slowly unbuttoned her dress. When he pulled away, his eyes were scorching hot and full of need. "I need to see you, Talya, now. The demon in me is greedy and impatient." Cayden pressed his forehead to hers.

"I've waited my whole life for a man I trusted to look at me the way you are right now." Natalya rubbed a hand over his chest, right above his heart. "This is becoming a night of firsts for both of us." She wanted to be wild and wanton with him, something she'd never done before.

A feral sound emanated from his throat as he spread the silk of her dress aside, and gazed at her black lace bra. "You're stunning. I've always thought so."

She'd longed to hear such sweet, honest words.

Cayden bent his head and sucked on her nipple through the lace. The heat from his mouth, and the graze of his teeth, became sensual overload. "Are you sure this is okay? Tell me to stop anytime," he rasped against her skin. "We'll take it slow. Baby steps."

"I don't want you to hold back, not this time." Then a thought popped into her head. What if she weirded out again? Would she allow her fear to get in the way of one of the greatest pleasures in life?

His fingers skimmed over her nipple, making her shiver. "You're sensitive. Everything about you is soft and feminine."

"You make me feel that way."

Sliding the straps of her bra down her arms, Cayden kissed her shoulder, and then tugged her bra off. He stared at her breasts with hunger in his eyes. The cool air brushed against her nipples. "I want to make you come, baby." He rubbed his nose along her neck.

"I want to, more than you know."

Switching to the other breast, he took his sweet time, giving it just as much attention. The devil himself swirled his tongue around the bud, licking and teasing, driving her out of her mind. "I can smell your arousal and it's driving me out of my freaking mind."

Her head fell back. "Keep going."

"There's another way I'd like to kiss you." Cayden set her on the mattress, and slid her panties off. His smile became wicked as he massaged her legs and moved his skilled fingers to her inner thigh.

"Cayden." Her skin flushed. Her breathing stuttered. "No man has ever gone down on me before." Did he have any idea how many times she'd fantasized about him doing this?

"I'm honored to be your first."

The way his blond head moved down her body got her hot. He ran his tongue over her belly button then blew on the spot. His warm tongue moved to her inner thigh. "You're beautiful here too."

Her body responded to his hungry perusal. Streaks of white–hot lightning sent heat straight to her soaking core. Everything he did felt amazing, and yet a small stab of anxiety threatened to overtake the mood. She ran her fingers through his thick hair, trying to stay grounded in the present moment, leaving the past behind where it belonged.

Cayden's hot breath on her sex snapped her right back to reality. "Are you okay?" The tenderness and concern in his voice helped her stay present.

"Yes, please don't stop." She'd never felt this kind of urgency before. Cayden took her body to new heights. He made her feel sexy and powerful.

The first brush of his tongue on her clit nearly jolted her off the mattress. Grasping onto the sheets, she moaned, and held on for dear life.

The soft, gentle strokes of his tongue drove her absolutely wild. His deep groan vibrated against her flesh. Cayden knew exactly what to do and how to pull every last drop of pleasure out of her.

The demon continued to sweep his tongue over her soft bundle of nerve endings and then added a finger, making her beg, turning her into a puddle on the bed. He murmured incoherent dirty words against her sex, while she whimpered.

She'd heard her friends talk about how some of the guys they'd been with didn't know what spot to hit, unlike Cayden, who needed no map of the female anatomy.

When he finally lifted his head, his lips were wet. His hair stuck up in all directions and his eyes burned like blue fire. "You taste hot and sweet. I could go all night."

His unhurried ardor enticed her on every level. She eyed the sizable bulge in his jeans. "We need to take care of you."

"Oh believe me, you will. But I can wait. You're first." His words made her hunger for him even more. "Do you think you can have an orgasm like this? Should I keep going?"

"Yes. I want to try." A tingling sensation spread inside her like flood waters about to burst through a dam.

"That's my girl." He bent his head again. An exquisite pressure built to a crescendo. He didn't let up, using his fingers and his tongue, creating the most exquisite sensations.

"Cayden, yes, right there. Don't stop. I'm going to ah ..." Natalya closed her eyes and just when she thought she might burst open and scatter to the wind, her core clenched. She went off like a bomb. A wave of pleasure washed over her, filling every part of her body. The colors around her became more vivid. The sound of their mingled breaths echoed in the room. He made her feel desired by giving her passion and tenderness. Satisfaction and joy raced through her bones. She laughed and stretched her arms over her head, feeling light and downright giddy. "I think we're on a roll, two out of two."

"Did that feel good?" Moving up her body, he kissed her eyelids and her nose, then brushed his lips against her forehead.

"Do you even have to ask?" She luxuriated in every tingly sensation.

"Thank you for giving me the most precious gift: your trust." Kissing her temple, he smoothed her damp hair off her face.

A sense of sweet, contented warmth radiated from her chest. After this, the line between their personal and professional lives would now be irrevocably blurred.

"I believe it's your turn." His care and patience emboldened her top make a move. Sitting up on her elbows, she eyed the enormous bulge in his jeans. She stroked him until he hissed out a breath. She fumbled for his belt buckle with clumsy fingers, wanting to give him the same kind of delicious pleasure.

His breaths came out shallow. "Have you ever done this before?"

"No, but it's something I've always wanted to. I can't stop thinking about how feral and sexy you looked the other day when you came apart." She slipped off her dress and placed it on the end of the bed.

He took off his jeans and set them to the side, leaving him in his boxers. Then he moved to his side and pushed her hair behind her ear. Reaching up, she ran her fingers over the scars and blemishes on his back, reminders of his strength. The man who lay before her with his legs hanging over the edge of the bed took her breath away. She wanted to be the one to drive him to climax. Licking her lips, her hand moved to the front of his boxers. She reached inside the waistband and ran her fingers over his erection. "Will you teach me?"

CHAPTER 36

"Is that a real question?" Cayden's cock hardened to the point of pain. Every brush of Natalya's fingers became torture.

The demon inside him wanted to take over, but he couldn't allow his cock to get in the way. He'd let Natalya take the lead and do this at her own pace, even if it killed him. Breathing in and out through his nose, he needed a moment to get his demon under control. A shockwave of pleasure rippled through him as she continued her exploration. Pulling down his boxers, his cock sprang free.

Her lips parted in wonder. "I'm not sure how I'm going to fit all of you in my mouth." The scent of her arousal filled the air. He loved that touching him got her aroused.

"We don't do anything you don't want to. You stop at any time." He couldn't tell her he was already halfway gone from watching her come. "I can still taste you on my lips and it's driving me insane."

As she ran her fingers over the base, he quivered in her hand. She explored his cock with gentle strokes. Her fingers moved to trace over the small tattoo on his right hip. "What do the numbers represent? I wanted to ask you about them the last time we were together."

"It's the mark of a slave. Every demon on Arcadia got one. The vampires who branded us used a special ink that never fades."

"I'm sorry you were forced to endure such hell." She placed a gentle kiss on the spot. Then her fingers moved lower, brushing back and forth. "Tell me what feels good."

"Everything you do, Talya ..."

"I want to kiss you the way you kissed me." The thought of her warm mouth on him forced his hips to push forward. Scooting to the edge of the bed, she bent her head and wet her lips. Her little pink tongue darted out to taste him, forcing him to hiss out a strangled breath through his teeth. She licked and sucked, then gave him another long, deep stroke. "A little help here. Am I doing this right?"

The combination of her hand and her tongue working him over almost made him shoot his load right there. "What you're doing feels amazing. Do it again, but swirl your tongue around the head." He touched her face and massaged her scalp.

"How does it feel?"

"Gods, yes, baby, right there." His breath became ragged, a sigh rumbled out from his teeth.

Natalya put the tip in her mouth and gagged. When she drew back, her eyes looked watery. "I'll just need to keep practicing." The wonder and innocence in her voice made him smile.

"Baby, you don't know what you're doing to me."

Silky strands of her hair fanned out over his cock. She licked him from base to tip with slow sweeps of her tongue. Tension rippled through his muscles and coiled down his spine.

His breath spiraled out from his lungs. "Talya." He couldn't hold on much longer.

She scraped her fangs against the tip and he went wild, jutting his hips forward. Moisture beaded on the crown.

"I'm ready to explode." He caressed her cheek, letting her know he was right there with her, every step of the way.

"This is more erotic than I ever imagined." Natalya alternated between slow and teasing and fast and urgent.

"Fuck, I'm going to come. You need to stop." He didn't want to scare the crap out of her. They'd gotten this far.

"Why?" The question sounded innocent. But there was absolutely nothing innocent about the way she took him into her mouth now. Her fingers wrapped around the base, pumping at the same time she sucked, so sweet.

"I won't be able to stop." His beast started to emerge. His thighs tightened. He'd been dreaming about her lips around his cock for months now. Reality blew the fantasy away. His balls tingled from the warm, wet heat of her mouth. Her eagerness and trust humbled him beyond words. When they'd started this, all he cared about was giving her pleasure—making her comfortable, but now he teetered on a razors edge, ready to explode. The way she took her time, learning what made him feel good was how she did everything else in life, with gusto. He loved that about her.

Whoa, where the hell did the L word come from? She tempted him to feel things he hadn't in years. She looked up at him with affection in her eyes, and he clung to it like a lifeline, tangling his fingers in her hair. He'd cut himself off to from any real emotional connection for so long, but with Natalya he couldn't do that anymore. Her sweet affection gave him a glimpse of what he'd been missing. She pumped from base to tip, and his control began to slip. Searing heat rippled through his veins, singeing every nerve ending. His vision blurred. Sparks flew through his body like flames. "Move your mouth away, baby."

She did at the last second and he spurted in her hand and onto the blanket. Cayden hung his head, sated and content. He collapsed next to her on the bed. "Let me get a towel." Wrapping the sheet around her body, she got out of bed and looked around. "Where am I going?"

"First door on the left."

She returned holding a towel and crawled into bed. She cleaned him up and set the towel aside. Sighing, she snuggled against his chest. "You look worn out."

"All thanks to you." Cayden pulled the comforter over them then kissed the top of her head. Wrapping her in his arms, he closed his eyes, and for one brief moment, all the turmoil hanging over his head melted away. Her ass brushed his cock and he instantly hardened.

"Are you kidding me right now?" She laughed. "How are you hard again?"

"It's a gift," he teased. "The demon in me can go all night long...with you." Nuzzling her neck, he inhaled the sweet smell of her skin. "What do you expect with your sexy, little body pressed up against me?"

"It goes both ways." His body warmed to the affectionate note in her voice.

When they lay together like this, it felt like their souls merged and their hearts beat as one. He could get used to the idea of having her here in his bed. But no matter how much he wanted her, he had nothing to offer. And he wondered if that made him a selfish bastard. Why couldn't he gather the strength to push her away for her own good?

His phone buzzed on the night table. "Shit. I should see who it is. I haven't checked my messages in a while." Untangling himself from her, he lifted the phone off the nightstand. He glanced at the screen, surprised to find a text from Erika.

Erika: Got something u need to c. Can u meet me @ Strbuks on Wash in thirty? It's about those gems. Bring the team.

Relief shot through his veins. As much as Cayden wanted to stay right here with Natalya, he needed to find out more about those gems and if they were somehow connected to the murders.

Cayden: I'll be there. Make sure one of the uniforms escorts you. C u soon.

He texted back and set the phone down, wishing he could spend the rest of the night cuddling and talking with Natalya, but it would have to wait.

"What's going on?" she asked and bolted upright. "Is everything okay?"

"Erika got a tip on the jewels and wants to meet up to fill us in. I'd text Denopoulos and Smith, but it's late. They're probably both asleep by now. We can head over there. I'll update them in the morning."

"As much as I'm curious to hear what she has to say, I can't. I need to head to the station. It's Mulroney's first night back and I promised to catch him up on what's been going on with his caseload."

"I understand."

"Is it safe for Erika to be out and about at night? I'm surprised she offered to meet you alone. Don't you think it's dangerous?"

"She's taking precautions." Crossing the room, he picked up her discarded clothing off the floor and laid her things on the edge of the bed. He then went to his dresser, pulled out a fresh pair of boxers, a pair of jeans and a hoodie and got dressed.

"I hope so. I wish we could stay here for a little while longer." When she stretched her arms over her head, the sheet slipped beneath her breasts. Suppressing a groan, his cock stiffened.

"What are you doing after your shift ends?"

Her eyes widened as her gaze landed on the bulge now straining against the front panel of his jeans. "Catching up on paperwork, laundry. Why? What did you have in mind?"

"I want to see how many times I can make you come."

"Cayden," she whispered his name in a voice thick with lust. *Damn.* He'd have to pry himself away. She slipped on her dress, covering all that beauty.

"Don't forget these." Picking up her heels, he walked over to her side of the bed. He kneeled before her and lifted her foot to his mouth.

"What are you doing?"

"The toes are erogenous zones. Let me show you." He bent his head and sucked on one pink-painted toe.

Her head fell back with a moan. "I see what you mean."

Pulling his lips away, he slipped her shoe on her foot. "Something to remember me by. I'd better go or I'll never get out of here. I can drop you at the manor on the way."

"Don't worry. I can take an Uber." Natalya pulled out her phone and shot off a text. "I don't want you to make Erika wait. I just pray she's being careful."

"Yeah, you and me both. Denopoulos sent me the computerized image he created from your description and there's no denying the likeness. It's Erika alright. I admit it's pretty damn freaky."

"I wish there was more I could do." He picked up on the worry in her voice.

He searched around for his boots and his gun. "If it were up to me, I'd spend the whole night holding you, but it sounded important. I don't want you to think this is like the last time when I bolted." He hated to leave her like this.

"It's okay. I get it, and this is different than the last time." She touched her new bracelet, now dangling from her slender wrist, and beamed.

"I never expected to open up to you." He could blame it on the moonbeams shining from the skylight and catching in her hair, or the intoxicating smell of her perfume. But it was her warmth and her heart.

"I'm glad you did."

"It meant a lot to have you listen without judging me. I feel like I can tell you anything."

"You can. I'm here for you, Cayden."

He huffed out a guilty breath as he holstered his gun. "It's time for me to come clean about all of my secrets and past indiscretions if we're ever going to be together for real. You deserve to know the truth."

"The truth about what?" she asked, buttoning her dress, and running her fingers through her tangled hair.

"I should've told you before. It didn't seem important at first, but now after what we've been doing, I think you have a right to know." Cayden exhaled, long and deep, and slipped on his boots. "I used to be involved with Erika."

The happiness faded from her eyes. "Why didn't you tell me, especially after I admitted to talking with someone else?"

"I never expected things to go this far with you, and Erika and I are ancient history. I'm sorry I didn't tell you from the get-go."

"I can't help but wonder if you have a pattern of getting involved with the people you work with." Hurt flashed in her eyes.

"Erika and I engaged in a brief fling. We both needed an outlet from the stress and ugliness of the job." Moving next to her, he reached out to touch her hair, but she pulled away.

"I'm not experienced in this arena." Blurring to the chair across from his bed, she curled up, and pulled her knees to her chest. "I think this explains why my visions of Erika kept popping up because of my connection to you. I must've been seeing the past, not the future."

"It makes sense. Look at me," he whispered. "Things are different with you."

"Are they?" She didn't sound convinced.

"I fucked up, and I'm sorry. I'm not used to being in a relationship or opening up to anyone."

"A relationship? Is that what this is?" Her big brown eyes widened in surprise.

"I know I don't want to share you with anyone, and from the look on your face you feel the same way."

Her lips tilted up in a breathtaking smile. "I do, but I wish you would've been up front with me from the beginning."

"You're right. When Abigail died, I tried to take away the pain by drinking and sleeping with random women, but nothing filled the emptiness inside of me until you came into my life." The confession felt like a balm to his soul

"I want to believe you with all my heart." Tears filled her eyes.

"Look, there may be nothing I can say to convince you with words. I can only do it through my actions." Scooping her off the chair, he sat down and rested her on his lap. He kissed her temple.

"You need to be up front with me, Cayden." She rested her head on his shoulder. "There can be no trust without honesty."

"I give you my word it won't happen again," he whispered, burying his face in her neck. "Are we okay?"

"Yes."

He looked up at her face, and sighed with relief. "There's something I've been wanting to ask you. We'll need to talk to our bosses first and make sure it doesn't affect your chances of getting promoted, but I want to be your date to the wedding."

Joy shined in her eyes. "I'm sure we can find a way to figure it out. I'm going to email my boss. I've been planning on doing it anyway. The answer is yes."

"Good." He smiled, loving her enthusiasm.

"No more secrets," she said in a soft voice.

"No more secrets," he repeated. He couldn't find the words to tell her he thought about her night and day, so he settled on a version of the truth. "Is it enough to know that you're the best part of my day?"

Her arms wound around his neck, warming him from the inside. "It is for now."

CHAPTER 37

*C*ayden walked through the door of the coffee shop, and found Erika seated at a table next to the window. Two large cups sat in front of her with a few packets of sugar. Luckily, the place was empty. "You're early. I hope you didn't come here alone." Taking a seat across from her, he removed his jacket. Even if Natalya's vision didn't come to pass, Erika still needed to be careful until the killer was behind bars.

"One of the uniforms followed me here when his shift ended," Erika said, sipping her coffee. "He escorted me from my car to the door and I rewarded him with a cold brew. You don't need to worry."

"I appreciate you picking up the ball and moving it down the field, but not at your own risk."

"Trust me, I'm being careful, following protocol, yada yada, yada."

"Okay then." Cayden smiled and pointed to both cups. "Are one of these for me? Or are you stocking up for later?"

"I took the liberty of ordering your favorite. If I remember correctly, two shots in a large cup of black coffee."

"Thanks. I could use this right about now." Lifting the cup to his lips, he blew on the top and took a sip. "I'm surprised you remembered." *Shit.* He hoped she still didn't have a thing for him. He cared about her. He always would. But now his heart belonged to Natalya.

"Some things you don't forget." Erika smiled. "Anyway, a friend of mine knows this retired antiquities professor who specializes in old coins and rare gems. I asked him to take a look at the ice that Pike tried to fence and send me a report."

"I can't wait to see what he found."

Erika pulled out her phone, pressed a few buttons and then set it on the table in front of his cup. "These gems aren't from this world. My guy is sure of it. They date back hundreds of years."

Shock rippled through his bones. Could they be the jewels stolen from his people, but how? Could Frost have brought them here after all these years? "I saw them the night of the bust, but nothing rang any bells. Then again, I'm no expert. Tell me how your prof came up with his analysis?" Scanning the report for a few minutes, Cayden swallowed hard. *Hell, it all seems legit.*

"A number of things like the weight of the gems, the historical era, the markings, the authenticity of the stones, the circa dating, and of course the lapidary techniques used to make them." Erika finished her coffee and set the cup aside.

"What kind of markings?" Cayden read over the words, trying to wrap his brain around the implications. After he finished, he took a screen shot of the report and sent it to the team in a group text.

Picking up her phone, Erika scrolled through her photos. "There were symbols on them he'd never seen before. I took pictures of a few. I looked them up. They're in Demonish. Do you recognize any of them?" She set the phone on the table in front of him.

Cayden studied the first rune and nodded. "A sword with a flame represents the eternal fortitude of my people. This can't be real."

"Hold on, so you do think these came from the lost demon plane of Arcadia?" Erika asked, staring at him like he'd grown another head.

"After the Coterie took over the plane, their ruling class claimed what was left of our treasures: gold, jewels, and ancient scrolls." Cayden sighed. Thinking about Arcadia even after all these years still made him nostalgic for all the people he left behind.

"None of this makes any sense," she said, sounding bewildered. "I checked the archives and the historical records. They say the jewels were destroyed hundreds of years ago. This is like finding artifacts from El Dorado or Atlantis."

"Arcadia existed, believe me." *I've got the scars to prove it.* "The plane was destroyed by the Coterie a long time ago. No one has ever been able to locate anything of value from there until now." Scratching his head, he couldn't help but think the jewels had turned up here for a reason.

She nodded. "Okay, let's assume these are real. Who brought them here and how do they tie into Andee Lyon's murder?"

"There are still members of the Coterie out there living under assumed names. They've been known to take on other people's identities. Our agency has managed to arrest most of them, but there are still some out there." Fiddling with the lid on his cup, he tried to connect the dots. "Let's say Frost is alive, and somehow managed to falsify the autopsy results. He could've used the gems to pay off Pike for helping him escape from prison. I sent him and his wife away for life. If he did manage to escape, he'd want revenge. I wouldn't put it past him to come after anyone close to me."

Erika rubbed her head. "You realize how crazy this all sounds?"

"I do. I need answers and the only way to get them is to make a pit stop at Hellios. I appreciate the update, but I need to book. I promise to keep you in the loop. You're aces, Erika. The next one's on me." He shot to his feet, grabbed their empty cups, and threw them in the trash.

"I'm holding you to it, demon." She smiled and reached for her things.

"Let me walk you to your car." He held the door open and followed her outside. A soft springtime breeze blew by, enveloping them in the crisp night air.

"I'm parked a few blocks away. I'm grateful for Natalya's warning, but it's hard to plan your day-to-day based on what appears in a crystal ball."

"I get it, but you need to play it safe right now."

The sidewalks bustled with people walking their dogs and leaving bars. The two of them headed across Washington Street then made a left on Clinton. Couples strolled by holding hands. His mind drifted to Natalya. He wished he could've held her in his arms until she had to leave for work.

"You've been with a vampire. I can smell her on you." Cayden caught the wistfulness in her voice.

No use denying the truth. "Yeah, I'm seeing someone. I never meant to hurt you, and if I did, I want you to know how sorry I am."

"I knew the deal going in, Cayden. You've always been straight up with me and treated me great."

Sure, he'd made mistakes with Erika, never giving them a chance. He'd been too closed-off to open his heart again. He didn't want to make the same mistakes with Natalya. He couldn't bear the thought of losing her now.

"I get it. You're taken. Whoever she is, you'd better treat her right." Erika gave his shoulder a playful bump. "We're cool. In fact, I'm seeing someone."

"I'm glad." Cayden smiled. "I want to see you happy. Is it serious?"

"It's still new. I'm headed over to his place now. You don't have to worry. I have the charms from the girls hung around my windows and doors."

They came to a deserted corner and stopped in front of her red Jeep. "Thanks for everything. You shouldn't be out at this hour all alone. Let me follow you to wherever you're going and make sure you get there safe. There's a killer still out there."

"Why would the killer come after me? I believe Andee's killer was a jealous lover who snapped." Erika gave him a hug and then got into her car and pressed down the window. "Let me know what you find out."

"Will do." Cayden tapped on the hood of her car, and then watched her drive away. He pulled out his phone and shot out a text to the Hellios warden to let him know he was stopping by. After that, he a group text to the team to see if anyone could meet him at the prison. But he wouldn't hold his breath, and there was no time to waste. His gut clenched as he thought about what he was about to do.

He just hoped he'd come out of it alive.

CHAPTER 38

"*H*ow does it feel to be back, partner?" Natalya glanced over at Mulroney, who sat in the cubicle directly across from hers. All around them the station buzzed with voices and a flutter of activity.

"I'm not sure. I'll let you know after I get through this mountain of paperwork." Mulroney motioned to the stack of files now on his desk.

"You want to play, you gotta pay." She teased. "Not all of us are taking tropical vacations and going to wild bachelor parties." One glance at the pile on her desk and she wanted to throw her hands up.

"Look who's talking." Mulroney chuckled. "I heard most of you were dancing on tables at the bar."

"Some of us were. It was a blast." She thought about what happened afterward and a hot flush spread from her cheeks to her neck. She'd never felt this cherished or in touch with her own body. These sensations all mixed up inside her weren't only about sex. She loved the way Cayden paid such close attention to her reactions and needs, giving her pleasure, taking his time. She'd already fallen for him hard.

"I've got something for you," Mulroney said, walking over to her desk, and setting a stack of files on top of the growing pile. "Don't say I never gave you anything."

"Gee, thanks. You know just what to give a girl." She tapped her mouse and clicked into her email.

"Any new leads in the Lyon murder?" he asked, taking on a serious tone.

"Everything points to Maverick as our rapist." Her hand hovered over her mouse. "I've been poring over the evidence, but something doesn't add up. "He's not our killer, and it doesn't gel with the testimony from our only witness. And we still haven't found out who drugged Cayden the night of the murder." Sighing with frustration, she let go of her mouse and pushed the pile aside. "What do you think?"

Mulroney knitted his brows together. "I think you've got to take Willow's vision into account and weigh it against the evidence. I'm going to review everything again. The captain wants me to assist on the case and it sounds like I'd better get up to speed."

One of the uniforms rushed into the open area looking harried. "We just got a call in from one of our patrol officers. He was one of the first responders on the scene at the Lyon murder," he said over the buzz of his walkie. "A young woman was found dead in her car with half her throat missing. The vehicle's parked in an apartment lot on the corner of Second and Adams."

His words thundered in Natalya's ears. "That's Cayden's building." *Crap, I just let the familiar out of the bag, so much for keeping our relationship a secret.*

The uniform gave her a curious look. "From all accounts, the Lyon killer struck again."

The drive up to Hellios had taken Cayden four and a half hours in the van. He'd gunned it two-fisted the whole way, maneuvering over treacherous terrain and wet mountainous roads. Thank the gods he hadn't taken the Challenger, or he'd be a twisted pile of metal at the bottom of the mountain right about now.

His caffeine jolt had worn off by the time he hit Poughkeepsie. He'd stopped and grabbed a large coffee and a greasy breakfast sandwich along the way. Now his stomach threatened to revolt.

As much as he didn't relish the idea of coming up here alone, both his partner and Smith were probably still catching z's and nursing some wicked hangovers right about now. Every fiber of his being told him that Stephen Frost was still alive and had managed to escape somehow.

The terrain began to change, growing more mountainous with rugged cliffs and narrow winding roads. His ears began to pop. Once he passed through the town of North Elba, he looked up and caught sight of the prison jutting out from the top of Algonquin Peak. From the outside, it resembled any other brick structure with a fifty-foot-high electrified fence surrounding the perimeter, but the inside housed a supernatural max prison.

No one except law enforcement knew that the world's most dangerous supernatural criminals lived and breathed behind its lead walls. It couldn't be found on a map or GPS, only through a series of coordinates. He'd been up here enough times through the years to find his way in the dark.

When he reached the security checkpoint, he lowered his window. "I'm here to see the warden." He flashed his badge and held his breath. They could turn him away. They didn't like outsiders entering their facility because of the dangers involved.

One of the many hulking demon guards covered from head to toe in body armor, stepped out from his post and walked up to Cayden's car. His horns poked out from the sides of his helmet. Glancing at his badge, he placed his hand on his weapon. "Step out of your vehicle, Agent Teague, slowly. Put your hands where I can see them."

"Of course."

"Have you been here before?" The guard pointed a scanner at him, and after a series of beeps, a green light appeared. The light moved from his head to his toes, taking his picture and doing a full-body scan. He wanted to say 'cheese,' but he figured it probably wouldn't go over well.

Cayden nodded. "A few times." It wasn't a place he'd forget, more like the kind that starred in his nightmares.

"No weapons allowed inside. You pick up your piece on your way out." The guard held out his hand.

After Cayden removed his gun from his holster, he handed it over. Going inside Hellios without a weapon made his skin itch.

If Frost did escape, Cayden wasn't sure how he'd managed to pull this off. If the vampire could make it past the computerized security blocks and the numerous armed guards, he'd still needed to traverse a mountain and hope like hell he didn't get turned into ash from the fire-breathing chimera roaming the grounds.

"This is for your ride." The guard handed him a ticket and then pointed to a footbridge that led to a cliffside elevator. "Take the bridge straight across and don't get off the elevator until you reach the top. The guards will meet you on the other side." He snickered. "Well, you know the drill."

"Thanks." Pulling out his cell, Cayden checked his messages and then remembered there were no towers out here, just their own in-house service. *Shit.*

After he made his way to the narrow footbridge, he took a deep breath and stepped on. Wind whipped across his face like a slap and blew his windbreaker in every direction. Cayden tried not to look down as he made his way across, wishing like hell he'd worn his sneakers and not these clunky-ass boots. His muscles bunched and tightened with every step.

The roar of the chimera pierced the air and forced his gaze to the two-headed beasts snarling beneath his feet. The creatures resembled a winged lion and a goat. They could swallow a person whole and grind up their bones for sport.

One misstep and he'd be their dinner tonight. He continued forward, putting one foot in front of the other. Holding his breath until he finally reached the end, he got off the bridge and pushed his head between his legs, panting.

Exhaling, he walked to the stone wall where the built-in elevator would take him to the main floor. He stepped inside and the wall lit up like a computer screen. The moment he pressed the button, he gripped the handrail. The elevator zoomed to the top of the mountain at lightning speed. He tried to stay upright and keep from hurling. By the time the doors opened, his whole body swayed. A wave of dizziness hit him hard. He practically crawled out the other side.

Two more guards rushed to meet him in the hall. "You'll need to follow us, Agent Teague." Cayden got his footing, and followed them to a security desk. Another guard stepped in front of him, holding a visitor's badge and a tracking device. They used green for visitors and red for prisoners.

The guard placed a small computer chip at the center of Cayden's forehead and it dissolved into his skin with a hiss. "This way."

He followed the guards down a long silver corridor with computer screens built into the walls. From previous experience, he knew cameras tracked his every move. Moving holograms of the inmates floated by. The familiar faces brought back memories. He'd nailed quite a few of them over the years.

Once they reached the tunnel to the main building, he felt his strength weaken and his senses dull. They embedded the walls with lead, the only known substance to zap a supernatural's powers completely. The guards and the prison staff took an antidote that kept them immune.

They crossed into a long corridor made up of glass paneled walls. Cayden swallowed hard as they walked through the prison area. Yelps and jeers echoed through the hall, reverberating off the walls.

A mad-looking wolf locked in an isolation cell stuck his face against the thick glass and screamed through one of the holes. "I want a piece of you," he growled, and proceeded to pull out his long, wild hair in hunks.

"Nothing like a warm welcome," Cayden murmured and kept on walking.

Many died in here from the lead exposure, the rest succumbed to madness.

They stopped outside the warden's office. One of the guards put his hand on the glass door and it lit up with his name and badge number. After a series of beeps, it slid open. "You may enter."

Walking into the room, Cayden passed a wall of laser guns, spiked batons, body armor and shields behind a digitally controlled steel cage. When he came face-to-face with Mark Andrews, the demon motioned for him to come forward.

"You said it was urgent, Teague." The warden stood almost as tall as Cayden with long, swirling black horns and grayish hair. He'd worked for the MBI pushing papers for years before he got promoted. They'd bumped into each other quite a few times over the years.

"Thanks for seeing me on such short notice." Cayden shook the demon's hand.

"I figured it makes sense to share information for both our sakes. I want to find out who killed Gregory Pike and confirm whether or not it's related to our recent break. Do you have any leads?" Andrews pointed to a metal chair across from his desk.

"We have a few," Cayden hedged, taking a seat. "I think it's fair to say our agency believes the break was an inside job."

"We've rooted out the guards involved and charges have been filed against them." Andrews said with a nod. "They've all been held accountable, all except Gregory Pike, our dead inside man."

"I have reason to believe Stephen Frost is still alive and responsible for killing Pike, Kyle Hawthorne and a CHS by the name of Andrea Lyon." Clearing his throat, Cayden unzipped his jacket. No sense in dancing around the issue.

Andrews frowned. "It's not possible. Frost's body was burned beyond recognition. The only way to identify him was through dental records."

"Can you take me through what happened the night in question?"

"Here's what we know, a fight broke out between Kyle Hawthorne, the prisoner in the cell next door to Frost, and his cellmate. Hawthorne got stabbed in the chest." Andrews pressed a button on his desk and it lit up with a layout of the prison. He pointed to a red dot. "Before the guards could get Hawthorne to the infirmary, a fire broke out here."

Cayden traced his finger along the map, and looked up. "I imagine all hell broke loose from there."

"Some guys never made it out of their cells." Andrews shook his head. "Our whole system went down, cameras, everything. But when the smoke finally cleared, we found Frost torched in his cell and Hawthorne gone."

"I believe Frost somehow managed to switch identities with Hawthorne." Cayden pointed to the monitor on the demon's desk. "What if he put him in his cell and changed the records? It's within the realm of possibility, considering the shit Frost was involved in when I arrested him."

Andrews sat up straighter in his chair. "The staff here is well aware he worked as a ghost hacker. Even still, there's no fucking way Frost could've pulled off what you're describing without us figuring it out."

"I'd like to watch the feed from the night in question to see if there's something you might've missed."

"Agreed." Andrews punched a few keys on his computer and black-and-white images filled the screen.

Cayden could barely make out the prisoners from the guards as flames and smoke engulfed the lurid scene, but nothing he saw indicated how Frost had managed to pull this off. "This is pretty gruesome stuff. "

"All of our computers were shut down temporarily."

"Speaking of computers, did Frost have access to your mainframe?"

Andrews switched screens. "I don't see how. Mind you, all of our inmates are assigned jobs. But Frost worked as part of the cleaning staff."

Cayden's horns tingled. "Then he had access to your offices? He could've used his own device to steal your passwords and then modify his identity in your system. Switching the records with Hawthorne would've been a cakewalk."

"I see where you're going with this, Teague, but there are guards in place at all times." Andrews rubbed his chin. "Frost was never alone."

"Can I get a list of your employees?"

Andrews nodded. "I don't like what you're suggesting." His horns elongated from his head. "I run a tight ship here. We got rid of our bad apples."

"What if Frost had a little help from some friends?" Cayden suggested. "What if some of your guards were on the take? Corruption's not an easy thing to stamp out. It wouldn't exactly be a stretch. I'm only asking if it's possible."

"Hell, anything's possible." The demon's expression turned contrite. "These guys risk their lives day in and day out for very little coin, but shit happens. Do you have any proof that Frost is still alive?"

Pulling out his phone, Cayden clicked on the jeweler's report and set it in front of Andrews. "Aside from circumstantial evidence, this is the closest thing I've got. We caught Pike trying to fence these jewels at a local pawn shop. There's no way he got these on the black market."

The warden tensed as he scanned the report. "I admit this is more than suspicious, but it doesn't prove shit."

"Maybe not, but it begs the question, who gave Pike Arcadian gems?" Cayden asked. "Where the hell do you think he got them from?"

"I don't have an answer for you."

"When we first brought Frost in, we confiscated his assets and froze his accounts, but we didn't get everything." Cayden swallowed hard. "We found a safe deposit box key at Pike's. We traced it to bank a few hours south of here. It stands to reason he used the gems to pay off Pike for helping him escape. It wouldn't surprise me if Frost still had a stash hidden elsewhere using different aliases."

Andrews shot him a look. "This is sounding crazier by the minute. Let's say by some miracle Frost is alive. I get why he'd whack Pike to cover his tracks, but why the hell would he kill the Lyon girl?"

Cayden heaved out a frustrated sigh. He laid awake thinking about this long into the night and only one thing came to mind. *Revenge.* "To frame me. Frost killed Andee as payback for putting him and his wife away. There must be a way to check if he could've hacked into your mainframe. Do the inmates get access to computers?"

"Every inmate gets their own tablet, but we have strict security and proxy service to keep certain sites from being accessed." Andrews pointed out. "We track all network activity per user."

"Can I take a look at Frost's tablet?" Cayden's mind reeled, trying to process this new info.

"I'm afraid it burned up in the fire, although there still might be some physical evidence for us to examine." The demon rubbed a hand over his face, looking shell-shocked.

"There's nothing to lose in checking. He could be out there killing other innocent women." Panic crept into Cayden's voice. "In terms of the timeline, Andrea Lyon was found dead a few days after the prison break. Don't you think that's too much of a coincidence?"

Andrews glanced at his screen. "There's only one way to know for sure. We'll need to exhume Pike's body."

Now we're getting somewhere. Cayden blew out a strangled breath. "Thank you."

When the warden stood, determination sparked in his eyes. He spoke into his mic. "I need backup, my office. Now." Pressing his thumb to a keypad on the cage, a red light scanned his print. Once his photo and badge number flashed across the screen, the door opened with a loud beep. He reached for a couple of body shields and tossed one to Cayden. "Prepare yourself."

"For what?" Cayden's adrenaline spiked. "Where are we going?"

"To have a little chat with the guards and see if your story checks out." Andrews crossed to the door. "If any of them were in on this, they'd be in a hell of a lot of trouble and have everything to lose."

Cayden followed him, gripping the shield. "Agreed. I'm guessing this will go over like rain at a picnic."

"If the staff figures out who you are and the case you're investigating, they could decide to bolt. We do it now while we have them cornered." Andrews stared at him long and hard. "Of course we run the risk of the guards pitting the inmates against us, and then we'll have a riot on our hands."

CHAPTER 39

By the time Natalya and Mulroney arrived at the apartment complex, both the sidewalk and parking lot had been cordoned off with yellow and purple crime scene tape. Foreboding rain pounded down in big fat drops. The static from walkie-talkies crackled in the distance and pierced her ears.

While Mulroney spoke to one of the uniforms, Natalya's gaze darted frantically around the lot, checking out the scene. Patrol cars and an MBI unmarked van were parked next to a red SUV. A stormy breeze blew the metallic scent of blood and body fluids around.

Did Cayden have any idea a homicide had just taken place outside his building? Natalya checked her phone again. After she'd read Cayden's text, she tried calling him, but it went straight to voicemail.

"You okay, Dubrosky?" Mulroney's gaze narrowed in her direction.

"What are we dealing with? Have they identified the vic?" Even after all this time, she'd never get used to this part of the job, the senseless act of violence committed against a woman. Natalya didn't envy the cops who'd have the unimaginable task of informing her family of the news.

"A witch with half a chunk of flesh missing from her neck was found bleeding to death in her car." Mulroney angled his dark head to the red SUV. "I overheard Smith says the vic bled to death from two fang marks to the neck. They've declared it a supernatural crime."

"Do you believe we have a serial killer on our hands?"

"Or a copycat. We'll find out soon enough." Mulroney pointed to the car. "They're ID'ing the body now. It's hard to believe we were all here less than twenty-four hours ago celebrating."

Natalya's throat tightened. His words struck with the force of the bolts above. "I wonder if she lived in the building." She bit down on her lip. How could this have happened right under her nose? But more importantly, how could she not have seen something that would've prevented a murder from taking place? Guilt gnawed at her gut.

"We should know more soon," Mulroney said, pulling on a mask and gloves. "We need to hang back and let the MBI agents do their thing."

"Any witnesses?" At this time of night and during a downpour, the streets remained empty, except for the occasional delivery truck passing by. To think the killer could be roaming the streets and possibly living or working near Cayden's building gave her chills. They wouldn't be able to conceal the murder out in the open like this. It would only be a matter of time before reporters swarmed the area.

"From the position of the body, she was killed somewhere else and then put back in her car. The coroner's on his way. I'm going to talk to the agents and find out if we can assist in any way." Her partner disappeared through the small crowd now gathered next to the vehicle.

Natalya couldn't stop thinking about the poor woman dead in her car and Cayden. Was he still at Hellios? Thunder boomed in the distance, matching the pounding of her heart. The wind picked up, swirling leaves in every direction. Pelting rain lashed across the sidewalk. This night had gone from magical to a complete nightmare in the blink of an eye.

When she spotted Smith and Denopoulos standing on the other side of the tape, pulling on paper booties, masks, and gloves, she blurred in front of them. "Who's in the car?" she shouted over the rain. A flash of lightning lit the sky, and an invisible fist twisted her stomach into knots.

Denopoulos sucked in a harsh breath. "I'm sorry to be the one to tell you this, Dubrosky, but it's Erika, our MBI lab tech."

Shell-shocked, Natalya staggered back. "No! It can't be Erika!" The image in the mirror had been a warning after all. Her stomach convulsed. "Cayden went to see her a few hours ago. How could this have happened?"

"We're doing everything we can to find out. I'll let you know as soon as we do. I'm sorry I've got to go." Denopoulos disappeared in the crowd of uniforms cataloging the scene.

Turning, Natalya slowly approached the car. Her knees almost buckled beneath her when her gaze landed on Erika's bloody body. The lab tech's head lolled to the side, revealing bite marks in her neck from razor sharp teeth. Her eyes remained open, frozen in death.

Nausea threatened. Normally she wouldn't be so sensitive to a scene like this, but she'd known this woman, and had been having visions about her for days. Taking a step back, her ears pricked at a conversation.

One of the uniforms pulled out a camera and began the grisly task of taking pictures of the body. "From the scratch marks on the seat and inside the car, it looks like she tried to fight him off."

"Look at this," another replied. "We checked her phone, and her last call was to one of the agents. The one common denominator between the two vics—special agent Cayden Teague."

CHAPTER 40

*B*etween the two of them, Cayden and the warden managed to get a few of the guards to come clean about their involvement with Frost without getting caught up in a riot. They admitted to being promised a payoff to look the other way while Frost attached his device to the mainframe. From there, he was able to download the employee passwords. Now all they needed was proof that Hawthorne was their corpse and not Frost. They'd get to the bottom of this one way or another.

By the time Cayden walked out of the main building and into the sunshine, bursts of orange and pink fire streaked across the sky, a stark contrast to the dim light of the prison. His stomach grumbled.

He'd stop for some grub and then catch a few z's in the van before making the trek home. Exhaustion gripped him hard. His mind raced with a million different questions, and scenarios; how long would it take to exhume the body of what had to be Hawthorne? And what measures would it take to find Frost?

He turned the corner and almost ran smack dab into two towering figures, Nick and Big Red. "What the hell are you two doing here?" he asked over the sound of whirring blades in the distance.

"Sup, Teague." Nick pointed to the roof. "The chopper's waiting for us on the helipad. I'll explain everything once we get in the air."

"The chopper? Are you shitting me?" Cayden stomach tightened. Did it have something to do with Natalya? "I'm not going anywhere until you tell me what the hell's going on." His heart thudded against his ribcage.

Big Red eyed the valet ticket now clutched in Cayden's hand. "There's no time. I'll drive the van to HQ."

Cayden's anger flared. His demon began to stir. He didn't like being kept in the dark. "Don't you think I have a right to know?"

"Easy, big guy," Nick said and held up his hands, palms out to soothe his beast. "No need to get your skivvies in a bunch. Smith sent us to fetch you because there's some shit going down and you're at the center of it."

"What kind of shit?"

They ignored his question and Cayden's frustration welled. Smith wouldn't have sent them if it wasn't something serious. He shouldn't direct his anger at them. He understood better than anyone what it meant to have to follow protocol. He handed the ticket over to Big Red. "Don't change my stations."

"Noted. See you on the other side, man." The demon saluted him and took off in the other direction.

Cayden followed Nick through a side entrance and up a staircase to the roof. The whir of spinning blades became deafening. The chopper sat on the helipad with the door open like it might launch at any moment.

They jogged across the helipad and ducked as they got into the chopper. After Cayden put on his headphones, he secured his seatbelt and glanced over at the other agent. "Look, Nick, you got me in this flying box. Now spill."

Nick signaled to the pilot. After a series of checks, they soared up into the air.

"I'm not going to ask you again." Taking a deep breath, Cayden tried to keep the explosion of anxiety in check.

"I'm sorry, man," Nick shouted over the spinning blades, his expression grim. "Smith wanted to give you a heads up. There's been another murder and I'm afraid all things point to you. We're headed to the Council."

Less than two hours later, Cayden sat in one of the courthouse's conference rooms facing his lawyer, Mike Sierpina. The moment they touched on the ground, he'd put a call in to him. Thankfully he was already there, finishing up a case. Sierpina sat across from him on a leather chair barking orders into his cell phone.

His partner had sent Cayden pictures—bloody, gory stills of Erika's body. Every time he closed his eyes, those images flooded his mind. When he thought about how hard she must've struggled, his stomach threatened to revolt. This nightmare never seemed to end.

Hearing the news of Erika's murder had absolutely gutted him. He knew deep down in his soul that Frost must be responsible. One way or another, he'd make him pay. Tears still stung his eyes and left him reeling.

A surge of emotions—anger, shock, and guilt swept through him with dizzying speed. One thing became patently clear—Frost wouldn't stop until he destroyed everyone Cayden cared about. He wanted to rip the monster apart and make him pay for what he'd done. But no punishment would ever suffice.

Trying to shake off his anger by being productive, he pulled out his phone and made some calls, first to the team to ensure Natalya's safety, and then to Mulroney to arrange for extra uniformed officers outside the manor. He refused to take a chance with her life. He made the next call to Natalya, to tell her the deal, but she didn't pick up. His fears mounted. Needing to hear her voice to know she was safe, he sent a group text to the witches to check on her.

His lawyer ended his call and glanced over at Cayden. "Here's the deal, you've been called in as a professional courtesy. You were the last person the vic texted. There's an eyewitness from the coffee shop who saw you leave with her around midnight. A few hours later, she's found dead in her car."

"We met to go over evidence on a case we're working on," Cayden said, running a hand through his hair. "Could they charge me with anything?"

"I talked to the Council members, and as of right now no formal charges have been brought against you. I suggest you voluntarily make a statement."

"I'll tell them everything." *Except for my involvement with Natalya.* Mental and physical exhaustion pressed down on Cayden like a heavy weight. Some of the adrenaline had started to wear off and he could barely keep his eyes open. Then a thought seeped into his veins like poison.

Natalya could be next.

He vowed to catch this maniac before he could touch a hair on her head.

"I just hung up with the warden and he said you've caused quite a stir." Sierpina opened his briefcase and pulled out a legal pad. "They sent a crew to dig up Hawthorne's body. Once they bring it to the lab, the coroner's going to check the DNA. We should know more soon."

Cayden rubbed at the scruff on his face. He needed a shave and a fresh change of clothes. What he wouldn't do right now for a clean bed and a hot shower. "Thanks, man." If a person was going to have someone representing them when getting accused of murder a second time, they'd want a badass like Sierpina in their corner.

"We're not out of the woods yet, not by a long shot." Sierpina scribbled notes on his legal pad before looking up. "There's a joint investigation going on between your agency and the RHPD. We've got a witness downstairs giving a statement on your behalf."

"Who?"

"I didn't get a name." Sierpina flipped through his notes. "Time isn't on your side. A four-and-a-half-hour window exists where no one can verify your whereabouts. You could've killed Erika before driving up to Hellios. Did anyone see you?"

"I stopped along the way for gas, but I paid in cash." Getting to his feet, Cayden sighed, and tried to clear the fog from his brain. He pulled out his phone and sent him the location of the gas station.

A second later, Sierpina's phone pinged with a text. "This is good. We might be able to get something off the security feed. You're not an easy guy to miss. Let me see what the other side has against you."

"Should I be worried?" Cayden asked, hoping for a miracle. This unknown territory felt like a vice around his throat.

Sierpina gave him a nod. "Tell me about your meeting. What was Erika's state of mind?"

Cayden blew out a breath. "She said she was headed to meet the guy she'd been seeing. He had to be the one who killed her. The proof must be on her phone." Could Erika have been meeting Frost?

"Unfortunately the RHPD found nothing. Did you get a name?" Sierpina asked, loosening his tie.

"No. And it wouldn't matter if I did, Frost would be using an alias." It wouldn't do Cayden any good to keep secrets from his lawyer, so he filled him in on the whole sordid tale, including his brief involvement with Erika.

When Cayden finished, his attorney drew his brows together. "The other side could say you met with the vic in an attempt to get back together and when she rebuffed your advances, you killed her in anger."

"I'd never hurt a female. Never." There had only been one time in his life when Cayden thought he could be capable of taking a life—the night he found his beloved bleeding in a ditch. He could still see the blood spurting from her neck. He never thought he'd get the smell out of his nostrils. A rage like he'd never known had pounded through his chest and clawed at his insides until he thought he'd go mad. He'd carried that rage with him every day of his life since.

"Is there anyone else who can corroborate your story or your whereabouts before the murder?" Sierpina asked, his voice bringing him back to the present.

Cayden couldn't tell him the truth, that he'd been with Natalya. It could ruin her chances of a promotion and sully her reputation to boot. The only way to keep her out of harm's way would be to push her away. This case was getting too messy, too personal, and he couldn't risk the killer going after her next. "No, no one. What happens now?"

"You have twenty-four hours to make a statement. You should go home and change, get some sleep." Sierpina glanced at his rumpled clothing. "You look like shit."

"Tell me something I don't know. I can't go home. Smith and Denopoulos texted me. There are reporters crawling all over my building."

"There's a motel close by. I'm headed to my office." Sierpina closed his briefcase. "I can drop you on the way. You should try to eat. You need to keep your strength up."

Yeah right. Cayden couldn't imagine eating something right now. Images of Erika's neck torn apart, sitting in a pool of her own blood flashed through his head. He should've gone with his gut and followed her. She might be alive today if he had.

Someone knocked on the conference room door. "Come in," Sierpina called out.

Cayden turned his head and found Natalya standing in the doorway. "What are you doing here?" Could she be the witness giving a statement on his behalf?

Their eyes met, and hers filled with concern. Seeing her in the flesh set his blood pumping. "Cayden, I'm so sorry about Erika. May I come in?" She looked all business in her crisp white shirt and navy suit.

"I'll give you some privacy." Sierpina got to his feet and left the room.

Cayden walked up to where she stood. "What have you done?" Inhaling her wild scent, he let the sweetness wash over the prison stench still seeping from his pores. He wanted to pull her into his arms and pretend this nightmare wasn't real. He'd give anything to whisk her off to some place safe and make love to her all night long. It might be the only way to take some of the pain and ugliness away. But he knew better, because nothing could.

"Something I should've done from the beginning," Natalya whispered in a voice full of remorse. "I told my boss we've been seeing each other and admitted we were together last night right before you left to meet with Erika."

"Natalya, you shouldn't have jeopardized your chances of a promotion for me. It's all you talked about. I would've found a way to get myself out of this without involving you." All things seemed to fall apart in his wake. He refused to bring her down with him into this living, breathing hell.

"I don't give a damn anymore about my promotion. There'll be other promotions. What I care about is you." Closing the distance between them, Natalya reached out and squeezed his hand. The warmth from her touch steadied him like an anchor.

"You shouldn't have." He wanted to say he felt the same way, but the words wouldn't form on his lips.

"Are you okay?" Natalya touched his face and he fought the urge to rub his cheek against her palm. "What can I do? This is so horrible I can't believe it's real."

"No one's worried about me in a long time." When Cayden thought about what she'd just sacrificed for him, his throat went dry. He understood her desire to prove her success to her snotty, stuck-up family and now because of him, she'd wear the mark of shame like a scarlet letter. Old-moneyed vampire families like hers would probably turn up their noses at anything they deemed messy.

"I'm prepared to deal with whatever the consequences are," Natalya said with concern in her voice. "Cayden, say something. You look so numb. I'm worried about you."

"You shouldn't have come here."

"Why not?" Her big brown eyes filled with confusion.

"You're in danger. I have reason to believe Frost is coming after you next." The overwhelming urge to pull her into a hug, and whisper against her hair, tell her how much he cared, assure her everything would be okay took hold, but he just stood there frozen.

Worry lines bracketed her mouth. His stomach twisted, knowing he'd put them there. "Please, stop being cryptic. I have a right to know."

"I'm sorry. I can't get into all of this right now. You have to trust me and take extra precautions." His voice came out harsher than he intended.

Tears filled her eyes and slid down her cheeks. "I do trust you, with my life."

You're killing me right now. "Please, don't go anywhere alone. Promise me."

"Fine, I promise, but I'm not leaving. I'm staying here with you."

"You can't. It's not safe. I'm sorry, but it's the only way." His gaze moved to her lips and it took every ounce of willpower not to ravish her mouth. He couldn't be this close to her and not be tempted to kiss her, comfort her, especially now. It had been years since he needed anyone, but right now he needed her more than he needed air to breathe. Her courage blew him away. He needed to get out of there. If he stood this close to her a moment longer, he wouldn't be able to drag himself away. Taking a step back, his chest ached from the pained look on her face.

"Don't do this, Cayden. Why are you pulling away from me? Why do you sound so detached?"

Gods. He hated himself right now. Now came the hard part, letting her go. "We shouldn't talk or be seen together from now on, not until the killer's caught." The moment he said the words, he felt the sucker punch to his gut.

Shock lit her features. "That's it? We're done?"

"It's the only way to keep you safe." He added an extra helping of BS to seal the deal. "We should've never gotten involved in the first place." The lie tasted bitter on his tongue. She'd been the only light in his life for centuries.

"I don't believe you. I can tell by your body language. I'm on your side, Cayden," she said with a sob. "I want to be here for you. I knew the risks of the job the first time I put on my badge. I want to help you get through this nightmare. Don't let this tear us apart."

"I get that you're a strong, capable female, and you probably think I'm acting like a caveman, but we're dealing with a madman who has nothing to lose." He took a shuddering, deep breath.

"What about us?"

"Don't waste your time on me. I've told you, I don't need anyone." *More lies.* "You were right about me all along. I'm a player and players never change." He imagined those words would haunt him for years to come.

"Don't be the noble savage for me." The hurt in her eyes felt like a physical pressure on his chest.

Talya, my Talya. How could this be happening?

"I'm sorry." He'd always been of the mindset to rip the Band-Aid off clean, even if it meant taking a layer of skin with it. As much as it killed him, Cayden did the one unselfish thing he could, he turned, crossed the room, and without looking back at Natalya, he walked out the door. *What have I done?*

The second the motel room door slammed shut behind him, Cayden passed out face-first on the bed, still in his clothes and his boots. After he woke up, he took a long, hot shower and shaved, starting to feel more like himself. Denopoulos had dropped off his shaving kit, a suit, shoes, socks, and a tie. He didn't know what he'd do or where he'd be right now if not for his friends.

Knotting a towel around his waist, Cayden walked out of the bathroom. He'd picked up a sandwich and chips on the way here and gobbled them down in Sierpina's car like a prisoner indulging in his last meal.

No matter how hard he tried, he couldn't stop thinking about how he'd treated Natalya. Swallowing hard, his esophagus burned with guilt. His phone buzzed with a text and he secretly hoped it was from her. He walked over to the desk, picked it up and glanced at the screen.

Andrews: The body we believed to be Stephen Frost is Kyle Hawthorne. Frost is alive & considered a dangerous missing person.

Cayden's heart pounded. He read the words over again. He wasn't crazy. *The pieces of this fucked-up puzzle are all starting to fit together.*

Someone banged on the door, but Cayden barely heard it over the buzzing in his ears.

Frost is alive. Frost is alive. The words reverberated through his head like a mantra.

Another bang. Denopoulos must've come back to drop off coffee.

"I'm coming." Cayden jogged to the door, holding his towel in place. He opened it and his chest tightened when he found Natalya standing on the other side.

Rain poured down on her, plastering her dark hair to her head. Shivering, she looked cold and miserable. "Natalya? What are you doing here?"

Anger formed a tight line around her mouth. "Getting to the truth."

CHAPTER 41

*N*atalya crossed the threshold into Cayden's motel room, dripping wet and shaking. Her eyes still burned with tears. She didn't know why she came. She just knew she couldn't stay away.

His jaw visibly clenched. "You shouldn't be here." His masculine scent, a combination of sandalwood and pure male, filled her head and made her ache. He shut the door and put the chain in place.

When their gazes locked, she stunned them both by reaching up and slapping him across the face, hard. "That's for shutting me out." She'd never struck anyone before in her life. And after everything he'd been through, it didn't seem justified, but he'd spurred her anger by making decisions about their relationship.

A part of her wanted to yell and rant, to shake Cayden for cutting her off at the knees. But then another part of her wanted to soothe him, considering how much he must be hurting. She stood on shaky ground by putting herself out there, something she'd never done before. He'd opened her up and now she risked getting hurt and maybe even rejected, but at least now she was willing to take the chance.

"I suppose I deserve that." Cayden touched his reddened cheek. "How did you find me?" The mouthwatering sight of him left her a little breathless.

"I asked the witches for help."

"Look, Natalya, I wish things were different, but they're not. You should go. It's not safe for you to be near me." His body tensed and his gaze remained defiant and angry.

"Stop leaving me out. I just read the coroner's report. I know Frost is alive. I get what you're trying to do, but I'm a big girl." Her voice rose. "You can't expect me to run and hide." She'd vowed to never leave herself vulnerable again. "I plan to go on the offensive and take Frost down if and when he comes after me."

"You don't get it." Closing his eyes, he shook his head. His stress and his pain became palpable, emanating off him in waves.

"Please, enlighten me." Her voice softened.

"Frost will stop at nothing, and I mean nothing, to destroy me." Sighing, he slumped to the edge of the bed. "How many more have to die before he's found?" A sob tore from his throat.

That's when she realized he never had time to grieve. She went to him and wrapped her arms around his big body while his shoulders shook. Anger and sorrow ripped from his chest. She held him and they both cried, feeling his pain like a physical ache until there were no more tears left.

"I'm so sorry, and I do hear what you're saying," she whispered, rubbing his back. "But I'm a trained professional. I can handle myself. Why won't you let me help you?"

Cayden got up and paced the small room, drawing her gaze to his muscular shoulders and rigid pecs, not an ounce of fat could be found on his sculpted torso. She shivered with appreciation. Why did he have to be naked except for a towel? When he turned around, her gaze moved to his scars. They didn't detract from his beauty. In fact, they only accentuated his resilience.

"I can't go there with you right now." He stopped pacing, and when he stepped closer, she sensed his turmoil. She couldn't think, couldn't breathe with seven feet of gorgeous demon so close. "Anyone close to me is a target. I've already put you in enough danger."

"I'm being careful. No one followed me." Natalya wanted to read him the riot act for not leaning on her, but then the overhead light caught on the shadows under his eyes and her anger melted away. "I can't imagine what you must be going through right now."

Cayden glanced at the door as though someone would break it down at any second. "Frost's a psychopath and a genius to boot. He's been one step ahead of us at every turn and now Erika's dead because of me." The pain in his voice broke her heart.

"It's not your fault. We have an all-out manhunt searching for him. One way or another he'll be found and then this nightmare will be over—"

"It's not over. Not even close." Rubbing his forehead, his features became hard and weary. He'd been through hell and back in the last twenty-four hours. She wanted to be there for him, even if it meant having him lash out.

His hungry gaze roamed over her wet hair and drenched clothing. She shivered again, but not from the cold.

"You're soaked. Let me get you a towel."

While he went into the bathroom, she glanced around the room. His computer and phone sat on a desk. When her gaze moved to the unmade bed, she caught a whiff of his scent on the pillow and it made her ache. It looked like he'd just gotten up from a nap. She wanted to crawl in there with him and pretend this nightmare had never happened. *Could this all be a bad dream?*

"Here." Cayden returned with a towel and wrapped it around her shoulders. He rubbed her arms until goosebumps broke out along her skin.

"Thank you." She wondered how she could be this physically close to someone and still be so far away. Pulling her wet hair from her ponytail, she ran the towel over the ends. Cayden followed the movement with his eyes. When she finished, she hung the towel on the desk chair.

"Feeling better?" His concern for her well-being confused her. She didn't know what to think anymore.

"Yes. I need to know why you're pushing me away." What if he didn't feel the same way?

"Gods, Natalya, my defenses are weak." The way he whispered her name warmed her more than the towel ever could. His gaze moved to her lips and then traveled lower to her soaked white shirt. At this point it probably left nothing to the imagination. "You're not helping matters," he said in a strained voice.

"Let me in on what's going on in your head, please."

Closing the scant distance between them, she craned her neck to look into his eyes. She sensed the war raging inside his head. She prayed for a miracle, hoping his attorney would find a way to get him out of this. But what if he didn't? What if charges were brought against him for Erika's murder? What if he got convicted and sent to Hellios? What if she never saw him again? The questions flitting through her head forced her to sway in her boots. If she didn't make the most of their time together, she'd regret it for the rest of her life.

"You shouldn't even be here right now. My life's in the shitcan."

"I want to help you." When she reached out to press her hands to his chest, his muscles bunched beneath her fingertips. She braced herself against his rejection, ready to walk out the door. But she wasn't the same person anymore. She'd wasted enough time being scared and lonely, living a half-life. The new Natalya took chances.

Standing on her tiptoes, she tried to place a kiss on his cheek, going for the spot where she'd slapped him, but it landed on his neck. "I'm sorry too for slapping you."

"I deserved it," he murmured, his voice filled with remorse. He rubbed his jaw. "Mulroney warned me about your right hook."

She smiled. "I lashed out because you hurt me. I know in my heart you were only trying to protect me."

"I never meant to hurt you, Talya, believe me." His arms wound around her waist. He pulled her against his chest and kissed her temple. "I have no doubt you can take care of yourself. I've lost every woman I've ever cared about. I can't lose you too. I didn't mean what I said, not a single word."

Something inside her ignited. She wanted to be with this man in every way possible and take away his pain. "I'm done living in fear. Cayden, please touch me."

His blue eyes flashed with unmistakable lust, blazing a trail of heat along her skin. "I'm not made of stone." Bunching her wet shirt in his hand, he skimmed his knuckles over the swell of her breasts.

"Cayden," she moaned and reached up to dig her fingers into his damp hair. Her body molded to his, the past fading from her consciousness, making way for the present. They could make new memories filled with passion to replace the dark ones. Her lips fastened to his, and she lost herself in the wicked flavor of his mouth.

He trailed kisses down her neck. "If something happened to you, I … couldn't live with myself." Hers stomach flipped from the rawness of his words. He cared.

His tongue trailed over her damp skin. She picked up on the thud of his heart and the race of his blood through his veins.

"I can't take it when you push me away." Her voice cracked with emotion. Her breasts rubbed up against his chest and her nipples grew tight with arousal.

"Talya," he growled. His warm fingers grazed her neck and then moved under her shirt to rub the bare skin on her back, torturing her with lazy circles.

She arched into his touch. She didn't know what would happen from one moment to the next. She only knew one way to make them both feel alive. Her hand moved to his heart where it pounded, needing to feel their connection. "I want you."

"No, not like this." Cayden groaned. Lifting his head, torment brewed behind his eyes. He let go of her, and she wanted to scream in frustration.

"Don't I get to make the choice?" If she walked out the door now in his time of need, she swore her heart would shatter into a million pieces. She decided to tip the scales in her favor. Swallowing hard, she undid the last of the buttons on her shirt.

"What are you doing?" Alarm laced his voice.

"My shirt's soaked. I'm taking it off to dry." Heat swirled between them like a volcano about to erupt.

Fire burned in his eyes like blue flames. "You don't play fair."

"Who says I'm playing?" Desire sparked low in her belly. She'd never done anything this bold in her life. But with Cayden, she could be herself. She could push him to the edge without any fear. And right now, he needed her just as much she needed him. The sight of his erection now tenting the towel emboldened her to keep going.

"Talya, don't." His deep voice filled with warning while the heat in his gaze intensified.

"Stripping for you is getting me hot." Shifting on her feet, her underwear became damp with excitement. She'd never felt this free or in tune with her body in her life. Her confidence surged with every sharp intake of his breath. She took off her shirt, glad she'd worn her new white lace bra. Cool air whispered across her skin. She hung her shirt on the back of the chair. Her boots came next. Kicking them off, she unzipped her slacks and slid them down her body.

"You're playing with fire." The hunger in his eyes turned ravenous. His nostrils flared. He must've smelled her arousal. She'd never seduced a man in her life. She couldn't imagine doing something so daring with anyone but him. His horns flamed red; his breathing became stuttered.

Time to poke the demon and lose the bra. Reaching behind her, she unhooked the clasp and flung it at the bed. "That's the plan."

Passion flared in his eyes and her confidence surged. He lifted her off her feet. She had him, finally. She wrapped her legs around his waist and exhaled in a rush. Crushing her lips to his, she flicked her tongue into his mouth with long, deep strokes.

A burst of heat shot between her legs from the passion in his kiss. From the tension in his body, she could feel his anger, his unrestrained lust, and his pain. Her heart melted.

He laid her on the bed and pushed her wet hair away from her face. His gaze filled with awe. "You're stunning. My cock's aching for you." Rubbing his erection against her, a jolt of electricity shot straight to her core.

"I want you, Cayden." Her breasts ached, begging to be licked and touched.

"I didn't want our first time to be this frenzied. But you've gotten me crazed." The deep rumble of his voice reverberated against her ear and ramped up her desire even more.

"I want to be here for you." *Body and soul.*

"I don't deserve you," he whispered in a voice thick with regret. Capturing her lips for another searing kiss, he swirled his tongue in her mouth. His fingers trailed over her stomach, then moved to the inside of her thigh. He rubbed his thumb over her thong, and heat rushed up her body.

She broke away, panting. "Don't ever say such things."

"I only wanted to protect you, never to hurt you, baby." He murmured words of apology and need against her lips.

Tears burned in her eyes. "Cayden, don't. Be here with me now."

"From the second you strolled in here with your big brown eyes and your wet shirt with those pouty nipples poking through it, I knew I was done for," he rasped against her neck.

Dipping his head, the hot, wet heat of his mouth closed over her nipple. His deft fingers slipped under the silk of her underwear to her dripping core. "You're wet for me." A shiver moved through her at the sound of his voice.

He added a second finger, pushing in and out of her in a slow lazy rhythm. She moaned and gripped the sheet. When he pinched her nipple with one hand and rubbed her clit with the other, her fangs slipped out. Desire spread from every pressure point on her body. Lifting her hips, she rubbed shamelessly against his fingers, loving the delicious friction.

"Don't stop," she whimpered as he increased the pressure on her clit, sliding long fingers in and out of her in a slow, tortuous rhythm.

"I want to make you come." Every touch and kiss overwhelmed her senses. He shattered the last of her defenses with his touch.

"It's so good, Cayden." Her breasts became full and heavy. Her clit throbbed along with her heart.

"You're so beautiful and brave." His words reverberated through her.

"Cayden, please."

"Are you sure you want this when I'm this raw and fucked-up?" His gaze brushed over her face as though committing every detail to memory.

"Yes. I want every part of you, good and bad.

"Then I need to get you really wet. It'll hurt less when my cock is balls deep inside you."

Natalya loved his dirty talk, and the incredible way he made her feel. She longed for this kind of irresistible sexual play with him, but then what? She didn't know what would happen from one day to the next, and it scared the hell out of her. How would she ever get him out from under her skin? "I was ready when my clothes were still on."

His thumb stroked and teased and then slipped deep inside and pressed her G-spot in lazy strokes, repeating the motion over again until her thighs began to shake. Her back arched while his skilled fingers brought her close to orgasm. Her body felt like it would combust. And she wanted more.

His chest pressed against her breasts. "I can feel you clenching around me. It's so fucking hot and all mine."

Mine? The fullness of his fingers and his words sent her teetering on the edge. The sensation of pleasure washed over her, igniting her desire. A hot current sizzled through her like lightning. She trembled on the edge. "I'm going to … ahh." She tightened and then everything released in a mindless surge of bliss.

When she came down from her orgasm and opened her eyes, his smoldering gaze raked over her body. The moment the spasm of pleasure faded, he didn't let up for a second. His gentle fingers continued to stroke and soothe her through the aftershocks of an intense orgasm. "I love watching you come apart." He removed his fingers, and a wicked smile spread across his handsome face. "I can't wait to feel you skin-to-skin."

She'd heard the rumors about demons having enormous sexual appetites. A host of nagging questions floated through her head. *Will I fulfill his needs? Will I be enough?*

"What's going on in your head?" He placed a long, deep kiss on her lips and some of her worries dissolved. He pulled back, leaving her breathless. Tracing the line between her brows, he gazed into her eyes like he could see inside her soul. "Talk to me?"

"It's nothing, just nerves. Please, keep going." *Stay present.* Natalya shook off any remaining doubts and pulled off his towel. His magnificent cock jutted out. Her thighs quivered in anticipation. "Gorgeous man." She didn't think she'd ever get used to the sight of his penis, but how would he fit? Fear worked its way around her brain. Her hand closed over his straining erection.

"Did you just give me the green light?" he asked, eyes blazing with desire.

"Yes."

"You tell me if it hurts. Do you hear me?" Brushing her hair away from her face, he kissed her temple. Everything about him radiated masculinity and strength, yet gentleness at the same time. His concern for her well-being shattered the last of her defenses. How did she once think of him as gruff? She could fall in love with this man. The realization sent her pulse racing.

"I promise I will." Their bodies pressed together and she caught a glimpse of the power in his muscles as he hovered above her with hunger in his eyes.

"Open your legs wide. Your body might just need a moment to adjust to me, and then I promise to make you come hard again." Nudging the tip of his penis in, inch by inch, his lips found hers again. His tongue delved into her mouth in hot liquid strokes, helping her relax, and he eased in a little more. The stretching of her most intimate parts bordered on pain. She cried out.

"I need a minute."

"Are you okay?" he asked with panic in his voice. "I'm sorry. Did I hurt you?" Sweat beaded on his forehead. He continued to hold himself up, not putting his full weight on her.

"I'm trying to adjust to you. I want to keep going, please. I know pleasure will eventually replace the pain."

Placing a tender kiss on her lips, he began to move again. Pain gripped her, but then came delicious tingles too. Unfamiliar sensations rocked her body. Would ecstasy and intimacy be sure to follow? All the things she'd always dreamed about but didn't have the guts to pursue until now.

"I'm afraid I'm going to hurt you. You're so tight." Cayden eased in a bit more. Her tender tissue stretched to accommodate the broad crown.

"Don't stop now." Natalya became aware of the softness of the sheet, the heat of his skin. She'd never felt this filled or connected to another person. She dug her fingers into his shoulders and moaned low in her throat.

"I've been fantasizing about doing this for months now." His pecs flexed as he moved. A sheen of sweat glistened on his body. His chest muscles tightened. The biceps in his arms bulged with every stroke.

"Me too. You take care of me in the most sensual way," she whispered, reaching up to touch his face. *Is this what making love is supposed to feel like?* "I finally understand what all the fuss is about."

"We're only getting started." Once he became seated to the hilt, the last of her pain became pleasure. The spicy scent of bonding pheromones filled the air. Their breaths mingled together. She shivered with anticipation at what would come next. *Hopefully me.*

Then something incredible happened as he moved deeper, the fullness of him got her hot in a way she'd never been before. Her skin burned. She masturbated all the time, but her vibrator didn't compare to this. Nothing prepared her for this kind of intense connection.

His jaw set as they moved together. The tendons in his neck strained and flexed. A fine sheen of sweat covered his body. "You feel so hot and snug. Do you need a break?"

It's too much. It's everything. "Don't you dare stop."

"I'm losing my mind." Cayden pulled out and then gently eased back in, stretching her, making her feel alive. "My Talya, taking all of my cock."

He continued to whisper sweet, dirty words in her ear as he took her to new heights of pleasure.

Could she have an orgasm through sex? If anyone could do it for her, it would be Cayden. Lifting her hips, her body kept adjusting to accommodate him, and then, with one deep stroke, he finally plunged all the way in.

"Fuck," he rasped. "I knew it would be like this." His lips fastened to her ear, brushing across her skin.

Sensations bombarded her, the fullness of his penis, and the intensity of their connection. Happy tears welled in her eyes, taking her by surprise.

Tension etched on his face. He reached between them and lifted her ass in the air, then hit that same delicious spot over and over again.

A cry fell from her lips as a surge of heat shot between her legs. Panting as another orgasm built and raced over her, the exquisite pressure blazed a hot trail through her limbs. She cried out, surrendering to its force.

A loud groan burst from his chest. "I'm close."

His hips bucked. He increased his thrusts. Cayden made a sound deep in his throat and his breath brushed her shoulder. She'd never seen him this abandoned. It filled her with feminine satisfaction.

His jaw tightened, his muscles bulged. "Ah … Talya, I'm coming." He roared and then erupted inside of her. The spasm shook her whole body. Her core clenched again from his liquid heat, and brought on another orgasm. *Scalding me.* Her fangs jutted out of her mouth, ready to pierce his skin and taste his blood.

"Kiss me." He bent his head and their tongues tangled together, leaving her breathless.

She melted into the mattress like a puddle. He treated her with exquisite care and tenderness while still managing to give her several bone-melting orgasms. She'd never felt this connected to another person, or this stripped and raw.

They both panted. Cayden lifted his head and smiled wide, then collapsed against her, gasping. His muscles twitched all over. "Holy crap, Talya. That was fucking out of this world."

"I thought we were going to break the bed." She couldn't remember feeling this sated or happy. Something shifted in her chest, something huge and scary—her feelings for Cayden.

After he kissed her forehead, he turned her on her side, and gathered her close. She wished they could stay there, sealed in the moment forever without reality setting in. Their bond was still fragile with rough edges that could easily inflict pain.

She found comfort in the steady beat of his heart, snuggling against his warm body. At some point, they must've dozed off.

His phone pinged, breaking into their cocoon. Jolting up, his gaze darted to the desk. Could it be the call from his lawyer? Their gazes locked and held without either of them saying a word.

They didn't need to.

CHAPTER 42

*A*fter another quick shower, Cayden slipped on his dress shirt and slacks, getting ready to head back to the courthouse. His lawyer said he should be ready to rock and roll anytime now. He glanced at his phone on the desk like a bomb ready to detonate at any moment.

"Let's make the most of our time together before you have to leave." Natalya's voice drew his attention to the bed. Lifting her arms over her head to stretch, she gave him a perfect view of her breasts.

"I could get used to the sight of you in my bed. I can't think of any place else I'd rather be." He picked up her clothes off the floor and set them next to her pillow. "I haven't yearned for anything in centuries, until now." She stirred cravings inside his heart he thought died a long time ago. Sharing stories from his past with her relieved the constant pain and grief he carried around. He'd forgotten what it felt like to be happy.

Natalya leaned up on her elbows. "No more pushing me away when things get tough."

"I won't. I promise." An outside light from the window danced across her black hair fanned out on the pillow. *I've got it bad. I'm so screwed.*

"Tell me what you're thinking about."

"I was worried about hurting you. Are you sore?" He sat next to her and toyed with a loose curl. Now he'd crave her night and day. As much as he wanted her, what could he offer her at this point with Erika's death hanging over his head? He should've never let her set foot through the door. Damn him for being weak.

"Yes, but in a good way." Slipping on her bra and panties, she got out of bed and walked to the dresser. She picked up his tie and turned to face him with a smile. "Let me help you."

"You're getting more comfortable around me." He gazed at her face and an emotion he couldn't quite identify lodged deep in his throat.

"Thank you for giving me the best sensual experience of my life." The trust shining in her eyes humbled him. She stood in between his legs, wrapping the tie around his collar, and then proceeded to expertly tie it in a knot.

""You look like you know what you're doing," he murmured, resting his hands on her hips. Now after all these years alone, he'd finally met someone he could see himself with for the long haul. Someone he looked forward to waking up to every day. She'd kick his ass in line and make him better in every way. Guilt twisted his gut for getting lost in pleasure and allowing himself to feel this happy so soon after Erika's death. He didn't plan it this way.

"I used to do this for my real dad." He caught the wistfulness in her voice. "I still miss him." She smoothed the front of his shirt.

Cayden lifted her hand and placed a kiss on her palm. "You deserve better than this hole-in-the-wall for our first time. I wish there had been candles, flowers, and soft music playing in the background."

"I kind of like this hole-in-the-wall, and being here didn't make it any less incredible or memorable." She sat next to him on the bed and put on the rest of her clothing.

He'd cherish these memories, praying with every fiber of his being they would have the chance to make new ones. He didn't know how to define their connection. He only knew that the thought of losing her sent him into a tailspin.

"I have questions." Curiosity sparked in her eyes.

"What do you want to know?"

"Whatever happened to Lilith and Stephen after you left Arcadia?" Reaching for his hand, she laced their fingers together.

"I never gave up trying to find them. I knew one day I would. I finally tracked them down through Interpol. After Arcadia was destroyed, the evil duo came here to the States and changed their identities to try and blend in to regular society." He gazed at her delicate hand in his, loving the way they fit.

"How?"

"Stephen became a ghost hacker. He found a way to obtain commercially available data and location trading from a third party who he believed to be a broker, but was actually an undercover operative. Stephen eventually led me to Lilith and I brought them both in. I made damn sure they stood trial for crimes against demon society. The last I heard, Lilith died in prison." Exhaling, his stomach tightened with every breath.

"And now you think Frost is hell-bent on revenge for putting him and his wife away?" Natalya massaged his neck.

He tried to relax, and leaned into her touch. "This is my worst nightmare come to life. I'm still trying to get proof. I'll let you know when we do. Be careful and make sure you carry your Summit Stake with you at all times."

She pointed to her purse on the nightstand. "I never leave home without it." Silence stretched between them. "I can't help but think there's more I could've done for Erika."

"You can't blame yourself." *Like I'm one to talk.* "You went out of your way and tried to warn her."

"Seeing what can happen in the blink of an eye puts a spotlight on the fragility of life. It makes you question things." Her breaths grew shallow like she needed to get something off her chest.

"What kinds of things?"

"Like how much time I've wasted. I may be immortal, but I'm at a point in my life where I don't want to waste anymore."

"What are you trying to say?"

"I wonder what this means for us."

"You're asking me to define our relationship now?" He heaved out a breath.

"I know my timing sucks, but I need to know if you've ever thought about being in a committed relationship after Abigail?"

Cayden swallowed hard. "I never saw myself getting tied down, between the job, and the long hours." He never imagined living through eternity with someone other than Abigail. But then he showed up in his life. "Things change."

Her deep sigh vibrated against his skin. Her gentle hands moved to the knot in his shoulder. Her fingers worked him over, alleviating some of his tension.

"What about you? After the first marriage, have you ever thought about doing it for real?"

"Yeah, I've thought about it, but I've never come close to meeting 'The One.'"

Could she ever see herself with a demon? It didn't matter how much he cared about her; the Dubrosky clan would never approve. He wasn't sure he cared about their approval, but it was clear she did.

"But it's like you said, things change." The wistful note to her voice tugged at his heart.

"Have you ever considered taking the potion Saje made for Mulroney to make you human again?" Cayden asked. "It seemed to work wonders for him. Alex says he's never looked back. Hell, now he and Gillian are even planning to have a brood of kids." *Who knew?*

"Garrett never enjoyed being a vampire, and in the beginning, neither did I." She smiled. "There are still some things I miss about being human. But now I can use my strength for good to help women who've been victimized or suffered from a form of sexual violence like I did. I don't think I could go back. I like moving forward. And this job makes me feel important. It may sound silly, but I like being strong."

"It doesn't sound silly to me, Talya, and as long as we're on the subject of the job, what about your promotion? I didn't want you to ruin your chances for me."

"It was my choice, and I don't regret a thing. I hope there won't be too much of a fallout, but I'll accept the consequences either way."

"No matter what happens, you're special in every way." He thought about admitting the depth of his feelings, but now wasn't the time.

Tears clung to her dark lashes. "I just know in my heart that no charges will be filed against you."

"Hey, no need to cry." He rubbed her tears away with his thumb. She knew how to keep him on his toes, the yin to his yang and the angel to his beast, although the fates might have other ideas.

"Cayden, there's something I need to say to you."

His phone buzzed. "Hold that thought." Untangling himself from her,

Cayden walked over to the desk and picked it up. He glanced at the screen and cursed. "It's time. I need to go."

Several hours later, Cayden leaned against the side of the van and sucked in a lungful of crisp night air. Exhaling a deep breath, he'd never been more grateful in his life to be outside.

His partner stood on one side of him, and Smith stood on the other. Cayden glanced around the now empty courthouse lot and then tilted his head up to gaze at the dark, cloudless sky.

The Council didn't file any charges against him due to the new overwhelming evidence, which included the positive ID of Kyle Hawthorne's body, confirmation that the Hellios server had been hacked, and the strength of Natalya's personal statement.

The gods must've been on Cayden's side because things could've turned out a whole lot differently. He'd asked his attorney to make a final request on his behalf, to allow him to assist the agency in finding Frost and bringing him to justice. They agreed, due to the extenuating circumstances and his intimate knowledge of all the players involved. He shot off a text to Natalya, giving her a heads-up.

"We checked Erika's phone, her home computer and the one at the lab, but found nothing that would lead us to Frost. He's probably using a burner phone, something untraceable. I think we're seeing a pattern here," Denopoulos said, pulling up the report on his phone.

Cayden's attention focused on the matter at hand, his friend, colleague, and former lover lay in the morgue while their killer roamed free. Guilt worked its way through his veins like a toxin. If only he'd followed her that night. She might be alive today. "She was on her way to meet someone. Now I know it had to be Frost. Shit, I should've called in a uniform. I should've trusted my gut."

Smith's gaze narrowed in his direction. "I didn't want to tell you this, but we checked the odometer on Erika's vehicle and here's what we came up with: The killer took her somewhere, killed her, and then dragged her into her SUV and brought her to your apartment complex to make it look like you did the deed."

Cayden's horns elongated and burned at the tips. He wanted to rip Frost's head off his body. "He must've tranced her like he did to Andee."

"Stop beating yourself up," Smith said with a shake of his horned head. "How could you have known Dubrosky's vision would come to pass?"

"I should've made it my job to know." Cayden swallowed the lump now lodged in his throat.

Denopoulos frowned. "Frost snuck under the radar. He's got to be using an alias."

Stalking across the lot, Cayden's anger and frustration mounted with every step. He wondered where the hell Frost was now. "What's the plan?"

"I've been texting with the warden." Denopoulos glanced up from his phone. "We uploaded pictures of Frost to every "most-wanted" list in the tri-state area. I don't believe he knows we're onto him at this point, which can work in our favor. We continue to piece together what we do have and track him down."

Smith took a swig from a water jug. "He couldn't have pulled this off alone. No doubt in my mind he has people working for him. I checked out the safe deposit box. It was empty. I'm still waiting for a warrant from the Council to get the bank to give me the name of the person who opened it. I'm hoping it'll give us a lead on Frost."

"Shit. Every time I think we're getting closer, Frost finds a way to cover his tracks." Cayden gritted his teeth, frustrated.

"Let's see if Julia can shed some light on the matter." Denopoulos pulled out his key ring and clicked the fob. The van doors slid open with a hiss.

Cayden walked over to the van and jumped in the seat as it swiveled around. He touched the dash and it lit up with a built-in keyboard. After he logged in, he pulled up Frost's record. His image filled the screen. The past came rushing back, leaving a cold fog on his skin.

Denopoulos and Smith slid into their seats and the doors automatically closed. The tinted windows prevented anyone from seeing in.

"Show me the Hellios mainframe, Julia." Smith directed the request to the speaker above his head. "I say we start there."

"Right away, Commander Smith," Julia answered back.

After a series of beeps, pictures flew across the screen at breakneck speed. "Their mainframe was infiltrated by background processes. The system became compromised by key logger scripts and apps used to record every keystroke when someone logged in to the system," Julia explained. "This allowed the hacker to get in and target the server. From there, a series of algorithms were attempted which gave the hacker access to every password."

Cursing under his breath, Cayden rubbed his temples, feeling the mother of a headache coming on. His phone beeped with an email. He glanced at the screen. "It's from the warden. He sent me their employee list with accompanying photos."

"Anyone look familiar?" Denopoulos asked.

After a quick scan of the faces, Cayden ran a hand over his chin. "Yeah, one guy, but I can't place him. I'll cross-reference the list with some of the other ones I've been compiling. What did you find on your end?"

Smith knitted his brows together. "The warden said there's a senior systems administrator investigating, trying to sift through the mess. He's going to get back to me when they do. In the meantime, we keep searching for Frost."

"Once we get a solid lead on Frost, we'll send the Bat out to surveil him." Cayden had sent their invisible drone out to take photos and record video on a multitude of cases. It would be a great help, but not as great as going out and finding the man himself.

Denopoulos turned to Cayden. "How in the hell could Frost have gotten away with this?"

"Typically hackers learn to encode scripts from analyzing and reverse-engineering other scripts. Once Frost had access to the passwords, he could change the records at will." A ball of dread worked its way around Cayden's gut. His association with Frost put everyone he cared about in danger. He reached into his pocket for a bag of nuts he'd gotten from the snack machine, ripped open the top with his teeth and dove in. He hadn't eaten a meal in twenty-four hours.

"When we're done, you should let me take you to the diner for some real food." His partner motioned to the bag of nuts. "I can't have my best man passing out on me."

"I almost forgot the wedding's only two days away. And the rehearsal dinner's tomorrow night?" Cayden didn't feel much like celebrating. Finishing the last of his nuts, he shoved the empty bag in his pocket. "We should take extra precautions in case Frost tries something at the wedding."

"Don't worry, buddy we'll find ways to keep the guests safe. Almost everyone in attendance will be carrying, and the witches can weave spells around the house and make charms for the guests."

Smith began typing on his phone. "Good point. We'll need to add a few agents to the guest list. We make sure we're heavily guarded from all vantage points. I'll talk to Ellen when I see her later tonight. Well, what are you waiting for people? We have a lot of work to do if we're going to pull this off before the rehearsal dinner. Let's fall out."

Cayden drew a breath. There were too many unknowns in the equation with a killer on the loose. "I hope like hell you're right."

CHAPTER 43

*N*atalya awoke to banging and the buzz of voices outside her window. She figured it must have something to do with the rehearsal dinner. Sitting up, she kicked off the covers and got out of bed.

Last night she'd been going out of her mind until she got Cayden's text. Hearing the news that no charges had been filed against him made her want to celebrate. But then the gruesome image of Erika's bloody body flashed through her mind and her stomach twisted into knots.

She shook her head at the irony. How could something so horrible coincide with something so beautiful? Could she have changed the outcome of Erika's death if she'd tried to warn her in person? The more she thought about Erika, the more darkness threatened to swallow her whole.

Her phone vibrated on the nightstand, breaking into her thoughts. Her heart fluttered with excitement when Cayden' number flashed across the screen. She pressed "accept" and put the call on speaker. "Is everything okay?"

"I'm fine," he murmured in his deep, gravelly voice. "I needed to hear your voice."

The words made her grin. Nothing in this world compared to the excitement of new love. "What time are you coming by?" She sat cross-legged on her floor.

"I'm not sure yet. I thought we should have a chat with our IT team. Can you meet me at headquarters?"

Glancing at her tank top and pj pants, she'd have to pass on this one, but at least he wasn't trying to be overly protective, or keep her out of the loop. "I thought it would make sense to stay here and keep a close eye on the witches, make sure there are no killer vampires lurking around." Allowing Frost to scare her into hiding was out of the question. On the other hand, she didn't relish the idea of the maniac coming after her.

"Please, be careful."

"I promise to take extra precautions. I thought I'd see if Willow and Alex need my help with anything before the big day."

"Fine. I'll head over as soon I'm done. Nothing will keep me from making the best man speech. I'm anxious to hear what happened with your boss. Smith shot me a text this morning and said he got a call from your captain."

Natalya toyed with the string on her pj pants. "After I left you at the motel, I met with my supervisor and told him everything. Technically, we haven't broken any fraternization policies since we work for different agencies. Luckily, I can still be considered for the transfer to the SVU."

He sighed, sounding relieved. "Good news for a change."

"I don't regret what I did. Not for a second." Her body still thrummed with delicious tingles.

"As much I admire and respect your independence, I'd never let anything jeopardize your dream. If it's important to you, it's important to me."

Her heart melted. She'd never imagined she'd find a partner who'd be invested in her dreams and goals as much as Cayden. "Thank you."

"Be prepared for extra security at the manor, in case Frost tries to crash the wedding and come after you." Cayden exhaled and she sensed the tension in his voice. "You don't need me to protect you, but I swear to the gods, I won't let him hurt you."

"I know, Cayden, believe me I know." Tiny explosions erupted under her skin from the possessive tone of his voice.

"What I still can't figure out is how he pulled this off. He must be getting help."

"He is. I've been cross-referencing the lists of names we've been given and sure enough, one name pops up on both the Wolf Tavern and the

Hellios employee list," Natalya said, going to her desk, and pulling up her spreadsheet from her laptop.

"Who?"

"A demon by the name of Jason Michaels. Do you recall the barback from the tavern who hasn't been seen since the night of Andee's murder?"

"Yeah, why? It seemed suspicious. How's he involved in all this?" Cayden asked, sounding tense.

"He used to work at Hellios as a former guard."

"Holy shit, Talya. You're brilliant."

His praise made her warm all over. "I don't know about that. In any case, I'm sending out a group text to let the team know." After she sent the text, she leaned against the bed and tried to relax. "We're getting one step closer to finding Frost. Enough about the case for now, we were discussing plans for tonight."

"I can bring my tux with me to the bonfire. I thought I could stay over. What do you think?"

Her heart thudded with excitement. "I'd love that." She couldn't wait to wake up next to him again. She craved his touch like a drug. In a few short weeks, he'd managed to turn her entire philosophy on sex, love, and relationships upside down. Now she couldn't imagine her life without him in it.

"Are you sure you want to fuel the rumor mill?"

"Trust me, everyone already knows we're together." She ran her finger over the bracelet he gave her, and smiled. She never thought she could feel this happy. "If they don't, they will soon enough."

"The only thing getting me through this nightmare is you. I think about the way your cheeks turn pink when you're aroused." His voice took on a husky tone and sent a shiver of awareness racing through her erogenous zones. "You squeeze me like a fist and make me come so hard it hurts."

"Cayden." Closing her eyes on a breath, her whole body thrummed.

The noise of beeping horns and the rumble of car engines echoed through the phone line. "I'm sorry, baby. I've got to go. I just pulled up to headquarters. I'll send you an update on any new developments. See you tonight at the bonfire."

"I can't wait." Natalya ended the call and couldn't stop smiling. *Is this what it feels like to be in love? No...* She couldn't be falling for Cayden. Her

heart seemed to disagree. She needed to get her head out of the clouds and
help set up for the bonfire.

Padding barefoot into the bathroom, she tied her hair in a ponytail.
After she washed her face and brushed her teeth, she came out and
rummaged through her closet, trying to figure out what to wear. She finally
settled on a pair of jeans and a soft, black sweater since she wouldn't be
going into the station today. Right before she headed out the door, she
swiped her compact off the nightstand and shoved it in the front pocket of
her hoodie.

She descended the stairs, and made her way into the kitchen. The buzz
of voices and banging echoed outside the door. Natalya headed to the
garden to check out the commotion.

Sunlight poked through the clouds in a bright blue sky. Strolling along
the stone path, she marveled at the breathtaking landscape bursting with
cherry blossoms. Flower beds bloomed with white and pink hydrangeas.
She inhaled, relishing their fragrant scent. The Bradford pear trees drew
her gaze up. Twisting branches loomed over the beds, creating a canopy of
silky white petals and spring light.

Voices drifted across the garden. The soon-to-be bride and groom stood
next to two demons dressed from head to toe in black. Small laser guns
were strapped to their belts. Cayden wasn't kidding about the extra
security.

Natalya recognized the MBI special agents, Big Red and Jax, having
worked with them in the past.

Ellen, Brooke, Delilah, Belinda, Saje, Gillian, Nadia, and Arabella stood
next to one of the patio tables stacked with silk pouches, ribbons, and dried
herbs, chattering away. They grew silent as she approached.

"What are you guys doing?" she asked, motioning to the herb pouches,
in an attempt to lighten the mood and stay productive.

Gillian shoved a handful of herbs into one of the pouches and then
handed it over to Arabella, who tied the end with a ribbon. "We're making
protection charms for all the wedding guests, and to use around the
house."

"Okay, I need everyone's attention." Alex held up his hands and waved
at the group. He then introduced the agents all around. "Every person that
comes in and out of here, florists, caterers, photographers, videographers,

hair and makeup people, will all need to stop and check in with security. No exceptions."

"I don't understand why we need extra security when we have Natalya, Cayden, Garrett, and Nick at the wedding?" Willow turned her attention from Alex to Big Red and Jax. "Sorry. No offense, guys. I'm grateful for everything you're doing. But when I pictured my dream wedding, it didn't include frisking the guests. Just sayin'..."

"It's going to be fine." Alex placed his hands on Willow's shoulders and kissed her temple. "You've got to trust me on this one, babe."

The private moment struck Natalya right in the heartstrings. She longed to have the same kind of partnership with Cayden.

Gillian walked up and pulled her into a hug. "How are you holding up?"

"I'm fine, thanks, still in shock." Her throat tightened. "I just want to make sure everyone's safe for the big day. Speaking of which, this place looks like a fairytale." She motioned around the newly transformed garden.

The next moment, a soft breeze caressed Natalya's skin. Pink and silver dust blew through the air. Wind chimes clinked together. Through the corner of her eye, she swore she caught a flutter of silver. Her head snapped around. "Did I just see a fairy?"

Gillian smiled. "Garden pixie. They come around on special occasions, typically around the spring equinox and make everything bloom."

"Nothing around here surprises me. I can't compete with pixie magick, but there must be something I can do to help."

"Did I hear someone offer to help?" Delilah walked over holding a giant bag of marshmallows and a box of graham crackers. "We could use an extra set of hands setting up for tonight's bonfire. How do you feel about taking over s'mores duty?"

Natalya took the bag of marshmallows and crackers out of Delilah's hands. "I say point me in the direction of the chocolate."

CHAPTER 44

ayden glanced at his friends huddled together on Adirondack chairs, drinking mulled wine and roasting s'mores over a crackling fire and his chest swelled with warmth. A lavish dinner of mushroom risotto, grilled vegetables and homemade ravioli followed the rehearsal. He cleared his throat. "I'm going to break tradition and make a toast before the reception, to pay tribute to a friend. I believe Emerson said, 'Let us make our glasses kiss and let us quench the sorrow-cinders.'" He held up his cup. "To Erika."

"To Erika!" everyone repeated and held up their cups.

Cayden took a swig from his mug. No one but Natalya knew he'd filled his with grape juice. His eyes teared up at the sentiment. Too bad it was bittersweet. Staring into the flames, he willed his grief to burn into ash.

"I loved the quote. It was beautiful," Natalya whispered from the chair beside him. Holding her marshmallow stick over the fire, she gazed at him with concern in her eyes.

"I'm glad." Cayden swallowed the lump now in his throat. Firelight caught in her hair and outlined the contours of her face. He'd never seen anything more beautiful.

"This has all been a nightmare." Handing the stick off to Gillian, Natalya turned to face him again. "Are you okay?"

"What? Yeah, I got smoke in my eye." He wiped his tears away. "Why don't we go for a walk?" Unbuttoning his flannel, he got to his feet, and held out his hand. "See you later," he announced to the group over the laughter and chatter.

"Okay, you two lovebirds, don't go doing anything crazy, like carve your initials into a tree," Alex shouted.

Catcalls and whistles ensued.

Natalya laughed. "They're incorrigible."

"I think this is payback." Draping an arm around Natalya's shoulders, Cayden led her away from the fire into the crisp night air. "I gave Alex a pretty hard time when he first got together with Willow. Look at them now. I still can't believe he's about to get hitched."

They walked along the stone path, now lit by flaming torches and cascading moonlight. Stars twinkled in a cloudless sky, casting a glow above their heads. The night couldn't be more perfect if someone drew it.

Once they reached the greenhouse, Natalya stopped and pointed to one of the towering oaks. "Have you ever carved someone's name into a tree?" she asked in a teasing voice.

"A long, long time ago." The more time Cayden spent with Natalya, the less he thought about Abigail. Her memory began to fade and now only fragments of their life together remained. He decided not to dwell on the past and lifted their joined hands. Lifting her hand, he placed a kiss on the inside of her palm. "What did you think of your first bonfire?"

"I think s'mores are seriously underrated." Natalya smiled. "There's something I need to say, but I don't think you're going to like it."

He tensed. "Okay, shoot."

"You were the one who said it's only a matter of time before Frost comes after me. Why not speed the process along and give him some help?"

"Where are you going with this, Talya?" Even with all the precautions they'd taken with the extra agents and magickal protections, he still felt like he might lose his shit at any moment.

"If I'm the one he's going after next, why put everyone else in danger? Why not turn the tables on him? I can't bear to see what this is doing to you."

"Don't ask me to dangle you out there as bait to a complete sociopath like Frost." He crossed his arms over his chest.

She sighed. "How's this any different than when we believed that

Maverick was our killer? Would you feel the same way if we weren't involved?"

"It's hard for me to say, because we are." The thought of losing her sent him into a tailspin. Pulling her into his arms, he placed a kiss on the top of her head. "There has to be another way."

"I'm sorry. I didn't mean to upset you." She wrapped her arms around his waist.

He tried to keep his emotions in check and breathed in her sweetness. They stayed there for a moment, lost in each other, both trying to will this nightmare to end. "I promise we're going to find Frost. He'll have to kill me before I'd let him get to you."

"Please don't say such things." Natalya touched his face. "What did the IT team find?"

"They managed to pull up Frost's data stream from the Hellios server and back-traced the link to the IP address of his computer. From there, they pinpointed his location to a studio apartment in the village."

"Are you serious?"

"He was long gone by the time our guys got there." Cayden frowned. "No big shocker."

"We're getting closer. It's only a matter of time before he screws up and then we'll find him."

"Let's hope you're right." Cayden exhaled. "I haven't been able to sleep. I'm not thinking straight. I've been going out of my mind."

"What about now?" Her voice softened.

"Being here with you is the only peace I've had all day," Cayden whispered. "I couldn't wait to get you alone."

Her face lit up with the admission. "Let's try and enjoy the rest of the evening. Are you ready to head back? I don't want to miss the fireworks."

"Oh, I'll give you fireworks." Moving his hand to the side of her face, Cayden bent his head and stopped inches from her lips. "I've been meaning to tell you, there's a piece of marshmallow right there." He ran his thumb over the corner of her lip.

All night long he'd been dying to devour her lips. Her sweater kept slipping off her shoulder, revealing smooth bare skin. He wanted to nip and taste the spot.

Her tongue darted out to lick the corner of her lip. "Did I get it?"

"Allow me." He pressed his lips to hers, craving a proper taste. His tongue darted into her mouth and tangled with hers in a searing kiss.

Threading her fingers through his hair, she kissed him back with deep, hungry strokes of her own. And he saw fireworks. How could he ever go back to the old way of living? His hands moved to her ass and squeezed.

Growling, he broke away and trailed open-mouthed kisses along her neck. He pulled her sweater down to nip at her shoulder. "I want to hold you in my arms and show you how much I want you." He'd take things slow and show her tenderness.

"Please, Cayden," she panted, and her pulse throbbed at her throat.

"All I can think about is being inside you and making love to you all night long." He kissed her temple.

"What's stopping you?"

"If we go now there's no coming back. You're mine all night."

"Let's hurry before anyone sees us."

CHAPTER 45

$\mathcal{N}$atalya's body pulsed with anticipation as they raced to the house. How could she be primed and ready simply from a kiss? Every time Cayden so much as touched her, she got hot.

Her gaze darted around the empty kitchen. Thankfully, everyone was still outside. They didn't need the whole crew to figure out what they were up to. They hurried through the hall and up the stairs to her room. Excitement sparked low in her belly. Her hands shook as she pulled her key out of her pocket and tried to shove it in the lock. Cayden didn't make it easy. His hands roamed over her back before settling on her waist. He brushed her hair off her neck and kissed her nape. He pressed his erection against her ass and she moaned. Shoving the door open, they tumbled inside panting.

Cayden kicked the door shut and bolted the lock in place. "Don't move. I'm checking the closet and under the bed for good measure."

Throwing her key on the desk, she sniffed the air. "I only smell you. There's no reason to think anyone broke in." Kicking off her shoes, she lit a candle and then pressed a button on her phone to her playlist. Soft notes of instrumental jazz music filled the room.

When he finished checking the place, Cayden took off his gun harness and laid it on the dresser. His gaze locked with hers from across the room. The ferocity in his eyes would've scared the hell out of her a few weeks ago, but not anymore. He made her feel confident and sexy. She'd never felt so wanted or cherished in her life. She trusted him with all her heart. She gazed into his soulful blue eyes and got a little lost.

"All clear," he murmured. His hungry gaze stayed locked on her, sparking heat to her belly.

She drank in his tall, broad frame and then her gaze moved lower to the thick bulge in his jeans. "What are you doing all the way over there?" The temperature in the room rose fast.

They dove at each other at the same time, kissing and touching, their breaths mingling as they tore at each other's clothing.

Natalya pulled away breathless. "Don't make me wait."

"I think I've created a monster." He laughed and the sound got her warm all over. He eased her backward, maneuvering away from the pile of clothing now on the floor.

"Your patience and care woke up my libido." She'd buried her sexual needs for far too long and now she wanted to explore everything with him.

When her knees hit the edge of the bed, she laid on top of her comforter. "You still have on way too many clothes. I think it's your turn to strip."

"Whatever the lady wants, the lady gets." Flashing a wicked smile, he kicked off his boots and socks. He undid his belt buckle. His sultry gaze stayed locked on hers as he took off his jeans and boxers. Her heart kicked up a notch when his cock sprang free. Cayden stood before her in all his magnificent glory.

"Come here." Licking her lips, she stared at his thick erection, and her mouth watered. They couldn't seem to sate this craving for each other.

He undid the clasp of her bra and slid the straps from her shoulders. "I don't think we need this." Next came her thong, and then he crawled on top of her body. He bent his head and sucked on her nipple, drawing the peak into his mouth in a silken caress, making her melt.

"Cayden," she breathed and slid her hands up his chest.

"I can smell you." He reached between them and rubbed her folds, opening her like a flower. "You're wet, baby." His finger brushed over her clit in slow, torturous strokes. He added another finger and then used his thumb to tease her, over and over again, sending her teetering on the edge.

She thought she'd break apart and scatter to the wind, but then he removed his fingers and switched their positions so she was on top. His hands wrapped around her waist.

"You're in charge now, Talya."

Her thighs trembled at the prospect of taking control. One hand moved her up until their bodies aligned perfectly. He pulsed between her legs, hard, hot, and ready to go.

His blue eyes glittered in the dark, full of sinful promises. But then she saw other things too, adoration, concern, affection. "Do whatever feels right. I'm yours." A hand went to her nape. Moving her lips closer, he kissed her again, soft and deep, replacing her apprehension.

Rocking forward, she slid on top of his cock, her wetness coating his shaft. At first she wasn't sure what to do, but then she went on instinct and rubbed her core against him, and she increased the pressure. She never knew anything could feel this good. Her breasts grew heavy and tender. Her nipples hardened into tight points.

After a few minutes, he hissed out a breath. "If you keep doing that, I won't last long. I want to be inside you." Cayden slowly guided the hard part of him into the slick part of her and this time she didn't flinch or hesitate. "Move forward a little." Holding her in place, he urged her on with silent moans and encouraging words.

"Cayden." Her breasts bounced as she moved, adjusting to the sensation of being filled.

"Is this okay?" Cayden's voice sounded ragged. He inched in deeper and she became suspended somewhere between pleasure and pain. He pivoted his hips, teasing her with shallow thrusts.

"Yes, it feels amazing." She squirmed under him from the sense of fullness. His cock slid deeper, and she cried out. When he became seated to the hilt, she began to move, slow and tentative at first and then a little faster. Power surged through her as sensations rocked her body and took her to new heights of pleasure.

"You take my breath away."

Her heart melted with the sentiment, solidifying their bond.

Reaching up, he caressed her cheek. "All the times we fought. I'd think about you when I was alone in my bed."

"What did you think about?" she whispered, moving forward to place a kiss on his chest. She never experienced this all-consuming passion before.

"Doing this." The intensity in his voice matched his lovemaking.

They moved together, finding their rhythm, and Natalya set the pace, focusing on every subtle thing, the catch of his breath, the creak of her bed, and the soft flutes of the music. She gazed into the eyes of this beautiful man, and when he looked back at her, she swore he could see into her soul. His hands went to her waist, holding her tight against his thrusts. A spark lit off deep inside her. The constant pressure and release forced her muscles to spasm. She'd never been this hot or frenzied ... never imagined sex could be like this. This time when he moved, her body stretched to receive him and it didn't strike her as scary, but intimate.

"You make me crazy," Cayden growled.

He began to pump faster, breathing in long gulps of air, and she figured he must be close. His hair became damp. His muscles tensed beneath his sweat-soaked skin. This time he hit her at just the right angle to make fire spark in her belly. The wicked man reached a finger between them and massaged her clit. She moaned, ready to explode.

"Cayden!" A fine sheen of perspiration broke out along her skin as she moved. Her core tingled. She sucked in a breath and blinding love rushed in with it. Lightning gathered in her limbs and blasted through every cell and nerve ending. The pleasure he gave her, the emotional connection they shared, brought tears to her eyes.

They moved together in a synchronized rhythm.

"I feel you, Talya. It's so good." His chest rumbled with a deep, primitive sound.

Her fangs jutted out from her teeth. The urge to bite him took hold with a force she didn't expect. She needed a taste of his blood. Her gaze locked on the vein pumping wildly in his neck.

"Kiss me." Reaching his hand behind her neck, he pulled her down for another sultry kiss. Their tongues tangled together and fire spread through her veins. He licked her fangs and her core tightened. He pulled away, panting hard. "Bite me. Do it. I know you want to."

"I can't. Not after what you told me about the guards drinking from the slaves as a way of shaming them." She stared at his vein, fighting the urge to pierce it with her fangs and taste his blood. She dug her nails into her palm until the craving passed.

"This is different. I'm asking you to. It will bond us even closer." His eyes became a little wild. "Do it." Cayden lifted his hips. The tempo of his thrusts quickened. "Please. I want this with you, Talya."

The words filled her heart. She moved her head to catch him at just the right angle and sank her fangs into his neck. The first taste of his blood transported her out of her body to a place of pure ecstasy. He tasted like salt mixed with a hint of spice. He must've enjoyed the sensation because he writhed beneath her in pleasure. She rode him as she drank, gasping as the heady sensation. She didn't want to take too much, so she licked the spot to seal it with her tongue. Nothing in this world had ever felt so intimate.

"I loved it, Talya." Her name came out as a strain on his lips. Rolling her onto her side, he pumped faster. The silent demands he strung from her body drove her to the brink. His liquid heat shot through her, spurring another orgasm. His whole body trembled. She never imagined sex could be like this, or that she'd feel this close to another person.

He pulled out and collapsed onto his back. Afterward, they both lay there, panting and gasping for air. She glanced over at him with a smile. His muscles twitched.

The spots of blood on her white sheets and smeared across his neck caught her eye. Guilt slid in her belly. "I'm sorry for biting you."

"Don't be. I asked you too. I know what you're thinking, but it's different with you." He kissed her temple and pulled her into his arms. Their legs twined together like vines. "I want to hold you all night long."

"Yes, please." As her eyes fluttered closed, she couldn't remember ever being this happy or satisfied.

Screams woke Natalya in the middle of the night. She sat up and found Cayden twisting in the sheets. "No, don't leave me! Don't…"

"Cayden? It's okay. You're having a nightmare." Touching his shoulder, she gently shook him awake. She hated to see him hurting. Her chest ached with physical pain.

His eyes flew open and darted around the room as though seeing it for the first time. Cayden's massive chest heaved with deep, panting breaths as he sat up. He blinked and some of the fog lifted from his eyes. "What did I say?"

"You were screaming, something along the lines of, 'Don't leave me.'" She tried to rub his shoulders. She knew firsthand the best way to push the nightmares under the bed was to be held and touched, but he pulled away and got out of bed.

"I'm sorry you had to see me like that." Moonlight cast a glow on the haunted look on his face. Rooting around for his boxers, he slipped them on and paced around the room.

Why does he now seem a million miles away? Her throat tightened. "Don't apologize. I want to be there for you. I want to know every part of you. There's nothing to be embarrassed about. Are you okay?" she asked, sensing a change come over him.

"I'm restless. I've got a lot going on in my head." From his hard, rigid stance, she could see the nightmare still clung to him, and it made her feel helpless.

"Talk to me, please," she whispered, trying to inject a measure of compassion in her voice. Tilting her head to the side, she stared at the sweat on his shaking body. "What's going on?"

"It's the stress of Erika's death, and I guess on some level it's making me relive Abigail's. And now there's a very real possibility of Frost coming after you." He ran a hand through his hair as he stomped around the room.

"I can see the toll this is taking on you. What do you do as an outlet when you're stressed?"

"The truth? I drink, and now that I've quit, I'm crawling out of my fucking skin." His words struck her like a knife to the chest. She hated to watch him suffer, knowing he faced these struggles all alone.

"Let me help you. I want us to be a team."

She got out of bed, went to her dresser, and pulled out a T-shirt. Slipping it on over her head, she went into the bathroom. After she grabbed a glass and filled it with water, she reached for a clean washcloth from the cabinet. She ran it under cool water, squeezed it out, and then came back into the room. She handed both to him.

"Here, put this on your forehead. Should I call someone? Maybe Saje has a potion for this."

"I told you, I'll be fine." His voice rose. The next moment regret flared in his eyes. "I'm sorry. I didn't mean to snap at you." Moving to the edge of the bed, he placed the washcloth on the nightstand. After he guzzled the water, he set the glass on the nightstand. "I have a sponsor. I'm supposed to call him when this kind of thing happens."

"Why don't you?"

He tensed right before her eyes.

"I didn't mean to overstep," she whispered, sitting beside him on the bed. "I want you to come to me with your problems, Cayden." *If you'll just let me in.* "I'm here for you. What can I do?"

"Nothing. It's all on me."

"How do you get through this?" she asked in a soft voice.

"The long-term effects of alcohol on demons aren't as bad as on other creatures, but it still sucks."

"It's okay to ask for help. You can't do everything alone." She rubbed his back.

"I know." The words seemed to get caught in his throat. He rested his head in his hands. "I used to drink to numb the pain. It made it go away, at least for a little while."

"I understand better than anyone what it's like to want to numb the pain, but it won't help you heal." She reached out and grasped his hand.

He blew out a breath. "I appreciate what you're trying to do, but I need to figure this out for myself. Let's talk about something else. I'll be fine. I promise. This will pass."

"Okay." She guessed warriors like him didn't ask for help. "What do you want to talk about?"

"You." Turning his head, he glanced at the bloodstains on the bed, a stark contrast against the white sheets. When he faced her again, some of the fog lifted from his eyes. "You've never told me how you became a vampire."

She sighed. "It's not a pretty story, one I'd rather forget."

"I'd never want you to relive a trauma."

He opened up to her about his drinking and about Abigail. She needed to do the same and tell him the whole truth, otherwise their relationship would never move forward. "It's okay. I told you how I was attacked by a group of young men, my former neighbor being the ringleader among them. What I didn't tell you was that when I tried to fight back, he pulled a knife and stabbed me in the abdomen."

"Jesus, Taylya." Lifting the edge of her T-shirt, his warm fingers traced over the small scar on her stomach. "This one?"

"Yes."

His jaw visibly clenched. He pulled her onto his lap and held her close. "We don't have to talk about this anymore." The concern in his voice gave her the strength to continue.

"I want to. Somehow I managed to make it home without bleeding to death."

"No one saw you? No one tried to help you?" The questions twisted inside her, along with the memories.

She shook her head, recalling every detail of that fateful night, the searing pain in her stomach, the blood smeared on the grass. "My biological father's business partner, Pavel Dubrosky, the vampire who eventually became my sire and adopted me into the family, happened to be at our house. I'd lost so much blood. I knew I was going to die. The only way to save me was to turn me before I bled out."

Brushing her hair away from her face, he kissed her forehead. "I'm sorry you went through something so horrific. Whatever happened to the men who attacked you? Did you press charges?"

Her stomach churned with regret. "No, I was too ashamed. I told everyone I couldn't remember what happened. They assumed I'd been so traumatized that I blocked the whole thing out. But I didn't. I found out one of them is in prison." She blew out a breath. "As for the rest, I don't remember what they looked like. I didn't even know their names. I just pray they didn't do what they did to me to some other woman."

"I'm so sorry, Talya." He wound his arms around her and she held on tight.

"It's all in the past. They can't hurt me anymore." *Only you can.* She rested her head against his shoulder and closed her eyes, refusing to let their pasts rip them apart. "I thought I'm the one who's supposed to be comforting you."

"You are just by being here," he whispered. The trembling in his hands subsided as he ran a hand through her hair. "You amaze me."

"I do? How?"

"You're the strongest woman I know. You've got steel running through your bones, but you're still kind and gentle." Cayden's voice sounded less tense.

Her heart squeezed at the compliments. "I get it from my human parents."

"Are they still in the picture?"

"Sadly, no. After they left me with the Dubrosky family, they went back to Russia. I found out a few years later they were killed during a political demonstration." The confession left her raw and filled her head with memories.

"Wait, I don't get how your parents ..."

"Could up and leave their only daughter?" Scooting off his lap, she walked around the room with her arms wrapped around her body. "They couldn't bear to be around me after the change, and I couldn't blame them. The craving for blood is 24/7 in the beginning."

"What did you do? How did you survive?"

"Eleanora and Pavel took me to a blood bank at first, which helped me get through the rough part. I found out later that the blood I was given was infused with witch blood, which may have ignited the predisposed trait."

"It seems as though my vampire is also a witch."

Natalya liked whenever he referred to her in the possessive. "If only I could've used my gift to help Erika."

"I don't think there's anything more you could've done. I'm guessing Frost pretended to be into her, to get close so he could move in for the kill."

Several minutes ticked by without either of them saying a word. The shock and pain over Erika's death still hung in the air like an anvil over their heads.

"I get how important your charity work is with SAAN." Cayden pointed to the brochure on her desk. "You have your big night coming up."

She followed his gaze to her desk and it caught on a photo of her with Eleanora and Pavel. "I've been working with Eleanora on the gala committee. I thought it might help our strained relationship. I'm still trying to repair the damage after my annulment."

"If they don't have your back, why bother?"

"They're the only family I have left."

"I understand your need to hold on to them, but at what cost?"

"You make a great point, but I'm not ready to let them go. I need them in my life. They're the last link left to my human life and my biological parents." Talking about them, even after all this time, made her sad.

"I understand."

Natalya needed to clear the heaviness in the air. "I still don't have a plus-one for the gala." She came back to the bed and stretched onto her stomach. "Are you sure I can't twist your arm into being my date?" She batted her lashes for effect.

"I'd do anything to support you and your charity work, Talya, but gala events aren't my thing. I'm sorry." The honesty in his words mollified her disappointment.

"The last thing I'd ever want to do is make you uncomfortable. Do you believe people like us can find their way to happiness?" She laid her secrets bare, no use trying to hold back anymore.

"I wish I knew." Resting his horns against the headboard, Cayden stared up at the ceiling. "I've been carrying around guilt and a fear of loss for centuries. It's the reason I've avoided being with anyone. I never imagined when I did find such a person, someone I could see myself with for the long haul, that she'd be a cop."

"I suspected as much, but I'm not a vulnerable creature, Cayden." She showed her fangs, still coated with his blood.

"Even vampires and demons can be vulnerable." After a few minutes, he got up, giving her a perfect view of his muscular back and his very fine ass encased in boxers. He picked up the rest of his clothing and placed it on her desk chair, and turned back to face her. "Look what happens to everyone who gets close to me."

It explained why he never got serious with a woman. They stared at each other in the dark, all their secrets out there on the table.

"Sometimes you need to take a chance," Natalya whispered on a sigh. "You don't have to be alone anymore."

"It's easy for you to say." Indignation sparked in his eyes. "You were married for a nanosecond. Shit, I didn't mean to lash out at you. I'm sorry. I'm stressing out and I'm not myself."

His words stung as if he'd slapped her across the face. Tears burned in her eyes. Nothing could hurt this much, nothing except love. This could only mean one thing. *I'm in love with Cayden.*

"You put Abigail on a pedestal." Natalya took a deep, calming breath. "But I'm sure she had flaws like the rest of us. And from everything you've told me, you didn't get to see hers, and you didn't let her see yours. Relationships take work. People fight."

Cayden's face became hard with frustration. "Talya, please, I don't want to do this now."

"You have to tell someone the truth even if it hurts. It's what you do when you care about someone." Her voice began to shake. "But hey, what do I know?"

His horns elongated and flared red, but he remained silent, brooding.

"I might not have experienced a love like you did with Abigail, but at least I'm trying to live in the present, not in the shadow of some fantasy." The harsh words did nothing to stop the yearning in her soul. They shared the most exquisite sex and deep, soul-bearing truths afterward. And now he hurt her. She'd chalk it up to his issues with booze and grief about Erika, but it didn't excuse his behavior, not for a second.

"I'm trying, believe me. But it's not easy."

"I feel terrible that you're struggling and in pain, but you can't take it out on me. When you want to stop living in the past, give me a call, or don't, your choice." Natalya went into the bathroom, slammed the door in his face, and let the tears fall.

"Talya, please, open the door." Cayden knocked on the door.

"Go away."

Swiping her tears away, she turned on the shower and stripped off her T-shirt. She got under the spray and let the hot water wash away her tears and her sorrow. Cayden's words hit her so hard she could barely breathe. She knew he could be mercurial, but his mood swings were maddening. Going out on a limb, she'd bared her deepest secrets and let herself be vulnerable, something she avoided at all costs—something she'd been working on with her therapist for a long time—and he threw it back in her face.

After she soaped up her body and shampooed her hair, she added conditioner, taking her sweet time. *Let him stew. He deserves it.* She rinsed and shut off the water, staying longer in the shower than necessary. She wanted to come across to Cayden like she had things figured out when she didn't, not by a long shot.

Once she secured a towel around her body and wrapped her hair in a turban, she stepped out of the tub. Taking a deep breath, she started to feel better.

Staring at her reflection in the mirror, she swallowed hard. Her red, swollen eyes would be a dead giveaway. She didn't hear anything on the other side of the door. Cayden may have fallen asleep or left. The thought made her eyes mist with fresh tears. Toweling off her hair, she set the towel on the rack, and slipped on her white terrycloth robe. Slowly, she opened the door.

"Natalya," he murmured and reached for her shoulders. "Everything you said was true. I lashed out at you because you were telling me the truth. I'm sorry. Forgive me, please."

"I want to go. Let me go." She pulled away from him and her body grew cold. His scent flared in her nostrils and made her ache. And despite everything, she wanted him again. He spurred a fierce physical reaction in her she couldn't ignore.

"I didn't mean the things I said," he murmured with such pain in his voice, her heart melted. His eyes grew stormy and hot as they trailed over her fresh from the shower.

"I need time."

He shocked her by dropping to his knees and pressing his face against her stomach. "I'm so sorry. Please, forgive me. I just need you to lay with me. Let me hold you." She couldn't bear to hear the torment in his voice.

Though she wanted to fall into his arms, she hesitated. She didn't think she could take getting hurt again. "You can't lash out at me when I say something you don't like."

"I know. I was wrong. I'm such an asshole." Pushing to his feet, the shadows faded from his eyes. He held out his hand. She took it and they got back in bed. He kissed her temple and pulled the cover over them.

"Yeah, but you're my asshole." Maybe she should've been afraid by the depth of his need, but she knew from the thud of her heart against her rib cage, she felt the same insane passion for him. She sensed how much he cared. His raw apology softened the last shred of her anger. Whatever might be left unsaid would have to suffice for now, because there was no doubt they were twisted up in each other for the long haul.

This time when he wrapped her in his arms, she let him and she drifted off to sleep.

CHAPTER 46

*W*hen Natalya turned on her side, something soft and fragrant tickled her cheek. The sweet scent of flowers perfumed the air. She opened her eyes and gasped. Her bed was covered in pink and white hydrangeas from the garden. Cayden must've done this while she'd been asleep.

He'd woken her up early this morning and couldn't stop apologizing. He'd whispered sweet, erotic words in her ear as he slid in and out of her, showing his remorse without words. Their lovemaking had been sensual and romantic, the perfect way to start the day before the wedding. She picked up the note next to her pillow.

Sorry, had to go. On best man duty. I need to rehearse my speech. I can't wait to hold you in my arms tonight. Cayden

The soft hum of need beneath her skin persisted even with all the orgasms Cayden had given her last night and this morning. She still wanted him. Picking up a flower, she held it up to her nose and inhaled. She basked in the sweet scent and the profound love she felt for him in that moment.

An hour later, she walked into the dining room which had been turned into glamour central. Hair dryers, curling irons, brushes, eyeshadow palettes and lipsticks of every variety were spread out across the dining room table. The bride, along with all the ladies in the wedding party, sat in a row of chairs getting their hair and makeup done.

As Arabella stared at her, her eyes lit with mischief. "Someone looks all bright-eyed and glowy-skinned this morning, and I think it has nothing to do with the bronzer, and everything to do with the sex. Have you and Cayden slept together?"

Natalya cracked a smile. "Please Arabella, a little louder. I'm not sure everyone heard you over the dryers."

"I knew you'd end up with him. I saw it in the leaves, and the leaves never lie." Arabella took a seat next to Willow who was getting the finishing touches on her hair by a young woman with a pink bob and sleeves of tattoos on her arms.

Natalya couldn't help but wonder if knowing Arabella's prediction would've changed anything. "In answer to your question, I'll simply say we've gotten closer." In fact, she'd never gotten this intimate with anyone. The thought made her smile. She took the empty seat next to Gillian.

All the chatter stopped. All eyes swiveled to her.

"I believe that's a classy way of saying you're banging the hell out of each other." Arabella winked and the other women laughed.

Heat swept up her chest. "A lady never kisses and tells."

"Aha, so you and Cayden are a thing?" Gillian caught her eye in the mirror. "Frankly, we've all been dying to know. There are no secrets with this group."

Natalya didn't know where they stood. He was hot and passionate one minute, cool and detached the next. Their relationship was messy and unpredictable to say the least, but she sensed with every fiber of her being, he was the one. "With everything going on, we're taking things a day at a time."

Gillian turned and gave her a playful poke in the ribs. "If I remember correctly, around this time last year, I believe the term 'misogynist' and some other more colorful words were used to describe a certain handsome special agent."

"What can I say? I misjudged him." Natalya never knew the pain he'd suffered or the challenges he faced. When she thought about all of his amazing qualities, her heart warmed. "He's passionate and charismatic. He's physically powerful, but he doesn't use his power to intimidate. He has a wicked sense of humor. He's intense and passionate." How could she not fall hard and fast?

"I think you're done for." Brooke walked up to her in a flowing purple bridesmaid's dress and practically beamed. She wore her blonde hair in an elegant bun. "Thanks for the fix-up with James. We haven't met in person yet, but he sounds cool on the phone. We've been talking nonstop. He slid into my DMs, which I thought was hot."

"If you say so." Natalya chuckled at her enthusiasm. "I'm glad I could help. When are you two getting together?"

Brooke applied lip gloss to her lips. "We're meeting tonight in the gazebo after the reception for a nightcap. Do you think it's too much too soon?"

Natalya shook her head. "It sounds fun, just let the agents know so you don't breach any security protocols." Normally, she'd say hell no with a killer still on the loose. But in this case, she'd checked James out.

"You look beautiful by the way." Brooke motioned to Natalya's champagne-colored halter dress, a Tessa original with zero back. She couldn't wear a bra with the cut, something she'd planned to torture Cayden with all night long.

"Thanks, so do you." She'd worn her hair in a chignon, a trick Brooke had taught her, and kept her makeup simple.

Delilah got everyone's attention by standing up on a chair. She looked like a wood lawn fairy with glittery eye shadow and ribbons braided into her wavy, blonde hair. "I think it's time to pop the champagne."

"Let me help you." Natalya blurred to the breakfront where several bottles of pink champagne sat chilling in giant cauldrons filled with ice. The pop of the cork echoed through the room. "It's officially a party." They filled a tray of flutes then set them on the liquor cart. Each woman grabbed a glass and held it up.

"I'm thrilled and honored to be Willow's maid of honor. I now know what real love looks like. It's given me hope that it just might happen to me and the rest of us who are still single." Delilah sniffled and her eyes filled with tears.

"You're going to make me mess up my makeup," Willow said smiling, dabbing at her eyes.

Natalya took a sip of champagne, her own eyes filling with tears, grateful beyond words to be a part of this special day.

The makeup artist motioned Willow over and then turned to Natalya. "I can fix you both. How do you feel about smoky eyes?"

Thirty minutes later, Natalya glanced at herself in the mirror. Her eyes looked bigger and more pronounced with an added sparkle to them. She barely recognized herself from the person she was a few months ago.

Saje whistled at her as she gathered up the bouquets and handed them out. "Cayden's going to lose it when he sees you."

A wave of emotions unfurled inside her, love, excitement, and nerves. Natalya's heart sped up and pounded in a steady rhythm. "I hope you're right."

Cayden stood at the center of the garden beside the groom. The rest of the guys in the wedding party were lined up behind them, looking sharp in their penguin suits. His gaze caught on the tall pillar candles glowing softly from the aisles where most of the guests had already been seated in fancy silver chairs. They were just waiting for the big game to start. The soft tones of a harpist strummed in the background.

He'd stopped by the checkpoint several times already and had a chat with Smith, Big Red, and Jax about the itinerary while Natalya remained inside with Willow and her bridesmaids. All of them were connected by radio and being extra cautious with who they let in. Once every wedding guest showed their invite, their name got checked off the list. Background checks had been done on anyone who set foot on the grounds. The security team stood at the edge of the garden. They'd been instructed to take their seats once the ceremony began.

He'd turned off his phone for the ceremony and transferred the itinerary to a slip of paper. He prayed everything would go as planned.

Turning to Alex, Cayden patted him on the shoulder. He'd never seen his partner this jittery. He kept glancing over his shoulder, probably hoping to catch a glimpse of his bride-to-be. "How are you holding up, buddy?"

"I'm nervous as hell." Alex smiled. "But I can't wait to start our life together and make Willow mine."

"I couldn't be happier for you both. I can't believe this day has finally come." Cayden choked up and caught Alex in a man hug. The magic of the day must've rubbed off on him and made him nostalgic.

"There's something buzzing in the air, my friend." Alex adjusted his boutonniere. "Be careful. It might just bite you."

Before Cayden could respond, all heads turned to catch a glimpse of Ellen walking across the lawn to stand behind the altar, now decked out with white hydrangeas and silver candles. "The high priestess is doing the honors?"

Alex nodded. "We're doing a handfasting ceremony. It's a Wiccan tradition."

The sun began to set in the sky in a dazzling burst of color. Cayden didn't think he'd ever seen anything more beautiful until Natalya walked into the garden. Lust tore through his chest and vibrated through his body like an electric current. The sight of her made him grin like a teenager. Could this be happiness? Did he have a right to feel this way when everything around him was going to hell?

She took her seat in the front row and flashed a smile. His heart swelled with an emotion he couldn't quite define. *I can't possibly love her, not yet. It's too soon.* He loved her sweetness and her strength. He loved everything about her, period. Pushing the sappy thoughts aside, he gave her a wink. Alex was right. Something was blooming in the air, and it had nothing to do with the flower spray.

The music started and Alex visibly swallowed. "Showtime."

A momentary flash of loss came over Cayden and then he realized as he saw the pure joy on Alex's face, *I'm not losing my best friend, I'm gaining a sister.* "Are you ready for this?" Cayden whispered to his partner.

"Definitely," Alex whispered back.

After the ceremony, Cayden followed Natalya through a doorway made of sheer white curtains tied back with greenery. Once inside the party tent, he looked up, taking it all in. Strings of fairy lights and chandeliers hung overhead. Tiny silver lights were strung into tiers at the top of the tent, meant to give off the starry sky effect. His gaze lowered to the floating candles on every table, along with tall vases of white flowers. "Holy shit. They went all out."

"This is breathtaking." Natalya gasped from beside him.

He turned and his gaze trailed over every inch of her in that sexy gold number. "Gods, Talya, so are you. I've never seen you look more beautiful." Reaching out to pull her close, his fingers slid over the satiny skin at her back.

She turned around in a circle, giving him the perfect view of her shapely backside. "Do you like?"

"Do I like?" An inch lower and he might have been able to see the curve of her ass. "I've been at half-mast from the moment I laid eyes on you. I can't wait to get you alone." He thought about sneaking into the solarium for a quickie.

"My plan involved driving you absolutely crazy." Her smile warmed his heart.

"You're unraveling me." He skimmed his knuckles across her cheek.

Last night she'd been there for him and hung in there like a champ. She accepted him, even when he was being difficult. He now knew he could depend on her, and she'd be there for him no matter what. *But am I worthy of a woman like Natalya?* The question burned in his gut.

They talked with their friends as they entered the tent. Once they got a moment alone, Cayden threaded their fingers together and led her into a private corner. "I'm sorry I had to leave so early." They ducked behind a column and he pulled her flush against his body,

"Cayden?" Her eyes widened. "What are you doing?"

"I haven't gotten a chance to say a proper hello."

He'd never been one for PDA, until now. Dipping her back, he sealed his mouth over hers in a blistering kiss. One arm stayed wrapped around her waist, and the other cradled her neck while he devoured her lips.

Natalya moaned and wound her arms around his neck, twining her tongue with his in deep, velvety strokes. Cayden became aware of the conversations and music surrounding them, but none of it mattered with her in his arms. The passion of the kiss took him by surprise. He growled and stroked deeper and then someone cleared their throat.

Shit.

Pulling back, he set Natalya on her feet. Her beautiful eyes looked hooded and still drowsy with lust. She smoothed her hair into her bun.

Cayden turned his head to find Big Red standing behind them with a look of surprise across his ruddy face. "What's up?" He shook the demon's hand.

Big Red raised his eyebrows. "Sorry to interrupt. I just wanted to give you an update."

"I think I'll go check the other side of the tent to make sure there are no breaches. You can fill me in later." Wiping her smeared lip gloss away, Natalya walked in the direction of the bar.

Cayden turned to Big Red and folded his arms across his chest. "Sorry, about that. You were saying ..."

"Our IT guys now have access to Frost's IP address, so they'll be able to locate him based on his next keystroke," Big Red said with a nod. "But it won't be easy by any stretch, depending on how many bounces and routers he's going through. The commander thinks we're getting close. I'll give the team a heads-up the moment we have something concrete."

"I appreciate the update." Once they found Frost, nothing would keep Cayden away.

Big Red glanced in the direction of Natalya, who stopped to talk to Gillian and Garrett, now standing beside her at the bar. "We've known each other a long time, Teague, and there's something I need to say."

Cayden's horns prickled. "Go on."

"A buddy of mine used to do security for the Dubrosky clan," Big Red said in a serious tone. "They're a tight-knit bunch and still believe in a class system. They sure as shit don't approve of anyone outside of their circles getting near their females, especially dudes like us, if you get what I mean."

Cayden swallowed hard, acid now coating his throat. "You're not telling me anything new." *Just confirming my suspicions.*

Big Red checked his watch. "I should get back to my post. See you later." The demon disappeared into the crowd, leaving Cayden to ruminate over the hot Pandora's box he just opened.

Why did it feel like he'd been sucker punched? Talya had been trying to get back in her sired family's good graces since her divorce. Being with him would only inflame the situation and alienate them even more. They'd never accept him for their daughter. He'd never be good enough and it would always come between them. She deserved so much more. No matter how much he wanted her, the only honorable thing to do would be to let her go. For now, he'd enjoy the rest of the evening and make every second count. A twisting pain filled his chest for a future with Natalya that would never be.

CHAPTER 47

"May I have the honor of the next dance?"

"I'd love to." A warm, contented sense of bliss moved through Natalya as Cayden reached for her hand, leading her to the dance floor as a slow song came on.

The reception winded down once the cake had been cut. Brooke ended up catching the bouquet, while Alex's handsome, brother Nico had managed to snag the garter in a flourish of claps and cheers.

"How are you enjoying the wedding?" Craning her neck, she looked up at her demon as they swayed to the music. The heels made no difference whatsoever. Cayden still towered over her by at least a foot. She smiled, lost in the splendor of the evening.

His smoldering gaze locked with hers. "One of the best nights of my life and it just keeps getting better." The sincerity of his voice almost sounded painful. "I get to hold you in my arms."

"Your best man speech moved me to tears."

"Weddings make people say mushy things," he murmured, holding her tight.

"I know what you mean." She'd contemplated admitting the depth of her feelings to him, but the right opportunity never came up. Her gaze raked over him for the umpteenth time this evening, admiring the mouthwatering way he looked in his tux. "You look incredibly handsome tonight." He'd even shaved for the occasion. "How are you feeling after last night?" she whispered. "You barely touched your meal. Does it have something to do with locating Frost's IP address?" Cayden had filled her in on the details.

"We're so close."

"I promise, we're going to find him." She saw clouds in his eyes. He'd been a little off since his talk with Big Red.

The song ended and Cayden placed a kiss on her cheek. "I could use some air."

They walked off the dance floor and out of the tent. The stars overhead drew her gaze up. Cayden took off his tux coat and draped it over her shoulders. It swallowed her up and hung past her knees. "You look adorable." He kissed the top of her head.

"Who are you calling adorable?" she joked, flashing her fangs. The coat brushed around her thighs as she walked.

Cayden wound his arm around her waist and led her past a couple she didn't recognize who appeared visibly wasted, drinking champagne straight out of the bottle. Following his gaze, she hated the stress lines on his face. It gave her the courage to say what had been on her mind. "There's something I'd like to talk to you about, although you might not like what I have to say."

They walked along the stone path and stopped at the gazebo. He leaned up against the side and gazed into her eyes.

"I wanted to make sure you're okay after last night. I hate to see you suffer. Have you ever considered going to talk to someone?" If she'd learned anything in therapy, it was that both people needed to be healthy for a relationship to work. She'd made too much progress to ever go back to the black hole she'd been in. They already had enough obstacles to overcome, and trying to sweep this one under the rug would be a huge mistake.

His eyes filled with storm clouds. "As of right now, I haven't had a drink since the night of Andee's murder."

Her shoulders slumped, immediately regretting her words. He'd been trying and she needed to give him encouragement and support. "I'm so proud of you. I'd never judge you."

Cayden reached out his hand and caressed her cheek. "I know your concern comes from a good place, but I need to figure this one out on my own."

"I'd never try to discount your choices. The stress of what you've been through would make any sane person crazy. It doesn't have to be this hard." Natalya bled for him, wishing she could take away his pain.

Disappointment drew a line across his forehead. "You're afraid I could slip?"

"Of course not. I'm not trying to crowd you." She understood what it meant to be proud better than anyone.

Their eyes met in the darkness. What she felt for him in that moment swept her up and became almost painful.

"I want to be there for you through the good and the bad. It's what you do when you love someone."

"What did you say?"

"I'm in love with you, Cayden." Natalya swallowed hard. "I can't hide my feelings anymore. I couldn't let another day go by without telling you. I know my timing sucks, but our connection is unlike anything I've ever known."

The deer-in-the-headlights look in his eyes pierced at her heart. "I ... I don't know what to say." His enormous chest heaved.

How about I love you too? Could he ever love her the way he loved Abigail? She'd gotten way ahead of herself on this. Tears burned in her eyes and constricted her throat. "I get that you're used to being alone and you just lost someone you cared about."

"Please, Talya." He reached for her, but she ducked out of the way, too raw to be touched or cajoled. "I'd never try to hurt you."

She'd read the whole situation wrong. She'd thought they'd made a real connection, only to have him look at her with uncertainty in his eyes. "You have the power to hurt me like no else can, Cayden." Closing the jacket tight against her body, she hoped he wouldn't see her tremble. Willow's words reverberated in her head. *Cayden never got over his lost love.* Maybe he never would. One thing became crystal clear, if she hung around, she'd be setting herself up for more heartache.

Cayden began to pace. "Your family will never accept me. You'd alienate them, and I won't let you do that. If you thought divorcing your husband caused shame to your family, how do you think they'll react to you being involved with me?"

"Don't you see? I want us to have a life speckled with beauty and messiness. My family will come around, and I'll be okay if they don't." She inhaled sharply, the tears now clogged in her throat. "This is a chance for us to start fresh."

"I wish I could believe people like me get second chances, but I'm too battle-scarred and fucked-up in the head to think otherwise." When he stopped to stare at her, he looked lost.

Her heart plummeted. "Look at everything Alex and Willow have been through, and what about Garrett and Gillian? Don't we deserve what they have?" The future looked uncertain, mainly because of all the wounds they could inflict on each other.

"I don't know what I deserve anymore." The finality of his words shot through her like an arrow. "Every woman I ever cared about has ended up dead because of me."

Tears splashed to her cheeks. Swatting them away with her hand, a sick misery spread through her joy. *Dammit, why do I have to cry?*

"Please don't cry, not for me." He closed the distance between them and wiped her tears away with his thumbs.

"You think I can't love you because of your flaws, but I do love every part of you. I know you're scared. I'm scared too." She didn't want his flight instinct to kick in. Even if he couldn't say the words back, she knew he cared, just maybe not as much as her. Natalya stretched to her tiptoes to touch his face. "If ever there were two people meant be together, it's us."

His eyes filled with yearning. "I never planned to love someone else after Abigail."

"I get that you had one great love before, but do you think you can open your heart again?" Her voice softened. "Please, tell me if I'm wasting my time."

Cayden wrapped his arms around her waist and squeezed. "I'm here with you now. Doesn't that count for anything?"

"I want more. I never believed I deserved it before." *I've changed.*

He closed his eyes, and when he opened them, she sensed his turmoil. "I've only told one woman I loved her and it didn't end well."

Her breathing became too quick and her heartbeat too fast. "You can't keep chasing ghosts. I'm flesh and blood … I'm real." She pressed his hand to her heart where it pounded wildly in her chest.

"You're killing me right now." His intense blue gaze seared into hers.

Their bond was fragile, wrought with open wounds and jagged edges. Could they put the horrors of their pasts behind them and focus on the present? She wasn't so sure, but she wanted to try. Self-preservation kicked in. "I'm sorry I brought this up. I have to go."

"Natalya, wait."

She hesitated, but then their radios buzzed.

He pulled his out of his pocket first and held it between them. "Talk to me."

"We got a break in the case. We got him this time. Frost's in Weehawken. Head over to the solarium." Smith's voice crackled through the static.

"We're on our way," Cayden answered back and then shoved his radio in his pocket.

He looked over at Natalya with concern in his eyes. "We've got to go check this out. Are you okay?"

"I'm fine." She refused to look him in the eye.

"I want to talk about this some more, but we need to head back."

What is there left to say? It wasn't supposed to end like this. They walked along the path in silence. When they got to the tent, their gazes locked and held. She could see the tightness in his face "You go on without me. I … just can't. I need to wash my face. I need a moment to myself."

Cupping her chin, he wiped her tears away with his thumb. "I'm so sorry I ruined your makeup. I never want to make you cry. I never want to hurt you."

As she angled her head in the direction of the solarium, her heart broke a little more. "The agents are waiting. You should go."

"Okay." He hesitated for a minute and then nodded.

"I'll be fine." She watched him walk in the other direction and all she could think about was getting the hell out of there. The agents could take things from here. She'd give them a heads up. As much as she hated to leave, at least she could take comfort in the fact that Frost had been found. Her gaze darted to the entrance of the tent as she contemplated what to do. If she went back in with half her makeup smeared on her face, she'd raise some eyebrows.

Maybe if Cayden hadn't rocked her world with mind-blowing sex and a baring-of-the-soul conversation the night before, she wouldn't be feeling this raw or vulnerable. And with every inhale of breath, her pain grew more intense. He didn't love her. Reality hit her with excruciating force.

Arabella walked out of the tent and her eyes widened when she saw her standing there alone. "Natalya? What's wrong? Have you been crying?"

"Cayden and I had a fight." Natalya's voice broke.

"What happened?" Arabella walked over and rubbed her shoulder.

"The gist is he can never get over his long-lost love."

Arabella shook her head. "I don't believe that for a minute. Especially the way he looks at you. Why don't you come back inside?"

"I need to be alone right now. I'm sorry. I don't want to ruin your night." Rubbing her temples, a wave of fresh tears threatened. Her surroundings became blurry. "I've got to get out of here. The manor will be noisy and milling with people. I'm too shaken up to bump into anyone. I need space. I'm going to my apartment. Please tell everyone I said goodbye."

"Of course." Arabella pulled her into a hug. "Let me know if you need anything. Did you want me to tell one of the agents that you're leaving?"

"I'll text Cayden on my way out." Otherwise he'd be frantic. She took off his jacket and handed it to Arabella. "Please make sure he gets this." Bolting might be childish and selfish, but she needed to lick her wounds and soak in a hot tub.

"I'm thinking you should let one of those big-ass bodyguards walk you to your car and escort you to your apartment," Arabella suggested, her concerned gaze focused on Natalya.

"I'll be fine." Natalya patted her purse. "The weapons go with the shoes. I'm going straight to my apartment."

"Okay, if you're sure."

"I'll text you the moment I get in." Natalya waved and blurred to the front of the house.

Cayden's words echoed through her head with brutal finality. *I've only told one woman I loved her and it didn't end well.*

She'd spent countless hours in therapy learning tools to help her through this kind of situation—a situation she'd been trying to avoid her entire life. Her emotional attachment to Cayden, coupled with her lack of experience, left her wide open for heartbreak.

They never talked about the future or even the possibility of one. Natalya never believed she was good enough for the fairytale, but she wanted it with a bone-deep longing. She'd made her decision, and as much as it would hurt, she couldn't waste her time wondering what if. Cayden was the love of her life, but if he didn't feel the same way—she'd have to move on and accept this as a fleeting moment in time. The thought made her heart twist with pain.

She exhaled and tried to see where she'd gone wrong. Maybe she'd put him on the spot with her declaration of love. But now she was too spent to even try and sort it all out. She felt like she'd crack open and break into a million pieces.

All those old, ugly insecurities rose to the surface with the force of a crashing wave. She'd never felt loved by her sired family, by the man she married, and now by Cayden. Dizziness hit her hard. If she didn't get out of here, she'd need to be swept off the pavement. Her eyes stung with fresh tears.

Taking a few deep breaths, she focused on the things she was grateful for—amazing friends, a rewarding career, magick, and a purpose—to help save the innocent. It was enough. It had to be.

She glanced over her shoulder, secretly wanting Cayden to follow her, and hoping he didn't at the same time. When she tried to get to her car, she found it blocked by three others. Natalya pulled out her phone to call an Uber and froze when a familiar male voice called out her name. *Crap*. She turned on her heel and found James standing at the curb. "What are you doing here?"

"I have a date with Brooke. I guess I'm a little early." He took a step closer and his gaze narrowed on her tear-stained face. "What's wrong?"

Mortification set in. "I can't talk about it right now. My car's blocked. I'm about to call an Uber."

"I'm happy to take you wherever you need to go. I'm parked on the next block."

"I don't want you to go out of your way." She waved him off. "Thanks anyway."

"Nonsense. I can't leave you like this. Think of it this way, you'd be helping me out." He motioned to the front door. "I don't want to look too eager. How about I drop you off and come back?"

His kindness lifted her embarrassment. "Okay. Thanks, I appreciate it."

She followed him to the end of the block, her head spinning in a million directions.

"My pleasure." James stopped at a shiny, red Porsche. Under different circumstances, she would've appreciated the beauty of the car. But right now, all she could do was concentrate on keeping it together on the drive to her apartment.

After James clicked the lock, he opened the passenger door for her and helped her into the car.

Resting her head against the cool leather seat, she pulled out her phone. A few missed calls from Cayden and a text. She didn't want to talk to him right now. She wondered how he'd react when he realized she'd left. The wounded part of her wanted to hurt him like he'd hurt her. But she couldn't. She shot off a group text to the team and then one to him.

Natalya: I'm headed to my apartment. Please don't follow me.

She hit send, and shoved her phone in her purse. After she fastened her seatbelt, she exhaled the breath stuck in her throat.

Once James got into the driver's side and belted in, he turned to her in the dim light of the car. "Where to?"

"Make a left at the end of Park and stay straight. There's a detour ahead. I'll direct you."

The locks clicked into place as the car veered down the block. The night came alive with the sounds of the city. Horns flared and yellow taxis bustled by. The clamor of the street roared in her ears like white noise. She'd never been more grateful for the distraction. She glanced out the window and sighed.

Mozart's "Rondo Alla Turca" flowed through the speakers as James maneuvered the car through the flow of traffic.

When she wiped her eyes, black smudges came off on her fingers. She almost laughed. *So much for smoky eyes.* Reaching into her purse, she searched around for a tissue. "Do you have anything I can use to wipe my eyes?" She pegged him for the monogrammed handkerchief type.

"There might be something in the glovebox."

"Thanks." She opened it and a pack of matches from the Wolf Tavern fell out in her hand. Closing her fingers around the matchbook, on instinct she lifted the cover. She found a phone number and the name "Michaels" scribbled across the top. She froze. She knew that name. Michaels was a barback and a former Hellios guard. Could this be a wild coincidence? The knot in her stomach told her otherwise.

"Is there something wrong?" His voice and manner came off as nonchalant.

"No, not at all." Shoving the matches back in the glovebox, a small brown bag with the name "Martindale's Cigars" emblazoned on the front caught her eye. Lots of people smoked cigars, she reasoned, but what were the chances James would frequent that particular smoke shop? An icy chill settled into her limbs. Her brain clicked into gear, fitting the pieces of this insane puzzle together.

I'm next.

The music stopped, along with her heart. A rush of adrenaline flooded her body as she looked out the window. They'd already passed Grand Street and were now three blocks from her apartment. "I didn't tell you where to go."

James remained silent. His gaze focused on the road.

She pulled out her phone to send a code three emergency text to the team, when he grabbed it out of her hands. Crushing it in his fist, he threw the pieces out his window. "Oh, don't worry, your beloved will find you, but not yet. I can't make things too easy. And I want him to suffer," he snarled.

Her heart went to her throat. Trying not to panic, she contemplated her next move. She could reach for her Summit Stake and demand he pull over, but this maniac might try and crash the car. She'd survive, even if it would hurt like hell. But what if he purposely caused an accident and put other lives in danger? She couldn't take the chance. When they stopped at a light, she reached for the door handle, ready to jump out.

"Don't bother trying to escape. I control the locks." James turned to face her and the mask of the charming gentleman slipped, replaced with the cruel face of a monster.

"To hell with this." Pushing her body against the door, she tried to shove it open, but it wouldn't budge. Pain exploded in her shoulder.

"I tried to tell you." He made a tsking sound with his tongue and turned onto Madison Street. He stopped outside her building and put the car in park. "I didn't think your boyfriend would make it this easy. You fell right into my lap."

"You're Stephen Frost." Coldness settled over her limbs like an icy blanket. "How do you know where I live?"

His gaze locked on hers and his pupils became wide and mesmerizing. No matter how hard she tried, she couldn't seem to look away. When his cold eyes pierced hers, she fell under his spell. She tried to reach for her purse, but her fingers wouldn't move. A scream surged up from her throat and died on her lips, her voice now frozen inside her body.

"I know everything about you." Frost smiled, revealing a set of razor-sharp fangs. "I've made it my job."

CHAPTER 48

*C*ayden met Smith and Mulroney inside the solarium for a briefing. They needed a plan before they swooped in on Frost. "We have to make sure this isn't a setup." The scents of lavender, tarragon, and mugwort floated through the air.

Stifling heat clung to his shirt, only adding to his apprehension. Natalya told him she loved him and he simply stared at her and said nothing. *Gods, I acted like a Grade-A prick.* If only he could go back in time and do over the last few minutes. He let his fear of loss get in the way of his happiness, and hers. The constant drip of water from the frond ponds mirrored the thump of his heart.

Smith sat on a bench against a backdrop of lush, green plants and loosened his tie. "Our IT guys sent the Bat to the last known IP address from Frost's computer. A vampire, six-foot-four and approximately two-hundred and ten pounds left a house on 7th Street in Weehawken at 10:38 p.m. and returned fifteen minutes later." He pressed a button on his phone and held it up. "Does he look familiar?"

"Holy shit. Let me see." Cayden walked over to Smith and stared at the image. His gut clenched. He'd know Frost's face anywhere. "The physical description is a match. That's him."

"I say we go in now and take Frost by surprise," Mulroney said, wiping the sweat from his forehead. His words hung heavy in the air.

"I want to make sure Natalya is safe before we head out. I've been calling and texting her and she's not answering." Cayden couldn't blame her, not after the way he'd treated her. What if she never talked to him again? He wanted her so much it hurt, but she deserved more than he could give. Pressing a button on his phone, he tried to pull up her location. The map showed it was unavailable, striking terror into his heart. She'd never forget to charge her phone. What the hell was going on? "I need someone to go to Dubrosky's apartment," Cayden said into his radio.

"I've got her address. I'm headed there now," Big Red shot back.

"Thanks, man." Cayden responded and then turned to Smith "What's the plan?"

"We could be walking into a trap, but the way I see it, there's no time to lose. This is the best we have to go on right now." Smith tapped his foot, clearly jacked up on adrenaline.

"True. It's a chance I'm willing to take." It felt surreal talking about killing his enemy amidst the tranquil beauty of flora and fauna surrounding them. One thing became clear, more blood would have to be spilled.

The three of them headed south on JFK Boulevard to Weehawken, passing through the modest tree-lined streets dotted with Victorian-style houses and brick apartment buildings.

When Smith stopped at a light, he glanced over at Cayden with a wry smile, the view of the New York City skyline over his shoulder. "If anyone can hold their own against you, it's Dubrosky."

"She's equal parts class and sass." Cayden tried to make a joke, despite the rock-size lump in his throat. Picturing her in his mind with tears running down her cheeks, twisted his stomach with guilt. Ignoring Smith's scrutinizing gaze, he downloaded a layout of Frost's house from the dashboard computer.

"I simply existed before I met Ellen. I wasn't living. She taught me how to stay present and frankly, how to love. I'm a hell of a lot happier as a result." Smith cleared his throat, along with some of the awkwardness in the air.

Cayden had seen the change in his boss over the past year. Smith's hair might be gray and his face creased with lines, but he had a boyish spark in his eyes when he talked about his woman. In all the years of working with the demon, they'd never engaged in this kind of heart-to-heart.

Before Natalya came into Cayden's life, he'd been surviving, but it was no way to live. How could he go back to his lonely existence now? He could get used to making love to her every night, and wake up to her sweet face on the pillow every morning. "I'm not sure what the rules are for fraternizing with a coworker."

"I'm getting a strong sense of déjà vu." Smith arched his brows, his gaze focused on the road. "I had this convo with Denopoulos when Willow was a witness and working with the agency."

"Look at them now," Mulroney chimed in from the back seat.

"Yeah, like you're one to talk." Mulroney fell madly in love with Gillian while protecting her from a blood-trafficking ring. "We're different," Cayden said and swallowed hard, hoping they'd both drop the subject.

Mulroney nudged Cayden in the shoulder. "Bullshit. Maybe Denopoulos hasn't lived as many lifetimes as you and me, but we've both seen our fair share of horrors in our day. All we can do is keep moving forward with someone we care about, and eventually the past has no hold on us anymore."

"He's right." Smith tapped his hand on the wheel. "Think of it this way, if you don't give Dubrosky what she wants, she'll start seeing someone else. Would you be cool with that?"

A combination of anger and jealousy tightened Cayden's gut like a vice. The idea of some guy touching her, or having sex with her, forced his hands to clench into fists. "Hell no!" He could hear the misery in his own voice.

"Yeah, that's what I thought." Smith maneuvered the van through swaths of row houses with brick walkways and imposing windows. Parked cars sat bumper-to-bumper in this slice of urban living.

The air in the van became thick and tense. The stress of the op and how he'd left things with Natalya weighed on him. He drew in a breath. When Smith went over a speed bump, Cayden smacked his horns on the roof of the van. Realization hit him hard. "I've been a damn fool."

"No kidding," Mulroney agreed.

Over these past few weeks, she'd managed to find a way into his heart. Natalya's love had brought him back to life. He hoped he'd get the chance to tell her as much. Thinking about the alternative wasn't an option. He'd get down on his hands and knees and beg if he had to. She accepted him even when he was being an ass and when he tried to push her away. At this point, words meant nothing. Action would win out in the end. He'd make sure Frost could never get to her, even if it meant sacrificing his own life in the process.

Smith cut to 7th Street, circled around the block, and found an empty spot a block away from the brick house marked number four. He parked behind a Suburban and cut the engine. "Let's go over the plan again."

"I go through the large bay window in front," Cayden said, turning his head and glancing at the houses lining the street. He'd have to remove the glass to fit inside.

"I'll go to the back and make some noise, distract Frost while you sneak up on him from behind." Mulroney met his eyes in the rearview mirror.

A criminal like Frost would be only too aware of this kind of ruse, which was why Cayden would have to act fast. The three of them sat there surveying the house for several minutes until a truck rolled down the street.

"I think it's time to go in." Smith swiveled in his chair and pointed to a nylon bag. "You two are going to need some weapons. I stocked up for the occasion."

Cayden moved to the back. He opened the bag and found a variety of Summit Stakes and different-sized machetes. "You weren't kidding." Pulling a pin gun from the gadget rack, he slipped it in the waistband of his dress slacks.

The plan was to take Frost in, but if he resisted, Cayden wouldn't hesitate to stake him in the heart or decapitate him. One hard strike to the jugular should do the trick.

Frost was the last remaining link to Arcadia, to his family, and to Abigail. Once he was dead, maybe Cayden could put the past behind him once and for all.

"You should probably change into something less conspicuous," Mulroney suggested, slipping off his tux jacket and replacing it with a Kevlar vest and a black windbreaker. "Whatever you do, try not to get blood on the rental."

"I don't plan on it." Cayden did the same and remembered he'd given his suit jacket to Natalya. *Where the hell is she?* He checked his phone and ice-cold fear settled into his limbs.

Big Red: She's not @ her apartment. We're looking everywhere.

Cayden: Go back to the manor. Check her room. Question her friends. Tear the house apart if you have to. Let me know the second you find her.

Shoving the phone in his pocket, a sick feeling of dread settled in the pit of his stomach. "No one's seen Natalya." But Cayden couldn't head back now, not when they were this close. He'd die a slow death before he let Frost harm a hair on her head.

"There's no way Frost could've gotten to her. We have every reason to believe he's here," Smith assured him. "Focus on the op, man."

Cayden nodded and reached for a machete from the bag, then secured it in his shoulder holster. Grabbing a couple of stakes, he stuck them under his waistband.

The tension in the van became thick. No one knew if they'd come out of this alive. For years, he'd been living in a self-imposed kind of hell until Natalya came into his life. She'd stormed the gates of purgatory and had dragged him back to the world of the living. "Let's go."

Smith stayed put. He'd act as their eyes and ears. "Go get this piece of shit."

The van door opened. Cayden got out with Mulroney hot on his heels. His gaze cut to the houses across the street, horrified to find children's toys scattered on the lawn. To think a killer lived among them made his gut clench.

At this time of night, the streets were empty. The team blended into the shadows. The glow of the moon lit their path, and for a brief moment, Cayden imagined kissing Natalya under the moonlight. He'd find a way to make it up to her for how he'd behaved for the rest of their immortal lives.

They crossed the street and approached the house marked number four. Five brick steps led to the door.

"Are you ready?" Mulroney asked, gripping his stake. The question hung in the air. Cayden stared at his human friend, his expression stark against the glow of a streetlamp.

"Let's do this. I'll see you on the other side." While Mulroney disappeared around the side of the house, Cayden scoped out the front. The house appeared dark and deserted, not unusual for his old notion of a vampire's lair.

"Go in through the bottom window. It leads to a living room," Smith said into his mic.

Cayden pulled out his pin gun and pointed it at the center of the window. A suction cup with an invisible wire silently shot out and landed on the glass. *Bullseye.*

"I'm looking into a kitchen," Mulroney said in Cayden's ear. "There's no movement, but there's a TV on in one of the bedrooms on the top floor."

"It sounds like he's home." Grabbing the suction on the window, Cayden gave it a good tug, and the glass slid out quietly in his hands. He set the pane on the side of the house and climbed inside.

A vampire would've heard him by now. "I'm in." He glanced around at the ratty drapes and disheveled-looking furniture. A rotten stench hung in the air. Stephen Frost wouldn't be caught dead living here. Cayden almost told them this couldn't be his place, but then again, the vampire was a fugitive, he reminded himself.

"No movement anywhere," Mulroney said in his ear. "I'm approaching a back door."

"He should be down here by now." Taking another step, Cayden reached for his stake and pointed it out in front of him. Adrenaline coursed through his veins. His breathing became ragged. He couldn't wait to get this over with.

The blare of the TV raised his hackles. "Something's up." Turning the corner, Cayden came to a staircase with a kitchen to the right. "All the rooms on this level are empty." Cold dread knotted his stomach. "He's not here. Where the hell did he go?"

"There are two bedrooms to the left and one on the right," Smith said with a note of caution in his voice. "Check it out."

"I'm headed up." Cayden took the stairs two at a time, his horns burning as his demon rose. He came into the first bedroom where the TV blared. *Empty.* He kicked the door so hard it came off its hinges and fell to the floor with a loud thwack.

Then he heard the scrape of chair legs. "Someone's here. I detect a heartbeat." When he got to the second bedroom, the heartbeat became louder, pounding hard and fast. He swung open the door and found a demon male with dark hair strapped to a chair. Silver tape covered his mouth.

"It's Michaels, the barback from the Wolf Tavern, the former Hellios guard." Natalya had been the one to make the connection. "I think we found our inside man. Shit, Frost knew we were coming." He'd been ready for them. Exhaling from pent-up adrenaline, Cayden needed his head to clear.

Shoving his stake in his waistband, he ripped the tape from Michaels's mouth. "You bastard."

Michaels cursed and gasped for air. "Frost double-crossed me." Before Cayden could ask how he got there, he heard the splintering of wood and loud footfalls. He turned his head and Mulroney and Smith appeared at the top of the stairs.

Gun in the low ready position, Smith came into the room and looked around. "I want Mulroney to question our guard while I call for backup. We'll need to get forensics in here ASAP."

"Frost's playing with us." Mulroney walked in and handed him a box marked "biohazard."

After the three of them cleared the room of other potential threats, they slipped on gloves and booties. Cayden walked around, taking in his surroundings. "We'll find him."

Smith moved to what had to be Frost's computer on the desk and attached a small black box to the back. It flashed red and began to buzz, downloading Frost's script and searching for his password.

While Mulroney interrogated Michaels, Cayden turned and inspected the closet. A black, heavy coat caught his eye. Moving closer, he touched the fabric, not at all surprised to find it was made of cashmere. Mrs. Pearse was right all along. He sorted through the clothing and boxes, not sure what he was looking for when a flash of gold caught his eye.

His whole body tensed as he lifted what appeared to be a broken, tarnished crown. Cayden stared at the piece of history. Rubies and sapphires glinted under the light. He recognized the tiara. It had been commissioned for Lilith and represented the colors of the Arcadian royal flag.

As his fingers skimmed over the rough edges, the past and the present collided, reminding Cayden of a war that left his family decimated, and a love he left behind. No matter how much he wished he could flee the past, it always caught up with him somehow. Maybe he was still chasing ghosts.

Sagging on the floor, he sucked in air, trying to stop the riot of emotions wreaking havoc over him. He didn't know how long he sat there until footfalls and voices filled the room. He stood and looked around as a slew of agents and officers began dusting for prints.

Mulroney walked over to him with a look of disgust across his face. "Michaels admitted to slipping a sleeping potion into your drink on the night of Andee Lyon's murder."

Cayden's mind reeled. "But why?"

"Greed. Michaels claims he helped Frost frame you in exchange for jewels," Mulroney confirmed.

While Cayden tried to process this new info, Smith called out his name. "I found a secret room." His boss stood in a cubby behind the wall of the desk. "You need to come see this."

The revulsion in Smith's voice beckoned him forward. His feet moved fast, considering his head remained in a fog. When his gaze landed on photos of Lilith, his stomach roiled. To the right, he found some of Andee, and even more of Erika. But when his gaze moved to the far corner of the wall, all the air in his lungs rushed out in a single breath. "Dear gods."

Photos of Natalya smiling and laughing covered the entire wall. The still shots said more about the photographer than the subject. A sick feeling spread through his veins like a cancer.

"He's been following Natalya all along," Smith said, pulling out his phone and snapping pictures. "What's this?" He reached for an envelope taped to the wall with Cayden's name across the front.

The floor dropped from beneath his feet. Cayden grabbed the envelope and tore it open with shaking hands. He found it hard to breathe as his gaze roamed over the black, scrolling writing

I've always loved the quote about revenge tasting like a bitter morsel in the mouth, savored and cooked in hell. No matter how hard we try, sometimes we can't hold on to the things we love the most.

Panic ripped through Cayden's chest at the implication. "The bastard has Natalya."

CHAPTER 49

*N*atalya tried to adjust her eyes to the bright lights inside her building. Frost walked her through the lobby to the elevator bank with his hand digging into her ribs. "Why are you doing this?" Her gaze darted frantically around the empty hallway, regretting her decision to move in to a building without a doorman.

Her head pounded. She tried to piece together what happened after getting into Frost's car, but it all became one big blur. Every time she gathered her strength to fight back, the bastard would put her in a trance again. She refused to let this psycho keep her down. The second she could grab her stake, she'd take him out. What did he do with her purse?

"Don't even think about screaming. If you do, I'll kill you before anyone will hear you," Frost taunted.

How could he have hidden such viciousness?

When the elevator dinged, Frost pulled her inside and pressed a button for the basement. He moved next to her in the confined space and it made her skin crawl. His crazy eyes gleamed under the fluorescent lights.

If Cayden came after her, he'd be walking into a trap. He knew she was headed here from her text. She had no way of warning him without her phone.

The elevator doors opened to the basement. Frost grabbed her arm and dragged her across the dark hall toward the storage lockers. He took her keys out of her purse and she used the opportunity to blur away. If she was going to die, at least she'd go down fighting.

Frost caught up with her and grabbed her by her bun, pulling at her roots. "I warned you." He spun her around and backhanded her across the face so hard it left a ringing in her ears.

Anger lit off a firestorm in her chest. The last time she'd been struck had been the night she'd been attacked. She refused to let Frost get the upper hand. Lunging for his throat, she knocked him into the wall. The move caught him by surprise, giving her a chance to reach for her purse. Before she could grab a weapon, he wrapped a hand around her throat in a death grip. Gasping for breath, he lifted her off the floor and held her above him while her feet dangled in midair. She landed a kick, aiming for the groin, but only managed to hit him in the thigh.

"Now there's your backbone. Try that again and I'll drain you." Frost set her on her feet then dragged her toward the storage room. Crushing the knob in his hand, he pushed open the door, shoving her over the threshold.

Damp, cold air hit her right away. She inhaled the dank, dusty air, wondering what Frost had in mind for her. Cobwebs hung overhead and dusted along her skin.

"You won't be needing this." He flung her purse across the room.

Her throat constricted. She shook it off by telling herself that she'd find a way out of this. She needed to keep him talking, in hopes of distracting him. "You put on an award-winning performance," Natalya's voice cracked as she stared at his face. "I checked you out on several sites. How did you create your fake persona?"

"I'm crack on computers," he said with pride in his voice. "If you know what you're doing, it's easy to trick even someone as clever as you." Frost pulled her over to one of the storage cages. He started to push her inside, but she held her ground, baring her fangs.

"I don't think so," he warned. "I've been saving the best for last." Pulling out a glittering scythe from his coat, he waved the blade at her neck.

This time when he pushed, she didn't resist. She'd seen the weapon slice the head clean off a vampire.

"What makes you think Cayden will find me?" Her voice started to break. She struggled to keep it steady as she moved to the corner of the ten-by-ten cage and took a seat on the concrete floor.

"I'm sure he'll figure it out. Too bad he won't be able to save you." After he shut the door to the locker, he held the scythe over his shoulder. "It's going to be a shame to mar such a pretty neck. It's a pity too, because I like you."

Fear closed around her throat. This time when a scream erupted from her lips, she made sure it rattled the walls.

Cayden couldn't remember much of the drive back to the manor. By the time the three of them entered through the doors of the solarium, he could barely keep his panic in check. A host of macabre scenarios kept running through his head.

"We sent the Bat out to Natalya's place right after you got the call, but the inside of her apartment was empty," Big Red confirmed. "I put a tracker on her phone. I found what was left of it in the middle of Green Street."

"Where the hell is she?" Panic gripped Cayden like a steel vice around his throat. He sucked in air, teetering on a razor's edge. Dread and anger raced through his veins in equal measure.

Smith gave him a sharp look. "Take it easy. Don't let your emotions get in the way or we could lose her for good. You're the link to get her out of this. You can still save her, Teague."

"How?" The question stuck in Cayden's throat like a rock. He'd do whatever it took, but would it be enough? "Frost could've taken her anywhere." Guilt squeezed at his chest. If he'd just told her how he'd felt, she never would've left the wedding.

"I've got an idea." Mulroney pulled out his phone and began feverishly texting. "There are other ways to trace her location. Frost couldn't have taken her far."

"Agreed." Cayden exhaled. "Frost wants me to find her." *Let her be alive. Let her be alive.* He repeated the words over and over again like a mantra. Every moment they wasted could cost Natalya her life.

A few minutes later, Gillian walked into the solarium looking panicked. "What's going on?"

When Arabella came in holding Cayden's tux jacket, his gut twisted. "Natalya asked me to give this to you." Her eyes filled with tears. "She said she was headed to her apartment. She promised to text me when she got in, but I never heard from her. I sensed something might be wrong."

Cayden filled them in, making sure to leave out the finer details. After he finished, his mouth became bone dry. How could he have let this happen? Rather than protecting her, he drove her into the arms of a killer. He could chastise himself all he wanted, but it wouldn't change a damn thing.

"Let us help. We can use your jacket to find her. It has Natalya's energy all over it," Arabella suggested, spreading his jacket out on the butcher block table.

"I'm begging you to do whatever you can." Cayden couldn't seem to get air into his lungs as he took a step back to let the witches do their thing.

With a nod, Arabella pulled a silver necklace with a black onyx attached to the end from around her neck "I'm going to use my pendulum to divine her location."

Gillian walked over to the table and removed a crystal from her purse. She blew on the top then placed it on his jacket. "This will give it an extra charge. We're going to find her, big guy." She reached out and squeezed Cayden's hand.

Arabella pointed to Cayden's phone. "Okay, we'll need you to pull up a map of the city."

Cayden pulled it up and then set his phone on the table, swallowing hard. "I pray this works."

Arabella held her pendulum over the map. At first, it swung back and forth, glittering in the dim light. After a while, it began to move in a circle. "I can sense her essence. Natalya's alive." Finally, the charm landed on Madison Street. "I thought you said she wasn't in her apartment?"

"We did remote surveillance. Her apartment's empty." Cayden shook his head, confused.

"What if she's below it?" Smith asked, stepping forward, gripping his phone. "Some of the older buildings have storage units in the basement. "I'm checking the layout now."

The temperature in the room had climbed to a sweltering degree, but Cayden couldn't seem to stop shaking. If he let fear get the better of him, it could cost Natalya her life. Snapping into action, he moved to Smith's side and glanced at his screen. Sure enough, there was a storage room. "I need to go alone. Frost could try and kill her if I come with backup."

"You can't go there half-cocked without backup," Mulroney interjected. "You'll be walking into a death trap."

"It's a chance I'm willing to take." Every moment Cayden wasted put Natalya in worse danger. *What if ...?* The thought was too horrible to bear. "She became the target in something that had nothing to do with her."

"We can follow at a distance and circle the perimeter," Smith suggested. "We'll catch Frost when he tries to leave."

If he tries to leave. "Frost won't be walking out of there, not if I have anything to say about it." *What if I'm too late?* Breathing in and out, Cayden couldn't stop the panic rising up from his throat.

"There's a possibility we have to consider, Teague." Mulroney's expression turned grave. "What if he's already killed Dubrosky and he's leading you there to kill you too?"

"No! I can't think like that." Cayden breathed in and out, trying not to panic. "I won't." Natalya was a part of him. He could feel her in his blood. He motioned to the agents. "You stay at a distance at all times. I need to get over there." All he could do now was pray with everything in him that just this once he'd get there in time.

CHAPTER 50

"You're taking a chance bringing me here." Natalya peeked through the slats on the locker, glancing at the door, willing someone to come in. If she distracted Frost, even for a second, she might be able to kill him before Cayden got there. She'd find a way to save them both.

A car alarm went off somewhere above their heads, she glanced at Frost. "What if a neighbor heard the scurry in the hall and called the police?"

He glanced at the door that led to a back staircase. "I'll blur away before the cops can get near me. It helps if you have a hostage."

I'm screwed. Natalya's gaze darted to the window, wondering if she could find a way to get past him, wrench it open, and haul herself to the ground level before he came after her. For a split second, hope flared like the glow of the streetlight above the window.

His gaze narrowed as though reading her thoughts. "Don't even think about running."

Her pulse thumped. She tried not to panic. It took a long time to work through her fears in therapy. In less than an hour, this psychopath had brought them all back with a vengeance. Angry tears burned in her eyes. "Why carry this grudge after all these years?"

Frost laughed and the creepy sound sent her heart racing. "Those of us who've lived for centuries don't have a sense of time. After my wife died, I thought maybe I should go too, join her on the other side, but then I decided to channel my grief in another way. I became obsessed with getting my revenge and evening the score."

"Revenge won't bring your wife back, and it won't change the past," Natalya said, trying to reason with him, all the while her gaze kept darting around the small storage locker in search of a weapon, but all she could find was a bike, some tennis rackets, and an antique-looking chair. Her gaze zeroed in on the wooden spindles on the back. Maybe she could fashion one into a stake.

"Maybe not, but I have the power to change the future." Frost set the scythe against the locker. "There are only so many ways to kill a vampire. I could break your neck, chop off your pretty head, burn you alive, or stake you in the chest. Hmm, then of course there's my personal favorite, draining all the blood from your body. Decisions, decisions."

Her stomach churned violently. "Why kill innocent women that had nothing to do with this revenge plot? Why make their loved ones suffer like you did?" Reaching behind her, she closed her fingers over one of the spindles. She gave it one quick tug, and it broke off in her hand. Thankfully, he didn't seem to notice.

His eyes flashed. "I want Teague to experience the constant torment I did."

"You won't get away with this. The law will eventually catch up with you. It always does," she said with a tremor in her voice. "It's karma times three for each life you took." Pretending to cough loudly, she scraped the end of the spindle against the floor, sharpening the tip into a point.

"You can skip the sanctimonious BS, Natalya," he snarled. "Any vampire who beds a demon is in no position to lecture me. There are laws in our world, and you've broken every one of them."

Frost must not have known that his precious Lilith had propositioned Cayden once upon a time. A heavy silence fell over them like a dark cloud. "How did your wife die?" She needed to keep him talking, and play to his ego to buy her time. Once he came closer, she'd aim for the heart. It probably wouldn't kill him, but it would buy her time to get away.

"She succumbed to a slow death from the lead-laden walls of Hellios. I was forced to watch the person I love most in the world die in front of me." For a split second, grief replaced the maniacal glint in his eyes.

"I still don't get how you managed to pull off the escape from Hellios." She tried to keep her voice calm despite the tornado twisting inside of her.

"I'd been planning it for years. I knew it would take time to execute," Frost said, moving closer. "But I was patient. I recruited help. Even behind bars, I still had money and means. I got the idea the night Lilith died when I watched Pike take her out in a body bag."

"And you bribed him to do the same for you?" Her hand tightened around the spindle.

"As a former king, I still managed to maintain some of my spoils of war."

Her heart thudded against her rib cage with the admission. "You used the Arcadian jewels to pay off Pike?" Cayden suspected as much all along.

"Pike was quite useful to me at first," Frost said, taking another predatory step closer. "He got greedy in the end, and when he no longer served a purpose, I eliminated him. But he wasn't the only one helping me. He told Michaels, one of the Hellios guards, about our agreement. Of course he wanted in on the loot and I gave it to him in exchange for his surveillance. He kept track of Teague's every move."

What a merry band of murdering accomplices, Natalya thought, but kept her mouth shut.

"After I framed Teague for the first murder, the evidence wasn't enough to put him away. I had no choice but to go after Erika and frame him for the crime. She fought until the bitter end. I can still taste the fear in her blood."

Her breaths came out in shallow puffs of air. "You're sick."

A huge smile spread across his face, as if her words made him proud. "Making Teague suffer has always been the goal, but adding you to the mix was an added bonus."

"He's already suffered," she said through panting breaths. The damage has been done. Pain stabbed at her heart. He's never gotten over losing Abigail. "How did you follow me without me noticing?"

"I'd been following Teague and saw you two together at the Wolf Tavern. I gave you my card in the hopes you'd call. When you clicked on the link I sent you, it downloaded a tracker onto your phone. It allowed me to spy on you from a distance. The closer I got to you, the closer I got to Teague."

Chills moved through her limbs. The methods he'd gone to in order to pull this off were even more diabolical than she imagined. "The MBI will find you and sentence you to death. If you leave now, you might get away."

"You don't get it. I've got nothing to lose anymore." His gaze zeroed in on her neck. "I've been wondering how your blood would taste since the night we met. I was waiting for your boyfriend to get here to find out, but I've grown weary." He opened the door to the locker, baring his fangs.

It was now or never. Reaching behind her for the makeshift stake, she surged to her feet and plunged the point into the center of his chest. Blood spurted everywhere.

"You little witch," he roared, pulling the stake out of his chest, giving her time to reach for the handle of the scythe.

She swung at his head, but Frost blurred out of the way. "I'm not going down without a fight."

CHAPTER 51

A soul-aching fury washed over Cayden as he descended the staircase to the basement of Natalya's building. Fire pulsed from his fingertips. He couldn't control his demon from emerging. When he got to the last step, a blood-curdling scream pierced the air.

Natalya.

The icy fear in her voice sent his heart thumping. Cayden cut across the space and found Frost holding Natalya in a headlock, the blade of a scythe angled at her neck. The sight forced panic to close around his throat. "Let her go. This is between you and me."

When their eyes met, hers filled with tears. "Take him down, Cayden! Burn this piece of shit to a crisp."

"Shut your mouth." Frost dug the edge of the blade into her neck, leaving a gash that started to bleed. His gaze flew to Cayden's. "Don't take another step. One swipe to the carotid and you'll be cleaning up her blood for a week."

Cayden held up his hands so Frost wouldn't make any sudden moves. He stayed rooted to the spot, even though he wanted to rip the bastard apart. He'd never been more ready to end this fight. "Natalya has nothing to do with ancient rifts. The way I see it, we've already settled the score."

"What fantasies are you spinning?" When Frost moved under the light, Cayden finally caught a glimpse of his face. He'd never forget the evil lurking behind those dark, hooded eyes, or the scar on his right cheek that he'd given him in battle.

"I rejected Lilith when she propositioned me. She got her revenge by killing the woman I loved." Cayden's gaze kept darting to Natalya, keeping her in his line of vision.

"You lie," Frost roared, releasing his hold on Natalya. Before she could get away, he slammed her head up against the steal post with so much force, Cayden heard her skull crack. Crumpling to the floor, she lay there still and bleeding. *No! Please, please, not Tayla.* If something happened to her he wouldn't survive it. Hysteria formed a tight knot in his chest.

There was time to check on her as the vampire moved to him in a blur. Gripping the scythe in his hands, Frost aimed a blow at his neck.

Cayden jumped out of the way just in time. The strike landed on one of the storage doors, the scythe sinking deep.

"I'll make you pay." While Frost pulled the scythe out, Cayden reached for the machete in his shoulder holster. He swung the blade in the air, aiming for his head.

Stumbling back with a curse, Frost's face contorted in rage. "After I kill you, I'm going to rip out your girlfriend's throat and drain all her blood. I'll savor the moments afterward when her body writhes beneath me."

Cayden clenched his teeth so hard he tasted blood on his tongue. He refused to let Frost's goading words get him whipped into frenzy. "Your sick plot for revenge has all been for shit. Your precious Lilith slept with countless soldiers as a power play."

"Don't you dare say her name," Frost hissed, doubt clouding his beady eyes. "She was my whole world."

"You set out to avenge the death of someone who wasn't even faithful to you, and killed two innocent women in the process." Stepping closer, Cayden pointed the blade at his face and swung out.

"Fuck off." Frost blurred out of the way. Swinging the scythe at Cayden's neck, he managed to duck as the blade whistled above his head. "She'd never cheat on me."

On instinct, Cayden inched closer to the staircase, blocking the exit. He wouldn't allow Frost to get out of there alive this time. "You must've been too busy conquering other realms and massacring innocents to notice," he taunted, with his fingers flexed tight around the handle of the machete, waiting for the vampire's concentration to slip. Every muscle in his body tensed to kill the bastard.

"I'm going to enjoy watching you suffer." His ghoulish smile revealed pointy white fangs.

Seizing his chance, Cayden dove at Frost, landing on him and knocking them both to the hard floor. With one hand clutched on the scythe, he wrapped the other around Frost's neck and lifted the blade to end him. Slippery as a snake, Frost twisted and managed to slip out of his grasp. Cayden's swing arced through empty air.

Through the corner of his eye, Cayden saw Natalya's hand move, heard a slight feminine grunt of pain. She tried to stand. Panting hard, relief flooded through his veins.

The distraction cost him. Frost lifted him and flung him headfirst into a post. Sharp pain exploded through his body, leaving a ringing in his ears. But there was no time to think. He shot to his feet. In an attempt to block Frost's weapon, he struck out. The clash of metal vibrated like a jackhammer.

Gritting his teeth against a wave of dizziness, Cayden lost his footing and stumbled backwards. This time when the blade arced above his head, the image of Natalya flashed through his head, along with the future they'd never have. He mourned over the words he'd never get to say to her, and tears filled his eyes.

A whooshing sound filled the air followed by a deafening thud.

Blood spurted all over Cayden. At first he didn't know if it was his. And then as Frost fell face-first onto the concrete floor, with a Summit Stake sticking out of his back, he realized the vampire was dead and gone, now a dusty pile of bones. He lifted his head to find Natalya standing behind Frost's body. A red mark slashed across her cheek and her hair looked wild around her face. Her dress was toast and covered in blood.

"Talya ..."

"Are you okay? Cayden?"

They ran to each other at the same time. Cayden crushed her to his chest and breathed her in. "It's finally over, baby."

"I thought you were going to die. I thought I was too late." Natalya sobbed into his chest.

"I'm fine and I'm not going anywhere. You can't get rid of me that easily." He kissed her temple and the top of her head, breathing in her scent, breathing in his life. All these years he'd been consumed by guilt and the memories of his former life. For the first time in over a century, he finally wanted to go forward with Natalya at his side.

Smith and Mulroney descended the stairs, swarming the storage room, followed by Big Red, Jax, and Nick.

"How in the hell?" Mulroney asked with shock in his voice.

"It was all Natalya. She saved my life." Cayden turned to his woman. "Good work, Detective." He pulled her away from prying eyes. "This whole thing is my fault. I'm sorry for everything I've put you through."

"This isn't your fault, Cayden. I survived and I've been through worse." She looked at him and smiled. "But I didn't have you."

"Let's get the hell out of this basement." Cayden pulled her into a tight hug and kissed her forehead. "We have a lot to talk about, and I'm not leaving your side."

CHAPTER 52

Several hours later, Natalya sat curled on Cayden's couch under a blanket. After a long, hot shower, she slipped on one of his T-shirts, sans underwear, grateful to be out of her ruined dress. No matter how hard she scrubbed, she couldn't get the stench of Frost out of her hair or off her skin.

Cayden had insisted she go to the hospital to get checked out, and despite her protests, he took her anyway. The whole way there in the ambulance, he couldn't stop checking her pulse and kept squeezing her hand.

Thankfully, her injuries hadn't been enough to cause any real damage. Her bruises had already started to fade, along with the throbbing in her head. Thankfully, she healed fast. She didn't want to think too much about what could've happened if she hadn't finished off Frost when she did.

The bathroom door opened. Cayden came out in a puff of steam. "How do you feel?" He walked over to her and placed a kiss on her lips. He sported a black eye. Cuts and scrapes were scattered across his handsome face. Black-and-blue marks covered his broad chest.

"I'm fine. I feel better than I have a right to considering the circumstances." Sighing, Natalya inhaled his delicious scent, a combination of sandalwood, musk, and body wash. "Things could've been a whole lot worse."

"I'm sorry for the things I said. I didn't mean them. I'll regret them till the day I die."

"It's okay, I forgive you." Her eyes filled with tears.

"Let me get you some tea." Cayden walked across the room and she got a chance to admire him as he puttered around the kitchen. Her gaze traveled over his bare chest and moved lower to his pj bottoms. The pants hung low on his hips, accentuating his sexy V.

"I don't need anything. I just want you." She heard cabinets open and close and then he pulled out a pot and heated something on the stove. After a few minutes, he came back holding a mug of tea.

"This might settle your nerves." Setting the mug on the end table, he sat down next to her on the couch.

"Thank you." She lifted the steaming cup to her lips and took a sip. "Talk to me. You need to stop blaming yourself."

"How can I not blame myself?" Cayden's voice broke. He lifted her legs onto his lap. "He'd been stalking you for weeks and I didn't figure it out until it was almost too late."

"Frost went to meticulous lengths to fool everyone. I even fixed him up with Brooke." She took another sip from her mug, savoring the taste of sweet warmth on her tongue, chasing some of the darkness away. "I was so happy. I wanted everyone else to be too."

"I'm sorry for driving you away. I should've never left your side." He visibly swallowed.

She sensed his pain like an open wound. She set the mug on the table. "The things I said to you about your drinking. I had no right. I didn't mean to overstep."

"You were right." Reaching for her hand, Cayden placed a kiss on her palm. "You said what I needed to hear. Getting help isn't a sign of weakness, but a sign of strength. We're in this together."

Warmth radiated from her chest. "Oh, Cayden." It finally felt like everything would be okay. "I could get used to this."

"Then you've caught on to my plan." Lifting her off the couch, Cayden carried her to his bed and set her on the edge. "There's something I want to show you." The depth of emotion in his eyes confirmed his feelings.

When Natalya turned her head, she found a framed photo of her on his bedside table. "How did you get this?"

"I saved one of the photos of "Loveseekingvampgirl" for myself. I want to wake up to your smile every morning." He sat beside her and his blue eyes bore into hers.

"Keep talking. I think I like where this is going." She ran her hand over his stubbly jaw. She wanted to believe with all her heart that maybe he'd fallen as hard and fast as she did, even if he couldn't say the words.

"I want to make new memories." His gaze trailed over her and filled with longing. "I want to wake up to the flesh and blood you, not a photo."

The fierce look in his eyes made her heart pound. "What are you saying?"

"I almost lost you. It forced me to put things in perspective." Cayden ran his thumb over her bottom lip. "I learned something these past few months, although it took me a little while. I never want to be without you, Talya. There are some things I need to say to you that are long overdue."

"I'm listening," she said, a little breathless.

"You make me feel things, right here." Cayden pointed to the center of his chest. "When you told me you loved me and I didn't say it back, I regretted it right away. I know I hurt you and I never meant to." Adoration lit his eyes. She'd never get tired of seeing it there. "Even when we were fighting, I loved you then, and I love you now."

Relief washed through her at the same time tears welled in her eyes. Cayden loved her. Her heart pounded with the admission.

"I'm in love with you, Talya," he repeated in a raspy voice. "I needed to make sure I could be the man worthy of your love before I said those words. I still can't believe I found someone with such a kind heart and a pure soul." His eyes appeared a little watery all of a sudden.

Happy tears fell to her cheeks as she stared at this strong, powerful man, with love shining in his eyes.

He pressed his forehead to hers. "The love I feel for you is all-consuming. There's this intensity about it that burns through me like a fire in my chest. You're a part of me."

"I understand, because I love you with the same intensity," she whispered and touched his face. He kissed her again, a tender brush of his lips. "I'm not going anywhere." She dragged her fingers over his chest and then moved lower to his rock-hard abs, enjoying his sharp intake of breath.

A heady wave of arousal sparked in the air between them. "I know you planned to move in to your apartment, but I want you to move in here with me. Or maybe we could get a different place." The hopeful look on his face crushed the last of her doubts. "Am I going too fast?"

A sense of bone-melting joy washed over her and made her smile. "I've been thinking the same thing. I can't move into to my apartment building. Not after this nightmare. I want to be with you, always."

"I was crazy to think I could ever walk away or let you go." He kissed her temple. "I couldn't go on without you."

"I think we need to celebrate being alive." She climbed onto his lap and wrapped her legs around his hips. The thick ridge of his erection pressed against her bare flesh in the most exquisite way.

"Talya," he whispered in a voice thick with lust. The familiar prickle of heat licked at the place where their bodies joined. "I've got your sweet scent filling my head." He reached under her shirt and cupped her breast, skimming a thumb over her nipple, replacing the darkness with ecstasy.

"I love you, Cayden." She rubbed against him, already wet and ready for her demon. "I need to feel our connection and our passion."

"I love you too." He kissed her long and deep. His tongue slid into her mouth, stroking back and forth in deep velvet strokes, driving her wild. He pulled away, breathless, caressing her cheek. "I want you so much. I'm going out of my ever-loving mind, but I don't want to hurt you. We should wait until you're healed."

Making love to her gorgeous demon boyfriend seemed like the best way to put this nightmare behind them. "I'm healing as we speak." She pressed her breasts against the hard wall of his chest. "I think we need to start working on making those new memories." Only Cayden could sate her hunger and make her forget, love her through this ordeal.

His eyes filled with hunger. "We have all night." Lifting her shirt over her head, he kissed her bare shoulder, making her shiver. "I have a few things in mind."

EPILOGUE

atalya looked out from the Rainbow Room's glass-paneled windows, admiring the panoramic views of the New York City skyline. She still couldn't believe three weeks had passed since that fateful night in the basement of her building. It all seemed like a lifetime ago. She'd moved in to Cayden's loft and now she got to spend every spare moment with her sexy demon.

They chose to celebrate life by making love each night. Whether it was slow and mind-numbing, or fast and passionate, it only made her fall deeper in love with him. Each morning before work, they parted with tenderness and kisses.

She never imagined being this happy or content, whether they were jogging together in the park, hiking in the mountains, or reading to each other in bed. Whenever they went to a restaurant, or to the movies, or when they hung out with their group of friends, their conversations never got boring.

These last few weeks with Cayden had been magical, the best of her life. They shared a deep, profound love and mutual respect. They'd found a way to work through their demons together. They'd fallen hard for each other in a short period of time, but after everything they'd been through together, it felt like many lifetimes.

Now she stood inside one of the city's most iconic landmarks about to be honored by a charity she loved. Life kept getting better all the time. She pinched herself to make sure this was real.

When she turned away from the window, her gaze darted around the reception room, now lit by a backdrop of dazzling lights and jam-packed with movers and shakers, a who's who of the vampire world.

The females were decked out in ball gowns and slinky dresses. They stood close to their vampire companions who all wore tuxedos. She glanced at the stage where an eight-piece orchestra played soft jazz in the background. All around her, the room buzzed with couples bidding on their silent auction items.

Cayden had jumped on the donation bandwagon with both feet and called in a few favors to add to the pot. She only wished he could be here in the flesh. She'd managed to twist his arm into being her plus-one, but sadly, he'd been forced to cancel at the last minute. He'd been called away to Cleveland on an assignment.

She understood, especially since starting her new position at the SVU. Working evenings and weekends had become the norm, but that didn't stop the momentary pang of disappointment when their plans got cancelled. She'd gotten more than a few curious glances by coming here alone. And for the first time in her adult life, she'd didn't care anymore.

Servers walked past with flutes of champagne. She declined when a waiter approached. She needed to keep a clear head before she delivered her speech. When she turned, she spotted Tessa in the crowd. She waved her over. "There you are."

Tessa walked over to her and kissed both her cheeks. She looked stunning in a strapless, black, beaded dress. "What's been going on?"

Natalya filled Tessa in on her new living arrangements, making sure to leave out the part about being kidnapped by a psychopath.

"I'm so happy for you both. Cayden's definitely a keeper. Is he here?" Tessa glanced around the room.

"No, he had to work." She tried to keep the disappointment out of her voice.

"I'm here for you. If any of these women give you a hard time about being here without a date, remember I've got your back. How did your speech come out? Are you nervous?"

"I've been practicing, but I'm not big on speaking in front of crowds." Natalya opened her clutch and pulled out her index cards. "By the time I sat down to write it, everything in my life had changed and shifted for the better. I'm not the same person anymore." Her speech reflected the transformation.

"You're going to be amazing. I can't think of anyone who deserves this honor more." Tessa's words loosened the knot in the pit of her stomach.

"I decided to tell the truth. Although I'm not sure how my family will react when I drop the inevitable bombshell."

"They'll have to deal. This isn't about them. I'm so proud of you, Natalya."

"You've supported me, Tessa. You've always been there for me no matter what." Natalya reached for her hand and squeezed. "I'm grateful to you from the bottom of my heart."

"I could see the beautiful butterfly emerging and spreading her wings." Tessa smiled. "You've got this, babe."

Her love for her friend deepened. "Thank you." She hugged Tessa with tears in her eyes. After a long moment, she pulled away, ready to take her seat.

"I almost forgot to tell you, an anonymous donor has been calling in and bidding on some of our pricey auction items."

Hearing those words made her tear up. Knowing the money would be put to good use. "Fantastic." Natalya grinned. The lights dimmed. "I should go to my table. I'll check in with you after the ceremony." She crossed the room, exchanging pleasantries with a few familiar faces, and then took a seat at her family's table. When she glanced at the empty seat to her right, her heart gave a little tug.

"Good evening, Natalya. I've been looking for you." Eleanora took a seat next to her at the table, looking like the epitome of class in a red ball gown. Pearls adorned her neck.

"It's good to see you, Eleanora." Natalya held her head high. They hadn't spoken in weeks, since the brunch.

"You look different from the last time I saw you." Eleanora's gaze moved from her face and hair to her blue chiffon dress.

It shimmered under the lights and made her feel like a princess. "I am different." Natalya smiled. She hadn't only changed on the outside. The heavy weight of shame had finally been lifted. She felt light and free. She could never go back to her old lonely existence.

"Where's your date? Are you here alone?" The shocked look on

Eleanora's face would've set Natalya on edge a month ago, but not anymore.

"Yes. I'm flying solo tonight." She didn't need to follow anyone else's rules.

"How could you embarrass us like this?" Eleanora angled her head to the couples waltzing across the dance floor.

A few of the women in earshot began to stare. Natalya ignored them, refusing to be intimidated by the old guard. This charity meant too much to her to let anything spoil her evening.

"This could've been avoided," Eleanora said with a frown. "Carter Henry agreed to come as your escort."

"I'm not interested in Carter Henry, or any vampire from a proper bloodline," Natalya whispered. "I'm with Cayden now. We're living together. He's a part of my life."

Eleanora's face fell. "You're with the demon?"

"Yes, and we can talk about it later. This night's not about me and you. I'm here to help women who've been abused, not kowtow to some archaic standard. You need to respect my decisions and my boundaries."

Eleanora's expression softened a fraction. "I've been told I can be controlling at times."

Natalya tried not to snort. "Don't forget meddling. In this century, women manage to function in society without a companion. You should try it sometime. It's quite liberating."

"I've lived for over four-hundred years. You can't expect me to change my ways now, Natalya."

And Natalya didn't think she ever would. "I'm not here to chastise you. I want to move forward, but there are things you need to do in order for that to happen. I know you mean well, but interfering in my life has only pushed me further away," she said with a sigh. "I'll always be grateful beyond words to you and Pavel for everything you've done for me, but I can't be beholden to you if it's unhealthy for me. Would you ever consider going to counseling with me?"

Eleanora stared at her without saying a word. Her silence stung.

Natalya swallowed hard. Maybe some things weren't meant to be.

Once the rest of the guests took their seats, the speaker came onto the stage to a round of applause. "Good evening, and welcome to the SAAN annual charity ball. We'd like to thank you for being here tonight. Your generous donations will go to helping survivors through therapy, research, education, rape kits, public service announcements, along with a center for the victims. We help individuals find support and resources. Let's get the evening kicked off with our awards portion in recognition of outstanding volunteer work."

One by one, the volunteers came up to the stage, made their speeches and accepted their awards. When Natalya's name was called, everything inside her churned.

Breathe, she reminded herself and stepped onto the stage and into the spotlight. She took the mic and looked out at the crowd. "Thank you." All eyes in the room were focused on her. Pushing her shoulders back, she tried to find her voice over the rush of nerves.

"Over Sixty-three thousand women and children are sexually abused each year. With awareness, we can bring this darkness into the light and someday turn that number to zero."

The lights dimmed further.

"Too many victims never come forward for fear of being taken seriously, or being ridiculed. I should know, because before I became a vampire, I was one of them."

The room fell into stunned silence. You could've heard a silver spoon drop. Natalya exhaled a breath, and then another. "I lived my life hiding under the radar. I never opened my heart, or let anyone in. I was too afraid they'd see the shame that lived inside of me. But I found out something, everyone deserves love, even me, and especially all of you." She motioned to the crowd with her hands.

"I don't want to hide anymore. I deserve happiness. I never thought I did, so I say to anyone out there who still feels the pain and shame of abuse, you too can be loved. Remember, you no longer have to be a victim."

She smiled. "Let someone know what happened to you. Don't hold back. If you know someone who's been abused, offer to get them help. After you finally acknowledge that this isn't your fault, that's when you heal." She held on to the corner of the podium to keep from swaying.

For a split second her throat constricted, and then she locked eyes with Tessa. Her encouraging smile gave Natalya a surge of confidence. All this time she thought she needed validation from these other women or her family, but she only needed it from herself.

She wanted to be the champion of her own story. She didn't need a man to make her happily ever after come true. Having one was simply an added bonus. She was in charge of her own destiny, and right now she felt pretty damn good about her life.

Somewhere in the back of the room, someone clapped loudly, breaking the uncomfortable silence. The spotlight shining in her eyes kept her from seeing who it was. The clapping grew louder and then as her heart began to pound in her chest, she caught a glimpse of Cayden as he stepped forward into the center of the ballroom.

Gasps pierced the air. When her gaze fell upon him, she sucked in a breath at how handsome he looked in his black tux.

A moment passed and then Tessa surged to her feet and applauded. Shock rippled through Natalya when the rest of the crowd followed suit.

Cayden walked up to the stage and kissed her on the cheek. "You nailed it." Lacing their fingers together, he led her down the steps to the side of the stage. "I'm so proud of you, Talya." He pulled her into his arms and hugged her tight. After several minutes of holding each other, he drew away and placed a sweet kiss on her lips, stealing her breath.

"I thought you had to work." She couldn't stop smiling.

"I wanted to surprise you. I wouldn't miss your speech, or seeing my girl receive her award. I'm here for you, always." He stroked her cheek.

Tear misted in her eyes. "Cayden."

"You've lived all this time believing you weren't good enough," Cayden rasped against her lips. "I can't let you go another day thinking you're not."

She began to sob now, her heart full of bone-deep love for her demon.

"For the better part of my life I didn't let anyone in, but somehow you managed to snag my heart." He wiped her tears with his thumb. His gaze seared into hers. "I'm better because of you."

"Then we're even." She laughed through her tears.

A flurry of noise and movement drew her attention to the back of the ballroom. Arabella, Willow, Brooke, Delilah, Belinda, Nadia, Gillian, and Ellen sauntered in. She turned to Cayden. Her heart beat so fast and hard she thought it might burst through her chest. "What's going on? Why are they all here?" A part of her already knew the answer.

"I asked them all to come. I figured you might want all your family and friends here to witness what I'm about to do."

"W-what are you saying?" She gave him a disbelieving look. This couldn't be happening.

"I don't want to go another day, or walk this earth, without you by my side. You're my heart and my soul. I love you more than I ever thought possible. I was dead before you came into my life, an empty shell of bitterness and misery. You made me feel things again. You see me for who I am. You're not afraid to call me out and tell me when I'm being a pain in the ass. And it's because you love me."

When Natalya stared into his eyes, all the love she felt for him was reflected back at her. "Cayden."

"I've never known a female as brave, or strong, or gutsy as you. I've got another surprise." He pulled out a brochure with the silent auction items circled in red and handed it to her with a wink.

"Wait a minute, you're the anonymous donor?" Her jaw dropped. "But how? Cayden, you don't have that kind of money."

"I was late because of my meeting at the Buckland Museum of Witchcraft in Cleveland. The curator offered to let me have some of the recovered jewels since they were the only things left of my people, but I gave most of them back." He shrugged. "I figured I'd hang on to a few."

Shock rippled through her when he got down on one knee and retrieved a black velvet box from his front pocket. He opened it and a gorgeous, round diamond ring with rubies and sapphires embedded in the band sparkled under the lights. The gesture took her breath away.

"Marry me, Natalya Galina Dubrosky and make me the happiest man in the world now and forever more. You are my soulmate, my better half, my destiny." He placed the ring on her finger.

"Yes! Yes!"

Rising to his feet, he bent his head and gave her a kiss so deep it felt like a merging of their souls.

Natalya knew she had someone who wasn't going to let a day go by without telling her how much he loved her. And she planned to say it right back to him every day for the rest of their lives.

"Forever, Talya. I will love you with my last breath."

A joyful sob tore from her throat. "Yes, for all eternity."

***

Thank you for reading! Did you enjoy? Please add your review because nothing helps an author more and encourages readers to take a chance on a book than a review.

And don't miss more in the *Raven Hollow Coven* series with book AFTER MIDNIGHT available now. Turn the page for a sneak peek!

Also be sure to sign up for the City Owl Press newsletter to receive notice of all book releases!

SNEAK PEEK OF AFTER MIDNIGHT

"I don't think I can handle another douchebag today." Brooke Howe cracked a smile as she glanced over at her best friend Arabella. She looked hippy chic in a white tee, ripped jeans, with strings of beads around her neck.

The two had become best friends while living together at a local coven with five other witches. Cutting through the rows of tarot cards, incense, copper bowls, and spell candles, Brooke's heels click-clacked against Enchantment's black and white tile floor.

"When I think about Nico Denopoulos, the words 'gorgeous' and 'hunk' come to mind, definitely not 'douchebag.' Did you forget you're doing a personalized match for him this morning?" Arabella asked, drawing her dark brows together. Reaching for a china mug and a tin of tea leaves off a shelf, she set them up next to the coffee table book she wrote about Tassography.

"Crap, that's today?" Brooke's heart skipped a beat. Nico was the hot younger brother of their friend Willow's husband Alex. They met at their wedding, and like the majority of the females there, she'd been riveted by his black, wavy hair and soulful dark eyes. He epitomized handsome and sexy in one unforgettable package. He'd shown up at the reception with a plus-one, but apparently now he was single and looking to mingle.

Rushing behind the counter to the spot where she kept her calendar, Brooke scanned her matchmaking appointments for June. Nico's name was written in pencil, next to a reminder to get her brows threaded and pay the electric bill. "You're right, as per usual." Having a psychic for a best friend meant it came with the territory. She reached for her still-steaming cup and took a sip from her Matcha latte, burning her tongue.

"What's up with you? You've been in a funk for the past few days." Concern laced Arabella's voice.

"Joe and I broke up. It's the start of a new season, I shouldn't be surprised." At this point Brooke knew the drill. Eventually, malaise would settle in and then she'd shake it off and start over. A deep ache moved through her. She forced a smile. "I'm either an eternal optimist or a sadist. At this point I'm not sure anymore."

"I'm so sorry, Brooke. I didn't know." Arabella walked over and pulled her into a hug.

Brooke eased back and shrugged. "You'd think I'd be used to it by now, but rejection still sucks." *Chalk one up to the curse of the matchmaker.* It was one of the reasons she started her business in the first place: to help others find love, something otherwise elusive to her. She'd been laser-focused on growing her client base by offering extra services like date-coaching and image consulting. Eventually, she wanted to branch out and write an advice column for a magazine.

"It always does." Arabella gave her a sympathetic smile and began rearranging the books on the shelf.

"It's not like I got that fluttery sensation in my stomach when we were together. And the sex wasn't anything special. So why am I feeling this sense of loss?" She'd dated her fair share of zodiac signs, from the crazy Geminis to the unyielding Capricorns, in an attempt to put herself out there in hopes of changing her fate. But every relationship ended the same way.

"You can't give up hope. There are other single guys out there—guys like Nico."

"You're right of course, but I don't know if I can withstand any more heartache. As for Nico, he's strictly off-limits. He's now an unofficial member of our friend group and a potential client."

Brooke had two choices: sit and wallow in self-pity, or seize the cosmic opportunity to help her next client find love and cater to his tastes, however vanilla or kinky. Thinking about Nico and some kind of kink brought a host of sultry images to mind. She redirected her thoughts to doing his birth chart. Once Brooke got that out of the way, then she'd search her database and find three women who would be perfect for him.

At least she could try and look human when he got there. She pulled out her mirror and checked her reflection. Her eyes looked dull, and her cheeks lacked color. Before she could swipe some lip gloss across her lips or add a little blush to her cheeks, the bell dinged, and the door swished open. Smoothing a hand down her black sheath dress, she was glad she wore her old standby. It was laundry day. This had been the only clean thing left in her closet.

Nico Denopoulos strolled into the shop, and just like the last time Brooke saw him, all the air left her lungs in one big rush. She'd seen her fair share of good-looking men, but Nico was in a class of his own, a six-foot-four Greek god, with a chiseled face, sculpted cheekbones, and a powerful build that hit every one of her hot buttons. Black scruff darkened his strong jaw. She could imagine it scraping against her skin in the heat of passion. The caramel color of his skin caught under the glow of the lights. She swallowed hard and tried not to drool.

"It's good to see you again, Brooke." Nico joined her at the counter and pressed a kiss to her cheek. A spark of electricity rippled through her and scattered her nerves. He smelled incredible, masculine and sexy, with a hint of cologne. He pulled back, and his appreciative gaze swept over her face. "You're looking well. I believe the last time we saw each other, there was a whole lot of clapping and cheering going on."

Her cheeks flushed at the memory. "And tequila shots being consumed." He was too much of a gentleman to say he'd caught the garter at the reception, while she'd been the one to catch the bouquet. There'd been an undercurrent of attraction pulsing between them from the moment they met. She'd never forget the hot glide of his fingers or the look of heat and amusement in his eyes when he slid the scrap of lace up her bare thigh. She'd been crawling out of her skin with embarrassment, and she couldn't get over the sensation that she'd known him before.

He smiled wide. "It was a fun wedding."

"Yeah, it was. Why don't we go into my consulting room?" Brooke motioned to the storeroom.

"Lead the way." Dark eyes rimmed with enviable lashes stared back at her. Everything about him was big and masculine, from his hands to his corded forearms. Joe had only been about an inch taller than her, so she'd traded in her heels for flats. She'd always feared he'd drop her on her ass when he tried to carry her, unlike Nico, who looked like he could lift her with one hand.

Nico's heavy footsteps trailed behind her as they crossed to the storeroom. The familiar scents of lavender and rosemary mingled in the air and put her at ease. They stepped through a purple drape into her cubby. "Please, have a seat and make yourself comfortable. I'm sorry it's the size of a matchbook." Arabella had helped her feng shui the small space by painting the walls cream and adding a few of her favorite watercolors. The finishing touch was setting her desk in a commanding position. A small fountain set on the opposite wall, bubbling with a relaxing stream of water. A piece of green jade sat on her desk, next to a cherished photo of her standing beside her brother Drew, right after they'd hiked up Bear Mountain.

"No need to apologize." Nico glanced around the room, nodding his approval. "I like it. You've made great use of the space."

Ignoring the fluttery sensation in her stomach, she smiled at the compliment. She pulled out her phone and turned on her jazz playlist, hoping it would get them both in the zone. "Thanks. Congratulations on your restaurant. I've been planning to stop in for dinner, but I heard it's hard to get a reservation." Nico looked like a giant standing in her tiny room. His blue cotton shirt stretched over his broad shoulders and what looked like slabs of hard muscle beneath.

"You don't need a reservation. You're welcome any time." His gaze slid to hers and got her warm all over. She'd never been so aware of a man in her life. He emanated a hot, sexual energy.

"I appreciate that," she said with a nod. "How did you come up with the name 'Gemini' for your restaurant? Tell the truth, are you a closet astrology buff?" she teased, hoping to calm the butterflies floating around in her stomach.

A deep chuckle rumbled from his chest. He sat down in the chair across from her and stretched out. When his leg brushed against her thigh, awareness prickled along her skin. Her physical reaction to him unnerved her. She ignored the sensation and leaned back in her desk chair. "No, not at all. My partner thought it sounded cool. It's strictly a coincidence."

"Trust me, there are no coincidences." This morning when Brooke checked her horoscope, it said she'd cross paths with someone that would change the course of her life forever. Did Nico have anything to do with the ominous prediction?

"Ah, a matchmaker who believes in fate."

If he only knew the half of it. "I admit, I'm one big cliché. But it's my truth." Nico didn't strike her as the type who'd have any trouble finding a date. Charisma rolled off his broad shoulders in waves. "Well then, if you're ready, we can get started. May I ask why you're interested in using a matchmaker?" Without thinking, she reached up and toyed with the blue topaz on the chain around her neck. The stone had been a gift from her dad and Drew for her twenty-fifth birthday.

"This was Willow's idea," he pointed out. "She raved about your matchmaking skills. When your sister in-law gives you a suggestion, you take it, even if magic and witchcraft aren't my thing." In the enclosed space, she caught another whiff of Nico's cologne and could smell summer on his skin.

Focusing on the man in front of her—and not the sexual fog flitting around in her brain— she tilted her head to the side. "Don't worry. This isn't about me putting a spell on you or another person, or making you drink a potion to fall in love. It's about using astrology to match you up with the perfect person for you, and to see if your stars align."

He leaned back in his chair and visibly relaxed. "It seems all the women I'm interested in already have boyfriends or are seeing someone. I guess my timing has been off."

The story of my life. "It's always about the timing. You can think of what I do as bringing the human element to getting matched. Do you mind if I ask about any previous long-term relationships, and what your current dating habits are like?" The second she posed the question, a flair of disappointment welled in her chest. While a part of her was still sad over her breakup with Joe, she couldn't stop imagining herself on a date with Nico. Shaking her head, she refused to go there.

"I don't have a lot of time to meet people. And when I do go out, I don't have much in common with the women I meet online. Their priorities are different. They're always looking over their shoulders for the next best-thing. The truth is I'm tired of swiping right." Nico ran a hand through his hair. His raw honesty softened her heart.

"Fair enough. I'm guessing you and your date from the wedding broke up?"

"The sparks just weren't there. I value family and my job keeps me pretty busy, so I want to share my off time with someone who's worth it, someone who's exciting. I want to explore the world with that person." His gaze locked with hers and the air shifted between them.

"Hmm, I think I can help. I appreciate your honesty and trusting me with your love life." Damn that sounded corny. "I assure you everything's strictly confidential. Okay, are you ready to get started?"

"You've certainly piqued my interest. How do you match me up?" His gaze narrowed as he glanced over at her computer.

"I use a combination of astrology, algorithms, and my Ephemeris." Brooke pointed to the leather-bound tome on her desk. "This book gives me insight as to what the solar system is doing, the planets' positions, retrogrades, eclipses, and, well, the signs from above."

"It's like your Escoffier, the main book we chefs use to learn how to cook."

"Exactly. Good analogy. I take your personality traits and goals, and then I match you up with someone who has similar ideals. These women will be vetted and background checked, as well as checked out on social media. Why don't you tell me what you're looking for?" she asked, holding her breath, waiting for his reply.

"I'm looking for my soulmate."

Brooke almost fell off her chair. How refreshing. "Wow, most of my clients don't speak in such honest terms." She didn't know guys like him even existed. His romantic heart spoke to her on every level, another reason to avoid gorgeous, charismatic men like Nico Denopoulos at all costs. Even if she was interested, things wouldn't work out. They never did.

A smile flashed across his handsome face. "I like to be upfront. So what's the first step?"

"I can do a personalized compatibility report to help you find your matches and get you started."

"Willow says you've got a gift for matching people up." A spark of excitement flared in his eyes.

"Thanks." She swiveled in her chair, angling her head to a collage of photos of some of her clients on the opposite wall. "We've seen seven marriages and seventeen engagements."

"I'm in your capable hands." A shiver moved through her at his intimate tone. An image of Nico in all his male glory flashed through her mind. From the size of his hands and feet, she'd bet her Ephemeris he'd be well-hung. She turned back to face him, trying to keep her expression neutral.

"Are you okay?" His gaze traveled the length of her, making her whole body tingle. "You're all flushed."

Busted. "Uh, this room tends to get warm." She cleared her throat and turned the fan on high. "If you decide to move forward, you'll be matched with three dates per week, for three months."

"And you personally choose them?"

"I hand pick every single one. I'll be matching you with women you're astrologically compatible with. We can discuss things like generosity, values, humor, chemistry, and hobbies beforehand. You can contact me anytime, day or night." She handed him her card with her cell number on the back. "I'm extremely dedicated to all of my clients." Why did her voice sound throaty on the last part?

Nico flashed a sexy smile that would make any of his dates lose their minds—and their panties. "I appreciate that."

"I typically start out by asking some questions and then doing a complimentary birth chart." She motioned to her screen. "It's based on the astronomical snapshot of where the stars and constellations were the moment you were born."

"Willow said you might ask me that question, so I called my mom."

From the sweet way Nico said her name, Brooke sensed their closeness and found the connection endearing. "Awesome. You came prepared."

"I was born March 21, 1996. At 2:00 p.m."

"An Aries." Brooke would've guessed it anyway. A fellow fire sign, Aries men were passionate and confident, with fiery personalities. They were known for their strong bodies, commanding presence, and dominating sex appeal. But Nico was on another level. She'd leave out the part about them being romantically and sexually compatible. She'd never been attracted to her astrological equivalent before, but none of those men had been as charming as Nico.

Humor lit his eyes. "So what you're telling me is that it's okay to ask a woman her sign?"

She laughed. "Well, yes and no. How about we leave that part to me for the time being?" Brooke picked up the astrological wheel on her desk and pointed to the center. "These wedges are the houses. Each one represents a different aspect of our lives. The creative house is what propels you cook up those culinary masterpieces I've been hearing about at your restaurant."

When he smiled, his eyes crinkled at the corners. "To be determined after you've sampled my food."

Brooke refrained from asking if that was a personal invitation and pointed to the pie-like sections of the chart. "The seventh and eighth houses are the most important, in my opinion. They're the houses of love, partnership, marriage, and sexual relationships. I'll be using them as indicators to find your soulmate."

His gaze narrowed. "You really take this stuff seriously."

"I do," she said with an audible sigh. "Our astrological charts hold the key to everything in the universe."

"I know a heavenly body when I see one." He winked and pointed to the circular sphere on her desk. "I'm referring to the stars and planets, of course."

"Of course." And the man could flirt.

When swallowed, his Adam's apple bobbed up and down in his throat. Strength and virility practically oozed from his pores. "What about fate? Do you believe some things happen for a reason?" The direct way he asked the question made her think of lazy days in bed and hot, sweaty sex.

"Absolutely." She tried to get her thoughts in check and stared at her screen. After she input his birthdate, a set of designed questions popped up. "Time for a quiz. I'll match you with the sign that you're best suited with romantically based on your score. How would your friends describe you? Passionate, smart, talented, cool, funny...?"

"Passionate." Every time Brooke looked over at Nico her heart raced.

"What about hobbies? Besides your exuberance for cooking?" She pounded away on her keyboard, focusing her attention on creating his profile.

"I enjoy watching football with the guys, going to sporting events, and running down by the river when I have the time."

"Those are all great." She added his responses to his profile then looked up. "What makes you mad?"

The humor drained from his eyes, and she sensed she'd hit a nerve. "Liars."

"Noted. Your sun sign can vibe with certain colors. What's your personal favorite?"

"Purple."

Brooke could guess his answer to the next question. "Which of these dates would you prefer the most? A fancy restaurant? Going for a hike? Talking under the stars? Parachuting? Or chilling on the couch and binge-watching your favorite show?"

A genuine smile spread across his handsome face. "Talking under the stars would be at the top of my list."

Mine too. She needed to stay in business mode and not get swept up by the hunger in his eyes when he looked at her. What was the point? Like all the others, he'd forget about her when the season changed. The fallout could put a strain on their friend group "What does love mean to you? A strong physical connection or a strong emotional one?" The question sent a flush of heat to her cheeks.

His gaze burned into hers as he leaned closer, forcing an involuntary rush of breath from her lips. "If you don't have physical attraction then there's nowhere to go, but there has to be a strong emotional connection, or you burn out fast."

"I agree." Her cheeks burned with heat from the intense look in his eyes. "There's another matter we should get out of the way. I strongly urge my clients not to engage in sex unless there's monogamy. Rule number one in the matchmaker's handbook."

He chuckled. "The matchmaker's handbook?"

"You can think of the book as guidelines that I strongly urge my clients to follow. What are your thoughts about kissing on the first date?" *Why the hell did I include that one?*

His gaze moved from her face to her lips. "I say yes, if we're both into each other and the moment presents itself."

His words made the room seem too small, and him too close. Those damn butterflies took wings and fluttered around in her stomach. "Let's move onto compatibility and intimacy. I'm going to recommend people who you're destined to click with, and let the universe pick your matches with a little help from me."

Amusement flashed in his eyes. "I'm game on everything except for your no-sex rule. Can we negotiate?"

A shiver moved through her at his words. "What did you have in mind?"

Don't stop now. Keep reading with your copy of AFTER MIDNIGHT available now.

And sign up for Shari Nichol's newsletter to get all the news, giveaways, excerpts, and more!

**Don't miss more of *Ravens Hollow Coven* series
with book four, AFTER MIDNIGHT, available now,
and find more from Shari Nichols at sharinicholsauthor.com**

**An ancient curse has prevented astrologer Brooke Howe from finding
true love. She hides her longing by matching others with the hope of
someday changing her plight.**

When Nico Denopoulos, the gorgeous younger brother of a friend, struts
into her shop seeking a soulmate, she's immediately drawn to his magnetic
presence and his romantic heart. She can't deny the intense sensation
drawing her to the sexy-as-sin chef.

An ugly divorce has kept Nico laser-focused on the opening of his new
restaurant. He's been single for years, but now loneliness has crept into the
cracks of his heart. Fearing that he's grown bitter, he has high hopes that
Brooke can help him with his problem, except for one thing…the more
time he spends with her, the more he wants her—in every way possible.

As much as Brooke wants to believe Nico is the real deal, she fears that
when the seasons change so will his feelings. Inexplicably drawn together,
she can't help but wonder if he may hold the secret to reversing the curse
and changing her destiny.

Will a secret from their shared past life bring them closer, or tear them
apart forever?

Please sign up for the City Owl Press newsletter for chances to win special
subscriber-only contests and giveaways as well as receiving information on
upcoming releases and special excerpts.

All reviews are **welcome** and **appreciated**. Please consider leaving one on your favorite social media and book buying sites.

For books in the world of romance and speculative fiction that embody Innovation, Creativity, and Affordability, check out City Owl Press at www.cityowlpress.com.

ACKNOWLEDGMENTS

An idea for this story came to me while writing book two in the series. This is an enemies to lovers story with a lot of twists and turns. I loved spending time with Cayden and Natalya, and truly enjoyed their bantering and slow burn to love. This book touches on sensitive topics like sexual abuse and addiction. The subject matter is close to my heart, affecting dear friends and loved ones. For anyone struggling with these issues, I'm with you in love and support. While this is a work of fiction, extensive research went into devising the plot. Any mistakes are truly mine. This book wouldn't be possible without the unfailing patience and kindness of my editor, Heather McCorkle. Thank you for always taking the time to talk me off the ledge, and imparting your brilliant wisdom into my pages. It takes a village to put a finished book together, a wonderful cover artist, whom I'm sure I drove crazy, and an amazing team that works together. Thank you to everyone who helped at City Owl Press. I want to shout out a big thank you to Mark B. for giving me his raw, honest feedback. I swear you know these characters better than I do. Thank you for encouraging me to turn this one little idea about a coven of witches into a four book series. Thank you to Lara Zee. You give a good beta read. And to the readers, thank you for letting me come into your lives. Your continued support means the world!

Xoxo

Shari

Would you like to stay up on all the latest news? Sign up for my newsletter here.

ABOUT THE AUTHOR

Shari Nichols grew up in a small town in Connecticut where haunted houses, ghosts and Ouija boards were common place, spurring her fascination with all things paranormal. Ever since she read her first Barbara Cartland novel, her life-long dream has been to write sexy, romantic stories. When she's not writing, she's reading, going to the gym, or hanging out with family and friends.

She lives in New Jersey with her husband, two children, and her golden retriever. Shari's a member of Romance Writers of America, New Jersey Romance Writers, Liberty States Fiction Writers and Fantasy, Futuristic, and Paranormal Romance Writers. Sign up for her newsletter here.

Awards: Golden Leaf Finalist, NJ Author Best Book Finalist, The Beverley Award, HOLT Medallion Finalist, Literary Titan Silver Medal Winner.

sharinicholsauthor.com

facebook.com/sharinicholsauthor
twitter.com/Shari_Nich
instagram.com/shari_nichols

ABOUT THE PUBLISHER

City Owl Press is a cutting edge indie publishing company, bringing the world of romance and speculative fiction to discerning readers.

Escape Your World. Get Lost in Ours!

www.cityowlpress.com

[f] facebook.com/YourCityOwlPress
[twitter] twitter.com/cityowlpress
[instagram] instagram.com/cityowlbooks
[pinterest] pinterest.com/cityowlpress

www.ingramcontent.com/pod-product-compliance
Lightning Source LLC
Chambersburg PA
CBHW020834030726
47496CB00001B/226